D0843391

IN HER TRACKS

Center Point
Large Print

Also by Robert Dugoni and available from
Center Point Large Print:

Her Final Breath
In the Clearing
The Trapped Girl
Close to Home
A Steep Price
The Eighth Sister
My Sister's Grave

**This Large Print Book carries the
Seal of Approval of N.A.V.H.**

IN HER TRACKS

ROBERT DUGONI

CENTER POINT LARGE PRINT
THORNDIKE, MAINE

*To all of those who lost their lives
or those they loved to COVID-19.
May we remember each, so we are not
doomed to repeat the past.*

PROLOGUE

October 30, Five Years Ago
Seattle, Washington

Seattle police officer Bobby Chin was late, and about to pay a heavy price.

Still in uniform, he hurried from his car and shuffled up the concrete steps of what once had been his home. The boyfriend had parked the Range Rover in what had been Chin's driveway. Brand spanking new vehicle. Supercharged, as if to add insult to injury, except no way a personal trainer could afford a $90,000 automobile. No way. The guy had to be dealing on the side—steroids was Chin's bet from the guy's bloated physique—though he also wondered if his monthly alimony and child support helped to pay for that luxury. Jewel, his soon-to-be ex-wife, wasn't about to ride in anything beneath her expensive tastes.

He reached for the lion's-head knocker, but Jewel pulled open the door, waiting for him, no doubt to chew him out.

"You're late." Her posture matched the tone of her voice. Attitude. She stood with a hand cocked on her hip and an accusatory tilt of the head. She'd had her nails done. This time, a royal blue. Gold necklaces and bracelets peeked out from her white cashmere sweater that, despite the cool October weather, barely met the beltline of her white jeans. She dressed in white when Chin picked up Elle. The color contrasted with her painted nails and complexion. Chin once told her how much he liked her in white, that it made her look sexy.

He regretted it.

"I called. You didn't answer, again," Chin said. "And I left you a text message. You didn't respond, again."

"You're always late."

"As I said—"

"I don't have time to be deciphering your messages," she said. "I have a date . . . a life. You should try it."

Chin bit his tongue. He knew what she was doing, and he wasn't about to take the bait. Not this time. Not again. He couldn't afford another domestic violence charge. His attorney said it would ruin his position in the parenting plan and likely land him in jail, meaning the loss of his job.

"Besides," she said, "I was preoccupied." She let the door swing open so Chin could see the puffed-up boyfriend—Spiffy Asshole, whatever his name. Chin didn't remember and really didn't care. Early twenties, the guy always looked like he'd just completed a set of bench presses.

Veins popped in his forearms and neck. His pecs stretched the fabric of his too-small T-shirt. Steroid Boy for sure. Total meathead.

"Hey, Bobby." The meathead grinned. His bleached white teeth matched Jewel's outfit. "You come to arrest somebody?"

"Greg," Chin said, taking a guess.

"Graham," the meathead said, losing the grin.

Greg. Graham. Whatever.

Chin spoke to Jewel. "Elle ready?"

"She was ready half an hour ago, when you were supposed to pick her up. You know the court order is to be strictly adhered to. I'm keeping a record."

"I know."

"Hi, Daddy." Elle appeared from behind the dragon statue at the foot of the stairs. It faced inward, to bring in wealth and prosperity.

Feng shui.

Feng bullshit. The only money flowing in was what Chin paid Jewel.

Chin dropped to a crouch. "Hey, Sunshine. What are you? No. Don't tell me. You're the most beautiful butterfly in the world."

"Yay! You guessed it." Elle spun so the colorful butterfly wings shook and shimmered. She wore a pink leotard and pink plastic shoes.

"You think you should change your shoes?" The corn maze he intended to take her to would likely be muddy from the recent rain.

"These are butterfly shoes."

"Okay," he said. Just get her and go, his lawyer had told him. "You ready to go?"

"The mortgage is due first of next week," Jewel said. "And you have her Thanksgiving weekend. It's in the court order. So get the time off."

She made Elle sound like a burden. "Grab your jacket, Sunshine. Let's get going."

His daughter took her coat from the bannister, picked up her backpack, and started toward him. Graham stuck out his arm, blocking Elle's path. Chin took a step forward, then caught himself, but Jewel and the boyfriend both noticed.

"Hold on a second, little princess," Graham said, grinning.

"Butterfly," Elle said.

"Give me and your mother a little sugar."

Elle looked stricken. It was all Chin could do to keep from snapping the bloated limb. Elle quickly buzzed Graham's cheek, then bolted out the door. Chin glared at the meathead before turning to leave.

"You sure that thing is going to start?" the meathead yelled from the doorway. "Why don't you buy yourself a new car?"

Chin turned. "You know, Greg—"

"Graham."

"I carry epinephrine in the car for emergencies. It might help to reduce the swelling you got going on."

10

Graham looked perplexed, uncertain. *Meat-head.*

Chin smiled.

"He only swells in the right places," Jewel quickly responded. Then she closed the door.

Chin sucked in several deep breaths as he drove away from the toxic, suffocating environment Jewel created. Jewel wanted to provoke—anything and everything to get under his skin, to gain any tactical advantage in the parenting plan. To use Elle. Chin took some delight in knowing that soon Jewel would be the meathead's problem, for a short while anyway. His ex would create another toxic environment, suffocate the meathead until she tired of him, then belittle and demean and eventually discard.

That's who she was.

That's what she did.

He shook the thought and looked at Elle's reflection in his rearview mirror. This was his night with his daughter. "How are you doing, Angel?"

"Butterfly, Daddy. I told you."

Elle's pink plastic shoes hung over the car seat. She was growing—and becoming more intuitive. Her teacher at the Montessori school said Elle had been reacting negatively to the divorce. She suggested that Bobby and Jewel not argue in front of Elle.

Good luck with that.

"I'm sorry. I meant to say how's my *butterfly* doing?"

"Can you take me trick-or-treating?"

"That's Mommy's night to be with you, Butterfly. But I get you Thanksgiving week-end."

"But I want you to take me."

"Mommy wouldn't like that very much, I don't think."

"Mommy doesn't like you, Daddy."

"No?" He looked again in the rearview mirror. What the hell kind of a mother told her daughter that?

"She said Graham is going to be my new daddy, and if I was bad, he would leave, too, and then I wouldn't have any more daddies."

This was the type of manipulative bullshit he had lived with, what he would continue to live with, long after the divorce, what he couldn't get his attorney or the judge or the guardian ad litem to understand. And if he accused Jewel, she would deny she said it and turn it against him. She'd say Chin had made up the story to gain leverage in the parenting plan, and what type of sick husband used his daughter that way?

And the guardian ad litem would agree.

This was his new reality.

"I'm not leaving, Butterfly. And I won't let Mommy take you away."

"When's the surprise?" Elle said, as if the matter were closed.

Chin had told Elle when he called that he had a surprise. "Just a few more minutes."

"I have to go to the bathroom."

"Can you wait? We're almost there."

Chin spotted a line of cars, most exiting a parking area delineated by hay bales and pumpkins. A bright-orange tractor and scarecrows glowed beneath decorative strands of lights. "We're here, honey. Isn't it beautiful?"

A young man dressed as Darth Vader directed Chin into the parking lot, and Chin helped Elle from her car seat, taking a moment to reattach her wings.

"Don't hurt my wings," Elle said. "Daddy, don't hurt my wings."

"I won't, Butterfly. I promise." Chin tried to help Elle slip on her jacket, but she protested, claiming it would crush her butterfly wings. He carried her over puddles from a recent rain into the tent. "It's a big Halloween party. Are you excited?"

"I have to go to the bathroom," Elle said again.

"Oh, right. Okay. Come on, we'll find the toilet."

He followed signs to a series of port-o-potties. They entered one that smelled like disinfectant. The butterfly outfit being a onesie, he had to remove the entire costume. He felt like Chris

Farley in the movie *Tommy Boy* changing his clothes in an airplane bathroom. Once finished, Chin reversed the process and put his daughter back into her costume. They used a hand sanitizer and stepped from the port-o-potty at 9:35 p.m.

"Okay. You ready for the corn maze?"

"I'm hungry."

Chin stifled a scream. Jewel refused to feed Elle when it was his night to have her.

Inside the tent he found bags of popcorn, caramel corn, cookies, soda, and bottled water. He was about to give up, promise food when they got home, when he spotted a signboard advertising hamburgers, fries, corn dogs, and chicken sandwiches. Perfect.

"Two hamburgers and fries," he said to a teenager behind the counter.

The teenager shook his head. "We're closed. I think all we have left are corn dogs."

Not great, but better than the alternative. "Fine. Two corn dogs."

The kid took Chin's money. Then he said, "I have to heat them in the microwave."

"How long?"

"Just a couple of minutes. Unless you want to eat them cold."

Chin couldn't tell if the kid was being a smart-ass or a dumbass. "We'll wait."

The kid shrugged.

"Let's take a picture," Chin said to distract Elle.

He lifted her onto a hay bale. "Okay, spread your wings."

Elle proudly lifted her colorful wings. Chin snapped her picture, then dropped to a knee and they took a selfie. When the food hadn't arrived, Chin went back to the counter, but the teenager was gone. "We're closed," a woman cleaning up said.

"I ordered two corn dogs from a kid working the counter five minutes ago."

The woman opened the microwave and found them. "Sorry about that. Jimmy must have forgot. I sent him to the corn maze."

Major dumbass.

Chin took the corn dogs and sat with Elle, watching to be sure she chewed each bite, so she didn't choke. He checked his watch: 9:42.

Elle ate half the corn dog and announced, "I'm done."

Chin threw the remainder of both dogs in the garbage, lifted her, and hurried to the corn maze ticket booth. Jimmy stood behind the counter.

"You left us," Chin said.

Jimmy shrugged. "They moved me over here."

"Two tickets."

"Can't," Jimmy said. "We close at ten."

"It's nine forty-five."

Jimmy explained that the maze took forty minutes to complete—if Chin stopped to decipher the clues and did all the rubbings. He wasn't supposed to sell any tickets past 9:20 p.m.

Chin ignored him. "Look, Jimmy, she's five. We don't care about the clues or the rubbings. We're just going to walk through. I get one night a week with my little girl, and I promised her a corn maze."

The boy sighed. "Fine." He sold Chin two tickets at full price. "But you have to be done by ten. 'Cause that's when we turn the lights out."

Chin took his daughter's hand and they entered the maze. The thick stalks exceeded six feet and made the path narrow. He moved as quickly as Elle's little legs allowed, not wanting to rush her, but wanting to get through the maze before the lights went out.

"Pretty cool, huh, Butterfly?"

Elle stared at the stalks of corn. Then she said, "Let's play hide-and-seek, Daddy."

"We don't have time for that, Elle. We have to get through."

"Please, Daddy."

"I'm sorry, honey. Maybe we can play at home."

Elle cried. Then she sat down in the dirt.

"Elle, get up, honey. You're getting your costume dirty."

"No."

"Honey, you have to stand up."

"I want to play. Mommy lets me play."

The counselor Chin had seen for his court-ordered anger-management classes had warned that kids going through a contentious divorce could become defiant and play one parent off the other.

"Elle. You need to stand up."

"No. Graham plays with me."

Chin felt his heart ripping apart. "Okay. One quick game. All right?"

Elle got to her feet. "Yay!"

"But when I say come out, you have to come out. Okay?"

"You count, Daddy. You have to hide your eyes."

"Okay, but if I say come out, you come out. Right?"

"Turn around when you count."

Chin turned and counted. It wouldn't be hard to find Elle's colorful butterfly wings among the green cornstalks. "One Mississippi. Two Mississippi. Three Mississippi."

At six he cheated and turned. He didn't see Elle's wings behind the cornstalks. "Here I come." He stepped forward. "I'm coming." He searched the aisle, looking under the drooping leaves. He turned the corner to another row. Then a third and a fourth. He checked his watch, felt himself starting to panic.

He shouted, "Okay, Elle. I give up. Come out." He turned in a circle, looking, hearing the wind rustle the stalks. "Don't let the lights go out," he muttered under his breath. He called again. "Elle? You have to come out. The game is over."

His heart raced.

He jogged, turning left and right, down the rows, shouting her name. "Elle. Come out. Elle? Elle!"

He turned a corner, disoriented.

Another corner.

Elle's colorful butterfly wings lay in the dirt. "Elle!"

Then the lights went out.

CHAPTER 1

Wednesday, October 30, Present Day
Seattle, Washington

Tracy Crosswhite inhaled deeply and slowly let out her breath, a meditative technique she'd learned in her counseling sessions to calm her mind. Following the traumatic events she had experienced in Cedar Grove the prior winter, Tracy started having nightmares and difficulty sleeping, then flashbacks in the middle of the day. A doctor diagnosed her with situational PTSD and recommended counseling and an extended leave from her duties as a Violent Crimes detective with the Seattle Police Department.

Already on maternity leave, Tracy took the additional medical time, and things slowly improved. With Therese, their nanny, already in place to watch Daniella, Tracy worked out daily and ate better, which helped her to clear her head and to sleep. She got in better physical shape than before she had Daniella. She couldn't recover the washboard stomach, but it was once again flat. She also spent time at the SPD shooting range in Seattle, and her most recent scores topped the scores of detectives at the Violent Crimes Section for the year.

But it was time to get back to work.

She'd miss Daniella. Tracy's counselor, Lisa Walsh, had three kids of her own and had warned that the first day back would be difficult. Having Therese helped, but this morning Tracy found herself teary, and short with Dan. The extended leave hadn't made the return to work easier—it made it harder.

Tracy pushed from her Subaru and walked across the secure lot adjacent to the Justice Center on Fifth Avenue in downtown Seattle. The brass now referred to the building as "Police Headquarters," but Tracy and the other veterans—old dogs—didn't easily learn new tricks or accept change. That thought made Tracy smile. She'd missed Kinsington Rowe, Vic Fazzio, and Delmo Castigliano, her colleagues on the Violent Crimes Section's A Team. The four of them had worked together for more than a decade and had become like family. Faz and his wife, Vera, were Daniella's godparents.

Tracy took the elevator to the seventh floor, already feeling comfortable again. She nodded to the detectives on the telephone and acknowledged others who called out to welcome her back. She stepped into the A Team's bull pen, one of four bull pens for the Violent Crimes Section's sixteen detectives.

Tracy noticed framed photographs of people she didn't recognize on her desk. Kins had called to give her a heads-up that Nolasco had hired Maria Fernandez while Tracy and Faz were out. Faz took medical then paid administrative leave after sustaining injuries while pursuing a drug dealer. He'd been back at work for roughly a month. Kins told her that he and Del had been up to their eyeballs, and they had asked their captain, Johnny Nolasco, for the help. Nolasco had offered the position to Henry Johnson, the A Team's overflow detective, also known as a "fifth wheel," but Johnson declined. He had four kids under the age of eight and needed the flexibility the fifth-wheel position provided.

"Hey, hey! The Professor's in early. Who died?" Vic Fazzio lumbered into the bull pen with a mug of coffee and a familiar greeting— an old homicide joke made colorful by Faz's perpetually hoarse voice and New Jersey accent. They called Tracy "the Professor" because she'd once taught high school chemistry.

"Hey, Faz."

"Welcome back." He burst into the theme song to *Welcome Back, Kotter*, a 1970s sitcom starring Gabe Kaplan and John Travolta with a song about dreams being your ticket out of your situation. "But the dream died!" Faz said, punctuating his punch line with a fist.

Faz set his mug of coffee on his desk, lowered his Windsor knot, and unbuttoned the collar of his shirt. He and Del were old-school—sports coats and slacks, despite the section's long-established dress-down policy. Others in Violent Crimes called them "Italian goombahs." Del and Faz called themselves "Italian stallions." Clydesdales was more of a reality. At six foot five, Del stood an inch taller and had once outweighed Faz, who pushed 260 pounds. A younger girlfriend, an improved diet, and vanity convinced Del to lose fifty pounds. He now referred to himself as "Del 2.0." Faz said he was "Half-a-Del."

Faz looked to what had been Tracy's desk. "You knew about Fernandez, right?"

"Yeah, Kins let me know."

"She's in a trial," he said. "A holdover case from her time working the Sex Crimes Unit. Like you, she gave up sex for death. Bada boom!" he said, making another fist.

Faz puffed out his jowls and gave a not-so-bad impression of a supersized Marlon Brando in *The Godfather*. "How's my goddaughter?"

"Growing like a weed," Tracy said. "Anybody know what happens to Fernandez with me back?"

"Don't know."

"Any other teams down a detective?"

"Not that I'm aware of."

An administrative assistant appeared at Tracy's cubicle. "Tracy. Welcome back. Captain Nolasco would like to see you."

Tracy checked her watch. This was early for

22

Nolasco. "Okay. Tell him I'm on my way." She looked at Faz, who shrugged.

Tracy and Captain Johnny Nolasco didn't have a complicated relationship. Their mutual animosity stemmed from Tracy's time at the police academy. Nolasco had been one of Tracy's instructors, and she broke his nose and nearly neutered him during a training exercise when he grabbed her breast. Then she'd beat his decades-old shooting score at the range, which was as much a blow to his ego as her elbow had been to his nose and groin. They tolerated one another because he was her captain, and she was too good a homicide detective to screw with—the only two-time recipient of the department's highest award, the Medal of Valor.

Tracy walked the inner hallway. Glass walls revealed a blue October sky. She loved the crisp fall temperatures and clear views. The gray gloom of November would hit soon enough, along with the persistent rain. She knocked on a closed door.

"Come in," Nolasco said.

Nolasco looked like he hadn't expected her, though she suspected he had. Nolasco rarely— as in never—got into the office early. Twice divorced, he'd long ago swallowed the bitter pill, but it hadn't kept him from working out mornings to keep in dating shape, or from getting the suspected vanity eye job that gave him the look of the perpetually surprised.

"Tracy. Welcome back," he said with a grin she didn't buy for a second.

"You wanted to see me?"

He gestured to one of two chairs across his desk. "Take a seat."

She reluctantly did so; the less time she spent in his office, the better.

"How was your maternity leave?"

She didn't take the time to correct him. "Fine. I'm looking forward to getting back to work."

Nolasco reclined, his chair creaking. "You were out a long time."

"What happened in Cedar Grove mandated the leave; the department approved it."

"No doubt, but . . ."

"Is there a problem?" she asked.

He squinted, as if fighting a headache. Another habit. "We promoted Fernandez."

"I heard."

"I didn't have a choice with both you and Faz out. We were short on manpower, like the rest of the department."

Tracy and just about everyone else in the department knew Seattle PD was down as many as ninety police officers and detectives, despite a concerted, three-year effort to hire two hundred more. Tracy's colleagues were fleeing King County for other police agencies as quickly as the homeless moved into the state. SPD had become the city council's whipping boy, and many officers were tired of it. The council ignored drug and alcohol addiction and mental illness and stuck to its mantra that homelessness wasn't a crime and shouldn't be treated as such. Meanwhile, Seattle's property-crime rate was increasing faster than Los Angeles's or New York City's, and annual homicides would exceed thirty for the first time in years.

"Faz came back first, so I had to slot him into the A Team."

"I heard that also."

"I offered a temporary position to Johnson, but he couldn't take on the extra responsibility with four kids at home."

Nolasco was stalling. Tracy's skin crawled with each minute in his office. "What's the problem?"

"I couldn't do a lateral move and offer Fernandez a temporary position. Sex Crimes wouldn't hold her position open."

More stalling and lying. He hadn't mentioned any of this to Kins. Tracy did her best not to show her aggravation. Nolasco was vague, but the picture was becoming more clear. He was nothing if not predictable. He'd done this before—hired a woman to take Tracy's position so Tracy couldn't allege discrimination, or argue that he was forcing her out of Violent Crimes, which was always his ultimate goal.

"Give her another position on another team."

"There aren't any openings at the moment."

"There rarely are."

"Unless someone goes out on maternity leave," he said.

"Or medical leave," she countered.

"It tied my hands."

Did he want her to apologize for having a child or for having a vagina and a uterus? "Give her a fifth-wheel position."

"All full."

"Then what do you suggest?" Tracy knew she was entitled to her position . . . if it was available. She didn't want to screw Fernandez, whom she knew well and liked. She and Fernandez had coordinated investigations involving sex crimes and homicides, and Tracy found her diligent and knowledgeable. Violent Crimes, however, was the pinnacle—the macabre joke once being that homicide detectives only left the section in a body bag. She was eager to hear what bullshit Nolasco had concocted this time to get rid of her.

"Nunzio is retiring. He gave word two weeks ago."

Technically, Art Nunzio worked in Violent Crimes, but for the past two years he'd been the section's cold case detective.

"You want me to take cold cases?"

"It's comparable."

"Only the pay."

"I'm offering you a position in the section at the same salary and the same benefits."

In other words, Tracy would be hard-pressed to win a complaint if she sought the union's help. She bit her tongue. The case in Cedar Grove had been a cold case that turned into a nightmare and nearly got her killed. The only other cold case she'd worked had been the disappearance of her sister, Sarah, and that had become an obsession that put her personal life on hold for nearly twenty years. To move forward she'd had to lock Sarah's files in her apartment closet and lock her memories in a mental box.

"When do you need an answer?"

"Art gave notice for the end of next month, but with accrued vacation days and sick time he's never taken, his last day is today."

Son of a . . . "You want an answer by the end of today?"

"I need someone in place, so Art can smoothly transition his files," Nolasco said, withholding a smile.

Tracy wanted to tell him where he could shove those files.

CHAPTER 2

Tracy hesitated as she approached the open door to Art Nunzio's cramped, windowless office. She wouldn't take the position. She'd tell Nolasco to shove it and retire. She and Dan didn't need the money; Dan made plenty as a plaintiff's lawyer. Tracy could stay at home and raise Daniella, teach her things like single-action shooting, like her father had taught her and Sarah. She'd take Daniella to shooting competitions. It had been a good life—until her sister's disappearance destroyed her family.

Tracy had been surrounded by death ever since.

Maybe it was time to surround herself with the living.

Maybe . . .

But the police department had not just been a job.

It, and her colleagues, had sustained her through dark years, gave her a sense of purpose and self-worth. The A Team had again provided her a family.

It had saved her life.

And she wasn't about to let Nolasco or anyone else take that from her or force her into a decision she didn't want to make.

She'd retire when *she* was damn good and ready.

She stepped to the open door. Nunzio had his head down. A bald spot peeked out from what had once been a full head of red hair. His reading glasses sat perched on his head like swimmer's goggles as he went through papers, tossing some in the nearly full wastebasket at his feet. Nunzio was fifty-eight years old, and simple math told Tracy he was retiring twenty-five years after reaching Violent Crimes, likely damn near to the day, she'd bet. Nunzio had worked on the C Team until a long and emotionally demanding murder trial took three years of his life, and no doubt a large portion of his soul.

Cold cases didn't require a detective to be on call 24-7 or otherwise require he put his life, and the lives of his family, on hold for someone he had never met and never would, but whom he would get to know as intimately as his own family members.

Sitting in his chair, Art looked as if the office had grown around him—the scarred walls, barely wide enough to fit the desk; the metal shelving filled with black binders, each neatly labeled with a white index card bearing each victim's name, date of death, and cold case number.

They looked like tombstones.

And these were just Nunzio's working files.

Tracy knew the rest of the cold cases, some three hundred total, were kept in a vault.

On Nunzio's desk sat a single cardboard box containing picture frames—likely his citations and other professional memorabilia that once hung on the wall behind him, which now displayed only gold picture hangers, proof Nunzio did not intend to hang his career on the walls of his home.

He was leaving death behind.

Tracy knocked on the door. "Hey, Art."

Nunzio looked up. The glasses fell onto the bridge of his nose. He quickly removed them. "Tracy."

"Heard you're retiring." She took one step inside the office.

"Heard you're taking my place." Nunzio stood. "Wasn't sure we'd have the chance to talk."

She smiled. "Who told you I would be taking your place?"

"Nolasco."

Figured. The ass had concocted the scheme before she'd even come in. "Not sure yet. Thought I'd take the opportunity to talk with you, ask you some questions. You have a minute?"

"I'm retiring, Tracy." Nunzio smiled. "Starting tomorrow, every day is Saturday, at least that's what my buddies on the golf course tell me."

"Sounds heavenly."

"I've officially written my last case file report.

I'm like a punch-drunk fighter nearing the end of a fifteen-round brawl. I want to be like Rocky Balboa, on my feet when the final bell rings." His eyes shifted to the clock on the wall. Counting down the minutes.

Tracy hadn't had time to formulate intelligent questions, and she didn't know a lot about the Cold Case Unit, which was just the one detective. She knew a homicide or missing person case didn't go cold at the department unless the detectives assigned to investigate the case exhausted all leads, explored all known evidence, and retired or left the department. Given recent developments, that was happening at an unprecedented pace.

"Not sure I'm cut out for this, Art."

"I wasn't either. They pitched the position to me as a place to work nine to five, with my weekends free. That appealed to me at the time."

"And was that true?"

"For the most part. You know how it goes when you're following a lead."

Tracy did. She looked at the ominous black binders. "I imagine it's hard, rarely getting a resolution."

Nunzio motioned to a stack of files on the only other chair in the office. Tracy put them on the edge of the desk and sat.

"Improvements in DNA analysis and other forensics are changing that. I solved twenty cases this past year, which is better than my predecessors ever did."

"I recall reading that. Congratulations." Only 280 more to go.

"But I'm not going to lie to you," Nunzio said. "It takes a certain personality to stomach this and keep it in perspective. You can only tell family members 'I don't have good news for you' so many times and in so many different ways, before you feel like a liar."

"Is that why you're leaving?"

"I'm leaving because I've put in my time." He shrugged. "It's time for someone new, someone with energy."

"And optimism?" Tracy asked.

Nunzio smiled but it had a sad quality to it. "This job takes years off your life. You know that. I'm the same age as my friends, and I look ten years older. And I'm tired. I'm ready for something different. Until I find it, there's fishing and golf."

Tracy looked at the sagging bookshelves. "Where does one start?"

"I looked for cases that interested me and treated each like an active case, like the murder just happened."

She eyed the binders and couldn't imagine where to begin.

"I made it a little easier for whoever follows me. I created a cheat sheet of the cases I pursued, and I summarized the known evidence. The brass wanted me to give priority to cases with the highest chance for a resolution, so I pushed sexual assault homicides with collected DNA evidence—samples of blood, semen, or saliva—to the top of that list."

DNA could now be analyzed and compared with the DNA profiles in CODIS—the FBI's Combined DNA Index System that contained profiles of individuals convicted of crimes.

"Here's the thing. If you look at it like you have three hundred unsolved cases, you'll drive yourself nuts. Just take one case at a time, with the same purpose as your active files—finding justice for the victim and the family. I'm not saying it's been easy," Nunzio continued, then stopped before he said anything more.

Tracy waited while he looked around his office. "Families call me regularly, Tracy, and it can be hard, but we have a great victim advocate team to handle expectations. Still, I'd be lying if I didn't tell you that walking out that door, leaving these cases unsolved, will be both the hardest and the easiest thing I've ever done."

"Why the hardest?"

He looked from the binders to Tracy. "Because I always believe I'm one phone call, one DNA hit away from solving another case."

"And why the easiest?" Tracy asked.

"Because I'm tired of lying to myself."

CHAPTER 3

Stephanie Cole was lost. Her GPS kept instructing her to turn right, but each time she did, she came to a driveway. She didn't know the neighborhood. She didn't know any of the Seattle neighborhoods, not after just a month since her move from Los Angeles. The streets were all NE and NW and hard to navigate, and she didn't know it got dark in the middle of the freaking afternoon either.

Frustrated, and rapidly running out of daylight, she spotted a middle-aged man walking the sidewalk and pulled her car over. She lowered the passenger-side window, letting in the cold autumn air, something else she'd need to get used to. Winter in LA had mostly been balmy.

"Excuse me. Excuse me."

The man stopped. He looked surprised.

"Can you help me?" Stephanie smiled. "I'm looking for the entrance to the park. My GPS has me driving in circles."

The man approached the window as if she might bite. Stephanie pulled back as cigarette smoke spewed from the man's mouth.

"Sorry." He discarded the butt in the gutter. "It's not really an entrance," he said. "It's more of a path. Not a big one neither. Are you going for a walk?"

"A run, actually." She checked her watch. "A quick one. I can't believe how early it gets dark up here."

The man pointed. "You go down there to the sign about not dumping no garbage."

"Thanks," Stephanie said.

"Did you just move here?" the man asked.

"A month ago, from Los Angeles."

"That's where they have Disneyland."

"Right," Stephanie said, sensing perhaps the man might be mentally challenged, or had a stroke, though he looked too young for a stroke. She didn't want to be rude, but if she wanted to get a run in before the sun set . . .

The man said, "Did your family move here?"

"God, no. My family is *why* I moved." She checked the time on her Fitbit: 4:34. "I better get going. Thanks again."

She shut the window and drove to the small sign and, behind it, thank God, the trailhead. The dirt path was no more than six feet wide and covered with leaves from the shedding canopy. She didn't see a parking area so she parked along the curb, stepping out into the cold, glad she wore the leggings and a long-sleeve shirt. She looked for the man, but he had gone.

Daylight had further faded when she reached the trailhead and quickly stretched beneath the tree canopy. She checked her Fitbit. Just 1,300 steps for the day. Sitting on her ass answering phones at work wasn't much of a job, but she needed the money. And she really needed this run. At five foot four and 140 pounds she wasn't fat, but she put the weight on in her legs and her butt, the worst possible places. She wasn't going to meet a lot of guys walking into parties feeling like an Oompa Loompa. She slipped a knit hat on her head and inserted earbuds, then hit her music library. Ed Sheeran and Justin Bieber's "I Don't Care."

He's at a party he doesn't want to be at.

She hoped she didn't feel that way later this night. The Halloween party would be her first work party. She hoped it would help her make some friends.

She looked for a trail map but didn't see one, just a sign advising people not to dump in the park, ironically posted above a wooden box with doggy poop bags. Priceless. She took a picture to post to Instagram.

She started a slow jog between lush green ferns and tall trees. The trail descended quickly, which was tough on her knees. Stephanie ran for ten minutes, waiting for the trail to flatten out or take a turn. It didn't. She came to wooden pallets creating a footbridge over a creek. On the other side, an elderly man with a small dog stopped and motioned for her to cross. Cole contemplated asking him about the trail but decided to keep moving in the interest of time. The man smiled as she jogged past.

The path's condition deteriorated. Fallen trees blocked the trail. She stepped over them, cautious of the slick moss. She deduced from the trail's poor condition, and the fact that she hadn't seen any other runners, that it was not heavily used. Being alone made her uncomfortable, especially because she did not know the run and was quickly losing what remained of the daylight.

The path turned and Stephanie ascended, hoping it would lead back out. It came instead to a certain and unceremonious dead end. She looked up at a sloping hillside with a metal guardrail, with a red stop sign, and a yellow "No Trespassing" sign.

Stephanie swore. "You've got to be shitting me."

She was at the bottom of a ravine with only one way back. She berated herself. This had been a bad idea. In her rush, she'd done everything wrong.

"Damn it," she said, and hoped it didn't get any worse.

CHAPTER 4

Tracy left for home without giving Nolasco an answer. Nunzio told Tracy he'd leave the list of his "active" cold cases on his desk, for whoever took the position.

Tracy maneuvered her Subaru around her home's circular drive, the Japanese maple in the center now the color of an autumn sunset. Gravel crunched beneath the car's tires. She parked beside Dan's Chevy Tahoe and quickly stepped out, anxious to see Daniella and get her mind off work. She hurried up the steps of their renovated home. "Renovated" was an imprecise term. They'd torn down all but the foundation of their four-room cottage and built a three-bedroom, three-bath, 2,500-square-foot home with nanny quarters for Therese.

Rex and Sherlock, their Rhodesian-mastiff mixes, greeted Tracy at the door, though not for long. They bolted past her, biting and playing with one another in the yard. Dan stood in the foyer dressed in his running attire, which explained the dogs' excitement.

"Hey," he said, giving her a kiss. "They haven't been out today."

"I see that. Therese didn't get them out?"

"Therese took Daniella to the zoo. They're stuck in I-5 traffic trying to get to the 520 bridge."

"That area is always a mess, but especially during rush hour. When does she expect to get home?"

"She expected to get home before five. I suspect she won't be home until close to six. Join me on a run before it gets too dark?"

Tracy really wanted her Daniella fix. "Ugh," she said.

"You have all the enthusiasm of a soldier starting the Bataan Death March."

"Less," she said. "I had a trying day at the office."

"Excuses, excuses. Do I make up excuses when I'm in trial and you're running me into the ground?"

"I think you just answered your own question."

"We have precious alone time. So, it's either sex or running, and I know Rex and Sherlock's vote."

"That makes it three to one." She hurried past him up the stairs to change clothes.

He called after her. "You could have at least contemplated the sex."

They ran the trail behind the house, the brown summer grass just starting to turn green from the fall rain. Final daylight bathed the trail and grass in a golden hue. Rex and Sherlock, as usual, took off as if shot from a cannon, racing up the hill. They'd soon slow down, panting and out of breath.

It took ten minutes before Tracy found her pace and her wind, at least enough that she could hold a conversation with Dan, who had been jabbering from his first step.

"You able to talk now without passing out?" Dan said.

"I can hear you huffing and puffing over there, too, Kip Keino."

"Kip Keino? The Olympic gold medalist? Wow. You're dating yourself."

"My mom and dad talked about him. What's your excuse?"

"I'm old."

"Some days I feel old."

"Okay, enough self-flagellation," Dan said. "Tell me about your day."

She told him about Maria Fernandez, and about Nolasco's offer that she work cold cases.

"What did you tell him?" Dan asked, the concern clear in the tone of his voice.

"Nothing yet, but he didn't leave me a lot of options."

"You could file a complaint with the union. You're entitled to get your job back."

"I could, and I would look like a woman whining. I don't have that luxury with two breasts."

"Well, for God's sake don't give up the breasts."

She laughed.

"Seriously," Dan said. "Your colleagues would know it's a legit beef."

"I'd lose," she said. "Nolasco was short two detectives with Faz out on medical leave, and Kins and Del both asked him for the help. I can't claim discrimination, because Fernandez also has breasts and she's a minority, which the department is pushing for promotion. And, technically, Nolasco is offering me a job in Violent Crimes."

"But not *your* job."

"I don't want to alienate Maria. She didn't do anything wrong. She deserves a position. Just not mine."

"When do you have to let Nolasco know?"

Tracy sidestepped Rex, who barreled out of the grass and ran across her path. "End of today."

Dan stopped running. "Are you kidding me?"

Tracy surged past him, then slowed. "Nolasco wanted an answer. I didn't give him one."

Dan caught up to her. "He could have called to give you time to think about it."

"You're mistaking him for human. I told you, he's a reptile."

The path narrowed, just wide enough for one person. "This is bullshit," Dan said. "You don't need it. Stay home with Daniella."

"I'm considering that." She glanced over her right shoulder. "A lot. But I don't want to be rash about this. There are advantages to think about."

"Such as."

The path widened and Dan pulled alongside her. "In cold cases I'm a team of one. Nunzio pretty much said he did what he wanted. He worked nine to five Monday through Friday, unless he was pursuing a lead, and that schedule is certainly advantageous with Daniella at home. We can spend weekends together. Unless you're in trial."

Dan didn't respond.

"Cat got your tongue?"

He stopped running. Rex and Sherlock continued, trampling the tall grass and occasionally stopping to chew the blades. Tracy jogged past Dan several steps, then jogged in place until she realized he wasn't just pausing. She walked back to him. She knew what he was thinking but asked anyway. "What?"

"I'm worried about you."

"I think you once said worrying is a part of loving."

"That was Faz."

"He's poetic for a big goombah."

"I'm serious, Tracy. I worry about you pursuing cold cases. The one in Cedar Grove . . ."

"I know," she said. "But that was an unusual circumstance."

"Maybe. Look, I don't know a lot, but I know the majority of homicide cases involve violence against women, young women. Am I right?"

"Most violent crimes are against young women, or gangbangers, and more recently, the homeless."

"And the investigations are cold because no one was able to solve them."

"And you think that because of what happened to Sarah I won't be able to separate my feelings for her from the cases I'm working on, and I'll have the nightmares, et cetera, et cetera."

"Will you?"

"I've been able to separate my feelings from my active files."

"Yeah, but the majority of those are either grounders," Dan said, a term Tracy used for an investigation where the killer was obvious, "where you get a confession right away, or it's a gangbanger, like you said."

"I didn't realize my job was so easy," she said.

"You know what I mean," he said. "What are you going to do when you come home night after night without making any progress?"

"Thanks for your faith."

Dan ignored the comment. "What is that going to do to you emotionally? You spent two decades working your sister's case. You didn't date. Didn't have a social life. You had Roger the cat."

"If I take the position, I'm going to have to readjust my expectations. I talked with Nunzio about that."

"Can you?"

"I don't know," she said. And she didn't.

"So, you're going to take the position?"

"I'm contemplating it," she said.

"Then contemplate this. Nolasco may be a reptile, but he's not a complete idiot."

"You're underestimating him. He's a complete idiot."

"I'm serious. Don't think for a second he hasn't considered these same factors. He knows your background with your sister, and he knows how you work, your obsession with finding justice, especially when the victim is a young woman. He knows what you just went through in Cedar Grove, that you're coming off administrative leave. Don't think he isn't hoping that by assigning you to cold cases, you'll emotionally burn out and quit."

"I realize that."

"And?"

"And if that happens, then it happens."

"Yes, but at what cost, Tracy?"

"I'm not going to quit and let him win."

"That's exactly the attitude that worries me. You never give in. You never give up. I'm afraid this is going to tear you up inside, take you down a dark road you once walked alone."

"I don't want to go down that road again, Dan, and I'm no longer walking alone."

"Wanting and not wanting doesn't make it so."

"Now you sound like a philosopher."

"At least talk to your counselor about it."

"I have to give Nolasco a decision tomorrow morning, though technically I needed to do so today."

"You know she'll get you in if you call."

Tracy checked her watch. "You've seriously screwed up our pace, O'Leary."

"We have time. Therese will be another hour."

She stepped toward him as if to kiss him. When Dan leaned in, she bolted past him, sprinting. "Beat me home and we still have time for sex before Therese and Daniella get there."

"Always has to win," Dan said, chasing after her.

"This could be a win-win for both of us."

CHAPTER 5

Franklin Sprague pressed the button clipped to the van's visor and waited for the garage door to rumble open. The racket was getting worse; either the engine was finally dying or the door rollers had worn out, both from decades of use. Just like the rest of the house. Franklin didn't have the money, the time, or the interest to fix any of it, though he'd contemplated repairing the door, but only because he knew the noise acted like an alarm. Just once he'd like to catch his two lazy brothers sitting and watching television.

He pulled the van into the garage of what had once been his parents' three-story home in Seattle's North Park neighborhood. The right side of the garage overflowed with used appliances, newspaper and magazine stacks, boxes of video-tapes, and other miscellaneous junk his father had hoarded. Franklin had to cram the shit on one side of the garage just to make space for the van. He pressed the remote-control button and waited for the door to rattle shut. He didn't like nosy neighbors watching him.

He stepped out, slid open the van's panel door, and grabbed two of the grocery bags, carrying them inside. He maneuvered down the hall, past more shit, filing cabinets, and an assortment of crap. His mother and father had both been hoarders. He'd seen a show on it once. People who couldn't throw shit out and didn't realize it took over their lives.

He stepped into the kitchen. Carrol stood with a glass in his hand, a bottle of Wild Turkey on the counter. Unwashed plates, glasses, silverware, and pots and pans still filled the sink and cluttered the stove. Enough shit for a dozen instead of just the three of them.

"Give it a rest, Carrol, and give me a hand. There's more bags in the van."

Carrol didn't move. He looked frozen.

Franklin set the bags on the floor; there was no room on the counters. "What are you, deaf? Give me a hand. I shouldn't have to do the shopping *and* carry in the bags. And I ain't putting this shit in the cabinets and fridge neither. Where's Evan? I told him to clean the damn kitchen this morning." Evan had the memory of an Alzheimer's patient.

Still, Carrol didn't move, and Franklin sensed . . . No, he *knew* something was wrong. Carrol didn't disobey him; Franklin made sure of that. Evan too. Franklin did most of the work, and he made most of the money. He'd *earned* their respect, and not just because, at forty-nine, he was the oldest. Carrol was two years younger, and Evan, who their daddy called "the mistake," had just turned forty. Chronologically anyway. Franklin was light-years ahead of both when it came to intellect and common sense. Evan couldn't help it; there'd been complications at birth. A lack of oxygen. He wasn't a retard. As their daddy used to say, "The elevator gets to the top floor, just takes longer than most."

Carrol had that wide-eyed look, like he'd just got caught doing something. The dumbshit never could lie. Didn't have the stomach for it. "What the hell is wrong with you? What happened?" Franklin asked. "You do something stupid?"

Carrol shook his head. He also stuttered when he got nervous and often chose not to speak.

"What the hell is it, Carrol?"

"Ev . . . Ev . . . Evan did something," he said in a burst. "You . . . you . . . you ain't gonna be happy, Franklin." He rambled like one of the damn ladies at the retirement home where Franklin worked as a janitor. Carrol continued, "I . . . I . . . I . . . told him you'd likely kill him."

Franklin stepped past him. "Where is that idiot?"

Carrol's stuttering got worse. "You . . . you . . . you got to promise me y . . . y . . . you ain't going to kill him, Franklin. He . . . he . . . he's your brother."

Franklin got in Carrol's face. "If that idiot did something stupid, I'll beat his ass." At six foot two, Franklin was three inches taller. He and Carrol each weighed 230 pounds, but Carrol was a fat ass. Always had been. Always would be. "So tell me what that dumbass did?" But even as he asked the question, Franklin suspected he knew what his youngest brother had done. He'd become obsessed with women. Franklin inhaled and exhaled through his nose, gritting his teeth. "Where the hell is he?"

Carrol reached out and grabbed his arm. "You got to promise . . ."

Franklin pulled his arm free. "I don't got to do shit, Carrol. Where is he?"

Carrol pointed to the pantry.

"Son of a bitch. Evan!"

Carrol again grabbed Franklin's arm. "D . . . d . . . don't kill him, Franklin."

Franklin ripped his arm free and grabbed Carrol by the throat, shoving him against the cabinets, then into the kitchen table. Stacks of papers toppled onto the floor. "Touch me again and so help me God, I'll kill you both."

CHAPTER 6

Tracy stood from the chair in the reception area and greeted Lisa Walsh. The two women made small talk as Walsh led Tracy down the hall to her office in the Redmond building she shared with other professionals.

"Would you like a cup of coffee or tea?" Walsh asked as they passed a universal kitchen.

Tracy declined. She'd awoken early, her thoughts spinning on the hamster wheel, going over the cold case debate and whether she should take the position. She'd drunk two cups of coffee, one more than usual, and was already jittery.

"Just a glass of water," she said.

"I can do that." Walsh grabbed a glass from a cabinet.

Walsh had not been what Tracy had expected when she started the counseling sessions following the case in Cedar Grove. She'd expected a dowdy woman with a soft voice who perpetually asked, "And how does that make you feel?" Tracy's mother would have called Walsh "black Irish." Tracy estimated early forties, with short dark hair and dark eyes but a light complexion. She had a runner's slim build and wore jeans and a light-blue sweater.

Walsh had decorated her office in soft colors and warm lighting. Shelves held an assortment of books on parenting, marriage, troubled teenagers, anxiety, and relationships. Tracy stepped to the brown leather couch on an area rug and sat with her back to a window that provided a view of the Redmond Library and other low-rise, red-brick office buildings. Walsh sat in a cushioned, leather armchair across a coffee table. She picked up a pad of paper and a pen and crossed her legs.

"Thanks for seeing me on such short notice," Tracy said.

"No problem," Walsh said. "How are you feeling? Any more nightmares?"

"No," Tracy said. "Nothing like that."

"How was going back to work?"

"Hard, just as you said, but I got through it."

"Do you feel guilty leaving Daniella?"

Tracy paused. Then she said, "No, not really, but I do worry about something bad happening to Daniella. I worry that I won't be there to protect her."

"Why would something bad happen to Daniella?"

Tracy smiled. "I've heard the families of victims say they never thought it would happen to them either. My family never thought it would happen to us. Not in a small town like Cedar Grove."

Walsh set down her pad. "Psychopaths represent four percent of the population."

"Four to eight percent," Tracy said and smiled, though without humor.

"Four to eight percent. But what are the odds that what happened to your sister and your childhood family would happen again to your daughter? What are the odds that a young girl, deeply loved and carefully watched over by two parents, will disappear?"

"It happened once," Tracy said, feeling herself digging in her heels.

"Yes, it did. But what are the odds?"

"Very small, I know, but that isn't why I asked to see you. Something unexpected has come up at work, and my husband thinks I should talk to you before I make any decisions."

Tracy explained her conversation with Captain Johnny Nolasco.

"Do you have any legal recourse?" Walsh asked.

"You sound like Dan. No. Not really," she added.

"But you think he hired this woman deliberately to freeze you out?"

"I do, but I'm not likely to prove it. Discrimination suits just put everyone on edge and don't play well with the men. I don't want that. I just want to do my job and be treated as a detective."

"What then are you going to do?"

"I still haven't made up my mind."

Walsh glanced up at the clock. "You haven't left yourself a lot of time."

"I think that was my captain's plan. He'd love to be rid of me, which is a strong reason for me to take the Cold Case job."

"Just to spite him?"

Tracy smiled. "We have a complicated relationship."

"I understand that. Put him aside for a minute. What do you want to do?"

Tracy sighed. "I don't know. Initially I was dead set against taking the job—"

"Because you feel it is being forced upon you, or you don't want to move laterally?"

"Both. But after speaking to the detective who is retiring, there are some advantages to accepting the position."

"Such as?"

Tracy explained what Nunzio had told her.

"What are the negatives?"

Tracy hesitated, uncertain how to answer the question. "You mean other than that I'd be capitulating to my captain?"

"Put him aside. You just gave a strong reason to take the position. What are the reasons making you hesitant, or is it simply to not let your captain have his way?"

"That's the problem. He'll have his way regardless of what I do."

"Is that it? Is it just that you don't want your captain to win?"

Tracy sipped her water, then said, "No. Dan is concerned the position could be emotionally challenging because a majority of cold cases are either unsolved homicides or sexual assaults and battery of young women, or women who have gone missing. He's worried how I will react when I can't solve a cold case."

Walsh said, "Pardon my ignorance, but aren't cases cold because they couldn't be solved?"

"It's more complicated than that, but essentially, yes."

Walsh paused. "I see." Then she said, "Why did you become a Seattle homicide detective?"

"Why?"

"I think you said once it was to find your sister."

"In part."

"To save your family?"

"Possibly."

"Did you save your sister?"

Tracy shook her head.

"Did you save your family?"

"No." She spoke softly, her voice almost inaudible.

"Does that bother you?"

"I've learned to live with it."

"Have you?"

"What do you mean?"

"Did you deal with it? Or did you just push it aside so you could move on, day by day?"

"I don't know. Maybe a little of both." She didn't tell Walsh about the mental box in which she'd put her sister's disappearance and death.

"Does it bother you that you couldn't save your sister or your family?"

"Of course it bothers me. That was my job—to save her. I failed."

"Why do you think it was your job and you failed?"

"Because she died. Because he killed her."

"Years before you ever became a homicide detective."

"Yes."

"You were a twenty-two-year-old woman just starting life, not a homicide detective."

"What?"

"It wasn't your job to save your sister, Tracy."

"I was older. I shouldn't have left her."

"But you couldn't have saved her."

"My father thought I could have. He never forgave me for leaving her."

"Why do you say that?"

"Because he killed himself. He never looked at me the same way after Sarah disappeared. He never treated me the same."

"Did he ever tell you that he blamed you, or that you were at fault?"

"Not in so many words, no. But . . ."

"Could he have treated you differently because he was grieving the loss of his child?"

Tracy took a moment. "Maybe."

"Not everyone can be saved, Tracy."

"I know."

"And you can't save everyone."

"I know."

"You can understand why Dan is concerned about what effect not solving cases, through no fault of your own, will have on you, can't you?"

"Yes."

"Are *you* concerned?"

She gave the question some thought. Then she said, "I don't know."

"I think that's the question you have to answer. When you do, remember this: You're human, Tracy, which means you're not perfect. You're going to fail, through no fault of your own. That's part of being human, being imperfect. The question is, can you live with being imperfect? Can you live with failure?"

CHAPTER 7

Tracy left Lisa Walsh's office with much to think about. Her father would have said she was stuck between a rock and a hard place; she didn't want to take the cold case job just to spite Nolasco, but she also didn't want to refuse the job and play into his hands, without recourse, except perhaps to retire. Tracy knew that whatever she decided, it shouldn't be to appease anyone but herself.

She needed to make an intelligent decision, and she needed a quiet place to make that decision. She didn't feel right about using what used to be her desk, even with Maria Fernandez sitting alongside a prosecutor in a King County courtroom. It would be awkward to sit in the A Team's bull pen, and it would likely make Faz and Del and Kins uncomfortable; she knew they felt bad about what was happening, though they had no control over it. She didn't want to make them feel worse by sitting at her old desk—like a wad of gum they couldn't get off the bottom of their shoes.

The door to Nunzio's office was closed but not locked. Tracy stepped inside and shut the door behind her. The room looked smaller without Nunzio at the desk, and the magnitude of the many binders, and the cold cases they held, loomed much more oppressively.

Nunzio had cleaned everything, a good-bye present, she supposed, for whoever was going to take his position. Tracy ran her finger over the desktop and didn't find a speck of dust. The computer monitor was dark. A mouse and a keyboard awaited use. A single door key rested on the desk pad beside sheets of paper stapled at the top—the list of the active files Nunzio had been working on and said he'd summarized for whoever took his place.

Tracy saw her name and picked up an unstapled sheet of paper. Nunzio had typed her a note.

Tracy:
If you are reading this, it means, well, that I am officially retired. Wow. You're the first person I've said those words to, and I'm not really sure how I feel. I guess it hasn't truly hit me yet.

If you're not reading this, then . . . well, I'm still retired, but now I feel like a jackass.

Tracy smiled.

But I'll be honest, I typed this note because it made it a little easier to walk out that door believing that I was leaving these files in good hands. Competent hands. Your hands.

I know your success rate in Violent Crimes is one hundred percent, and that says a lot about you and about your commitment to your cases and to the victims and their families. In my humble opinion, that's what separates good detectives, like you and, formerly, me, from the ones just playing out their hand. You give a shit. Something to be said for that. Sure, it can make investigations more painful, like when we only confirm a family's worst nightmare, but that's what makes us human too. We care. It's one of the reasons I decided to step down. I stopped caring as I once had.

So . . . no pressure. Ha! Ha!

Seriously. You do what's best for you. Nobody walks in your moccasins but you . . . or whatever the saying. I know now that life's too short to do anything less.

Okay. There's a round of golf with my name on it.

And as of five o'clock today, every day is now Saturday.

I hope I don't regret this. You know

the saying, right? It's easier to live with failure than with regret.

Art

P.S. At least try out the chair. It's supposed to be ergonomic, so your ass doesn't fall asleep sitting in it. If you decline, just drop off the key with the captain.

Tracy laughed to herself. She should have just come to work and read Nunzio's note rather than going to see Lisa Walsh.

It's easier to live with failure than with regret.

She looked up at the binders. They didn't seem as intimidating as just a moment ago. She rolled back the chair and sat, getting a feel for the place. It was nice to have privacy.

Maybe she couldn't save them all.

Maybe she couldn't find justice for them all, or for their families.

But maybe she could find justice for one. And wasn't that better than not even trying?

She could live with failure. She couldn't live with regret.

Start with one, Nunzio's voice spoke in her head. *Just start with one.*

She flipped over the note and glanced at Nunzio's case summaries, uncertain what she

60

was looking for but diving in anyway. She opened desk drawers and found an assortment of colored highlighters. She took Nunzio's advice and looked for sexual assault cases, cases that could have DNA evidence to be processed. She highlighted those in yellow. More-recent cases she highlighted in blue. She pulled cases off the shelves that had caught her attention on Nunzio's summary and went through half a dozen. Her attention was drawn to one case in particular—the abduction of a five-year-old girl, Elle Chin, from a corn maze the night before Halloween. The timing seemed prophetic. Nearly five years to the day. She remembered the case, though she hadn't worked it. It had involved an officer in the North Precinct.

She read Nunzio's summary.

The father, twenty-eight-year-old Bobby Chin, had been a Seattle police officer going through a nasty and violent divorce. He'd picked up his five-year-old daughter, Elle, following his watch and had taken her to a corn maze and pumpkin patch. In his interview, Chin was adamant his ex-wife and her boyfriend had snatched his daughter and intended to blame him and put him in jail. The wife, Chin said, was crazy and vindictive. The police had been called to the house several times, but not because of the wife. Chin had pled to a domestic violence charge.

Tracy sat back. Chin sounded like a guy

rationalizing his bad behavior by blaming the wife. Anything was plausible. Of import, the little girl had never been found, and the file contained no updates. Tracy shuddered at the thought of losing Daniella.

She finished Nunzio's case synopsis, stood, found the corresponding binder on the shelf—Nunzio had alphabetized them—and pulled it out to read the contents for herself.

It was a parent's worst nightmare. Her worst nightmare. She noted significant dates and details. The case wasn't as old as some of the others, but of the two detectives who had worked it, one had retired, and the other had moved to a police department in another county.

Tracy set aside the binder and looked for other recent case summaries. Two grabbed her attention, prostitutes who had disappeared along the Aurora strip within nine months of each other. Like the Chin case, neither case was old, but the investigating detectives had moved on and the cases had gone cold. It seemed far too soon for Tracy. She had spent months tracking a serial killer of prostitutes known as "the Cowboy" working the same strip of motels and hotels. A quick review of each file provided another reason the cases had gone cold. There was no DNA evidence. No witnesses. No evidence of any kind. The women had simply vanished. She pulled out the correlating binders from the shelves and put them with the Elle Chin binder.

Keys rattled in the door. She glanced up as it pushed open. Johnny Nolasco looked surprised to see her. "Crosswhite, how'd you get in here?"

"The door was unlocked."

"The door is always supposed to be locked."

She held up Nunzio's key. She suspected from the key and the personal note that Nunzio had purposefully left the door unlocked, knowing she'd be back. The thought made her smile. *You give a shit.* "You could fire Nunzio," she said.

Nolasco's eyes roamed over the binders on the desk and the sheets of paper. "What are you doing?"

Tracy looked up at the clock on the wall. It was nearly two in the afternoon. "Going through files."

"The cold case files aren't for casual reviewing."

"Nunzio left me a summary."

"He left . . . Did you . . . Did you meet with Nunzio?"

"Yesterday. It was the only time he was available. Yesterday was his last day."

Nolasco ignored the jab. "Why didn't you tell me yesterday you decided to take the position?"

"I didn't make up my mind yesterday."

"Then what are you doing in here now?"

Tracy looked around the office. "Making up my mind."

"What's that supposed to mean?"

"It means I'll take the position."

Nolasco did his best to keep a straight face but she heard the surprise in his voice. "You will?"

"On one condition. A spot opens on the A Team, I get right of first refusal."

"I can't promise that."

Tracy smiled. "Yeah, you can."

Nolasco looked like he was biting his tongue. "There's some paperwork—"

"I'll take care of it."

Nolasco nodded. Now looking uncertain.

"Something else, Captain?"

Nolasco shook his head and left the office.

CHAPTER 8

Late in the afternoon, Tracy pulled into a parking lot of a one-story business park in Kirkland and found the Amazon warehouse. She'd spent the remainder of the afternoon going through the Elle Chin file, reading the missing person report, the police reports, the statements of witnesses, family members, friends, and portions of the massive police investigation that followed up on more than 2,000 tips that eventually came through a dedicated tip line. Chin was one of SPD's own, and they'd spared nothing to find his daughter. Despite the police effort, the use of dogs, a search of the homes and the cars belonging to Chin, his wife, and the wife's boyfriend, the little girl was never found.

The case had generated a significant amount of press because of the juicy circumstances: Chin being a Seattle police officer, and his wife alleging physical and verbal abuse that had led to a domestic violence arrest, a restraining order, and a custody hearing that had limited Chin's contact with her and his daughter until he completed an anger-management course and community service. The newspaper articles and news reports on the TV had liberally quoted Jewel Chin after her daughter's disappearance, and it was clear she had initiated a lot of the coverage to draw attention to her husband as the prime suspect and, in the process, make herself out to be a victim.

Neither was a new tactic. Tracy knew from experience that the husband and wife, especially in these circumstances, were always the prime suspects. The detectives handling the case had spoken to both Bobby and Jewel Chin and noted this. They wrote that both had become agitated when the detectives suggested they were responsible for their daughter's disappearance. Each blamed the other. Tracy would have to tread lightly and strategically when she spoke to them. She might only get one chance, if they spoke to her at all. She had questions for others and hoped to educate herself fully before she took another shot at either Bobby or Jewel Chin.

Tracy parked beneath autumn leaves clinging to the spindly branches of small trees in parking lot planters. She loved the fall in Seattle. Parts of it, anyway. She loved the colors, which reminded her of her childhood in Cedar Grove. As the years passed, though, the falls seemed to get shorter, the colors faded more quickly, and the dark days of winter descended more rapidly. Now, the sun set at four thirty in the afternoon and didn't rise until seven thirty in the morning, if it rose at all. Pewter-gray clouds hung over the city, at times an oppressive curtain. Kids would be trick-or-treating in the dark, though hopefully not the rain. She and Dan had discussed taking Daniella to the closest neighborhood for her first Halloween. Tracy knew taking a ten-month-old out for candy was ridiculous, but she also wanted her daughter to experience the holidays, the way she had.

As she approached the one-story office park, a glass door opened and a young man stepped out dressed in a warehouse uniform—black shirt, blue pants, and a matching jacket. "Are you Detective Crosswhite?" he asked as Tracy neared.

Tracy extended her hand. "I assume you're James Ingram?"

"Yes," he said. Ingram looked and sounded nervous, though he was putting up a pretty good front. Five years ago, Ingram had been a seventeen-year-old working a seasonal job at the corn maze. Now twenty-two, he had an AA degree from Bellevue College and worked a warehouse job for Amazon. "I thought we could talk next door. It's a coffee shop."

"That's fine," Tracy said. "Lead the way."

Ingram pulled open the door and sat at a table near the windows. Java House clearly catered to the office-park employees, with minimum window signage. In addition to serving coffee and tea, a glass case displayed juices, muffins, cookies, and prepackaged sandwiches.

"Can I get you anything?" Tracy asked.

Ingram shook his head. "We have coffee and stuff at the warehouse."

Tracy hadn't eaten since having a protein shake that morning. She ordered a black tea and a whole-wheat muffin, bringing both to the table. As she set down her cup, the table wobbled, tea spilling from the brim. Ingram, a veteran customer, folded a napkin and slipped it under one of the four legs to steady the table.

"Thanks for talking to me," Tracy said. "Are you under any time constraint?"

"I get off at five."

Tracy had made her intentions known in their telephone conversation, but she liked to look witnesses in the eye and hear the tone of their voices when they spoke. She had a notebook full of questions, not all for Ingram.

"You saw the little girl with her father that night, correct?" Tracy asked.

"That's right."

"Tell me what you remember."

"Has there been some kind of break in the case or something?" Ingram asked. He looked sheepish. "I told the other two detectives everything I could remember about that night. I was questioned about it several times."

"I understand. But those detectives have retired, so the case is now mine."

"But that was five years ago," Ingram said. "I'm not sure what more I can remember."

"I'm just taking a fresh look at the evidence," Tracy said. "And trying to determine if maybe there was something that somebody might have missed."

"Okay." Ingram shrugged, not sounding convinced or enthusiastic. "I guess the first time I saw them I was working the food tent. He came in pretty late; we were shutting things down."

Ingram told her about Bobby Chin ordering corn dogs and seeing Chin later at the corn maze entrance. "I told them it was too late, that we stopped selling tickets at nine twenty because it took about forty minutes to get through the maze."

"But you sold the father tickets anyway?"

"I told him no, but he was like, 'Hey, I only get my daughter once a week, and I promised her I'd take her to the corn maze.' He was pretty adamant, so I said, 'Fine. But be done by ten 'cause the lights shut off.' "

"He knew the lights went off at ten."

Ingram shrugged. "I told him."

Tracy had found that interesting when reading the file, that and the fact that Chin said his daughter slipped away when he closed his eyes to play hide-and-seek. She thought the lights going out to be convenient, and a father agreeing to play hide-and-seek with a five-year-old little girl irresponsible.

"How did the father seem to you?"

Ingram shrugged. "Like he was in kind of a hurry. And he really wanted to do the maze."

"Why do you say that?"

"He just seemed like he was on edge."

"Nervous? Anxious?" Tracy asked.

"No. I wouldn't say that. More like it was a really big deal that he take his daughter through the maze."

Tracy wondered if that was because Chin knew someone was to meet him and Elle in the maze.

"I don't know," Ingram continued. "I mean, I don't have any kids or anything, but she was like four or something. How big a deal could it have been to her? Don't kids that age get excited about candy and stuff? I thought it was more important for him than her."

Interesting. "You thought maybe he had another agenda?"

"A what?"

"Another reason to get into the maze."

"I thought about it after everything went down—you know? I mean, not that night, but when I started getting asked all these questions. I thought that if he had it set up, you know, that maybe that was why he wanted to go so badly. And maybe that was why he timed it so close to the end of the night."

Tracy was thinking the same thing.

"Had you sold tickets to anyone before the father and daughter?"

"I didn't. I'd just gotten transferred over there to shut it down."

"Do you know if others were still in the maze?"

"There were still a few cars in the parking lot, so I guess it's possible. I can't say for sure."

"Can people get into the maze without going past the booth?"

"Well, yeah," Ingram said, suppressing a grin. "I mean, it's just a big cornfield."

Tracy smiled. "Tell me about the next time you saw the father and his daughter."

"You're asking about when I saw the girl and the woman?"

"What did you see?"

"Well, like I told that other detective, it was only like a couple of seconds. I was picking up the trash and putting it in the can, and I thought I saw the little girl walking with a woman and a man—not really with the man as much as the woman. I mean, he was like a few feet ahead of them."

"What else do you remember?"

"She was holding the woman's hand."

"The little girl was holding the woman's hand?"

"Yeah and then, *bam*. The lights went out."

"You said in your statement the little girl didn't have her wings on then?"

"My memory is she had a dark coat on."

"And the woman?"

"Also a dark coat."

"Did you see their faces?"

Ingram shook his head. "No."

"How do you know it was the little girl you saw earlier that evening?"

Ingram started to answer, then stopped. The prior detectives had not asked him this basic question. "What do you mean?"

"You didn't see her wings or her face. How do you know it was her and not another little girl?"

His face contorted. After a moment, he said, "I don't know. I guess . . . I guess because given the time, and I don't recall any other little girls at that time . . . Not that age."

"But you had just been transferred over there."

Ingram again looked stumped. "I guess it could have been somebody else. Another family. I never really thought about that." He shrugged. "I guess I don't really know."

"You recall the little girl holding this woman's hand, at least in that brief moment you saw her. Did she appear to be walking with the woman willingly?"

"Willingly?"

"Did the little girl look like she was struggling or resisting, trying to get away?"

72

"No. They were just walking along together."

"And you didn't hear the little girl scream or yell?"

Another shrug. "No. Nothing like that."

Which was why, when Tracy read Ingram's statement in the file, her first thought was he had been led to his conclusion that the little girl had been Elle Chin by the detectives questioning him. The facts were, Ingram never saw the little girl's face, she wasn't wearing the colorful butterfly wings Elle Chin had been wearing, and she wasn't resisting. In his police statement, Bobby Chin said Elle had been proud to show off her wings, so much so that she wouldn't let him put on her coat. He'd also said that she had become upset when he initially would not play hide-and-seek, that she had sat in the dirt and cried. The little girl was clearly capable of being defiant— or Chin was lying.

Either way, Tracy didn't put much stock in what Ingram claimed to have seen.

"Can you describe the woman?"

"Not really. She was wearing a baseball cap."

"What about the man?"

"I didn't really see him either, but I think he was wearing a baseball hat also—I mean the style, you know."

"You didn't see his face?"

"No."

"What do you recall happening next?"

"After the lights shut off? I heard a man yelling. You know, 'Elle! Elle! Come out!' Like that. The father came running out of the maze like it was on fire. I mean, he was going crazy—telling me to turn the lights back on and to have everyone lock down the parking lot and stuff, but we couldn't really do that."

"Why not?"

"The lights were on a timer and it was a farm so, I mean, there was a parking lot, yeah, but anyone could have just driven in or out. Anyway, people came running, and the father was telling us where to go and what to do. He was telling everyone what his daughter was wearing, how tall she was. And then there were a lot of police. I mean, they were everywhere, and they had dogs. They kept us all there most of the night asking us questions."

"Did you see the car that the little girl got into?"

"No. Like I said, everything went dark."

Tracy thanked Ingram and stood from the table even more convinced that Ingram had not seen Elle Chin. Kidnappers would have picked Elle up, or covered her with a coat or a blanket. And, at five, Elle would have been terrified. She would have been screaming, kicking. Something. Tracy was about to ask the next question but paused at a thought. Terrified, unless perhaps she knew the woman and the man.

"Just to clarify. The little girl didn't appear to be struggling at all?"

"No," Ingram said. "She was just walking along."

CHAPTER 9

The morning after Halloween, Tracy stepped from the elevator onto the seventh floor and turned for the A Team's bull pen out of habit. "Old dogs," she said, changing direction and making her way to the Cold Case office.

She had rushed home following her interview with Jimmy Ingram, and she and Dan had pushed Daniella's stroller through a Redmond neighborhood. She was surprised to find entire families dressed in matching costumes, characters from the movies *The Incredibles* and *Frozen*, even *The Wizard of Oz*. Tracy had not even contemplated dressing in costume, though Dan apparently had. He'd worn a Frankenstein mask, an Elvis wig, and a hideously colorful jacket. Leave it to him—people thought Franken-Elvis was hysterical.

Tracy had dressed Daniella in a bumblebee outfit, which everyone said looked adorable. Daniella only lasted an hour before falling fast asleep in her stroller. They returned home to a mess; Rex and Sherlock had eaten chocolate bars Dan bought and left on the kitchen counter. Lucky for the dogs, they'd thrown up. Not so lucky for Dan. Since the chocolate bars had been his idea, in the unlikely event a child trekked to their remote home, Tracy gave Franken-Elvis the privilege of cleaning up the mess and calling the vet to determine if the dogs needed to go in. Considering the amount of chocolate and kibble Rex and Sherlock had thrown up, the vet didn't need to see them.

She'd spent much of the remainder of the night going through the Elle Chin file, looking for something the prior detectives had missed, some clue hidden in the photographs and witness statements that would unlock what had happened to the little girl. Experience had taught her that detectives could get so close to the evidence during an investigation, their focus becoming myopic, they'd let something significant slip past, unnoticed.

That's when Tracy sought fresh eyes. A fresh opinion. A fresh start. She reviewed the Elle Chin case as if just beginning the investigation.

The Chin divorce had been bitter and ugly in just about every sense of the words. It had also been violent, at least according to Jewel Chin. The detectives had run a background check on Bobby Chin but found no prior incidents of physical or verbal abuse of women—his wife, the notable exception. Was this an allegation just to get leverage? Tracy didn't think so. Her mother used to say tigers didn't change their stripes. Once a cheater, always a cheater. Once abusive, always abusive.

She decided to find out if Bobby Chin was a tiger. The burning question was whether he could have hated his ex-wife so much he might have harmed his daughter. Tracy didn't want to believe that was possible but, sadly, she knew it happened far too often. SPD had also appeared to give Chin the benefit of the doubt; he was one of their own. Tracy would not do so.

Chin had graduated from the University of Washington, where he'd been a member of the Phi Delta Phi fraternity. The investigating detectives found no police reports evidencing he'd ever abused woman, though he certainly could have. Many college women chose not to report such incidents. They didn't trust the system, and they feared spending their college years as a leper. Chin's plea to domestic battery, and the two other documented incidents that brought police officers to the home, indicated a propensity for violence, and Chin's only "excuse" was his wife had baited him into hitting her, which wasn't exactly an admission of remorse or regret.

She added a note to her list to find and talk with some of Chin's fraternity brothers.

The file also did not contain any evidence that Jewel Chin had a psychological disorder, or an addiction, as Bobby Chin alleged, though again, that wasn't necessarily something someone walked into a shrink's office and volunteered. Jewel certainly could have a psychological problem that had gone undiagnosed. The guardian ad litem's report made no such reference, but again, Tracy presumed both Jewel and Bobby Chin would have been on their best behavior when meeting the person who would determine their parental rights.

As for Jewel Chin being a suspect in her daughter's disappearance, the file contained multiple statements from both Jewel Chin and her boyfriend, Graham Jacobsen, that supported each other's alibis for that evening. The two claimed to have stayed at home—except for approximately fifteen minutes when Graham left to pick up Chinese food at a nearby restaurant. The restaurant had confirmed the order and the pickup. Detectives had obtained receipts. Bobby Chin dismissed this as a planned alibi. At his urging, the detectives had put together a timeline and determined that, even with the boyfriend's drive to the restaurant, there would have been sufficient time for him and Jewel Chin, or someone else, to drive to the maze and snatch the little girl, and still be home in time before all hell broke loose. If the little girl Jimmy Ingram saw that night had been Elle Chin—unlikely, Tracy thought—the timeline could explain, perhaps, why that little girl did not appear to be struggling. She'd been walking with her mother.

The case-file detectives had also contemplated this scenario, but they found no further evidence to support it. Bobby Chin could label his ex-wife a nut job all he wanted. He was throwing stones from a glass house.

Bill Miller, the first officer to the Chin home the night Elle went missing, filed a report that was strange, to say the least, and it made Tracy wonder if Miller had seen the detectives' reports before writing his own and had been looking out for a fellow officer. He and Chin both worked out of the North Precinct. Miller was also on Tracy's list of people to speak with.

Reading the file made Tracy think of that line in *Parenthood*—a movie she and Dan had watched prior to Daniella's birth. Keanu Reeves played a son-in-law and said something to the effect that you needed a license to buy a dog or to drive a car, even to catch a fish, but they let any asshole be a father . . . or a mother for that matter.

Too true.

"Knock. Knock."

Tracy looked up. Kinsington Rowe, her former partner on the A Team, stood in the doorway.

Kins flashed a cautious smile. "Came by earlier to see if you wanted to get a cup of coffee."

Tracy knew Kins's unspoken intent. He wanted to talk about Fernandez.

"Don't worry about it, Kins," she said. She had expressed doubt to Kins when he told her Nolasco said Fernandez's promotion was temporary, but she didn't want to get sideways with Kins by throwing an *I told you so* in his face.

Kins stepped into the office holding a folded sheet of paper. He wore a collared shirt beneath a brown V-neck sweater, jeans, and tennis shoes. His eyes scanned the daunting shelves of black binders. "You're going to take the position?"

"I don't really have much choice," she said, unable to entirely mask the bite in her tone.

Kins winced. "Look, Tracy—"

"Forget it, Kins. Seriously, this might give me more flexibility to spend time at home." As she spoke, she had another thought. "How'd you know I took the position?"

"Well, you're sitting at the desk, and . . ." Kins handed her the folded sheet of paper.

"What is it?"

"It went up on the website about an hour ago and, I assume, was sent to the news media."

Tracy felt her pulse race as she read.

Update: Decorated Detective Will Lead Seattle's Cold Case Unit

Written by Public Affairs on November 1, 2019, 11:22 a.m.

11/1: Decorated Violent Crimes detective Tracy Crosswhite will lead the Seattle Police Department's Cold

Case Unit, renewing the department's commitment to resolving past crimes and bringing justice to victims and their families. "The assignment of Detective Crosswhite reiterates the department's dedication to resolving crimes, no matter how old, and putting the perpetrators behind bars," new police chief Marcella Weber said. Crosswhite is a two-time recipient of the Seattle Police Department's Medal of Valor, its highest honor, for her investigative work. Last year the Cold Case Unit resolved twenty cold cases, Weber said, which she attributed to both improved and evolving forensics and devoted investigative work by Violent Crimes detective Arthur Nunzio.

The language of the news release had Nolasco's hands all over it. He'd released Nunzio's statistics as a benchmark, something he could and would use to evaluate Tracy's performance, which was unreasonable since the large majority of the cases Nunzio resolved were due to the evolution in DNA analysis, and there was no guarantee that evolution would continue or provide a new tool Tracy could use to solve other cold cases.

She also knew other detectives wouldn't want to hear her plight. *Back between the rock and the hard place.* She shrugged. "My bed. I'll lie in it."

"Don't get too comfortable. I could use your help."

"On what?"

"Katie Pryor called." Pryor had been a patrol officer Tracy mentored and helped to get a position in the Missing Persons Unit, so Pryor could better schedule time with her family. "A young woman is missing. The mother filed a missing person report and—"

"Why isn't Katie handling it if it's a missing person?"

"She said she has a hunch, given the circumstances, that this isn't going to turn out well."

Katie's hunches were usually accurate. "Why? What do we know?"

"I talked to the mother this morning. The room-mate called her and said the young woman"—he looked at a notepad—"Stephanie Cole, hadn't come home for two days, which isn't like her. Apparently Cole just moved here from LA. With Fernandez in trial, and Del and Faz up to their eyeballs with that bar shooting in Pioneer Square, I was hoping you had time to give me a hand." Kins flashed the charming smile that must have been a killer with the girls in college.

"You run this by Nolasco?"

"Nope. But I did run it by Billy," he said,

meaning Billy Williams, the Violent Crimes Section's detective sergeant.

"And Billy was good with it?"

"Billy said bringing you in sounded like the prudent thing to do, given that we're short-handed." Again, Kins smiled. Billy and Tracy were close. As a black man, Billy well understood discrimination, both overt and subtle.

"Is this a pity case, Kins?"

"I don't know. Are you taking pity on me? You are, after all, the twice-decorated detective in this room. It would be a real honor to work a case with you."

"You're a jackass," she said, and grabbed her purse.

CHAPTER 10

As Kins drove the pool car from the secure lot, he gave Tracy the *Reader's Digest* version of the case.

"High risk?" Tracy asked as she looked through the notes of the mother's statement. She wanted to know if Stephanie Cole was a prostitute, or an addict, or simply one of the homeless said to be moving to or being bused to Seattle by other states to take advantage of its homeless resources.

"Doesn't appear to be. She's nineteen, just moved here a month ago from LA, and works as a receptionist at a trucking company in Fremont, though she didn't show up for work yesterday or today—I confirmed with her employer—which coincides with what the roommate told the mother."

"Is the roommate Scott Barnes?"

"Affirmative."

"Roommate or a boyfriend?" Tracy asked.

"Just a roommate, though I haven't talked to him yet."

"How old is the roommate?"

"Barnes is twenty."

"You run his ID?"

"Clean. Not a scratch on him. He's a student at

UW Bothell and works as a barista at a Starbucks and as a dog walker."

"It's always the boyfriend, isn't it?" Tracy said.

"Seems to be."

Barnes had suggested he and Kins meet at Green Lake's east parking lot so he could perform his afternoon job walking two dogs. The lake was the basis for the neighborhood's name, and it included a three-mile walking path.

"That's him," Tracy said as they pulled into the relatively full parking lot and saw Barnes standing near paddleboats stacked on their sides and holding the leashes of what looked like an aging golden retriever and a spry rat terrier. Kins parked, and he and Tracy approached.

Kins took the lead and made introductions.

"Do you mind if we walk?" Barnes said. "I have to get the dogs their exercise or they drive the owner crazy the rest of the day."

"Not a problem," Kins said.

Tracy was glad to keep moving rather than stand in the cold. The temperature hovered in the upper thirties, and their breath was visible as they walked around the lake. The two dogs walked ahead of them, though they were relatively well behaved. Barnes called "heel" a few times, and both dogs obeyed. Tracy zipped her jacket closed and slid on gloves to protect her hands from the cold.

As lead detective, Kins asked the questions.

"Tell me why you called Stephanie Cole's mother."

Barnes said, "I got up this morning and Stephanie wasn't home. That was two days in a row. I thought maybe she could have driven home to LA. I really didn't know who else to call. I didn't want to freak out her mother, but . . . She kind of freaked out anyway."

"And what's your relationship to Stephanie?"

"Just roommates," Barnes said. They stepped to the side to accommodate two approaching women. Joggers, bikers, mothers with strollers, and walkers of all ages were taking advantage of clear blue skies. "She moved up here about a month ago from the San Gabriel Valley. I was looking for a roommate . . . to save on rent."

"You don't share a room?" Kins asked.

"With Stephanie? No. It's a two-bedroom apartment. We're not boyfriend and girlfriend, if that's what you mean."

"Could Stephanie have come home and left before you got up?"

"I don't think so."

"Why not?"

"First, her bedroom door was open the same amount each morning. Second, I didn't hear her get up yesterday or today. And her clothes weren't on her bedroom floor or in the bathroom."

"Do you always hear her get up?"

"Tuesdays and Thursdays I do. I don't

have classes until ten, so I try to sleep in, but Stephanie is pretty noisy. She turns the radio on in the bathroom. I can hear the music and the shower and the hair dryer. I would have heard her yesterday for sure if she had been there."

"And she didn't come home last night either?" Kins asked.

"This morning I got up and she wasn't there."

"You said something about her clothes being on the floor?"

"She runs when she gets home from work, which is right around four, four fifteen. She leaves everything on the floor in her room or the bathroom."

"When *was* the last time you saw her?"

"Wednesday morning before she went to work."

"Did she have any plans Wednesday night?" Tracy asked. She walked behind them to accommodate the joggers and walkers coming from the opposite direction. She flexed the fingers of her hands against the cold and regripped the pen she used to take notes.

Barnes spoke over his shoulder. "She said she'd been invited to a party by someone at work Wednesday night, and that she was thinking about going, but she hadn't made up her mind yet."

"Do you know if she went to the party Wednesday night?" Tracy asked.

"I don't know for sure, but I don't think she did."

"Why not?" Kins asked.

"She was making a costume. She'd cut up a skirt and a shirt she'd bought at a thrift store, so she'd have something to wear if she decided to go. She didn't have a lot of money; she had to put down a first and last month's rent on her share of the apartment."

"I'm not following," Kins said. "So why don't you think she went to the party?"

"Because the skirt and the shirt are still on her bed. Seemed weird given the effort she went to."

It did seem odd, Tracy thought.

"Oh, and she also didn't go to work yesterday or today."

"How do you know that?"

"Her mother called the trucking company where she worked."

"And it wasn't like her to miss work?" Tracy asked.

"I've only known her a few weeks, so I wouldn't really know, but from what she'd told me, she needed the money. She said she and her mother didn't really get along, so Stephanie was paying for everything herself. She took the first job she could find." That information had also been in Katie Pryor's report, and was part of the reason Pryor had called Violent Crimes. "I think they're going to fire her. Sounded that way."

"Do you know the name of the employee who had the party Wednesday night?" Kins asked.

"No. No idea."

"What did you do Wednesday night?"

"Me? I was out with friends in the University District."

Again, Tracy wrote down the specifics—the friends Barnes had been with and their phone numbers. "What time did you get home?"

"Around one in the morning. We took an Uber."

"Did you call the Uber?"

"Yeah."

"The receipt for the ride is on your phone?" Kins asked. Barnes said it was, and Kins provided his email at Seattle PD for Barnes to send the receipt. "What did you do when you got home?"

"Wednesday? I went to bed."

"Had you been drinking?"

"Some."

"Drugs?"

"No."

"Any of your friends spend the night?"

"No. We all had class Thursday morning."

"What time did you get up Thursday?"

"Around nine. I had class at ten."

Barnes detailed the classes he'd attended that day and the people he'd had lunch with.

"What time did you get home?"

"I worked at Starbucks that afternoon, so not until around six thirty."

Tracy again took down the details.

"Did you go out last night for Halloween?" Kins asked.

Barnes shook his head. "No."

"No parties?" Tracy asked.

"The parties at school were Wednesday. It keeps the high school kids away. There's too much liability for the fraternities."

"You said Stephanie runs after work?"

"She's pretty religious about it."

"Where does she run?"

"Usually here, around Green Lake, or in Woodland Park." He pointed across the lake to the tops of trees.

"Does she have friends she runs with or goes out with?"

"Not that I'm aware of. Usually she just comes home, runs on her own, then eats a salad, watches television, and goes to bed."

"What did you do last night?"

"Studied in my apartment."

"All night?"

"Until about eleven. Then I watched a *Jack Ryan* episode and went to bed."

"How did you have the mom's number to call?"

"It's the emergency contact on Stephanie's rental application. I called the apartment manager."

Kins asked for and Barnes provided the apartment manager's name and phone number.

"Does Stephanie have any issues with mental illness, anything you know of?"

"Not that I know of."

"You never saw prescription bottles in the bathroom drawers or on the counter?"

He shrugged. "No."

"Drugs?"

"Not that I know of."

"She never indicated she wanted to hurt herself?"

He shook his head. "Not to me."

They told Barnes they wanted to come by the apartment and have a look around Stephanie's room. He told them he'd be home around five that afternoon.

Tracy and Kins left Barnes to finish his dog walk and headed back to their car. "Did you put in a request on Cole's car?" Tracy asked.

Kins nodded. "According to her mom, and the California DMV, she drives a 2010 Prius with California plates. I had them send a picture."

"Shouldn't be hard to find. Barnes said she ran around Green Lake or Woodland Park every afternoon," Tracy said. "This parking lot has cameras atop the light poles. I'll get the video and we can check to see if Cole showed up Wednesday or Thursday afternoon."

"What do you think of Barnes?" Kins stepped aside for a woman jogger pushing a baby carriage.

"At first I questioned his calling the mother; most guys his age wouldn't have bothered, but he seems like he's responsible," Tracy said. "Goes to school and holds down two jobs."

"A lot more responsible than my sons," Kins said.

"Maybe he really was worried about her well-being."

"Or wants it to appear that way," Kins said.

"I thought I was supposed to be the skeptical one," Tracy said.

"It's rubbed off on me." Kins pulled open the car door and lowered himself inside.

"Let's drive over to Woodland Park since we're close and determine if the parking lot also has any cameras," Tracy said.

Woodland Park comprised nearly a hundred acres of running trails, picnic spaces, gardens, and open space. The park also was home to the Woodland Park Zoo.

"We had a zoo pass when the boys were young," Kins said. "I think it kept Shannah sane." They did not see video cameras in the parking lot and decided to walk a portion of a running trail that zigzagged through the well-kept grass. The deciduous trees displayed full autumn colors, though some had begun to shed their leaves, littering the dirt path. "My boys ran cross-country meets here," Kins said. "The trail is well defined and popular among joggers and walkers. I don't think anyone would be bold enough to snatch a runner here."

With time to kill before Barnes went home to his apartment, they drove to the trucking company in Fremont and spoke to the company's employee manager. The woman confirmed Cole worked as a receptionist Monday through Friday from 7:50 in the morning until 3:50 in the afternoon. She confirmed Cole worked Wednesday as scheduled, but didn't show up Thursday or today. They asked the woman about a party Wednesday night. She had no personal knowledge, but she did know of a party and called in a woman who worked in dispatch.

Ame Diaz said she'd invited Cole to the party, but that Cole did not attend. Diaz was in her midtwenties, short, and heavyset. Though her last name sounded Hispanic, the woman looked like she could be Filipina. She said she coordinated the drivers' routes and fielded calls from customers expecting shipments.

"Did Stephanie tell you she was going running before the party?"

"I don't recall her saying she was going for a run. She might have, but I just don't recall it. It sounded like she ran every day."

"Did other people here at work know she was a runner?"

Diaz shrugged. "It's possible."

"Do you know anyone who would have known

94

Stephanie was going for a run Wednesday afternoon?"

Diaz shook her head. "No one I can think of."

"Was Stephanie close to anyone here at work? Did she have someone she hung out with?"

"I can't really say."

The manager added, "Stephanie just started working here a couple of weeks ago. Most of our employees are older and married."

"She ate in the lunchroom with the rest of us," Diaz offered. "But I'm not sure there was anyone she was particularly close to. Everyone just sort of eats together."

"Do you know if she was seeing anyone?"

"You mean dating someone? Here at work?" Diaz did not sound like that was likely.

"Did she ever mention anyone?"

"Not to me. She mentioned her roommate once, but it wasn't anything in particular."

"What did she say?"

"I think I just asked where she was living, and she said she had rented a room in an apartment with some guy. I think he was a student."

"She didn't express any romantic interest in him?"

"Not to me. I'm pretty sure she left LA and came up here alone. So I would say she wasn't seeing anyone, but I don't really know for certain."

"She didn't express any interest in anyone?"

Diaz smiled, but it was nerves. "Not to me."

"Did anyone express any interest in her?"

"Again, not to me."

Tracy looked to Kins, who shook his head to indicate he had no further questions. They thanked Diaz, and the manager excused her. "Did Stephanie have any interaction with the drivers or warehouse workers that you're aware of?" Tracy asked the manager.

"She shouldn't have," the manager said. "She didn't act as a dispatcher. She was a receptionist."

"You didn't see anyone hanging around reception talking to her?"

"That's not really allowed here."

"Allowed or not," Tracy said.

"No," the manager said. "I didn't see anyone."

Kins sat forward. "Do the warehouse workers or drivers wear a uniform?"

"They have a company shirt."

"What does it look like?"

"It's light gray with black pinstripes and has the company name and logo over the breast pocket."

"What about uniform pants or shoes?"

Kins was thinking ahead, in case they found a witness who had seen Cole with someone or they found shoeprints.

"They're supposed to wear black pants. They can wear whatever shoes they want."

"Are there cameras in the parking lot?" Kins asked, knowing many trucking companies had cameras to deter theft.

"In the parking lot and the loading bays."

"We're going to need the video for Wednesday afternoon. Say, from three thirty to four thirty. Would you please send it to me?" He handed the woman a business card that included his work email address and cell phone. Kins and Tracy would review the video, then have it sent to the video unit at Park 90/5 on Airport Way. The building housed CSI, the Latent Print Unit, SWAT, and other SPD forensics units.

Tracy and Kins thanked the woman and left. Near five o'clock, they drove to the two-story apartment complex where Cole and Barnes lived. On the way there, Tracy called the number Barnes had provided for the apartment manager and set up a meeting in the parking lot. Tracy wanted to ask about video cameras.

The manager, a man, met them dressed in a long down coat, knit hat, and gloves.

"You ever have any complaints about either of them?" Tracy asked.

"Had a couple complaints about him and his prior roommate playing loud music, but nothing since Cole moved in."

Tracy noted cameras in the parking lot, but the manager told her the cameras were mainly just a deterrent. "They haven't been operational in more than a year." He then showed them Cole's designated parking spot, which was empty, and confirmed Cole had listed a Prius with a

California license plate on her rental application.

After speaking to the manager, Tracy and Kins walked to the second floor of the building. Barnes was not yet home. They knocked on the apartment next door. A midthirties woman answered. She didn't know Barnes or Cole, other than in passing. She said Cole was quiet and largely kept to herself.

"You ever hear any arguing? Yelling or screaming?"

She shook her head. "No."

"Any indication they were more than room-mates?" Kins asked.

"You mean romantically involved?" She shrugged. "I never got that impression. But I was never in their apartment either, so I don't really know."

"Never saw them holding hands, kissing, anything like that?" Kins asked.

"No." She shook her head. "This generation is not like your generation. Young people now don't have a problem living as roommates with members of the opposite sex."

Tracy and Kins glanced at one another. Tracy hadn't felt old before, but she did now. They thanked the woman and went back to the car to wait for Barnes.

"The last statement about our generation got to you, didn't it?" Kins said.

"How old does she think we are?"

"Old enough," Kins said. "Get used to it now that you have a kid."

Tracy had. She'd tried a PEPS class for mothers and their newborns but felt like a dinosaur.

When Barnes got home, he let Tracy and Kins into the apartment. Things inside looked exactly as Barnes had described. Cole's bedroom door was open, a mattress and box spring on the floor covered beneath a light-blue down quilt. On the quilt lay the cut-up white T-shirt and red skirt, and an unopened package of black fishnet stockings.

"Looks like she intended to go to the party," Tracy said.

"Like Barnes said, a lot of effort if she was going to just blow it off."

Tracy noted a laptop—a MacBook—also on the bed. She made a note to have CSI—if they needed CSI—grab it, and have the Technical and Electronic Support Unit find out if there were any emails or if Cole had conducted any searches of interest.

Cole's closet door was also open. Though it was a mess, they didn't see anything disconcerting. Tracy noted several pairs of running shoes. All New Balance. They checked the bathroom Barnes and Cole shared, but they did not find any prescription medications, or anything suspicious or of particular interest. They looked for blood-stains in the tile cracks and on the carpet but could not detect anything with the naked eye. They didn't smell bleach. They photographed Cole's bedroom and the bathroom, then shut the bedroom door and sealed it with yellow-and-black crime scene tape.

"Why are you doing that?" Barnes looked and sounded concerned.

"We're going to get a court order and have a CSI unit come by and take a closer look. Are you all right with that?" Kins asked.

"Sure," he said. "I'll be here."

As they left the apartment, Kins said, "He's way too calm and open for someone who's guilty."

"Let's wait and see if they find anything in the apartment before we exonerate him."

"We need to find her car," Kins said.

"Let's have Katie get out a news release with photographs of Cole and her car. We're too late for the six o'clock news tonight, but maybe the ten o'clock news and the news tomorrow. Maybe somebody saw her or her car."

Darkness had descended, and they returned to a parking lot cast in pools of light. Tracy recalled from Elle Chin's file that Bobby and his ex-wife had lived in Green Lake. There being no time like the present, while Kins made his phone calls, Tracy pulled up what had been the address to the Chins' home and plugged it into the map on her phone. It was nine minutes away.

CHAPTER 11

Tracy parked across the street from what once had been Bobby Chin's home on Latona Avenue near Northeast Sixty-Second Street. A one-story house with dark-green wood siding that Tracy estimated to be no more than 1,000 square feet. A white picket fence with a trellis enclosed the front yard, a dormant and gnarled wisteria vine growing over the wood slats. With the property lots so small, no more than fifteen feet separated Chin's home from his adjacent neighbors.

Tracy left Kins making phone calls in the car and approached the house to the right. The man who answered told her his family bought the home just two years ago, and he never knew the Chins. She tried the house to the left, a light-blue stucco home with an arched doorway atop three brick steps. Blinds covered the two front windows, but the porch light burned bright. A woman answered Tracy's knock. Mid to late seventies, she looked tentative. A television— what sounded like the news—played inside the house.

Tracy held up her identification and told the woman the nature of her visit.

The woman made a face and gave a slight eye

roll. "I figured it had something to do with them. Did one of them finally kill the other?"

The statement caught Tracy off guard. "Why would you say that?"

"You're standing here asking about them."

"I wanted to talk about the disappearance of their daughter."

"Oh. Sorry. That had to be what, five years ago now?"

"It is," Tracy said.

"Something new develop?"

"I'm taking another look at the file," Tracy said.

The woman identified herself as Evelyn Robertson. She and her husband had purchased the home and raised two kids before he passed away.

"I'm assuming from what you said that the Chin house was volatile?"

"That's a polite way to put it. I thought it would be nice having a police officer living next door. Never knew I'd have the whole department over here. More than once."

"Do you know what for?"

"I knew," she said. "Bobby left the house in handcuffs one time. He came over later to apologize. He said he was embarrassed and sorry about it."

"How well did you know him?"

"Not that well. We'd see each other in passing.

He wasn't a bad man. At least I didn't think so when we talked."

"Did you talk much with the wife?"

She shook her head. "No."

"Sounds like you had a run-in with her?"

Robertson pursed her lips. Then she said, "I'm not sure what she did, before the baby anyway. After the baby, she stayed home, mostly. I used to see her in running gear pushing the stroller, and a big guy would come by the house, *a lot*."

"Do you know who he was?"

"I asked her one time, and she told me he was her trainer, and I should mind my own business. Said it just like that. 'He's my trainer. Mind your own business.'" Robertson made a face like the trainer had been more than a trainer.

"Can you describe him?"

"I could, but no reason to now. He shot himself."

This gave Tracy pause. There had been no mention of this in Elle Chin's file, and it raised several red flags. "When did this happen?"

"After the little girl went missing. About a year later, if I'm remembering correctly. And I don't always."

"And you said he shot himself?"

"It was in the paper. I didn't hear it or see anything . . . That's not true. There was an ambulance and a lot of police that night. I guess you could say I saw the aftermath."

"He shot himself inside the house?"

"Yep."

"Did the police interview you?"

"Just asked if I saw or heard anything. I didn't. Until the police showed up, that is."

Tracy wondered if the death was, in fact, a suicide. She could think of reasons why either Bobby or Jewel Chin might want the boyfriend dead. "Was his first name Graham?" She fumbled through her notes from the case file. "Graham Jacobsen?"

"I don't know. Like I said, the wife told me to mind my own business. I did. I was glad when they finally sold that house. So much tragedy there. First the little girl disappears, then the trainer shoots himself."

"Did the trainer come around before the Chins were divorced?"

"Before, after." She shrugged. "Seemed like he was always there."

"You think Jewel Chin was having an affair."

"Don't know. Didn't ask. Didn't care to know." But she did think it.

"Sounds like you weren't too fond of Jewel Chin."

"She wasn't real friendly, and based on some things I heard coming from over there, I chose not to get too close."

Tracy made a mental note to ask Robertson what she had heard, but first asked, "Other than talking with Bobby Chin in passing, what else can you tell me about him?"

"He worked a lot and he had odd hours. I'd hear him leave early and get home late."

Tracy deduced that had to do with the nature of Chin's watch. "You live alone?"

"Since my husband passed away, going on ten years, but I have two sons who come by often and take good care of me."

"You said on occasions you heard things coming from the house next door? What kind of things?"

"Arguing. Fighting. And the language . . . I couldn't believe the language she would use with that little girl in the house."

"The wife?"

"She had a mouth like a sewer."

"What about Bobby?"

"He was no angel, but I never heard him swear. Not like the wife anyway. At times he'd just leave the house. I'd be watching television and I'd see him get in his car and drive off. I looked to see if he took the little girl with him. He didn't, unfortunately."

"Why do you say that?"

"Because the wife drank. I think that was part of the problem."

"How do you know she drank?"

"Because she was always worse at night than during the day. I'd see her some mornings and she'd be pleasant. By night she got cross. My father drank at night. I know a drinker. She was a drinker. Bobby would leave the house and she'd be standing in the doorway, yelling and swearing at him. Got so bad one night I finally called CPS."

"Child Protective Services?"

"That house was no place for a little girl. They figured I was the one to report them and it didn't sit well with either of them, let me tell you, though Bobby said he understood why I did it. Not the wife. If I saw her, she shot daggers at me."

"Did the Chins' arguments ever become violent?"

"I heard things banging around. My kitchen window is on that side of the house. And, like I said, the police showed up a couple of times. The last time is when they took Bobby away in handcuffs. I felt sorry for the little girl. She was standing right there in the middle of it, watching her parents fight like that. Watching the police take her father in handcuffs."

"Did you see Elle often?"

"Every so often. She'd be in the backyard and I'd see her over the fence, or she'd be out walking with her father when I was watering the lawn and they'd stop for a minute. Sweet little girl. He seemed to really care for her too."

"Were you home the night Elle disappeared?"

She nodded. "Sure was. I was watching television. The next thing I knew there were police cars and police officers all over the house. I thought one of them finally killed the other, there were so many officers. And then they sent in the people wearing masks and rubber gloves."

"CSI."

"Is that what they call them? The little girl's disappearance was all over the news."

"You saw the wife and the boyfriend together after Elle disappeared?"

"I saw them *before* she disappeared. He came to the house, and he was there when the police showed up. Like I said, he was there all the time. It was more of the same, just different participants."

"More of the same?"

"The yelling and the screaming and the swearing. Different guy but same thing. Except he swore back at her."

"Did you ever call the police?"

"No," she said emphatically. "I didn't want any part of that."

"The night Elle went missing, did you see the wife or the boyfriend leave the house?" Tracy asked.

"No," Robertson said. "But I wasn't looking. I believe I was watching television. I usually keep the blinds down this time of year to keep the heat in. I do recall the police came later. So sad they never found that little girl, but . . ."

Tracy waited. "But . . ."

Robertson shook her head. "Nothing," she said. "It's just sad."

CHAPTER 12

Following a late shift at work, Franklin set his plate and his Budweiser bottle on the collapsible TV dinner tray and sat to view the 10 p.m. news on the twenty-six-inch Sharp box television. Piles of newspapers, magazines, VCR tapes, and other things their mother had collected took up most of the rest of the space. The three brothers had learned to live around it. Franklin could not bring himself to discard the stuff. More than once he'd contemplated getting a Dumpster and just throwing the shit out, but he never seemed to get around to doing it, and there was never any impetus to do so. It wasn't like any of them had unexpected guests drop by.

He picked up the remote and changed the channel from a college football game to the news. "Evan, bring in the salt and pepper, and some of that steak sauce while you're at it."

Evan walked in with a limp and a swollen lip. The bruises on his arms were a sickly yellow and deep purple. He carried his own plate and handed Franklin the salt and pepper.

"Did you hear me say 'steak sauce'?"

Evan gave him a puzzled look.

"Go get the damn steak sauce."

Evan did, and Franklin applied the sauce

liberally to his steak and to his baked potato. Evan cleared a space on the sofa by shoving everything to the side and set his plate down on a stack of books atop the coffee table. Franklin shook his head. If there was a shortcut to doing work, Evan would find it. He was lazy, in addition to being stupid. A bad combination.

"Move the damn books so you don't knock them over," Franklin said. "And didn't I ask you to clean up around here?"

"I like the books stacked. It makes my mouth closer to my plate."

"Move the books and get after this mess when you finish up dinner."

Evan cut into his steak and spoke while chewing his food. "What happened to football?"

"It's over. I want to watch the news."

Evan frowned. "Same news every night. I like football. You don't know who's going to win. I like the Seahawks."

"Keep quiet. I'm watching the news because I want to find out if there's anything on that girl in the park. I got to do everything around here—think for the three of us. So shut your trap for five minutes." He pointed the remote at the television and tried to increase the volume. Nothing happened. "You change the batteries in this remote?"

Evan gave him a blank stare.

"Get your ass up and get me two double-A

batteries. I just bought a pack the other day. They're in the drawer to the right of the stove."

Evan set down his fork and knife and limped into the kitchen.

"Turn up the TV volume while you're up." Evan did. "And bring me another beer too," Franklin shouted over his shoulder.

Franklin watched the news while eating his steak, which he charred top and bottom but left blood raw inside. He could hear Evan rummaging in kitchen drawers and predicted what was to come next.

"I don't see no batteries."

"Your right is the hand you throw a baseball with."

"I know my . . ."

The rummaging stopped. Then it started again. The dumbshit had been looking in the wrong drawer.

"Here they are."

Franklin groaned. Taking care of Evan, and Carrol for that matter, was a lot of work, but he'd promised his daddy he'd look after the both of them, though their daddy had done little of it himself while alive. When he hadn't been at work, he'd either be down in the cellar or up at the cabin. And he hadn't given Franklin much choice in the matter, not after Franklin discovered what was in the cellar. Not like he could just sell the house and move on.

Evan called out from the kitchen. "You want a Bud or a Bud Light?"

"What did I say? Did I say Bud Light? That's Carrol's piss water. I don't drink that shit. Just bring me a Bud."

"They ain't cold."

Franklin was ready to explode. "I put two in the freezer so they'd . . ." Franklin swallowed the rest of the sentence when the picture of the young girl appeared on the television.

Evan walked back into the room. "I took the second one out so it don't explode—"

"Shh." Franklin stared at the television. "Turn up the volume."

"I got the batteries."

"Quit running your mouth and turn up the volume." A name appeared under the photograph. Stephanie Cole. "Shit," Franklin said under his breath. He put down his fork and knife.

The news report didn't provide a lot of particulars or details, but it didn't need to. One thing was clear. The police were looking for Cole. The newscaster said she had last been seen leaving work in Fremont Wednesday afternoon, and that her usual routine was to jog around Green Lake or Woodland Park. There was no mention of North Park. One good thing. The newscaster also reported on Cole's car, a blue Prius with a California license plate and, as the plate number flashed on the screen, a number

112

for a dedicated police tip line followed. The newscaster ended with a plea that anyone with any information should call that number.

Franklin closed his eyes and ran his fingers through his hair. His stomach gripped and his ulcer burned. The doctor said the ulcer was from stress. No shit, Sherlock. You try living here and have no stress. " 'Nobody's going to look for her.' Isn't that what you said, little brother?"

Evan paled. "I didn't know, Franklin."

Franklin stood. His thighs toppled the dinner tray and his plate of food onto the throw rug. " 'Nobody is going to look for her.' Isn't that what you said?"

"But—"

"No buts, Evan. I told you not to do it. You just screwed all of us, all the work I put in."

"They didn't say they knowed nothing."

"They're not going to give details of their investigation over the television. The police never say what they know and don't know. The point is, they're looking for her hard, and now, so is everybody else. How hard you think it's going to be to find a car with California license plates?"

Franklin ran his hand over the stubble on his chin, thinking about what to do. He'd had Carrol deal with the car, but who knew what type of job the lazy shit had done. Maybe this would blow over, like the others. Maybe this girl wasn't worth finding neither. Maybe the police would make a run at it, then give up. He doubted it. This one was different. This wasn't no prostitute. This was a damn cheerleader. They'd keep looking, and that meant Franklin needed to do something now.

He looked at his food strewn on the carpet and took Evan's plate. "That's yours," he said, pointing to the carpet.

Evan didn't protest. He held out the bottle of beer. "You still want your beer?"

Franklin reached for his beer. When Evan stepped forward to hand it to him, Franklin slapped him hard across the mouth, knocking him to the ground.

CHAPTER 13

Tracy had spent a quiet night at home with Dan and Daniella. It had rained hard, and they'd lit a fire in the family room and read books until the workweek caught up to her and she fell asleep on the couch. Not that her slumber lasted long. During an investigation, her subconscious often worked a case after she'd gone to bed, then when she woke up. This morning her thoughts had prevented her from going back to bed after feeding Daniella.

Tracy unlocked the door to the Cold Case office and moved quickly to her desk. When she took the cold case position, she thought she had worked her last weekend, but here she was, again. She and Kins had agreed to meet later that morning.

She found the summary of cases Art Nunzio had put together, the files he'd been working. She'd awoken that morning thinking of Stephanie Cole, which triggered a recollection of the Cowboy—the serial killer who had tied up and murdered female prostitutes working the motels on Aurora Avenue in North Seattle. Tracy had put the Cowboy in prison, but foremost on her mind, what had triggered the recollection, was something she had read in

Nunzio's summary of the cases he'd worked.

She ran her finger along the typed words, flipped the page, and ran her finger down the second page. She stopped and read the summary more closely. Angel Jackson, age thirty-two, disappeared from Aurora Avenue, a known prostitution area. Tracy continued down the page past several additional summaries. Three months after Jackson's disappearance, Donna Jones, age twenty-nine, vanished from roughly the same area. Jones was a known heroin user with multiple arrests for prostitution, narcotics, and, in one instance, for stabbing a john in the leg.

The same detectives who had worked Elle Chin's file also worked the missing prostitutes. When the detectives left the department, all three files were transferred to the Cold Case Unit.

Tracy left her office and made her way to the stairwell leading down to the room just off the sixth-floor landing, what was now a storage room, but what had once been the room for the Cowboy task force. The metal staircase thrummed as she descended. She pulled open the door and flipped on the light. Case files rested on high-density movable racks several rows deep. Tracy walked to the back of the room and retrieved the map she'd mounted on the wall that she and her team had used to mark the locations of each Cowboy killing. She hurried back to her office and removed Nunzio's now empty corkboard and taped the map to the office wall.

She wrote "AJ" on a sticky note and placed it on the map where Angel Jackson had last been seen. She marked a second note "DJ" for Donna Jones and put it on the map to mark her last-known whereabouts. Both were within a block of each other on Aurora Avenue North, or State Route 99, which ran north to south and was a straight shot to Green Lake and Woodland Park, the two places where Stephanie Cole routinely ran. She put a third sticky note with "SC" in that area, since they didn't know specifically where Cole had gone missing.

The facts of the two cold cases were certainly different than the information Tracy and Kins had so far uncovered regarding Stephanie Cole's disappearance, which wasn't much, but the location and the circumstances certainly were of interest. Women seemingly abducted without witnesses. No bodies found. No video, no DNA, no blood or other evidence of substance to follow up on. Through the years, Seattle had more than its fair share of serial killers, which was likely why the two prostitute cases had been assigned to the same detective team.

Someone knocked on her door. "What are you doing?" Kins asked.

Tracy explained her middle-of-the-night epiphany.

Kins didn't look impressed. "I could have saved

you the trouble. Patrol officers from the North Precinct found Cole's car early this morning. CSI is heading out there."

"Out where?"

"A parking lot in Ravenna."

"Anyone report finding a body?"

"Nope. Just the car."

Tracy placed the sticky note roughly in the area of Ravenna Park—north of the University District and the University of Washington, and less than two miles east of Green Lake—grabbed her purse and jacket, and hurried from the office.

As Kins drove the SPD pool car, Tracy called the Public Affairs Office and provided an updated news release on Cole's Prius. She requested that anyone who might have seen Cole or her car in or near Ravenna Park phone the dedicated tip line. She then spoke with the weekend patrol sergeant, advised him of the change in the case, and asked that North Precinct patrol officers, armed with Cole's photograph, canvass the homes near Ravenna Park and the park itself to determine if anyone recalled the young woman. After, she called Scott Barnes, waking him, and asked whether Cole ever ran in Ravenna Park. Barnes wasn't certain but said he'd never heard her say that she had.

Tracy disconnected and turned to Kins. "Do we

know if there are cameras in the Ravenna parking lot?"

"Not yet. What did Barnes say?"

"He didn't know. He said Cole asked him about other places to run besides Green Lake and Woodland Park, but he isn't one for exercise and told her to Google it. What about Cole's cell phone? Did you hear from the carrier?"

After obtaining Cole's cell number from the roommate, Kins had called the carrier, Verizon, told them they had exigent circumstances, and asked them to track the phone.

"Late yesterday. Verizon said the cell phone has been turned off since Wednesday night."

"Turned off? How many kids her age ever turn off their cell phone?"

"None. Including my boys and all their friends."

Tracy gave it further thought. "Cole would have listened to music while running, wouldn't she?"

"Again, I don't know anyone who doesn't," Kins said. "At least not her age."

"Was Verizon able to track her phone before it was shut off?"

Kins nodded. "Wednesday afternoon it pinged in Green Lake and in Fremont, then again in the North Park neighborhood to the north. That's where they lost the signal."

"Green Lake is where she lives. Fremont is

where she works. What was she doing in North Park?"

"Don't know."

"If the phone shut off there, that has to be where she went missing."

"Then how did the car get to Ravenna?" Kins asked, the question rhetorical. "The trucking company sent over the video for Wednesday afternoon. Cole left the building alone, dressed in running clothes and carrying a gym bag. She drove from the lot at 3:56 p.m. No car appeared to follow her from the lot."

"Which direction did she drive?"

"North out of the parking lot."

"Not south?"

"No."

"North Park is to the north."

"I know. I've asked Anderson and Cooper to canvass the nearby businesses and streets for any private cameras or traffic cameras that might have caught the street and determine if her car shows up."

Kins pulled into the lot at Ravenna Park and stopped beside the gray CSI van. Several detectives wearing gloves were going over a blue Prius with a California license plate, as well as the surrounding area. Tracy noted the car was parked in the slip closest to the park's edge, farthest from the street. She looked about for a running trail, thinking that Cole, a young woman, would park as close to the trail as possible, wouldn't she?

She and Kins greeted the CSI sergeant in charge, Dale Pinkney. Pinkney advised that a Seattle Parks and Recreation employee called in the car after finding it parked in the same spot for several days. He first recalled seeing the car Thursday and thought someone might be living in it, but he never saw anyone near it, and he finally decided to call it in. He had no knowledge the car had been on the evening news.

The car did not look to have been damaged, and there was nothing to visually indicate it was undrivable. Pinkney planned to go over the car in place, then tow it back to Park 90/5 for DNA and fingerprint testing and other forensic analysis.

"Anything inside the car?" Kins asked.

"A cell phone, a gym bag containing clothes, and a bag from a Bartell's drugstore."

"Her cell phone is in the car?" Tracy asked.

Pinkney nodded.

"Can we see it?" Kins asked.

They walked to the car, and Pinkney handed Tracy and Kins blue N-DEX gloves before giving them the plastic bag containing the cell phone. Tracy hit the screen buttons through the plastic, but the screen remained dark. She hit the power button on the side and the phone powered up, but the screen was password protected.

"Plenty of battery," she said, showing the phone to Kins.

She'd have to get Andrei Vilkotski at the Technical and Electronic Support Unit to do a dump of Cole's emails, text and phone messages, any numbers called or received. She'd also look through Cole's photographs for recurring pictures, people they'd want to talk to, possibly a boyfriend or want-to-be boyfriend.

Kins gently lifted articles of women's clothing from an athletic bag—jeans, a blouse, a sweater. Likely what Cole had worn to work Wednesday before changing into running gear. The clothes didn't appear to be torn or soiled, and neither he nor Tracy detected blood.

Pinkney handed Kins the Bartell bag. "It was behind the backseat."

"Pirate accessories," Kins said to Tracy as he lifted an unopened plastic package with a wide black belt, gray plastic sword, black eye patch, and red bandanna.

"Further indication she intended to go to the party," Tracy said.

A receipt recorded the Bartell store address and Cole's time of purchase: 4:18 p.m. Wednesday.

"Where's Twenty-Fourth Avenue Northwest?" Kins asked.

Tracy plugged in the address on her phone. North Park.

"I guess we now know why she drove to North Park," Kins said.

Tracy shook her head. "Why wouldn't she just go to a local drugstore in Green Lake near where she lived, or Fremont? Why drive to North Park?"

"Maybe there isn't a local store, or the local store didn't have pirate accessories," Kins said.

Tracy took out her spiral notepad and pen and made a note to check the phone log after Vilkotski opened it to determine if Cole called the store or did a search before driving there. She doubted Cole would have driven out on a whim that the store stocked pirate accessories, especially if she was trying to run before the party, which looked to be the case. That would also seemingly dictate against her driving all the way back to Ravenna to do so. "Why not just run around Green Lake or Woodland Park? Why come here?"

"She could have been bored with Green Lake or Woodland Park. Barnes said she was looking for different places to run. I'm wondering why she made a point of getting those accessories. Makes me wonder if there was going to be somebody at the party she wanted to impress."

"Let's take a drive out to the store and see if anyone remembers her," Tracy said. "The store might still have video."

Kins told Pinkney to call if they found anything else. DNA hits and positive hits for latent fingerprints could be days, maybe even weeks, even with a rush.

They didn't have that kind of time. Not if they hoped to find Cole alive.

Tracy spoke as they got back into their pool car. "I'll call Oz, tell him time is of the essence, and see about getting any DNA expedited." She was referring to the Washington State Patrol Crime Lab director Michael Melton, whom she called "Oz" from *The Wizard of Oz*. Others called him "Grizzly Adams," because Melton's hair and beard were similar to Dan Haggerty's, the actor from the television show.

"They're backed up," Kins said. "I have another case I'm waiting on. Likely weeks."

"They're always backed up. I know Mike's weakness."

The first forty-eight hours after an abduction were critical. Statistics showed the chances of locating a missing person alive decreased dramatically after that point.

And Tracy and Kins were already behind.

They spoke to the Bartell store manager in North Park. The woman did not recall Stephanie Cole, but the store had cameras in the ceiling tiles, and the manager suspected they still had the data for Wednesday at 4:18 p.m. They followed her into a room in the storage area at the back of the store and she logged onto a computer, then pulled up the video for that date and time.

"There," Tracy said, viewing the monitor. "That's her."

Cole entered the store in her running clothes. It was just a video, but something about seeing Cole alive, walking into the store, made the image compelling and personal. It also gave Tracy hope. She prayed it wasn't false hope.

Cole walked to the back of the store, where she found the package of pirate accessories. After less than a minute, she moved to the front of the store.

"She was on a mission," Tracy said.

"Certainly didn't waste any time," Kins agreed.

"Makes me think she called ahead," Tracy said.

Tracy watched other people in the store to determine if anyone took an interest in Cole. She didn't see anyone suspicious as Cole walked to the registers at the front of the store, where she was assisted by a young woman. "Who is that?" Tracy asked, pointing at the female cashier.

"That's Denise," the woman said.

"Is she working today?"

"No. She's off."

Tracy took down the woman's full name, and the manager promised to provide her work schedule. The exchange between Cole and the cashier was brief. At one point on the video, Cole considered the Fitbit on her wrist.

"She's worried about the time," Tracy said.

The monitor at the bottom of the screen

registered Cole leaving the store at 4:19 p.m. Again, Kins and Tracy watched to determine if anyone had followed her.

No one did.

The manager typed on the keyboard and pulled up footage from the parking lot. They watched Cole leave the store and move quickly to her car. A slow jog. Another indication she was rushed. Again, Tracy watched the people and cars around her. Cole pulled from the parking lot and departed on surface streets.

"If anyone followed her, this would be the time," Kins said softly.

They watched the tape. No car pulled from a space to follow.

They asked additional questions and provided the manager with business cards. Tracy requested that the manager email Kins the video, which he'd also send to the unit at Park 90/5.

"You got any ideas?" Kins said as he and Tracy got back inside their pool car.

"One. She bought the costume at 4:18. No way she drove back to Ravenna in that traffic in time to get a run in. Not in daylight anyway, which would seem to be a priority for someone who didn't know the running trail and was trying to make a party."

"Maybe she didn't know it gets dark at four thirty, not being from up here," Kins said. "Maybe she thought she had more time."

"Maybe," Tracy said, though she was not convinced. "Or maybe she didn't run there."

"Her car is there."

"I know. But so far there's no indication she ever was."

"We're speculating. Maybe someone near Ravenna recalled seeing her or the car."

"I think we should look up running parks and trails around here."

"Okay, but let's get some lunch. We can go over our notes, and talk this through, see if we're missing anything. We can look up running trails and give Pinkney a call and determine if CSI has found anything more or if anything came in on the dedicated tip line."

Tracy checked her watch, not realizing it was already 12:30. She wanted to talk to Bill Miller, the North Precinct patrol officer who had been the first officer at Jewel Chin's home the night Elle had gone missing. She'd confirmed the night before that Miller continued to work out of the North Precinct, and the patrol sergeant said Miller had been scheduled to work the First Watch last night, which meant he'd be just getting off.

Tracy told this to Kins.

"Give him a call. Maybe we'll kill two birds with one stone," Kins said.

"You need a different idiom."

"Not to mention a better vocabulary. Idiom?"

CHAPTER 14

Tracy reached Bill Miller on his cell phone as he left the North Precinct following his watch. Tracy had questions regarding the report Miller filed the evening Elle Chin disappeared. She felt Miller shaded his report to benefit his fellow officer. Miller was just about to eat before a workout, then go home and sleep, but said he'd be happy to talk to Tracy at the IHOP restaurant on Aurora Avenue not far from the North Precinct.

"See," Kins said. "Two birds with one stone."

Miller wasn't hard to find, and not just because he remained in uniform. Almost as wide as the booth he sat in, Miller looked to be early thirties, with boyish facial features, a broad chest and back, and biceps that strained his shirtsleeves.

"He looks like Li'l Abner," Kins said as they approached the booth, referencing a very dated comic strip character.

"You really are old," Tracy said.

"Raise three boys," Kins said. "They zap the youth out of you faster than you can say 'vasectomy.'"

Miller had a half-eaten plate of food in front

of him, steak and eggs, as well as an—as yet—untouched stack of pancakes.

As Tracy and Kins made introductions, Miller looked sheepish at the amount of food on the table. "I'm carbo loading before my workout."

"What are you curling, small cars?" Kins said with a smile.

Miller laughed. "I'm training for a competition coming up. It's tough when I'm working the First Watch." His voice was higher pitched than Tracy expected, given the man's size. "But at least I can get to the gym."

"What kind of competition?" Kins asked. Tracy figured this was a male bonding exercise and let Kins continue.

"Powerlifting. I got into it when I was at the U."

"Did you play football there?" Kins asked. "You must have been the entire offensive or defensive line. I would have loved to have run behind you."

"No football," Miller said. "My dad is a neurologist. He didn't want me hitting anybody with my head. I had a track-and-field scholarship. Hammer throw, shot put, discus. You played at the U?"

"Four years, one year in the NFL. Wish I had your dad advising me. Could explain a lot of things."

"Concussions?"

"A few, but I retired when I hurt my hip. I got a new one before I turned forty. Lucky me. I don't let my boys play football."

Tracy and Kins ordered from the waitress as she filled their coffee mugs. Kins chose an omelet. Tracy selected a Danish.

"You're the detective that caught the Cowboy," Miller said to Tracy.

Tracy had received considerable recognition inside the department and from the news media for arresting the Cowboy. She wasn't surprised Miller, working out of the North Precinct, knew the case. "I am," she said.

"I thought I recognized the name when you called. You're working cold cases now?" He sounded surprised.

"I am," Tracy said.

"You said this had to do with Elle Chin. Something new come up?" Miller poured half a jar of syrup over the stack of pancakes and cut into it with his fork, taking a wedge the size of a slice of cake.

"Just giving it another look," Tracy said.

Miller cut to the chase. "I imagine you want to talk to me about my report the night the little girl went missing."

"First, let me ask, how well did you know Bobby Chin?"

Miller swallowed his pancakes with a drink of milk. Then he said, "Not that well. Bobby and I were close in age. I think he was the class ahead of me at the Academy, but we didn't hang out or anything."

"What kind of guy was he?"

Miller shrugged those big shoulders. "Good guy. I liked him. Like I said, we didn't hang out or anything. He was married." Miller made a face when he said it.

"Did you know his wife?"

"I'd never met her, until that night, but I knew *of* her. All the patrol officers in the North Precinct knew about her."

"Bobby talked about her?"

"Not like you're thinking." He shook his head. "But he'd get phone calls while he was on patrol, and his partner would overhear and let some of the guys know. You know how that goes. You can't keep secrets in the station."

"I know."

"Then there were the reports about Bobby beating on her, and the domestic violence charge she filed against him," Miller said. "That was also pretty hard to keep quiet."

The police department, like many organizations, was a fishbowl. If you didn't want everyone to know your personal business, you kept your mouth shut—or threatened to shoot your partner, which had always worked for Tracy and Kins.

"Did you believe it?" Tracy asked.

"The DV? I didn't. Not at first. Thought she

was making up stuff. Heard the divorce was ugly. But then Bobby pled. So I guess it was true."

"You ever ask Bobby about the DV charge?"

"No. I figured that was his business. But what I heard was Bobby fessed up to it. Said he slapped her, I think. No excuse for that."

"Did Bobby ever strike you as violent?"

"No," Miller said without hesitation. "But I didn't work with him. He seemed pretty even-keeled to me, though he liked heavy metal music. Drove his partner crazy."

"I heard Bobby left the department. You know anything about it?"

"Shortly after his daughter disappeared. He was put on leave," Miller confirmed. "Had to be tough for him—the uncertainty, I mean. And his wife was in the news quite a bit, saying she believed Bobby took their daughter. She didn't have any evidence of it, but that didn't stop her from using it as a bat to beat him over the head in the media, that's for sure. From what I understand, Bobby was blowing the same horn, saying his wife and the boyfriend took the daughter."

Tracy wanted to ask Miller about his report. "You were first to arrive at the Chins' house that evening?"

"I got the call to haul ass and find out if the wife and boyfriend were at home or not."

"Who told you to do that?"

"Patrol sergeant."

"Do you know who called him?"

"I don't. I assume Bobby, but I don't know for certain."

Tracy could only imagine the preconceptions the officers had about Jewel Chin, and what Bobby had said to his patrol sergeant to get patrol cars to the house.

"Sounds like your perception of the wife wasn't good when you got to the house."

"Not sure I had a perception, but I guess you could say I'd heard enough to not know what to expect."

The waitress brought their food. Kins shook hot sauce and ketchup on the omelet and the hash browns.

"And was the wife at home?" Tracy asked, breaking off and eating a piece of her Danish.

"She was," Miller said. "With the boyfriend."

"Tell me about what happened when you arrived." Tracy knew that reports were the bane of every officer's existence, and for that reason, most officers kept them brief and to the point. They also didn't want to offer too much for a potential defense attorney to use. Miller's report was no exception. Tracy wanted to know his impressions, not just the facts about what had transpired.

"I think 'odd' is the word I used to describe it in my report."

"Odd how?"

"I mean, I was younger then—not even married—and I don't have kids, but . . ."

"But . . . ?" Tracy asked, setting down her mug. The neighbor, Evelyn Robertson, had also ended her comments with a "but."

"You have kids?" Miller asked Tracy.

"A daughter."

Miller looked to Kins. Kins laughed. "Shit, I got three boys."

"Wouldn't you think that the mother's first reaction to a police officer showing up at her door to tell her that her daughter is missing would be to ask about the daughter?"

The question gave Tracy pause. It would be Tracy's first question. "I would."

"I was fretting the whole drive over there about what I was going to say, hoping I wasn't the first one to arrive and have to tell her. Then when I get there and I tell her, she starts going off on Bobby, saying this was all 'bullshit,' that Chin took the girl, that she'd had a restraining order against him. I was like, whoa! Where the eff was this coming from?"

"Did she eventually get around to asking about her daughter?"

"Later, when the detectives showed up. While I was there, alone, she just kept swearing and telling me to radio in that Bobby took the girl and to have him arrested. The boyfriend was on me also."

"How long was it before the detectives showed up?"

"A lifetime—felt like it anyway."

"Tell me about the boyfriend."

Miller smiled. "A bodybuilder type with the spray-on tan and the big biceps and teeny waist. Steroids for sure. Sorry. It's an old prejudice."

"What did he have to say?"

"For the most part he couldn't get a word in edgewise because the wife was ranting. No one could. She was going on about how we needed to arrest Bobby and throw his ass in jail, and about how he beat the shit out of her and all he got was probation, how we were all just protecting one of our own."

"Were you?"

"Not me. I had nothing to do with that arrest, and when I heard about it, I didn't condone what Bobby had done. My dad taught me better. You don't put your hands on a woman. Ever. That night, I was just doing my job. I didn't know the details about what had happened except the girl had gone missing in a corn maze."

"Did you get the impression his wife knew where the daughter was?"

"The other cold case detective . . . What was his name?"

"Art Nunzio."

"Right. He asked me the same thing once. And I think I told him I don't know what I was thinking, if I even had an impression other than *Why the hell is she going on about Bobby and not asking about her daughter?* Like I wrote in my report, it was odd."

The detectives had said much the same thing. They said Jewel's ranting continued even after they told her that Bobby had called in Elle as missing and prohibited anyone from leaving the corn maze parking area. Witnesses had described him as "distraught." Jewel Chin dismissed it as an act. She'd said Bobby put on "an act for the police" and the police had bought it.

Kins slid from the booth and headed to the bathroom.

Miller continued. "When the detectives got there and asked her about her evening . . . you know, where she and the boyfriend had been, she got even more upset and started dropping more F-bombs and saying she wasn't saying another word until she spoke to her lawyer. Then she clammed up. Didn't say a word except that Bobby was responsible. She basically provided no help. Never did, either, from what I recall."

The detectives who initially handled the case had also noted that Jewel Chin seemed more concerned with her personal liability. After first going to the press to pin the daughter's disappearance on Bobby, Jewel went to a hotel room to avoid the media. She later refused to answer the detectives' questions. In his final report, the investigating detective speculated that Jewel, the boyfriend, or somebody they knew—or paid—took the child, probably to inflict pain on Bobby Chin. Little evidence supported the theory.

"What were your impressions?" Tracy said. "What didn't you put in your report but thought?"

"She was a piece of work," Miller said without hesitation. "How someone like that ever got a kid, or why she even bothered, is beyond me." He shook his head. Then he pushed aside half the stack of pancakes, as if he'd lost his appetite, which did seem unusual given his size. "Bobby was no saint either, like I said." He shook his head. "I don't know what happened that night. I don't know if it was the mother and the boyfriend or Bobby or somebody else. I just hope, for the little girl's sake, that she's alive somewhere. Alive and safe and that neither of them has any further contact with her. That's the kid's only hope for a normal life, in my opinion."

The neighbor, Evelyn Robertson, had said much the same thing, without actually saying it.

Kins stepped back to the booth, but he didn't make a move to sit down. He looked at Tracy. "We may have a witness who saw Stephanie Cole."

"Where?"

"In the North Park neighborhood."

"That's close to Bartell's."

"I know. You just may be right about us looking in the wrong place."

CHAPTER 15

Kins drove to a single-story brick home across the street from what looked to be an elementary school in the North Park neighborhood. Tracy suggested they drive around and get a feel for the area. She deduced North Park to be middle class, with modest, one-story homes and neat, well-kept yards. On this wintry Saturday, Tracy noted many dog walkers, mostly what appeared to be retirees bundled in down jackets against the cold, some with scarves and gloves or knit hats. The neighborhood had a friendly feel; at least the walkers were smiling. Some talked to one another on the sidewalk. A good thing if Cole had indeed been spotted here.

Kins parked in the street and they climbed steps to a brick rambler with large plate-glass windows on both sides. The door pulled open before they had the chance to knock; the tall, gray-haired man who answered had been waiting for them. A Jack Russell terrier sprang up and down beside him, tail whipsawing back and forth.

"Mr. Bibby?" Kins said.

"You must be the detectives." The man looked down at the dog. "Okay, okay, Jackpot. Settle down now and let them get inside." He looked back to Kins and Tracy. "He gets excited when we have visitors." A woman came into the room, expressed greetings, then bent and scooped the dog into her arms.

"Come on in," the man said. "Let me get the door shut before he runs off." After doing so, he said, "I didn't expect you this fast."

The woman put the dog on the ground as Kins made introductions. He explained they had been nearby when the call came in. Brian Bibby introduced his wife, Lorraine. Tracy estimated both to be midseventies.

"Can I offer anyone something to drink—coffee or tea? A glass of water?" Lorraine asked. Tracy and Kins declined. Bibby asked for coffee.

The home, like the yard, was simple but well kept and cared for. The main room had wood paneling, hardwood floors with a large area rug, and a leather couch pushed against a window that offered a view across the street to the school. A futuristic leather reading chair was angled to see out the window, as well as to view a flat-screen television mounted to the wall. Behind the chair, neatly arranged books, what looked to be mostly nonfiction—biographies—filled a tall bookcase along with family photographs. The Bibbys apparently had two grown children, a son and a daughter. Beside the bookcase, a redbrick fireplace spewed warm air from an enclosed insert.

Bibby took their coats and invited Tracy and

Kins to sit on the couch. He adjusted a back pad in the leather chair before sitting, explaining that he'd hurt his back working as a machinist at the Boeing plant in Everett.

"I gutted it out until retirement," he said. "But it was still too early. I'm not one to sit around."

"How do you spend your time?" Kins asked.

"We keep a Boston Whaler at the Edmonds Marina. When the salmon are running, Lorraine and I are out just about every morning, regardless of how my back feels. I smoke the salmon in a smoker out back, freeze-dry it, and give it to all the neighbors. I have a whole freezer full in the garage. Can I interest either of you?"

Again, Tracy and Kins declined.

Lorraine returned with Bibby's cup of coffee. He thanked her, sipped it, and set the cup on a coaster on the table near the floor lamp. Lorraine pulled up a folding chair and sat beside her husband.

"Mr. Bibby—" Kins began.

"Bibby is fine," he said. "Everyone has always called me Bibby."

He sounded like he took pride in it.

"You think you might have seen Stephanie Cole?" Kins said.

"You got a photograph of her?" Bibby asked.

Kins pulled up the photograph they'd used for the news release and handed his phone to

Lorraine, who handed it to her husband without looking at the picture. Bibby studied the photograph. Then he said, "Is she a runner?"

"Why do you ask?" Kins said.

"Because the young lady I saw was running in the park down the street."

"That's where you saw her?"

"That's where Jackpot and I go walking. That's our usual route. We walk down the street to the park entrance and walk until the trail dead-ends, then walk back."

"And is this the woman?"

"Sure looks like her," Bibby said. "She had her hair pulled back in a ponytail. That's the only thing keeping me from being a hundred percent certain, but I'd say ninety percent." In the photograph Cole's hair hung to her shoulders. "She live around here? I've never seen her before, but I figured if she was running in the park maybe she just moved in."

"Why do you say that?"

"Because it's not really a park for running. There's just the one trail and, as I said, it dead-ends at the bottom of the ravine. It's also steep, which I imagine is hard on a runner's knees going downhill, all that pounding, and the back, I suppose. And, what goes down must come back up again, which would not be pleasant. Beyond that, the entrance to the park isn't easy to find, if you don't live here. I figured she must have recently moved to the neighborhood and didn't know any better."

"What time do you and Jackpot go for your walk?" Kins asked.

"Depends on the time of year. Jackpot and I leave the house so there's enough daylight to make it there and back. We walk in the afternoon because it helps to settle Jackpot down for the night and helps me stretch out my back."

"When did you see the woman going for a run?" Kins asked.

"It was Wednesday." Bibby looked to his wife as if calculating the time. "So Jackpot and I would have left the house at about 3:45."

"Do you walk with your husband?" Tracy asked Lorraine.

"Sometimes, but not always. I still work part-time. I didn't walk with him Wednesday."

"So then what time did you see Stephanie Cole?" Tracy asked Bibby.

"I thought you might ask me that, so I checked the sunset calendar. The sun set at 4:48. Jackpot and I saw her right around 4:35 to 4:40, as we were walking back up the trail. I'd just put Jackpot back on leash . . . He got to chasing after a squirrel or a rabbit or some damn thing and was running in circles all over the brush. I had just got him back on leash when the young woman came running down the trail. I recalled thinking it was getting dark and the young lady had better hurry if she was going to finish with any daylight."

"What was she wearing?" Kins asked.

"Running clothes. Leggings, long-sleeve shirt, sneakers. She had those buds in her ears for listening to music. The kind without any wires. Not sure what you call them."

"Wireless," Tracy said.

"Makes sense to me," Bibby said.

"Was she carrying a phone?" Tracy asked.

"In her hand."

"You said you and Jackpot walk that route every day?" Kins asked.

"Occasionally we'll stray, but why, when the park is right there? I'm a bit of a creature of habit. Lorraine will agree, I'm sure."

"Did you have any interaction with the runner?" Kins asked.

"Nothing verbal. She smiled, and I nodded and pulled Jackpot out of the way. She was a little thing." He set out his hand, palm down. "Not even as tall as Lorraine, I'd say."

Kins asked and Lorraine told him she was five foot five. Cole was five foot four.

"Do you think she went missing in the park?" Lorraine asked, looking and sounding concerned.

"We don't know," Kins said. "We're doing our best to retrace her whereabouts that afternoon. I take it that you didn't see her come out of the park?" he asked Bibby.

"I did not. Jackpot and I would have been home by then, or close to it, I'd guess."

"Did you see anyone else as you completed your walk? Anyone on the trail or who looked to be waiting around it?"

"No. I thought Jackpot and I were the last ones . . . until she ran by."

"What about on the street as you came out of the park? Did you notice anyone?"

He shook his head. "Sorry."

"Anyone sitting in a car?"

Bibby shook his head. "Don't recall seeing any cars. I mean, cars park along the curb all the time, but mostly during school hours. Most are gone by three o'clock."

"When does school get out?"

"Two thirty," Lorraine said.

"Lorraine taught there thirty-seven years," Bibby said. "Easiest commute a teacher has ever had."

"Is that where you still teach part-time?" Tracy asked.

"I don't teach any longer, but I help with some of the administrative work."

"How did you hear that the young woman was missing?" Kins asked Bibby.

"The news." He made a gesture to the television screen. "As I said, I'm a creature of habit. After Jackpot and I walk, we sit down to watch King 5, and I have a cup of coffee. I was watching the news yesterday, and they put up the woman's photograph and said she was missing. I turned to Lorraine and said, 'I think I walked by that woman in the park Wednesday.' "

Lorraine nodded.

"I said, 'Does she live around here?' Lorraine often knows before me because new parents will enroll the kids in school, though this girl looked too young for kids. Could have moved here with her parents, I suppose. Did she?"

"Did she what?" Kins asked.

"Move here," Bibby said.

"We're still piecing everything together. This helps. Thank you. Anything else you can think of?" Kins asked.

"No. Nothing. I sure hope nothing bad has happened to that little girl. This is a peaceful neighborhood. Good people. We all know one another and get along."

Tracy turned to Lorraine. "Do you know if the school has security cameras for that parking lot?" She pointed out the window.

"It doesn't. Last January thieves stole a wheelchair ramp that provided access to a portable classroom. It would have been nice to have caught them on camera."

"Can you believe that?" Bibby said.

"We were the second school targeted," Lorraine said. "But we don't have much recourse without security cameras, and we won't get them if the voters don't approve two school levies to allocate funds for all Seattle elementary schools."

"You said the entrance to the park can be difficult to find?" Tracy said to Bibby.

"I'm getting ready to take Jackpot out for his walk. We can go a little earlier if you'd like me to take you," Bibby said.

"We'd appreciate that," Tracy said.

Bibby stood and grimaced. "No worries. My back could sure use the walk," he said.

After Bibby slid on his winter gear and tethered Jackpot to his leash, Kins and Tracy followed them out the door. Kins walked beside Bibby and Jackpot. Tracy walked behind them, surveying the school parking lot as they passed, then the house kitty-corner to what Bibby described as the park entrance. The entrance wasn't well defined, though there was a park sign. Someone had sprayed graffiti on it—gang symbols.

"You have any gangs around here?" Tracy asked when they stopped at the park entrance.

"Only of the septuagenarian variety," Bibby said.

The obscure park entrance made Tracy wonder if Cole had trouble finding the running trail. She made a note in her notebook.

Did Cole ask for directions?

Across the street from the trail entrance, Tracy noted a two-story house with floor-to-ceiling plate-glass windows. She looked for security cameras over the front door and over a sliding glass door on the side, but she didn't see any. She made a note to talk to each homeowner with a view of the park entrance, then followed Kins and Bibby into the park.

A signpost at the trail's entrance did not include a trail map. If it was Cole's first time running in the park, she might not have known the trail descended into a ravine and came to a dead end.

"A few years back the trail had become a dumping spot for garbage, used appliances, tires, you name it," Bibby said, starting down the path. "A neighbor got funds from the county to clean it up, and the neighborhood did the work. It's looking a lot better now."

She followed Kins and Bibby down the steep grade into a wooded ravine with maple trees and ferns. Tracy agreed that going back up the grade would be a killer, and it made her wonder why Stephanie Cole chose to run here when she had seemingly better running paths closer to her home that circumnavigated a beautiful lake and weaved through one of Seattle's best parks.

After fifteen minutes of walking, the trail flattened, and they stepped across wooden pallets creating a footbridge over a small creek. Bibby said, "This is where I passed her. As I said, I'd been chasing Jackpot all through these bushes and had just got ahold of his collar and got him back on the leash when she came jogging along."

Tracy could not hear street traffic, just the wind rustling the leaves of the small, tranquil forest. Not that Tracy felt peace. The lack of sunlight and the quiet brought a sense of foreboding. She looked from the trail to the plants, at broken branches and depressed leaves. She looked for footprints in the dirt, anything to indicate a woman had been dragged along the ground. She looked for disturbed soil or a mound of dirt.

Winter light faded, blocked by the canopy, though many trees had shed most of their leaves. They continued along the trail. Tracy's head remained on a swivel, searching for unnatural colors in the bushes. Already she was making plans to come back in the morning with cadaver dogs and CSI detectives. She'd also call Kaylee Wright, a sign-cutter who could re-create what had happened at a crime scene from shoeprints and broken vegetation. If this was a crime scene, they'd need Wright. Given the amount of time that had passed, and the hard rains last night, she doubted search-and-rescue dogs could track a scent, though she'd call to confirm. Kaylee was as good as the dogs, maybe better.

They came to an unceremonious but clearly marked dead end. Thick brush sloped up a steep hillside. Halfway up the slope, on two metal guardrails, someone had posted signs identifying this to be the end of the public trail.

"This is where Jackpot and I turn around and start the walk back up the hill."

"Give me a hand," Tracy said to Kins and held out her hand. Kins helped her step up onto the guardrail, but she couldn't see above the slope. "What's up there?" Tracy asked Bibby.

"Backyards," Bibby said as Tracy stepped down. "That's why it isn't a continuous loop. Some of the land is private property."

Tracy again studied the vegetation. She noticed a gap in the heavy brush, a small game trail that led up the hill.

"We're losing light," Kins said.

Tracy checked her watch. If this was roughly the time Cole had run through the park, she, too, would have almost been out of daylight.

They made their way back to Bibby's house and left business cards and indicated they might have further questions.

"Anytime," Bibby said. "Old Jackpot and I will be here. Sure hope nothing bad has happened to that little girl."

In the car, Tracy said, "Let's call the North Precinct and have them post an officer at the entrance, in case anyone saw us go down there."

"You thinking what I'm thinking? That Cole's body might be down there?" Kins asked.

"Unfortunately, I think it's a good possibility," Tracy said.

"I'll get CSI lined up. You call Kaylee?"

Kins asked. After years as partners, they often anticipated the other's thoughts and actions.

"I'm on it."

"Then let's talk to the homeowners in the houses across the street from the park's entrance and those in the houses with backyards that abut the ravine," Kins said. "Something stinks. Bibby seeing her here but her car being in Ravenna. I got a bad feeling."

"That makes two of us," Tracy said.

CHAPTER 16

Tracy and Kins canvassed the homes across the street from the park entrance. Unfortunately, it was not the best time to catch owners at home. People who worked either still remained at work or were stuck in Seattle traffic, and stay-at-home parents likely waited to pick up their children from after-school athletics and other activities.

They moved down the street from one house to the next, noting those in which no one answered so they could have a detective team return the following day. Those homeowners they spoke with either weren't there Wednesday afternoon, or didn't recall seeing Cole or her car. No house had a security camera, but some homeowners indicated that neighbors regularly walked, many with dogs. Several mentioned Bibby, but none could be precise about Wednesday afternoon. No one heard anything coming from the park. No shouts or yelling. One resident confirmed what Bibby had said, that the neighbors kept an eye out, and likely would have noted an outsider—or an unfamiliar car. Kins called Detective Sergeant Billy Williams and asked that he have North Precinct officers canvass as many

151

of the homes and businesses in North Park as possible with a photograph of Cole.

On the positive side, Tracy and Kins could now account for Cole's whereabouts up to approximately 4:45 p.m. Wednesday afternoon, though it didn't explain how her car ended up at a Ravenna parking lot.

"She got off work at 3:50," Tracy said as Kins drove along the street and looked for lights in windows. "We know she left work six minutes after changing into her running clothes. She left Bartell's at 4:19 p.m., and Bibby passed her in the ravine somewhere between 4:30 and 4:45, so it's unlikely she made any other detours after leaving Bartell's."

"I agree." Kins continued to survey the houses.

"We now know she ran in the park, which means she had no reason to drive to Ravenna, especially if she was in a hurry to get home, shower, change into her costume, and get to the Halloween party, which certainly seemed to be her intent."

"Seems to have been," Kins agreed.

"The roommate says she didn't come home. She didn't change into her costume. Which makes Bibby the last person to see her before she disappeared."

"Looks that way," Kins said. He pulled to a stop at the curb in front of a home with lights on, and they got out.

"So we have a young woman who disappeared seemingly without a trace. We have no witnesses, no evidence yet of a crime, and no body."

"Yet," Kins said. "Where are you going with this?"

"I'm just thinking of the two other cases I told you about that Nunzio was investigating."

"The two missing prostitutes?" Kins asked.

They crossed the street. "They also just disappeared. No witnesses. No evidence of a crime. No bodies. And not far from here."

"Let's focus on Cole," Kins said. "If she leads us in that direction, we can go down that path. Right now, she's still warm. If we find her, maybe we get lucky and solve the other two, or find out she isn't related at all."

Kins noted a camera over the front door, facing the street. "Maybe we get lucky." He knocked. The woman, midthirties with dark-brown hair, introduced herself as Nancy Maxwell. She said her husband had installed the camera when they moved in, but did not put up a camera at the back of the house that led to the ravine.

Maxwell invited Tracy and Kins inside. Her husband and two sons were at soccer practice. She replayed the video footage on her computer for Wednesday afternoon between 3:30 and 5:30. They did not see a blue Prius pass by the home, or Stephanie Cole, but they

153

did identify a man walking the sidewalk at 4:22 p.m.

"Who's that?" Tracy asked.

"That's Evan Sprague."

"He lives here?"

"The Sprague brothers live two houses down."

"Does he walk every day at that time?" Kins asked.

"I can't say every day, not like Bibby, but I've seen him out before."

"Can you speed it up?" They watched the next two hours at high speed. They did not see Evan Sprague return home, and Kins asked Maxwell if she knew why not.

"I'm pretty sure he walks around the block," Maxwell said. "Evan is a little slow. 'Challenged' is probably the proper word. It's not pronounced, but . . . I think he keeps to the same walk, you know, so he doesn't get lost and his brothers can look out for him."

"You said he lives two houses down? In which direction?" Kins asked.

"I'll show you." Maxwell stepped onto her front porch, crossing her arms against the cold. She pointed down the block. "The house is a bit dilapidated. It belonged to their parents. They're real nice people, but I don't think they have much money to spend on repairs. Franklin works at a retirement home and Carrol works at a Home Depot."

"Carrol is a man?" Kins confirmed with Maxwell.

Something about the relationship struck Tracy as odd. "Are the parents dead?"

"They are," Maxwell said. "Since before we moved in."

"But the brothers still all live together?"

"Three of them."

"How old are they?"

"I would guess Franklin is in his late forties or early fifties. He's the oldest. Then there is Carrol and Evan. Evan is younger."

"Were any of them ever married?" Tracy asked.

Maxwell shrugged. "I'll admit I thought it was odd at first, but as I said, they're great neighbors. Mostly they keep to themselves. We brought the kids by Halloween night, and Evan and Franklin gave away full-size Hershey bars. It was very generous of them."

"Does Evan work?" Tracy asked.

"He does odd jobs in the neighborhood. He mows the backyards of several of the houses. Franklin takes care of him. He's very sweet with him."

"Are there other siblings?" Tracy asked. "Other than the three brothers?"

"I don't know. I know how it sounds, three brothers living together. I can hear it in the tone of your questions, but sisters live together all the time, and nobody thinks anything of it."

They copied the video and sent it to Kins's work email, thanked Maxwell, and walked two houses down the street. The sun had set, the darkness interrupted by patches of light from the street lamps. The trees behind the homes swayed in the breeze and the air was heavy, like it could rain again.

The dilapidated house sat atop a small knoll. Unlike the other yards, the front yard was barren, without flowers or plants, the lawn mostly crabgrass. A cracked concrete walkway led to three wooden steps and a porch.

"Looks like Norman Bates's house at Universal Studios," Kins said as they approached. "If I see an old lady sitting in a rocking chair in the window, you're handling this interview on your own."

"You're a baby," Tracy said.

"And I readily admit it," Kins said. "I'm afraid of the dark, horror movies, and sharks. When I go to Hawaii, I don't swim in the ocean because I'm sure Jaws lurks below the surface."

Tracy peeked around the side of the house. The yard extended back thirty feet or so and looked to continue to the wooded ravine, roughly in the area where the trail came to a dead end, though the darkness made it hard to be certain. She did not see a fence at the back or separating the three adjacent properties. The lawn continued uninterrupted across the yards, but for an occasional flower bed.

Tracy and Kins climbed the wooden steps to a dark porch. Drawn shades prevented them from seeing in the windows. She had concluded the Sprague brothers were not home before Kins knocked on the front door, a dull, almost hollow sound. The porch light flickered on, and the front door pulled open.

"Can I help you?" The question came from a broad-shouldered man who looked to be the age the neighbor had said for the oldest brother. He had long black hair that showed traces of gray and which he combed back off his forehead. A wave of curls extended almost to the collar of his white T-shirt. He wore jeans and, despite the cool temperature, was barefoot.

"Franklin Sprague?"

"Who wants to know?"

Kins introduced himself and Tracy. They flashed their shields. "We're sorry to intrude on your evening."

"Oh, that's okay. I was just watching some television. Thought you might be solicitors or religious freaks. You can never be too careful nowadays. What can I do for you?" He crossed meaty arms. Tracy thought he had to be freezing, standing in the cold barefoot and in a T-shirt, but he didn't invite them inside.

"We're asking all the neighbors if they might

have seen a young woman who went running in the park late Wednesday afternoon."

"Is she missing or something?" Sprague asked.

"She is," Kins said.

"What time did she go running?"

"Between four and four thirty," Kins said.

He shook his head. "I was at work, and I went shopping Wednesday after I got off. Didn't get home until well after dark."

"One of your neighbors recalled seeing her in the park."

"Bibby?"

"You know him?"

"I know he walks in the park just about every day. Everybody does. You talk to him?"

"He's the one who called, said he saw her."

"There you go then."

"So, neither you nor your two brothers saw her?" Tracy said.

"Bibby tell you about my brothers?"

"No. Another neighbor."

"I sure didn't see her. Let's see. Carrol would have also been at work Wednesday that time of day." He shrugged. "What does this girl look like? You got a picture of her?"

Kins pulled up the photograph on his department cell phone and held it out to Sprague.

"Hang on a second." Sprague stepped back inside, partially shutting the door.

Tracy looked to Kins, mouthed "Norman

Bates," and mimed striking him repeatedly with a knife. The door pulled open and Sprague stepped forward, slipping on a pair of half-lens reading glasses.

"I don't see so well without my glasses," he said. "Let me have a look."

He took the phone from Kins and looked down his nose at the picture. "Nice-looking young lady, but no, I haven't seen her." He handed back the phone.

"Where do you work?" Tracy asked.

"I work at a retirement home in Seattle."

"What do you do there?" she asked.

"I'm a brain surgeon," Sprague said, straight-faced. Then he smiled. "I'm just giving you a hard time, Detective. I'm an environmental services engineer, which is a fancy term for a janitor. I clean the floors and the bathrooms, strip the beds when the people wet 'em or pass on, those kinds of things. It ain't glamorous but it's a job. Been there for years. I can give you the name of my supervisor if you like."

Kins smiled with him. "You said your other brother was also at work Wednesday afternoon?"

"Carrol works at the Home Depot in Shoreline. I'm not sure what his schedule was this week, but he wasn't yet home when I got home Wednesday. I know because I was looking for a little help with the groceries. He likely was still at work, but I can't say for certain. He hits a

159

pub up that way some days when he gets off."

"And your other brother?" Tracy asked.

"Evan? Evan would have been home. He don't work. He's not capable."

"Is either brother home now? We'd like to speak to them."

"Carrol's out. Again, I assume he's either working a later shift or getting a beer and some dinner. Evan is home, but he's sick. Came down with a bad flu and has a high fever and has been throwing up most of the evening. He's asleep in his room at the moment. I'm hoping I don't get it."

Tracy and Kins handed Sprague business cards. "Could you have your brothers call us?"

"I could, but I got to warn you, the chances of Evan remembering anything aren't real good. He don't have much recall. Not anything long-term. Maybe it would be best if you came back when I'm home, just in case he don't understand something you're asking him."

"When would be a good time?" Kins asked.

"Just about any night, except when he's sick. Just curious, Detectives, but is this the girl whose picture they showed on the news?"

"Yes," Kins said.

"That's where I saw her then. That's a shame, a girl that young. I sure hope you find her, and no harm has come to her."

Tracy and Kins thanked him and stepped down

from the porch. Behind them the door closed, and the porch light went dark.

"Man, my skin was crawling," Kins said when they reached the car.

"Yes, but we've established that you're not exactly a heroic figure," Tracy said, moving to the passenger side.

"Are you telling me your skin wasn't crawling?" Kins said across the car's roof. "The whole thing is kind of creepy—three brothers living together in what was their parents' house."

"You have three sons. What if they lived together?"

"I'd call hazmat to clean the place before I went to visit them. And I do have hope they'll get married someday and move out, but live together? That's just weird."

Tracy slid into the passenger seat and buckled her seat belt. "They're lucky they have the house, given the real estate prices in Seattle. And it's like the neighbor said."

"What?"

"You wouldn't think twice about it if it was three sisters."

Kins pulled from the curb. "Three sisters living together would be spinsters, wouldn't they?"

"If this was the 1850s."

"What do they call three brothers living together?"

"Bachelors, I guess," Tracy said.

"Horny, Randy, and Todd," Kins said, laughing.

"You just make that up?" Tracy said, not wanting to humor him.

"I did." He looked at the road, then back to her. "Come on. That was funny. You have to admit that was funny."

"Todd?"

"That's what makes it funny . . . The first two are obviously . . . oh, forget it. A guy would have gotten it and laughed."

"No doubt," Tracy said. "Let's stop at the North Precinct and see what arrangements have been made to get patrol officers canvassing this neighborhood, and make sure they have Cole's photograph and the car information. When we get back to the office, I'll confirm a CSI team and cadaver dogs are set up for the morning."

"I'll handle that. You go home and take care of your daughter," Kins said. "It's Saturday night. I'm sure Dan would appreciate you being home."

"What about Shannah?"

"She's out with girlfriends. If she has a couple pops, though, I may get lucky."

Tracy rolled her eyes. "Okay, Todd."

"You see, that *was* funny," Kins said.

Dan greeted Tracy at the door with a mischievous smile that meant something was up. "Come here. You'll want to see this."

He led her into the living room where Therese

sat on the floor. Daniella stood with one hand holding onto the coffee table. She was smiling and drooling and reaching with her other hand for a rattle Therese held just out of reach. "What's going on?" Tracy asked.

"Your daughter has reached a milestone early," Therese said.

Tracy stepped forward and dropped to her knees. Daniella immediately turned her attention to Tracy. "Don't distract her, Mrs. O," Therese said. She shook the rattle, drawing Daniella's attention. "All aloney," Therese said lyrically. "All aloney."

Daniella slapped at the wooden table, then unsteadily, she let go, took a wobbly step, a second step, and grabbed the rattle, falling into Therese.

Tracy laughed, which caused Daniella to smile and to kick her arms and legs. She picked up her baby and kissed her cheeks.

"She's not supposed to be able to do that for another month," Therese said. "This baby has some strong core muscles, I'll tell you that."

"She takes after her father," Dan said.

"Fat chance," Tracy said, continuing to coo and smile at her daughter. "This kid is all Crosswhite; Sarah was always ahead of the curve in everything she did."

"Fat chance?" Dan said. "That's a little harsh, don't you think?"

"It has nothing to do with your physical shape," Tracy said.

"Ouch again," Dan said.

Therese stood. "I'm sorry to have been first to see it, Mrs. O, but she surprised me as well. I left her for three seconds to grab my phone, and when I returned she'd pulled herself up and took two steps before falling back down."

Tracy smiled. This was the trade-off for working. She knew she'd miss some milestones. "It's okay, Therese. I'm glad we could all share it."

"Phew. I thought you might be upset with me. Well then, I'm headed out with friends. I'll leave her to walk for you two. There's a stew on the stove."

"Is that what smells so good?" Tracy said.

"I used what vegetables I could find," Therese said and left the room.

"Hungry?" Dan asked.

"In a minute. I want to play with Daniella, and she probably needs to be fed. At least I hope so."

"I waited for you," Therese yelled from the nanny's quarters.

Tracy laughed.

"She's going to be walking all over the place," Dan said, holding out his finger to his daughter.

"And she's already a handful," Tracy said.

"Like you said, she's definitely all Crosswhite," Dan said. "How was your day?"

"Interesting." Tracy filled Dan in on what she and Kins had learned. "It's a start, but . . . I'm afraid we're going to find her body somewhere in that park tomorrow. We're going back out with a CSI team and cadaver dogs in the morning. I'm sorry to work all weekend."

"Is this dog walker legit? Could he be a suspect?"

"Always a suspect, but unlikely. He's married and just about everyone told us he walks his dog every day at the same time. More likely a coincidence. Besides, I'm not sure why he'd be eager to tell us he saw her in the park if he was somehow culpable."

Tracy picked up Daniella and got off the floor, carrying her daughter to the couch. She raised her shirt and fed Daniella while talking with Dan.

"How are you doing with all of this?" Dan asked.

"I'm okay. Thanks for asking though. I think keeping busy helps. I don't have much time to think about things."

"And this case isn't hitting too close to home?"

"They're always going to hit close to home, Dan. That's just reality."

"Yeah, but how are you going to feel if the cadaver dogs find a corpse tomorrow?"

"Sad," she said without hesitation. "Sad for that young girl and her family, and all the more determined to catch the son-of-a-bitch responsible."

Dan smiled.

"What?"

"All Crosswhite," he said.

She smiled. "What do you call three middle-aged sisters living together?"

"Spinsters?"

She rolled her eyes. "What do you call three middle-aged brothers living together?"

"I don't know. What do you call three middle-aged brothers living together?" Dan said, his tone indicating he now realized this was a joke.

"Horny, Randy, and Dan," Tracy said.

"Dan?" He looked confused but also curious.

"Kins said 'Todd,' which he said is what makes the joke funny." She carefully laid Daniella down on the cushions. "But I'm hopeful for Dan."

CHAPTER 17

Sunday morning, Tracy found the CSI van parked at the trailhead. Yellow-and-black crime scene tape strung between the trees blocked access. Kins stood near the wooden sign talking to Pinkney and a handful of CSI detectives dressed in blue N-DEX gloves, black BDU pants, and jackets with "Police" on the front and "Crime Scene Investigator" on the back. Cadaver dogs and their handlers from the King County Sheriff's Office lingered on the periphery. So much for subtlety. At least in the ravine no one could see them, but already people looked out windows, and a few neighbors had ventured onto the sidewalk, talking with a uniformed officer, no doubt asking if the flurry of activity related to the girl they had been asked about door-to-door.

"My thought is we start at the bottom and work our way back up the trail to the road," Kins said when Tracy stepped up.

Tracy agreed and Kins gave Pinkney and the other CSI detectives a rundown of the terrain before leading them down the path to the trail's end. The temperature in Tracy's Subaru that morning was forty-eight degrees, but down in the ravine, where the trees and foliage blocked the sunlight, it felt colder. Tracy slipped on a knit hat and gloves.

As the dogs worked, Tracy updated Kins on what she'd learned speaking to Search and Rescue. "The detective sergeant confirmed that, given the amount of time that has passed since Cole was last seen, and the fact that it's rained hard, it's unlikely the dogs could pick up a scent to follow."

"What about Kaylee?" Kins asked, referring to the King County tracker.

"She got back from a conference in California last night. I told her to sleep in and give CSI a head start. She said she'd be here by noon."

For the next several hours, the dogs searched for any scent of a cadaver. Tracy hoped she was wrong.

Not long after starting, Pinkney approached with clear, sealed bags. "We've found blood. Mammalian."

"You're sure?" Kins said.

"I ran a Kastle-Meyer test," Pinkney said. "It's blood. We'll run a precipitin test in the van and see if it's animal or human," he said. "But if I was a betting man, I'd bet human."

"Why?" Tracy asked, knowing there was more to Pinkney's willingness to bet.

"Because we also found these."

Inside the first of several clear evidence bags was a white, wireless earbud, the kind Brian

Bibby recalled seeing Cole wearing on the trail. Coupling it with the blood, Tracy felt sick. In the other bags, CSI had collected cigarette butts. One looked recent, unsoiled. The others looked to be older, more weathered from the elements.

"Where did you find the earbud?"

Pinkney turned and led them to several red flags. "Near where we found the blood."

"And where did you find this one?" Tracy asked, holding up the bag with the butt that appeared the most recent.

Pinkney pointed behind them, to the dead end. "Just up that hill, beside a tree stump." Tracy could see red evidence flags protruding above the stump and foliage. "The earbud we found down here, in the bushes, near where we found the blood." Another evidence flag protruded from the shrubbery. "We're searching for the second one."

Tracy turned to Kins. The cigarette butt was in an unusual location, not on the trail or flicked from the trail into the bushes. More likely it had been left by a person waiting behind the stump, a perfect place to hide and watch the trail.

Tracy looked over her shoulder at the trail and imagined Cole running down the path, coming to the dead end, perhaps stopping to search for where the path continued, or to find another path. Not seeing one, she would have turned her back to the hillside to face the daunting and long ascent back up the trail. It would have been the perfect time for someone behind the stump to strike. It also explained the location of the blood, and the vegetation looked to have sustained damage. Tracy crouched and saw dark spots on the leaves of a low-growing bush.

"How long before Kaylee gets here?" Kins asked, looking at his watch.

"I'll call and find out her ETA."

Tracy stood and pulled out her cell phone. As she called, she looked around the area for disturbed soil, though the dogs had been through the ravine and didn't scent on a buried body. Not yet.

Tracy and Kins would call Cole's family and determine her blood type. If it matched the blood found on the bushes, they'd run it for DNA and compare it with DNA obtained from something in Cole's apartment—a toothbrush or strand of hair. They asked Pinkney to instruct his detectives not to further disturb the location behind the stump or the bloodied bushes until Kaylee Wright had a chance to review the scene.

Wright would be able to tell them what had happened, whether the body had been dragged off, and in which direction.

The dogs made their way up the trail toward the trailhead. They would now go over each of the greenbelt's ten acres. They did not scent buried remains in the ravine. Good news. Maybe. But a long way from Cole being alive.

Wright arrived at the site just after the noon hour. She came down the trail in jeans, hiking boots, and a warm jacket with her head down, scanning one side of the trail to the other.

Like Tracy, Wright was tall—five foot eleven. Dark hair extended to her shoulders from beneath a navy-blue skullcap. A former volleyball player at the U, she had studied criminal sciences, joined the Seattle Police Department, and eventually became a CSI detective. She and Tracy first met at the Park 90/5 complex. Tracy went on to become Seattle's first female Violent Crimes detective. Wright became King County's first certified tracker, often referred to as a sign-cutter.

Wright held yellow flags and occasionally stopped to put one in the ground. Over her shoulder, she carried a satchel with blue index cards she used to draw the sole patterns of each shoeprint she found, and to record each print's size and depth. She also carried a camera, though she relied more heavily on her eyes. Wright had located some of the Green River Killer's victims. She operated under Locard's principle that a person cannot move in or out of an environment without disturbing, taking, or leaving behind evidence. In a world of ever-evolving DNA and high-tech forensics, Wright was a throwback to a science that evolved two hundred years ago. She looked for footprints, kicked-over rocks, broken branches of plants, trees, and shrubs, changes to and trampled vegetation, blood, hair, and clothing fibers, and any other disturbance to the environment that most people, including some detectives, passed over. She could tell a person's ingress and egress to a site, the number of people who had been present, provide roughly a four-to-six-hour window of when they had been there, and a strong assessment of what they had been doing.

As Wright approached, she studied the CSI team processing the site, then glanced at Tracy's and Kins's shoes. To her, shoeprints were like fingerprints. She would obtain the type of shoe and the sole pattern of everyone at the site so she could eliminate them. Neither Tracy nor Kins provided Wright any details of the investigation. They did not want to influence her findings and make her potentially vulnerable to cross-examination by a skilled criminal defense attorney.

While Wright went to work, Tracy and Kins stepped away to speak with Pinkney, who had just disconnected a call.

"We finished with the apartment," Pinkney said. "A lot of fingerprints to analyze. We took the roommate's elimination prints."

"Anything?" Kins asked.

"From a superficial view, we didn't find any bloodstains on the carpet, the walls, or in the bathroom drains. We'll confirm that, of course.

Also, no physical evidence of a struggle. The roommate had no physical bruising or scratches to indicate he'd been involved in a struggle."

"What about the car?" Tracy asked.

"We're still going over it for fingerprints and DNA, but I can tell you someone wiped down the interior."

That got Tracy's and Kins's attention.

"The door handles, steering wheel, emergency brake, anything that someone would have naturally touched, were wiped with a disinfectant wipe. We found trace amounts of isopropyl alcohol and alkyl dimethyl benzyl ammonium chloride. As in hand sanitizer."

Tracy looked back to the scene, at Wright and the CSI detectives. "Have them check for dirt on the floorboards. If they find any, we'll want to compare it to the dirt behind the stump where you found the cigarette butt."

"Already noted it," Pinkney said. "And Andrei Vilkotski is working on the phone and the laptop. I'd imagine he'll have both unlocked and everything downloaded to us no later than first thing tomorrow morning."

They spoke for another twenty minutes, then Tracy said to Kins, "Let's go talk to the neighbors we missed last night while we're waiting."

The two detectives climbed back to the trailhead, which left them both winded. They walked around the block to the back side of the park and climbed the steps to Nancy Maxwell's front door, hoping for her permission to go into the backyard. No one answered. They went around the side to an unfenced backyard. Roughly fifty feet of grass extended before the terrain sloped down to the ravine. Tracy looked to the right, two houses down, to the Sprague backyard, which appeared to be directly above where CSI had found the cigarette butt behind the stump.

"You thinking what I'm thinking?" Tracy asked.

"He did say to come by anytime," Kins said.

"We need to make sure CSI checks the backyard lawns for any blood."

"That too."

They walked down the block and climbed to the Sprague porch. Tracy knocked three times. No one answered. She knocked again, but again got no answer.

"You'd think the one brother would be home," she said.

"If he was that sick," Kins said.

After leaving, Kins called into the North Precinct and put the duty sergeant on speaker-phone so Tracy could participate. The sergeant said officers had spoken to more than seventy-five homeowners and business owners in the North Park area. None recalled Cole or her car. They had obtained video from residences with cameras and had sent the video data to the unit at Park 90/5 for analysis. He also said the dedicated tip line had received more than 150 tips, and he had officers following up on each, though none seemed particularly hopeful.

Kins disconnected. "Maybe Kaylee has better news."

They made their way back down the trail. Wright stood speaking to Pinkney. "Just getting ready to wrap it up," Pinkney said. "We'll be running out of light down here soon, and what we have left to go over doesn't justify generators."

"Anything?" Tracy asked Wright.

"I was just explaining it to Dale." Wright led them up the trail to a series of yellow flags, in a relatively straight line that demarcated a path.

"People walk this trail. Dogs also. I've marked those prints that are relatively fresh, made within the last few days." She knelt. "These prints I've marked were made by someone who was running. The shoe impressions are consistent all the way down the trail."

"What can you tell us about the person?" Tracy asked.

"The person is petite. The foot is narrow, based on the width at the ball of the foot and at the heel, and the length of the stride is about sixteen to seventeen inches. This usually coincides with a woman, though not always. The stride interval is consistent, as is the route choice, indicating the person was running with a purpose."

"How clear are the prints?" Tracy asked.

"Some are better than others. The recent rain didn't help, but I'm used to it up here. There are enough to get a good impression. I'll check when I get back to the lab, but I know that print. The shoe is a New Balance, I'm sure of it."

Tracy and Kins had found several pairs of New Balance running shoes in Cole's closet.

"Another thing," Wright said. "A running strike is more heel to toe. The impressions at the top are consistent. As the runner descended the trail, the foot strike became more solid at the ball of the foot."

Wright led them to the trail's end. "She stopped here. Unlike the impressions on the trail, which point in the same direction and are a consistent stride interval, you'll notice the imprints down here point in a number of different directions."

Wright crouched and showed them what she was talking about. "The overlapping impressions and stutter steps show a change in mental state, unsureness. Looking at the location, I would surmise from the sign evidence that the person didn't expect the dead end and stopped to look around her environment."

"To determine if the path continued or there was another path?" Kins said.

"That's a working hypothesis for sure," Wright

said. "But the sign evidence also indicates a struggle occurred here."

"How can you tell?" Tracy said.

"First, from the number of and varying depths of different impressions, and the damage to the environment." Wright showed them broken bits of vegetation.

"How many different impressions?"

"Three," she said. "You'll notice scrape marks, upturned soil and stones, and stomped vegetation. I also noted dog prints here in the path and off the path in the vegetation. Based on the vegetation discoloration, I'd say it was broken and stepped on three to four days ago. I've taken a few samples to examine in the lab. Also, I found blood."

"Setting aside the blood evidence for a moment and assuming that it's human, why do you say the vegetation indicates a struggle? Why not just people who left the trail?"

"People are like animals. They take the path of least resistance. They don't normally walk into the brush unless they are chasing something or running from something."

Tracy thought of Bibby, and his comment that he had chased Jackpot into the brush, trying to get him back on leash. Lord knows Sherlock and Rex could get going when they got on a scent.

"They follow the trail, as the runner did, or they follow game trails," Wright continued. "Also, the sign evidence is not indicative of someone stepping lightly, such as to leave the trail to look for mushrooms or berries. And at some point, the runner was dragged backward, into the brush. You can see heel marks from the runner's shoes in the dirt." Wright showed them examples of those marks going off the trail and into the vegetation.

"So, if the body isn't here, then what? Someone carried her?" Kins said.

"Again, that would be a working hypothesis."

"How many people?" Tracy asked.

"How many carried her? Just one, based on the sign evidence," Wright said. "Here, let me show you what I think happened." She moved again, up the game trail, where she had placed additional yellow and red flags. "The flags mark areas where I either found a boot impression or a partial boot impression, or vegetation damage. Every impression faces the same direction." She pointed up the hill toward the back of the houses. "The person who came down that hillside moved with a specific intent."

Wright continued up the slope to the tree stump where the CSI detectives had found the cigarette butt. "Someone was here." She pointed to two shoe depressions, half-moons in the soil, and to more damaged vegetation. "They're not easy to make out, but that's the toe of a hiking boot of some kind." She turned toward the sloped hill.

"The person came down that hill and crouched here with his weight on the balls of his feet." Wright demonstrated.

Tracy crouched down. She was no more than ten feet above where the trail came to an end, but she would have been concealed, especially in the fading light. She looked up at Kins. "They could remain hidden but still see down the slope."

"The person was lying in wait," Kins said.

"Who?" Tracy asked, standing. "Who knew Cole would be running here?"

"The roommate," Kins said, shotgunning ideas. "Or someone who followed her. Bibby?"

"We watched the tapes. No one followed her from work or the Bartell's."

Tracy looked to Wright, knowing what she could determine from the sign evidence. "What can you tell us about the person who wore the hiking boot?"

"It's wide at the ball of the foot and the heel, and it measures at thirteen and one-third inches, about a size 12."

"Someone big," Kins said.

"Small people can have big feet," Wright said, "and the depth of a depression can vary with the type of soil, saturation, and other things. I looked instead for high signs."

"High signs?" Kins asked.

"Large men walk and move differently than men who are short or have a slight build. Look at the bush where the person crouched. I found broken branches several feet off the ground that likely caught on the person's clothing as he pushed through it to come down the trail quickly. This is someone moving with a purpose."

Tracy thought of the roommate, Scott Barnes. She had not looked to see what type of shoe he wore when they took the dogs on a walk, but he wasn't a big man. He was slight and not as tall as her. She estimated five foot nine at best, and guessed he weighed no more than 150 pounds. She thought also of Franklin Sprague and Brian Bibby. Sprague was a large man. Bibby was tall but not big. Plus, his bad back made it unlikely he could climb a slope, especially carrying a body.

And he had the dog.

"If the person lying in wait came down the slope and grabbed her, where did he take her?" Kins asked.

"Up the slope," Wright said.

Wright went up the slope, where she'd planted additional flags in the dirt and brush. "The boot impressions are deeper and inconsistent, indicating the person stepped carefully and was working to maintain his balance while carrying something heavy up the slope."

"That's a pretty steep grade," Kins said.

"Definitely challenging," Wright agreed. "It's another reason to conclude the person was not small and was in decent physical shape. And we can assume from the blood I located that perhaps the runner wasn't conscious," Wright said, meaning Cole would have been dead weight—much more difficult to balance and to carry.

"It would explain why no neighbor heard her," Tracy said. "Did you find a rock or stone with blood or hair on it?"

"No. If she was hit with a rock, the person took it with him." Wright looked up the slope. "The impressions lead to the backyards of those houses. That's where I lose the trail, and I doubt I'm going to pick it up again. Someone mowed that yard within the past day or two . . . all of the yards actually."

Tracy thought of the neighbor, Nancy Maxwell. She said Evan Sprague did odd jobs in the neighborhood, including mowing the lawns.

"The lawn is also mostly crabgrass, so the blades don't depress or bruise as easily as regular lawn. The mower cut and mulched the grass. I'm going to have to do more work to see if I can find a trail, blood evidence, perhaps after the person stepped from the lawn."

Tracy didn't think that likely. "He wouldn't carry the body past homes with windows, then be exposed on the street while he dumped the body into a car."

"He or they could have waited until it got dark," Kins said.

"Could have," Tracy said. She gave that some

thought. "If we make that assumption, then we have to assume Cole was either still alive, or the person wanted to draw attention away from this neighborhood to Ravenna, or possibly both," Tracy said. "Which would indicate the perpetrator lives around here, wouldn't it?"

"Possibly," Kins said.

"If he didn't live here, he would have just left the body, wouldn't he? It's too big a risk. He'd have to have a good reason to take that risk."

"It's also a lot of moving parts, isn't it, for one man to undertake?" Kins said.

"Seems that way," Tracy said. "Though it certainly could be done by one person."

"Or three," Kins said.

"We don't have enough to get a search warrant," Tracy said, knowing what Kins implied.

"No. But it's another reason to talk to the brother who was sick. What was his name?"

"Evan."

"And the other brother, while we're at it."

"Carrol."

They packed up and made their way to the trailhead as the sun set. Wright intended to return and go over the site in greater detail. Tracy and Kins would seek permission to enter the backyards of the homes. They focused, for the moment, on what they had not found more than what they had found, leaving at least a slim hope that Stephanie Cole remained alive.

CHAPTER 18

Franklin Sprague drove through the small town of Cle Elum, which was quiet on an early Sunday afternoon. He proceeded north onto Summit View Road and continued into the foothills, then turned right onto the dirt road that descended into Curry Canyon. The few houses in this remote area could not be seen from the road, and all were nearly inaccessible in the winter, when the snow came. Not even four-wheel-drive vehicles were assured of reaching them when the heavy snow fell.

Franklin pulled up to a locked fence with rusted signs: **NO TRESPASSING**, **PRIVATE PROPERTY**, and **TRESPASSERS WILL BE PROSECUTED**.

Their father had enforced his privacy since obtaining the land some forty years ago. He'd said he wanted land to hunt and fish, a place where he wouldn't be bothered. He'd fixed up a dilapidated cabin and pump house, along with a barn—though they had no livestock and never did. Like the basement in Green Lake, the barn was a forbidden zone. Summers, their father came out to the property frequently, and often alone. When he brought the family, Franklin and his brothers knew better than to go near the barn or to ask about it, knowing they'd get a beating just for being curious.

"Get the lock," he said to Carrol. "You remember the combination?"

"I remember." His brother pushed open the van door and stepped down.

"Don't you be touching that girl," Franklin said, eyeing Evan in the rearview mirror.

Evan lowered the tarp covering the women lying on the floor of the van. Before leaving Green Lake, Franklin had Evan remove one of the van's two backseats to accommodate their cargo.

"I was just looking," Evan mumbled.

"What did you say?" Franklin turned in his seat.

Evan winced. He still had bruises on his arms and his back from the belt buckle. In his lap he held a couple board games, Monopoly and Risk, and a pack of cards.

"Don't mouth off to me, boy," Franklin said. "Or you'll get another beating. We wouldn't be in this mess if it wasn't for you. Seems like I'm always cleaning up your and Carrol's shit. Seems like I'm always pulling your bacon out of the fire."

"I just wanted one to play—"

Franklin raised his hand as if he was about to strike. "Don't you talk back to me." Evan flinched. "You hear me? I'll beat you upside your head and leave you right here in the road for the wolves and coyotes. You understand me?"

Evan looked down.

"And put down them damn games. You're like a twelve-year-old."

Evan set the games on the floor of the van but slipped the pack of cards into his jacket pocket.

The chain rattled as Carrol pulled it from the metal fence, and the gate squealed when yanked open. The hinges needed oiling. Franklin drove far enough in for Carrol to close the gate and re-secure the chain and the lock. After he got back in the passenger seat, they drove another quarter of a mile. The branches of the thick brush and the trees along the edge of the road scraped the van. They hadn't been cut back since Franklin found mountain bike tread on the trail. He didn't want people getting too near the property.

Franklin drove up a small rise to the circular parking area. The place looked the worse for wear. The wood siding of the house needed staining, and the metal roof leaked, which was likely causing dry rot in the rafters. It all took time and cost money, neither of which Franklin had. He'd come up in the spring and work on the roof with Carrol and Evan since that was a priority. Neither brother was worth a shit nor had much of a work ethic. Hell, Evan couldn't keep focus long enough to pound a damn nail.

Franklin drove the van past the house to the

back of the barn. Carrol again got out, unlocked the padlock, and pulled open doors meant for unloading hay. Franklin backed the van inside and climbed out, and Carrol shut the doors.

"Evan, get out here," Franklin shouted.

When Evan reached the back of the van, Franklin removed the three tarps covering the three women—the runner Evan had grabbed in the park, and the two prostitutes he and Carrol took off Aurora Avenue.

They'd tied and gagged all three, though fear now did more than the ropes and the gags with respect to the prostitutes. If they tried to escape, or yelled to get someone's attention, a beating would be fast and furious. The young runner wasn't at that point yet.

"You and Evan bring them to the room," Franklin said to Carrol. As with the basement that the boys had dug beneath the house for their daddy, Franklin had never entered the room hidden behind a horse stall at the back of the barn until after their daddy died.

"We gonna leave them all here?" Carrol asked, looking and sounding concerned.

Franklin hadn't told either brother his plan on the drive because he had not yet made up his mind. Only one thing was clear at this point. "We don't got much choice now, do we? Not with the police looking for the girl Evan snatched damn near in our own backyard. They were searching in the ravine yesterday and this morning. Just a matter of time before they start searching the houses door-to-door."

"What . . . what . . . what are we gonna do?"

"Leave them here until I can better assess the situation."

He was trying to be smart about this. The night he'd gone down into the cellar and found the girl, he sent Carrol back to the street to move the car. The girl had the car fob tied to one of her shoes. He gave Carrol a knit hat and gloves and a box of disinfectant wipes, and told him not to leave behind fingerprints or possible DNA. He'd hoped that moving the car would keep the police away from North Park; he hadn't counted on Bibby seeing the girl in the ravine on his daily walk though. That changed everything. The detectives were now all over the neighbors and the park. Would just be a matter of time before they focused on Franklin—twice convicted of solicitation—and his brothers.

He made sure everything looked normal. He and Evan passed out Halloween candy—and not the tiny pieces neither. He'd bought the big bars, so the neighbor kids would remember them. Remember Evan. And he'd been sure to have Evan mow the lawns, as was his usual routine. He came up with Evan being sick on the spot when the detectives showed up. He needed time to prepare the idiot, Carrol for that matter, too, before they were interviewed. And he needed time for Evan's bruises to heal.

"I brought enough food and water to last them awhile. That should give me time to figure out what kind of shit Evan stirred. Evan, go put down them damn games and help Carrol carry the three of them to the room in back. And make sure you chain them to the posts."

Franklin carried the groceries from the car to the cabin. The temperature had dropped in the canyon. He'd have Carrol throw blankets in with the women so they didn't freeze to death . . . though that could take care of his problem for him.

The inside of the house smelled of mold, dry rot, and disuse. He left the door open, despite the cold, hoping to air out the smell. He made a sandwich and drank a beer at the kitchen table while he contemplated his next move.

He'd miss the regular visits with his girl while she was here at the cabin, but Evan hadn't left him much choice. Evan had compounded the problem by bringing the runner into the basement and letting her see the two other women. If he hadn't, Franklin might have had a chance to find a way out of this situation. He could have just turned the girl loose somewhere and hoped she didn't remember what had happened to her. The blow to her head had been significant enough to draw blood.

But now she knew about both the cellar and the other two women. The stairs leading down to the cellar were hidden behind a door their daddy had cut in at the back of the pantry. He had the three boys dig out a room below the foundation and reinforce it with railroad ties and four-by-four pressure-treated posts set in concrete. They'd dug for nearly a year, carting the dirt out by wheelbarrow at night and dumping it into the ravine at the back of the property. They stopped when they'd dug roughly six feet deep and eight feet square. Their daddy said they was building a wine cellar, but Franklin had never seen him buy so much as a single bottle of wine—he was a Jim Beam man, always had been. 'Til the day he died. Franklin didn't know what his daddy used the room for. Not back then. He had forbidden the boys from entering the basement, just like the room at the back of the barn, and he'd beat the hell out of each of them with his belt buckle just so they'd know what would happen, the pain they'd be in, if they ever disobeyed him. They hadn't. Not even when he'd gone into the home for people with Alzheimer's. Not 'til the day they'd buried him in the ground and covered him with six feet of dirt.

It had been the perfect spot to keep the two women. Franklin had thought through his plan for a long time. He had to be careful. The judge had made it clear after his second arrest that Franklin would do serious time if he got caught again, and that meant losing his job. Same for Carrol, who'd also been pinched once. Neither could afford the prostitutes anyway, not on a regular basis, not with the money they each brought in. Franklin figured that had been his daddy's rationale as well. Why pay for what you could take? And nobody was going to miss a couple prostitutes. They were . . . what the hell was that word? Sounded like "fungus," but that was a mushroom. Fungible. That was it. The prostitutes were fungible. They could be replaced. Nobody cared. Shit, the Green River Killer got away with it for decades. Franklin figured he could simply dump the two if he and Carrol tired of them, someplace far away. Yeah, they'd seen his face, but they didn't know where he lived. They hadn't seen anything but the basement. He'd put the fear of God in them. Scare them so bad they wouldn't say a word.

But Franklin hadn't prepared for something like this, for his brother being a dumbass and disobeying him.

There was always the alternative—though Carrol kept reminding him otherwise. "We . . . we . . . we ain't killers, Franklin."

Not yet.

As Franklin put his plate in the sink and his bottle in the garbage, Carrol and Evan came into the kitchen. "What do we do now?"

"Now?" Franklin pulled another beer from the fridge. "Now you and Evan are going to take them cutting shears in the barn and cut them branches narrowing the road, but not too much. Just enough so they don't damage the car."

"Wh . . . wh . . . what are you gonna do?" Carrol asked, clearly not happy.

"Is that any of your business?"

"J . . . j . . . j . . . just asking."

"Well, since you're j . . . j . . . just asking. I'm going to make myself busy in the barn for a bit. I think I earned it. Any objections?" Neither Carrol nor Evan said a word. "I didn't think so."

The one they called Franklin had walked to where Stephanie Cole sat on the scrap of rug and undid the belt buckle of his pants. When Stephanie pulled away from him, as far as the chain allowed, he'd laughed. Then he'd walked to Angel Jackson, unlocked her chain from the post, and took her to the back of the room like a dog on a leash.

Stephanie hated to admit it, but she was just so scared . . . She'd prayed, prayed that he wouldn't take her, that he'd take one of the other two, Angel or Donna, and she'd been relieved when he chose Angel. Still, she knew it was just a matter of time. She figured that's why she was there.

Half an hour after he had walked in, Franklin

rechained Angel to the post. He looked at Stephanie with a scowl, his eyes dark and hardened. Then he walked out, without uttering a word.

Stephanie had done her best to listen when they'd put her in the van, hoping maybe to learn something, where she was or where they were taking the three of them. She knew the men were brothers from the conversation they'd had in the dirt room. She knew Franklin was the brother in charge and that Evan had disobeyed him, though about what exactly she did not know. She'd watched in horror as Franklin beat his brother with a belt buckle until she thought he might kill him. She'd almost felt sorry for Evan, whom she suspected was slow. Almost. Mostly she was afraid. If Franklin could inflict so much injury on a blood relative, what could he do . . . What had he already done to Angel and to Donna? What would he do to her?

Stephanie looked across the room to Angel Jackson. "Are you all right?"

Angel had her head back against the wall, her eyes shut.

"Angel? Are you all right?"

"Let her be," Donna Jones said. "She's dreaming she's somewhere else."

In the light peeking between the slats of the room, Stephanie could better see the two women than in the darkness of the room where she'd first been chained. Angel had dark skin, African American or Hispanic. Donna was fair, with light-brown hair. She had track marks inside her arms. Heroin. The new drug of choice.

Stephanie and Angel had spoken in the basement. Donna mostly kept quiet. Angel had told Stephanie the men had abducted her first, a few months before they abducted Donna. She said the men brought them both to motels, then drugged them.

"Why didn't Franklin touch me?" Stephanie asked Donna. "Why only Angel?"

"He didn't touch you, or me, because we don't belong to him," Donna said.

"Don't belong to him?"

"Angel belongs to Franklin. I belong to Carrol. I guess Evan's got you." She smiled. "Look around, Little Miss Sunshine. Look at the scraps of carpet, the flattened cardboard, the chains. We ain't nothing but junkyard dogs to them. Pets. They own us."

Stephanie wiped tears. "Is there something wrong with Evan? He seems . . ."

"Retarded?" Donna said. "They're all retarded. A bunch of inbred motherfuckers. But Evan . . ." Donna laughed. "I see the way he looks at you. He looks at you like he's got something special planned for you."

"What?" Stephanie asked, fear welling inside.

"Oh yeah, Evan will be coming for you.

Franklin's just put his ass on probation for the time being, but your time is coming, sweetheart. He's going to have his fun with you. What's he keep asking you? If you want to play?" She shook her head, chuckling. "I'd be scared shitless if I was you."

"Leave her alone," Angel said. She did not lift her head from the wall or open her eyes.

"You've seen it too," Donna said to Stephanie. "The way he looks at you—like a kid staring at presents under a Christmas tree that he just can't wait to unwrap."

Tears streamed down Stephanie's cheeks. How did she get here? How did her life come to this? She should have stayed home. She shouldn't have been so eager to get away from her parents, but she couldn't take the constant bickering and fighting. She thought it would get better after the divorce but it only seemed to get worse. Battles about money, about the cost of Stephanie's education, which is why she chose not to go on to college. She had the grades. She had the ambition, but she was tired of being the pawn between them. She just wanted a fresh start. Life had to be better, she thought. She had no idea how wrong she had been.

"Why you got to do that?" Angel said, opening her eyes.

Donna rested her head back against the wall. "What else am I gonna do?"

Angel looked to Stephanie. "You listen to me. When your time comes, you just close your eyes and try to think you're someplace else. You think of that boy in high school you always liked. You think of him and just drift off, go someplace else. Then it won't be so bad."

When Franklin reentered the kitchen, Carrol and Evan sat at the table whispering like two girls. Each had a beer in his hand. Carrol picked at the label, a nervous habit, like his stuttering. Evan stared at the tabletop.

"You get those branches cut back from the road?" Franklin asked.

"We . . . we . . . we got as far as we could."

Meaning the lazy shits quit. "Stop stuttering."

"I'm try . . . try . . . trying."

Franklin took Evan's beer from the table and drank from it. "What are you two idiots talking about anyway?"

Evan looked to Carrol.

"Something you mean to say?" Franklin asked Carrol. "Then get on with it. Say what you have to say."

"Me and Evan, we . . . we . . . we . . . don't think it right that you got to be with your woman, and we can't."

Goddamn idiot stuttered even when he tried to act like a tough guy. "Yeah?" Franklin looked to his youngest brother. "That what you think, Evan?"

Evan lifted his gaze from the tabletop. "I want to play with her."

"I . . . I . . . I . . . didn't do nothing wrong. I d . . . d . . . done what you said from the start. Waited my turn and f . . . f . . . found my girl the right way, just like you said. I don't see w . . . w . . . why I'm being punished for something Evan did."

Franklin laughed. "So you're throwing Evan under the bus? How you feel about that, little brother?"

"What bus?" Evan said.

Franklin laughed. "The one that just ran you over, and you don't even know it." He looked to Carrol. "Who was supposed to keep an eye on Evan when I went grocery shopping?"

"Evan's a grown man," Carrol said.

"Yeah," Evan said. "I'm a grown man."

"Well, the circumstance we are currently in would be serious evidence to the contrary, now wouldn't it?" Franklin looked to Carrol. "You know he's a dumbshit. Couldn't find his ass with both hands if he was sitting on them."

"I don't sit on my hands."

"I . . . I . . . I was at work."

"Really? What time did you get off?"

Carrol lowered his gaze.

"You think I'm as big a dumbshit as the two of you? I know when you got off. If you had come home instead of going to the bar, we wouldn't be in this mess, now would we? So, you're both to blame. Him for doing what he done and you for letting him do it." He took another drink of Evan's beer. Then he said, "Evan, get in the van." He turned to Carrol. "You got your cell phone?"

Carrol looked from Franklin to Evan and back to Franklin, uncertain. "Yeah. I got it."

"Keep it close, in case I need to get ahold of you."

"I . . . I . . . I don't understand."

"You're staying here a couple days to make sure nothing else happens."

Carrol became animated. Then he said, "I . . . I . . . I got work tomorrow."

"You call in sick, just like today. You told your boss you had the flu, right?"

"Yeah."

"Call tomorrow morning. Tell her you're still under the weather and you're coughing and sneezing and you don't want to get all the other employees sick. She won't want you coming in and spreading flu germs all over the store."

"Where are you going?"

"Me and Evan are going back to Seattle. I want to take him into the doctor, so we have a record he was sick. And the detectives want to talk to him. So I need to get him ready."

Carrol smiled like a jack-o'-lantern.

"Wipe that shit-eating grin off your face. This isn't a pleasure trip. There's plenty of things to get done up here, and the police want to talk to you as well."

"M . . . m . . . me? Wh . . . wh . . . why do they want to talk to me?"

Franklin pulled a sheet of paper out of his shirt pocket. "I wrote out some things for you to say. Read this and memorize it. In a day or two I should have a better idea if we got anything to worry about and I'll coach you up. Evan, get in the van."

"I want to—"

Franklin put his hand on his belt buckle and stepped toward his youngest brother. Evan slid back his chair and hurried from the table. Franklin swatted him in the back of the head as he passed. Carrol sat grinning. "You think something is funny?" Franklin asked.

"N . . . n . . . no," he said, quickly losing the grin.

Franklin picked up both bottles of beer and poured what remained down the sink. "Stay off the sauce and keep your ass sober. I'm going to call you, and if I think you been drinking, I'll haul ass back up here and give you the beating of a lifetime. We clear?"

"We're clear," Carrol said. Franklin turned and started for the kitchen door. "Franklin?"

Franklin turned back. "What?"

"What about my woman?"

Franklin gave it a moment of thought. Who

knew what Carrol would do if he didn't give him a chance to get out all that pent-up anxiety.

"Yours," he said. "After you get work done. Don't touch mine."

"I won't."

"And don't touch Evan's none neither. There's still a chance we could get out of this," Franklin said, though at the moment he was uncertain how. "Maybe we put the blame on Evan if we have to, plead he's retarded and didn't know better and throw ourselves on the mercy of the court."

"Y . . . y . . . you think that will work?"

Franklin didn't. But he wasn't about to tell that to a stuttering fool and just make it worse. "Read that script. I'll call and we'll go over it again. Right now I got to get Evan prepared." Though Franklin didn't think Evan would remember much. He'd make sure of it.

CHAPTER 19

Sunday, early evening, Tracy and Kins returned to the houses that backed up to the ravine as CSI and Wright departed. They noted two cars in Nancy Maxwell's driveway. She didn't seem surprised to see them again, and this time her husband stood beside her. Tracy immediately assessed him. He was over six feet, medium build. Tracy looked down at his slippers. They didn't look particularly large, but then she couldn't really judge. Maxwell introduced her husband as Paul.

"I heard you closed down the park," Paul said, sounding on edge. "Can I ask what's going on? Is it related to that girl who went missing? Everyone around here is a bit freaked out."

"How did you hear the park was closed?" Kins asked.

"I talked to our neighbor, Brian Bibby," Paul said. "He said you spoke to him yesterday about a young woman he saw running in the park last Wednesday, the girl who's been on the news. He said he went to walk Jackpot this afternoon and found the park was closed, with police tape strung across the entrance."

"We have two small children," Nancy said. "Do we need to be worried?"

"We're still trying to find the young woman,"

Kins said in a calm voice. "And we're looking for clues to confirm she was there."

"Then you didn't find a body, is that right?" Paul asked.

"We can't discuss the details of an ongoing investigation."

"What the hell does that mean? That park is in my backyard. If someone got murdered down there, I have a right to know. As my wife said, we have two kids."

"We didn't find a body." Kins spoke calmly. "We just wanted to follow up and ask you a few more questions."

Headlights preceded a car turning the corner. It drove past the house—a white van.

"That's Franklin Sprague," Nancy Maxwell said, noticing Tracy watching the van.

Tinted windows prevented Tracy from seeing the driver, but as the car passed under the street lamp, she thought she saw someone through the windshield in the passenger seat. The van turned into the Sprague driveway.

"Did you see anyone in your backyard Wednesday night?" Kins asked.

"Oh God," Nancy Maxwell said.

"You think someone hurt that young girl and was in our backyard?" Paul asked.

"Right now, she's just missing, and we're trying to find her. Did you see anyone in your backyard?" Kins repeated.

"No," Paul said. Nancy shook her head.

"And you didn't hear anything?"

"No," Nancy said. She looked pale, like she might be sick.

"It looks like your lawn was recently mowed," Kins said.

"I told you," Nancy said. "Evan Sprague mows it every other Thursday. It gives him a job and, I think, something to do. And since there are no fences in the back, it makes sense for the neighbors to share in the cost."

"And he mowed it this past Thursday?" Tracy asked.

"Yes."

"Was that his regular day?"

"Thursdays. He keeps to a schedule because Franklin says he doesn't remember well."

"How well do you know Brian Bibby and his wife?"

"We're friendly. Neighborly," Paul Maxwell said. "Lorraine used to teach at the school across the street. I think Bibby worked for Boeing. They're both retired now. They like to fish. He does anyway. I think his wife humors him. They keep a boat out at the Edmonds Marina during the summer months."

"They'll let us know if they're going out of town," Nancy Maxwell interjected. "They have a motor home. When they travel we keep an eye on the house."

"Does Bibby smoke?" Tracy asked.

"I don't know," Paul Maxwell said.

"And the Sprague brothers? What can you tell us about them?"

"Mostly they keep to themselves," Paul Maxwell said. "We don't know them well, but they're friendly."

Tracy and Kins thanked the Maxwells for their time and told them they would keep them apprised of what they could.

As they walked back to the sidewalk, Kins said, "Let's go talk to Bibby."

"Let's talk to the Spragues first. I'm fairly certain I saw someone in the passenger seat."

They walked down the street and knocked. As before, the porch light flickered on just before Franklin Sprague pulled the door open. "Detectives. I noticed some activity in the park today and saw you talking with Nancy when I drove by. Has something more come up? Did they find that young girl?"

Tracy looked down at Sprague's feet, but he wasn't wearing shoes. He stood in his socks. When she looked up, Sprague was watching her.

"Are your brothers home?" Kins asked.

"Evan's home. Carrol is still at work."

"That's the Home Depot in Shoreline?" Tracy asked.

"That's right. I gave him your card. Did he not call you?"

"No," Kins said.

Sprague shook his head. "I'm sorry. I'll remind him again when he gets home."

"Is Evan up to talking to us?" Kins asked.

"Sure. He's still under the weather and looks pale, but he's feeling better. I took him into the doctor this evening to make sure it wasn't a bacterial infection and he didn't need antibiotics. Did I mention last time that Evan is a little slow?"

"You did."

"Let me get him."

Again, Sprague did not invite them into the home or leave the door open. Tracy heard him call out to his brother from the other side of the threshold. "Evan? Come on out here."

Franklin opened the door accompanied by a man as tall as him though not as stout. Tracy estimated Franklin Sprague to be 230 to 250 pounds—certainly large enough to carry a young woman. Evan had a slighter build, perhaps two hundred pounds, though it was hard to be certain because he wore baggy sweatpants and a gray sweatshirt with the hood up. He kept his hands in the front pouch. Like Franklin, he was also wearing socks but no shoes. His face looked sallow under the porch light.

"These two people are detectives," Franklin said. "They want to ask you a few questions about Wednesday night."

"Okay," Evan said.

"I understand you like to go for walks," Kins said.

"I do it to get exercise."

His speech was slow, but the words clear. "What time do you usually walk?"

"After I get my chores done, but I've been sick. I haven't walked the last few days."

"Did you walk Wednesday?"

Evan seemed to give that some thought. "I'm not sure. I don't remember."

"What about Thursday?"

"That was Halloween, Evan," Franklin said.

"I gave out candy to the trick-or-treaters on Halloween." Tracy recalled Nancy Maxwell saying Evan had given full-size Hershey bars to her kids.

"Do you remember what you did Wednesday afternoon?" Kins asked.

Evan shook his head. "I don't remember."

Franklin Sprague shrugged and put a hand on Evan's shoulder.

Kins showed Evan the picture of Stephanie Cole. "We're trying to find this young—"

"I haven't seen her," Evan said.

"Let them ask you the questions before you answer, Evan," Franklin said. He gave Tracy and Kins an eye roll.

"She was wearing running clothes," Kins said. "Did you see her?"

Evan shook his head. "I don't remember."

"Look at the picture, Evan," Franklin said.

Evan looked to his brother, then at the photograph. "I didn't see her," he said.

"Do you ever walk in the park, Evan?"

"We all walk in the park," Franklin said. "That's what it's there for."

Tracy thought he seemed a little too quick to answer. "How about you, Evan? Do you walk in the park?"

"That's what it's there for," Evan said, mimicking his brother.

"Do you remember the last time you walked in the park?" Tracy asked.

Evan shook his head. "No."

"It wasn't recently?"

"I don't . . ." He looked to Franklin.

"He doesn't remember things real well, Detectives," Franklin said. "I think I told you that. I usually have to remind him to do things, and I write it down for him."

"I understand you cut the lawns for the neighbors," Kins said.

"Every other Thursday," Evan said.

"Did you cut them last Thursday?"

Evan looked to Franklin. "He wants to know if you cut them a couple of days ago."

"Uh-huh. I cut them. But not this Thursday. Every other one."

"I remind him Thursday mornings and we

206

put the days he cuts the yards on the calendar," Franklin said. "So he doesn't forget."

"When you walk in the park, how do you enter the park?"

Again Evan looked to Franklin. "How do you go into the park?" Franklin asked.

"At the entrance," Evan said, looking at Tracy.

"You ever take a path through the backyard?" Tracy asked.

Evan again looked to Franklin. "There isn't an entrance," Franklin said. "And the hillside is pretty steep."

"You've never seen anyone go into the park that way?" Tracy tried again.

"Take the hillside into the ravine?" Franklin said. "No."

"Can I ask what doctor you took Evan to see?" Tracy asked.

"I don't remember his name," Franklin said. "I took him to the emergency room at Northwest Hospital. A doctor looked him over and took some blood. We're supposed to get word tomorrow whether he needs antibiotics."

They spoke for a few more minutes. Tracy and Kins thanked the brothers and departed. As they walked down the street to their car, Tracy said, "He doesn't remember if he walked in the park Wednesday, but he remembers cutting the lawn Thursday and handing out candy."

Kins looked at her. "Franklin said he reminded him and put it on his calendar so he didn't forget. It sounds like a set thing. And he was excited about Halloween. Walking doesn't sound like it's a set thing."

"Yeah, but we know he did."

"Doesn't mean he remembers. What are you getting at?"

"Seems strange. That's all. And he's big, like his brother, big enough to carry a woman's body up that incline."

"How would he have known she was in the park?" Kins asked.

"He could have seen her when he went for his walk," Tracy said. "The timing is right, based on when he crossed the Maxwells' front yard. He could have seen her go into the park."

"And what? Walked home and climbed down the hillside to wait for her to get there? He doesn't exactly seem like the type to attack a young woman."

"It's possible."

"Doesn't seem likely."

"Did you smell cigarette smoke when we were talking to them?"

"I'm not sure I did. Why? Did you?" Kins asked.

"I thought I did. You want to drive up to Shoreline and talk to Carrol?" Tracy asked.

"Let's talk to Bibby since we're here," Kins

said. "Then we can swing by Cole's apartment and talk to the roommate."

"I want to stop at the Northwest Hospital emergency room."

"You think he's lying?" Kins said. "Why would he say something if he didn't go there?"

"Let's check it off anyway."

Bibby didn't recall seeing Evan on Wednesday but did say he saw him walking Tuesday. He also didn't hear anything coming from the park while he walked Jackpot, or after he got home. He didn't recall seeing anyone in the backyard, though his house was situated at the street corner, and his backyard wasn't contiguous with the four houses that shared the large lawn. It had a side fence. Kins asked him what kind of shoes he walked in and the size, telling Bibby they needed to eliminate his shoeprints in the park.

Bibby's shoes were in a shoe bin outside the front door. "My wife doesn't want me tracking dirt inside," he explained. He handed Kins a pair of Hokas. "My doctor recommended them for old, dilapidated men like me. He called them a miracle shoe because they allow men to run past the age of fifty. I'm happy just to walk."

Tracy and Kins noted the make and the size— 10½—and Tracy photographed the shoe and the soles for Kaylee Wright. The sole pattern was different than the waffle pattern Wright found in the park, but the shoe was muddy and looked to have been recently worn.

They drove from Bibby's home to Northwest Hospital and spoke to a Dr. Dan Waters. Waters confirmed he had seen Evan Sprague earlier that evening, and that Franklin thought Evan could have the flu and wondered if he might need antibiotics. He would not say anything further without a court order, citing the patient-physician privilege.

From the hospital they drove to Stephanie Cole's apartment. Scott Barnes let them in. Barnes had no objection to showing them his shoes. He owned a pair of Merrell walking shoes, size 9, that looked to have a different waffle pattern than the pattern Kaylee Wright found in the ravine. Tracy photographed them anyway. Barnes said he did not know Cole had driven to North Park, and he was unaware whether she knew anyone who lived there or had any reason to go there.

Before heading home, Tracy checked the tip line, and also called the North Precinct. Neither had any further information or promising leads.

It was as if Stephanie Cole had just disappeared.

CHAPTER 20

Franklin sat in the kitchen drinking a beer, feeling like he'd just dodged a bullet. He was glad he'd taken Evan into the emergency room and worked with him on how to answer the detectives' questions on the drive home from Cle Elum. For once, the idiot hadn't disappointed him. Still, it was clear that the detectives weren't letting this go. He knew when he saw them standing on the Maxwells' porch that they would come by the house. He needed more time to work with Evan, but he wasn't about to get it. He made sure Evan knew what to say and what not to say. The idiot's memory wasn't good, but he could remember in short spells, which was why he could play cards and board games. It was anything beyond an hour that he had trouble recalling.

The detectives would now turn their attention to Carrol, and he'd start stuttering and spitting all over the damn place. Carrol couldn't lie to save his life. Franklin's only hope was to take his daddy's advice to heart—that the best defense was a good offense.

He dialed Carrol's cell phone. His brother answered on the first ring. "Wh . . . wh . . . what's going on?"

"You having a nice time up there?"

Carrol didn't respond.

"You touch my girl?"

"No. I swear it."

"Evan's?"

"No. I mean . . . she . . . she . . . she was crying, and I might have slapped her to shut her up, but that was it. Wh . . . wh . . . why? Wh . . . wh . . . wh . . . what's going on, Franklin?"

"What's going on is I seen those two detectives talking to the Maxwells when we drove home, and they came down here to talk to Evan."

"Oh shit."

"That's right, oh shit. Evan did just fine though. Someone told them Evan goes walking the same time that girl went missing. They were asking him all kinds of questions about when he walked last and if he went into the park."

"Wha . . . wha . . . what did Evan say?"

"He said what I told him to say, but I'm worried they might have some evidence putting him there."

"B . . . b . . . but the woman isn't there," Carrol said.

"No, the woman isn't there, but the police can do all sorts of shit nowadays to prove things. They can get DNA off almost anything. Fingerprints. Hair fibers." Which reminded Franklin of something. "You wiped that car down like I told you?"

"Everything," Carrol said, continuing to stutter. "And I wore the gloves and the ski hat like you said."

Franklin gave that some thought.

"Fr . . . Fr . . . Franklin?"

"Shut up and listen. Tomorrow you're going to call that female detective first thing—"

"What am I going to tell her?"

"Shut up and listen. You're going to call her so she don't come around here or the Home Depot looking for you. You go over that script I gave you." Carrol didn't answer, meaning he hadn't. Lazy shit. "Get it out now and go over it. When you're ready, you'll call and tell her you can't make personal calls while you're working, that you had to wait for a break to call her."

"Okay."

"And for God's sake, don't go stuttering all over the phone. It'll make you sound suspicious. Hold it together."

"I'll try."

"You better do more than try," Franklin said. "Or you'll be in a cellblock."

"What are you going to do, Franklin?"

Franklin reached down along the side of his chair and grabbed two white plastic garbage bags. Evan's shoes were in one and the clothes he wore the previous Wednesday were in the other. The detectives asked if Evan ever walked in the park, and Franklin caught the woman looking at his and Evan's feet. That likely meant they had shoeprints. This time of year, when the ground was wet, a shoeprint would be like a fingerprint.

"Right now, I got to get rid of some stuff," he said. "You practice. When I get back, I'll call and we'll go over it until you get it right."

Franklin knew Carrol wanted to ask him the next question but was too afraid to do so. Franklin didn't have an answer anyway, not just yet, but if he suspected the detectives knew more than they were letting on, he'd have to make the decision to get rid of the women at the cabin and bury them somewhere in the wilderness.

"We ain't killers, Franklin," Carrol said.

Maybe not yet. But they had it in them. Franklin knew that for a fact. He'd seen the evidence of what their daddy had done, what he had gotten away with.

They had killing in them.

And a whole lot more.

Stephanie stood. Her chain was just long enough to allow her to stand and stretch. She put one leg back and felt the stretch in her other Achilles and her calf. It hurt, but it felt good. She switched legs and stretched her right Achilles and calf.

"What the hell are you doing?" Donna asked.

"I'm stretching," Stephanie said.

"I know you're stretching. Why?"

"Because I'm tired of just sitting here. I'm tired of being stiff and cold."

She lifted one knee to her chest, then the other. God, it felt good.

"Sit down before you hurt yourself."

"You should do it."

"Why? So I can stay in shape? For what? They're going to kill us. That's why they brought us up here in the middle of nowhere. They're going to kill us and bury us, or leave us for the animals to eat."

Stephanie shook her head, not wanting to listen. She didn't have enough chain to do jumping jacks, but she could jog in place. She lifted her knees, speaking while trying to catch her breath. "It doesn't change the fact that we have to sit here day after day," she said. "You want to sit there, go ahead."

She dropped back to the ground and did five push-ups. She felt weak and dehydrated, but she pushed through it. She did five burpees, then ran in place again. Five sets. She'd do five sets. Then she'd do yoga. She could remember most of the moves from the class she took at home. What she couldn't remember, she'd fake. After yoga she'd meditate for thirty minutes. She didn't have her phone so she couldn't follow the meditation app, but she'd done it enough to know how to breathe and count, and that was all there was to it.

She heard chains rattle and looked over at

Angel Jackson, who had got to her feet. Stephanie paused.

"Don't stop," Angel said. "Show me what to do."

CHAPTER 21

Early Monday morning, Tracy stopped at the Redmond business park for a scheduled session with Lisa Walsh. She told Walsh she had accepted the Cold Case position.

"Did you take the job because you wanted it, or to spite your captain?" Walsh settled into her chair. The room felt warm, cozy.

"Probably a little bit of both," Tracy said. "I want to keep working. I love what I do. And I didn't want my captain to be the reason I walked away from something I love and that I'm good at. But really it was the detective who preceded me in Cold Cases who said something that resonated with me."

"What was that?"

"He pointed out that the victims and their families have no voice. I can provide one. I can be their voice, and maybe find justice for some victims that others have forgotten."

"It's certainly admirable."

"He also pointed out that what I thought could be a negative, something we discussed at our last session, could actually be a positive."

"And what is that?"

"I care. In his words, I 'give a shit.'" Tracy smiled at her recollection of reading Nunzio's note. "He said that's what separates the good detectives from those just going through the motions."

"How did you take that?"

Walsh's question surprised her. "I took it the way he intended me to take it."

"Which was what?"

"That it was okay to empathize with the victims—people I've never met and never will—to empathize with them and their families because I care. I know what it's like to lose someone you love to a violent crime."

"Yes, you do. But do you see how that could also be a negative? How it might impact you?"

Again, Walsh's question surprised her. The counselor was clearly concerned about the emotional impact the cases would have on Tracy, but again Tracy was prepared. "I think it can be, if I allow it to control me. If I become obsessive about the cases I work. But I'm not that person I was back then. My life has changed."

"How has it been being back at work, with respect to your leaving your daughter with the nanny?" Walsh changed gears.

"It's hard leaving Daniella. I missed her first steps the other day, and it was bittersweet, but Dan missed them too. I guess it's just a part of parenting in this day and age. I'm also working an active case in addition to my cold cases, so I've been crazy busy and . . ."

"And . . ."

Tracy's train of thought had been interrupted, as it often was when working a case. Though she was physically present, her subconscious went over forensic evidence. Or something a witness had said would suddenly become significant. "Sorry. I was just thinking about one of my cold cases, about a mother whose five-year-old daughter disappeared."

"What was it you were thinking about?"

"The loss of my sister tore my family apart, as I've explained. But everything I've read about this woman . . . the mother . . . It was as if she wasn't impacted, that she was more concerned with the police arresting her ex-husband than finding her daughter. That's odd, isn't it?"

"I can't really say. She may have compartmentalized her feelings rather than deal with them. The two are not the same."

Tracy had done the same thing with Sarah's case, but that had been long after the incident, unlike with Jewel Chin. "That's what was so shocking about the responding police officer's report. He was first on the scene the night the little girl vanished. He said he got the impression that Jewel Chin didn't care. He didn't say she had compartmentalized her pain. He said it was as if she didn't have pain to compartmentalize. She was too busy being angry at her ex-husband. I'm just wondering, is that some fundamental flaw in her character?"

"I don't know. It certainly could be, but without speaking to her it isn't possible to guess. I think we should get back to you."

"A flaw, or she knows something the rest of us don't, that maybe her daughter isn't really gone."

"I think we should stop for the day," Walsh said.

Tracy looked at the clock on the wall. "You do?"

"I don't think this is productive," Walsh said. "You're in what I'd refer to as combat mode; you're in a battle. Your mind is singularly focused, and you've pushed aside thoughts that might interfere with the battle."

"I'm sorry. I didn't mean to . . . Do you think that's a bad thing?"

Walsh set down her pad. "There are instances of people achieving incredible success because they have the ability to be intensely, singularly focused, Tracy. It allows them to work relentless hours with little sleep, food, or outside distractions. Da Vinci, Edison, Alexander Bell, even Bill Gates have been described that way."

"I like that company," Tracy said, but Walsh wasn't smiling.

"Did you watch the documentary *Free Solo*?"

"No," Tracy said.

"It's about a young man, a rock climber who wants to ascend El Capitan in Yosemite without any ropes or clips. No one has ever done it. He becomes so singularly focused he can recite every move of the nearly three-hour practice ascent from memory. But when they did a scan of his brain, they determined that the portion of the brain that detects danger and fear was virtually turned off. As if he didn't register the possibility that he could fail, that he could fall and die, despite his knowing many rock climbers who had."

"Why are you telling me this?"

"Because I want you to be careful, Tracy. We know the men I named because they lived and achieved what they set their minds to. We don't know the many others who slipped and fell. Every man I named was on a similar wall. Every one of them could just as easily have fallen, and we would never have known their name."

CHAPTER 22

Tracy left Walsh's office less than certain about what had transpired during their session. Walsh intimated that Tracy was headed for a fall—at least that was how Tracy interpreted it. Tracy didn't have a lot of time to dwell on it. She had an interview with Elle Chin's former teacher that morning and hoped to gain further insight into both parents. Then she had to bust ass to get into the office so she and Kins could determine their next step with regard to Stephanie Cole. The clock ticked, and the odds of finding Cole alive grew worse by the minute.

The preschool was located inside a church in the Green Lake neighborhood. Tracy arrived early and parked to review the investigative file the North Precinct emailed her that morning on the death of Graham Jacobsen, Jewel Chin's boyfriend. She pulled up the report, reading it on her phone. The police had concluded Jacobsen shot himself in the head at close range with a Glock 9 mm pistol he had purchased on Craigslist several years before. Jewel Chin provided a statement that she had discovered Jacobsen's body after returning from a Green Lake bar. Her alibi had been confirmed. Based on a subsequent autopsy, Jacobsen had been drunk and had several known steroids in his system including prednisone and methylprednisolone, which, in conjunction with the alcohol, could have acted as a depressant. Nobody had checked to determine where Bobby Chin had been that night.

The police did not find a suicide note. They had Jacobsen's phone, however, and noted dozens of text messages to Jewel Chin and her very infrequent and brief responses. In one, she told Jacobsen she thought it best if he moved out of the house. The detective's report the evening of Jacobsen's death was eerily similar to Officer Bill Miller's report the night Elle Chin disappeared. Jewel Chin, the detective said, seemed largely detached from the suicide and had been more concerned with the mess, and whether the death could impact the sale of the home. She even asked whether she had to disclose the suicide to interested purchasers.

In short, Art Nunzio would have said that Jewel Chin "didn't give a shit." Tracy wondered if it was a fundamental but undiagnosed flaw in her character.

Tracy made her way to the preschool. Inside the church facility she passed young moms dropping off children and imagined herself doing so with Daniella. Orange-and-black Halloween motifs and scrawled pictures of witches and ghosts and pumpkins decorated the classroom windows. Tracy stepped into the lobby and approached a woman standing behind the reception desk, thumbing through files in a three-drawer file cabinet.

"Are you Detective Crosswhite?" the woman asked when she saw Tracy.

"I am," Tracy said.

The woman reached across the desk to shake Tracy's hand. "I'm Lynn Bettencourt. We spoke on the phone."

Bettencourt, the executive director of the preschool, appeared younger than Tracy expected. Over the phone Bettencourt said she had been at the school for eight years and had taught Elle Chin the year of her disappearance, which is what prompted Tracy to seek to speak to Bettencourt in person.

"I'm just looking for Elle Chin's file," Bettencourt said. "I planned to do it earlier, but I have a teacher out sick so we're scrambling."

"Take your time," Tracy said, though she was eager to get into the office to meet with Kins.

Bettencourt opened and closed several file drawers, searching. "We keep most everything on the computer, but I printed this file out for the divorce and custody proceedings, and I kept a copy. Here it is." She pulled a two-inch-thick file from the drawer and slid the drawer closed. "Come on back."

She led Tracy to an office with skylights. Windows looked out on an empty playground with climbing gyms on rubber mats. Bettencourt sat behind her desk and moved the extension arm to her computer monitor so she and Tracy could see one another.

After Bettencourt settled in, Tracy asked, "When did you teach Elle Chin?"

"I taught Elle the year that she disappeared," Bettencourt said. "That was five years ago. It was really a tragedy for everyone here at the school, as I'm sure you can imagine. You don't forget something like that. She was a sweet little girl. Smart."

Tracy nodded to the file on the desk. "You said you printed out the file for the divorce proceedings?"

Bettencourt flipped open the file, thumbing through the pages. "They had a child psychologist involved in the parenting plan who met with Elle."

"Did he talk to you?"

She nodded and closed her eyes. A habit. "Yes."

"Before we get to that, how well did you know the parents?"

Bettencourt shrugged and gently shook her head. "Not well. We encourage the parents of our students to become involved in their child's education, but it isn't mandated."

"Neither parent was involved?"

"I'd say sporadic. Not on a regular basis."

"Which parent was more involved?"

225

"Mostly the father." Bettencourt hesitated, as if about to say something more, then said nothing.

"You look like you wanted to say something else," Tracy said.

Bettencourt paused. "Judgments are often unfair."

"What was your judgment?" She paused. Bettencourt was contemplating her words, what to say. "I'm just trying to find out more about the parents," Tracy said, trying to alleviate any concern.

"The mother seemed preoccupied with other things."

"Working out?" Tracy recalled the neighbor Evelyn Robertson's impression of Jewel Chin.

Bettencourt smiled, but it was pensive. "Yes."

"Did you encourage her and Bobby Chin to become more involved?"

"We encourage all the parents, with varying degrees of success. I said judgments are unfair because some parents don't have a choice. They have to work. Not working isn't an option."

"Did Jewel Chin work?"

"I'm not sure. The father was a police officer; I know that. The kids got a kick out of it when he came in dressed in his uniform." Bettencourt smiled.

"So would you say Bobby Chin was more involved?"

Bettencourt looked troubled. She let out a sigh.

"As I said, he worked a lot. There were days he was scheduled to pick Elle up from school and he'd get stuck. He'd send his sister mostly, and, less often, his mother or father."

"Not his wife?"

Bettencourt shook her head. "The sister and grandparents were on our list of people approved to pick up Elle."

"Did the wife list any family members?"

Bettencourt flipped through the file. After a moment, she said, "No."

"Are the names of the grandparents and sister in that file?"

"They're here, yes. Along with phone numbers."

"How long did you teach Elle before she disappeared?"

"I taught Elle for about thirteen months, starting in September and ending the following October." Bettencourt looked as if she were about to cry.

"Are you okay?" Tracy asked. Bettencourt reached for a tissue from a box on her desk and dabbed the corners of her eyes.

"Take your time," Tracy said.

"It was a pretty big shock here at the school; we've never had anything like that happen before or since." She blew out a breath.

"Your reaction indicates you were close to Elle."

She blew out another breath. "You can't help but love these kids. They're so innocent. They come here bright-eyed and eager to learn. Our job is to foster their enthusiasm and inquisitiveness. You develop a bond. That's what I miss the most about the teaching."

Bettencourt seemed like a genuinely good person.

"Tell me about Elle. Did you notice any changes in her behavior?"

"You mean because of the divorce?"

"Yes."

"We have many children of divorced parents. Depending on the divorce, it can impact the children to varying degrees."

"What about Elle?"

Bettencourt said, "Give me a minute," and she pulled out a sheet of paper, reading it.

"What are you referring to?" Tracy asked.

"It's a report I did for the psychologist who put together the parenting plan."

"What does it say?"

"I noticed changes in Elle's behavior during the school year. Bear in mind that a child acting out during a divorce is not unusual, especially one as young as Elle, who doesn't have the emotional maturity to understand what is happening. They become frustrated and stressed."

"How did Elle change?"

"There were instances of anger—fighting with

other children, sadness, depression. She missed her father."

"She told you that?"

"She did. She also expressed it in some of her drawings." Bettencourt handed Tracy a crude drawing of a young child holding someone's hand. Tracy immediately thought of the witness who said he saw Elle holding the hand of a woman as she walked away from the corn maze.

"Did she say anything about her mother?"

"Not directly."

"Indirectly?"

"Elle would say things like her daddy was always late; that her mommy didn't love her daddy anymore; that her mommy had a boyfriend and he was going to be her new daddy—things that, more often than not, come from one parent speaking negatively about the other parent."

"You don't think the mother was handling the situation with Elle's best interest in mind."

"Are you asking for my judgment?"

"Based on everything you knew about the family and Elle."

"It's not really my place. I didn't live in the home . . ."

"I understand."

"I don't think either parent handled the divorce with Elle's best interest in mind," Bettencourt said. "That's my judgment. The husband moved out and there were allegations of domestic violence that limited his time with Elle. Then the boyfriend moved into the home soon after the husband moved out."

"How do you know that?"

"The sister told me one afternoon when she came to pick up Elle. I asked to speak to her because Elle was having difficulty understanding the situation—why her daddy wasn't home and why the boyfriend was living in their house."

"Did Elle say anything about the boyfriend? Or was there anything in her acting out that made you think she was being abused?"

Bettencourt paused. Then she opened the file and handed Tracy another crude drawing, a stick figure of a little girl. Blue teardrops flowed from the little girl's face all the way to the floor. She'd also drawn the stick figure of a man. He had an angry face. Tracy looked up at Bettencourt.

"I told the sister when she came that Elle said the little girl was sad because the man slapped her."

"I assume you submitted this in the civil proceeding."

"Elle drew it after the psychologist had prepared and presented the parenting plan, but I did submit it, and I notified Child Protective Services."

"What came of it?"

"Nothing. The mother said Elle was mistaken. She said Elle had told her the stick figure was her father, and she drew it after the father got angry and hit her mommy."

"Did you ask Elle again?"

"No. She disappeared."

Tracy asked Bettencourt additional questions, then made arrangements to get the school file copied. She stood to leave.

"Detective?"

Tracy stopped. Bettencourt looked troubled. "Something else?"

"Earlier, you asked for my judgment."

"Yes."

"I don't think either living situation was a healthy environment for that little girl."

"I understand," Tracy said.

Bettencourt still looked troubled, as if Tracy didn't comprehend what she was trying to say. "Let me put it this way. I see a lot of kids in difficult home situations, and usually one of the parents is more to blame—they're lashing out and blaming their spouse for what has happened. The other spouse becomes the child's protector, the person who swallows their own pain or pride and puts the child first."

"But not here."

She shook her head. "Unfortunately, not."

CHAPTER 23

Tracy met Kins in the A Team's bull pen. Faz and Del had left to conduct further interviews of witnesses to the shooting in Pioneer Square, and Fernandez continued to sit with the prosecutor in a King County Superior Court murder trial.

"Pinkney called," Kins said, referring to the CSI sergeant. "The precipitin test on the blood sample came back as human. I put a call in to Cole's mother and asked Stephanie's blood type. That wasn't much fun. She's type A positive, the same as the blood sample CSI located. We have hair samples from a brush in Cole's bathroom, but I called the lab and told them to concentrate on the cigarette butts. At least for now, I think we can assume from the earbud and the blood type that it belongs to Cole." Kins handed Tracy several pages. "Andrei Vilkotski from TESU sends his undying adoration for ruining his weekend."

The documents were Cole's cell phone records and her computer records.

"Anything?" she asked.

"No calls or texts while she worked. She did send text messages and made phone calls to area codes 626 and 909, cities in the San Gabriel Valley."

Tracy read the time of the calls, which were between ten to ten fifteen in the morning, twelve to one, and two to two fifteen. "Her breaks," Tracy said.

"Appears to be. The photographs are unremarkable," Kins said. They had hoped to find recurring pictures of a man, perhaps a boyfriend no one yet knew about. "Take a look at the last photograph on the phone."

Tracy did. It was a picture of the trailhead sign at North Park. Cole had photographed the "No Dumping" sign above the doggy poop bags.

"So we know she had a sense of humor," Kins said.

"And didn't exactly feel threatened," Tracy said.

"And a nineteen-year-old who abides by an employer's rule not to send text messages from work doesn't exactly sound like someone who would blow off work two days in a row and jeopardize getting fired, does it?" Kins reasoned. "The last text was to Ame Diaz at 3:55, just before she left work. She said she was going for a run and hoped to make it to the party."

Kins motioned for Tracy to turn the page. "Tuesday night she called a costume store in North Park. I phoned the store and asked if anyone remembered a woman calling about a pirate costume two days before Halloween."

"Any luck?"

"Nah, not over the phone. The lady said Halloween is their crazy season. I asked Billy to have officers follow up with the costume shop and see if anyone remembers her coming in. I doubt she did."

"Why?"

"Because I asked the woman in general what a pirate costume would cost to rent. She said that, because it was Halloween, anywhere from fifty to seventy-five dollars."

"Ouch," Tracy said. It explained why Cole went to the thrift store and cut up the skirt and blouse herself and opted for the $9.99 accessory pack at Bartell Drugs.

"She also looked up Bartell drugstore locations, as you speculated," Kins said. "And she used the map app to locate the stores and several public parks."

"So she intended to go to North Park?"

"Maybe more out of necessity, as you also speculated. Something else," Kins said. "She didn't map Ravenna Park, which indicates she didn't plan on going there—or she knew the route."

Tracy set down the pages. "Now what?"

"The mother and father called this morning looking for an update. I'm just getting ready to call. You want to handle it?"

"Not a chance."

Kins smiled. "Thought I'd ask." He picked

up the phone and dialed. From his end of the conversation, Kins sounded like he was doing his best to keep the family calm.

While Kins spoke on the phone, Tracy made a list of suspects and known evidence. That list included Brian Bibby, Scott Barnes, Franklin Sprague, Evan Sprague, and Carrol Sprague. She also listed the "unknown psychopath." Next to each name she noted evidence that seemed to exonerate each, like Brian Bibby's bad back and his choice of walking shoe, and Scott Barnes's physical size as well as his shoe size. Franklin Sprague and Carrol Sprague were unlikely because both had been at work Wednesday at four thirty; they'd confirmed Franklin's employment and work history with the retirement home but had not yet reached the correct person at Home Depot to confirm Carrol Sprague's employment. Driving to the Home Depot was on Tracy's to-do list.

In making the list, Tracy realized they'd failed to ask Franklin and Evan for the shoes they wore when they walked in the park. She made a note. She would tell the Spragues, as she had told Bibby, that she needed the shoes to eliminate them from the prints they'd found.

She looked back over her list and circled the name Evan Sprague. She wondered about Franklin's too-quick excuse for his brother's faulty memory, particularly whether Evan recalled walking Wednesday afternoon, and his supposed illness. He had certainly been healthy enough to mow the lawns on Thursday, and to hand out Halloween candy that night.

Tracy wrote a note by his name. *When did he come down with the flu?*

She also made a to-do list, which included returning to the Fremont trucking company and to Bartell Drugs. Finding out who knew Cole was running that afternoon seemed to be the key. It was unlikely the perpetrator would have waited to grab just anyone, especially since runners did not regularly use the park, though the perpetrator did likely know that the trail came to a dead end and that the stump would be the perfect place to hide. That also coincided with the evidence that someone had purposely moved the body *and* the car away from the neighborhood. She made a note to have another detective run background checks, particularly of any young men who lived nearby, and determine if any had a criminal record, particularly of violence against young women.

Tracy made a few more notes, then used Faz's desk phone to call the Washington State Patrol Crime Lab and leave a message asking Michael Melton to call her the first chance he got. She wanted to be certain Melton prioritized the DNA analysis on the cigarette butts. Violent Crimes got priority, with homicides at the top of that list, but the lab remained backed up. She wanted to be sure Melton understood there was a young girl missing, and time was of the essence. Melton had six daughters of his own. It didn't hurt to play the empathy card every now and then.

Tracy had just called the Home Depot in Shoreline to speak to Carrol Sprague when Johnny Nolasco stepped into the A Team's cubicle and gave her a quizzical look.

"What are you doing *here?*" he asked.

Tracy set down the receiver. "I'm working a case with Kins."

Kins turned but, still on the phone, didn't respond.

Nolasco had his sleeves rolled up and several sheets of paper in hand. "What about your cold cases?"

"I'm working those also."

Nolasco looked to Kins, who had just ended his conversation. "Why didn't you come to me if you needed help on your files?"

"I ran it by Billy," Kins said.

"Why?"

"This one came in the other day from Missing Persons. Fernandez is still in trial, and Faz and Del have the shooting in Pioneer Square. Tracy was here when it came in. I asked Billy if I could get some help."

"Why are we working a missing person case?"

"The circumstances."

"Which are?"

Kins gave him a brief summary.

Nolasco looked to a calendar on the wall. "Where are you on it?"

Kins explained their progress to date.

Nolasco turned to Tracy. "And what are you doing?"

"At the moment I'm putting together a list of suspects based on interviews, known evidence, and known exculpatory evidence. I'm also coordinating with CSI, Kaylee Wright, and with the crime lab."

"Why the crime lab?"

"We found cigarette butts in the park. Wright believes the butt was left by someone lying in wait for this girl. We're hopeful the lab can pull DNA. We also found blood."

"Who knew she was running in this park?"

"That's what we're trying to find out," Tracy said.

"What cold cases are you working?"

Tracy told him about the two missing prostitutes and about Elle Chin.

"Nunzio worked sexual assaults, cases that had collected DNA evidence and had a chance to be solved. Do any of those cases have DNA evidence?"

"Not yet," Tracy said, knowing the question had been rhetorical.

"Sounds like you're starting off on the wrong

foot. You do realize Nunzio had a breakout year last year, clearing twenty files."

"It was made abundantly clear in the press release," Tracy said. "I was wondering who provided them the specifics."

Nolasco smirked. "We celebrate the successes. We also hold ourselves to them."

"I'll remember that," Tracy said. "When I solve these cases." Her cell phone rang. Grateful for the excuse to get away, she stood and checked caller ID but didn't recognize the number with the 206 area code. She answered, "Detective Crosswhite."

"Detective?" A male voice, high-pitched. "This is Carrol Sprague. I believe you spoke to my brother, Franklin, and asked that I give you a call."

"Thanks for getting back to me, Mr. Sprague."

"I'm at work today. I can't make personal calls except if I'm on break. I don't get a lot of free time." The voice sounded affected, but she couldn't quite place how. Tracy asked Carrol the same questions she had asked Franklin and the other neighbors—his whereabouts Wednesday at dusk and whether he had seen Stephanie Cole.

Carrol confirmed he had worked that day and said he went out for a beer at a place called the Pacific Pub on Aurora Avenue. "So I really wasn't in a position to see or hear anything."

"Did you get a beer with anyone from work?"

"No."

"Did you meet anyone at the bar?"

"No. But they know me in the bar. You could ask the waitress."

Tracy would. She asked if Sprague ever walked in the park.

"I don't get a lot of opportunity on workdays, and I'm not much of a walker to be honest."

"What about your brothers?"

"Evan has more time to do those sorts of things. I think Franklin told you Evan is slow?"

"He did mention it."

"He has more time."

Tracy continued to get a weird vibe from the conversation. It sounded almost as if Carrol was talking an octave higher than normal. He was deliberate with each word. "How's he feeling?" Tracy asked.

Pause. "Evan? He's fine."

"Did he get over his cold?"

"Oh . . . uh, yeah. Th . . . th . . . that was nothing. He's h . . . h . . . healthy as a horse." There was another pause.

Tracy quickly asked, "Is he taking his walks again?"

No answer.

"Mr. Sprague?"

The pause became pregnant. Sprague again spoke deliberately, as if carefully choosing each word. "I'm sorry, Detective. I think maybe we got cut off for a second. I didn't hear your question."

"I was just wondering if Evan was taking his regular walks again."

"I don't really know, Detective. Like I said, I'm not home most afternoons. I . . . I . . . I haven't been getting home until late, so I . . . I . . . I can't really say what Evan was doing."

It sounded like a recovery and not a very good one. She wondered about the stutter, if that was the reason his voice sounded stilted.

"I have to get back to work."

Tracy thanked Sprague and hung up. When she walked back into the A Team's bull pen Nolasco had, thankfully, departed.

"That was Carrol Sprague," she said to Kins.

"What did he say?" Kins asked.

"He said Evan got over his cold and was healthy as a horse."

Kins squinted. "I thought he had a bad case of the flu and went to the emergency room?"

"So did I," Tracy said.

CHAPTER 24

Tracy and Kins drove to the Home Depot in Shoreline. Tracy was certain Carrol Sprague had lied when asked about his brother's health; she wanted to determine if he was lying about his work history the past week as well.

On the drive, Mike Melton called. Tracy put him on the speaker so Kins could participate in the conversation.

"Tracy Crosswhite," Melton said. "I thought you were home with your new baby, not out chasing bad guys. To what do I owe this pleasure? Or is this about your voice mail telling me to push your DNA analysis to the head of the line? Nice touch, by the way, telling me the victim is a young woman. As if I don't worry enough about my girls."

"Sorry about that." Tracy smiled. "Just wanted to let you know what we're dealing with."

"I know. And I've asked everyone and anyone to bust ass. I've turned in all the chits I have."

"You're the best, Mike."

"That's what they tell me."

"Kins and I will buy you dinner."

"Just pick your favorite taco truck," Kins said.

"Not me. I'm on a diet."

"What?" Kins said. "That's blasphemy."

"My daughter the nutritionist says my high blood pressure is related to what I eat. She's got me on some diet. I can't remember the damn name, but I've never eaten so many vegetables in my life."

"That's the price you pay for raising smart and caring daughters, Mike," Tracy said.

"Yeah, yeah. I'll call when I have something for you. In the interim, picture me eating a carrot . . . and enjoying it."

Tracy had no sooner disconnected than her phone rang. Caller ID indicated Kaylee Wright. Again, Tracy switched to speaker.

"I was correct about the shoes," Wright said. "The running shoe is a New Balance 880v10, which is relatively new and retails for a hundred and thirty dollars."

"We can conclude from that price that a woman working as a receptionist who just put down a security deposit and last month's rent on an apartment was serious about her running," Tracy said.

"It's a serious shoe," Wright said.

"What about the boot?" Tracy asked.

"Made by Merrell. A men's Yokota 2. It's a midline hiking shoe, waterproof. The wear on the sole indicates it's well-worn by someone who pronates when he walks."

"Help the uneducated," Kins said. "Is pronates the inside or outside of the foot?"

"Outside."

"Can the average detective observe a person pronating, as opposed to . . . walking with most of his weight on the inside of the foot?" Kins asked.

"The word is 'supinate,' and no, I don't think you could. Not unless it was highly pronounced."

"But if we get a suspect and a court order asking for his shoes, you could do a comparison?" Kins continued.

"If it's the same brand of shoe, the wear on the sole would be like a fingerprint," Wright said. "Assuming that the size is the same."

Tracy and Kins arrived at the Home Depot and, through a series of questions, an employee directed them to the office of the store manager, Helen Knežević. The woman looked besieged, seated at a utilitarian desk covered with paper. She stared up at a computer monitor and didn't divert her eyes when Kins knocked on her door. "Yes, what is it?" she asked.

"Ms. Knežević," Kins said.

She looked from the monitor to the door. Then picked up a pair of glasses from a stack of papers and slipped them on. "Can I help you?" She spoke with an Eastern European accent. Tracy guessed Russia or one of its neighboring countries.

Kins made introductions. "We just have a couple questions about one of your employees."

"Who is the employee?" she asked, sounding cautious.

"Carrol Sprague."

Knežević invited them into the office, motioning to two seats across the desk. She looked concerned. "What is it you want to know? I cannot tell you any personal information. It is against company policy."

"We just want to confirm the days he worked this past week," Kins said.

"May I ask what this is about?"

"We're investigating a case. Mr. Sprague may be a material witness. We just want you to confirm the days and the hours he worked—specifically Wednesday, Thursday, and Friday," Kins said.

Tracy knew Kins was trying to get as much information as possible before they spoke to Carrol Sprague. They would then give Sprague as much rope as they could to hang himself.

"That's it?"

"That's a start." Kins smiled.

Knežević sat and removed her glasses. She stared up at the screen with a scrunched face, typed, and used the mouse. "He worked Wednesday, October 30, from nine in the morning until four thirty."

That was as Franklin and Carrol Sprague had both said.

She again squinted and moved the mouse on

the desk pad. "And he worked Thursday and Friday the same hours."

Tracy looked to Kins, who shrugged. "He didn't call in sick then?" Tracy asked.

"Last week? He was scheduled to work yesterday and today, but he called in sick both those days."

"Wait. He's not working today?"

"No. He called in and said he has the flu and did not want to get others sick."

Carrol had lied. He told Tracy he was calling while on a break at work.

"Is an employee who calls in sick required to get a doctor's note of any kind?" Tracy asked.

"No. Employees don't get sick days. They get sick hours each month. Full-time is eight sick hours per month. If you are sick more than that, it is a point against you."

"Did Mr. Sprague get a point against him?"

"No. He had accumulated enough sick hours."

"Does he get sick often?" Tracy asked.

Knežević again moved the mouse and squinted up at her monitor. After a few minutes she said, "No. First time this year. He is a good worker. He has good reviews."

Kins and Tracy thanked Knežević and departed.

In the parking lot Tracy said, "Carrol lied."

"About today," Kins said, "but Carrol was at work Wednesday, so he wasn't in the park."

"No, but his brother Evan could have been, and

Franklin and Carrol could be covering for him."

"You think Franklin and Carrol were getting rid of a body yesterday and today?" Kins asked.

"I think we should ask the retirement home if Franklin worked yesterday and today." Tracy called the human resources director at the retirement home and learned Franklin also had Sunday off, but he was at work today and scheduled from nine to five thirty.

Tracy thanked the woman, disconnected, and provided Kins the news. She looked at her watch. "This is just about the time Evan goes for his walk. Let's go see if we can catch him out, away from his brothers. Maybe he remembers more than Franklin says he does."

CHAPTER 25

Tracy and Kins knew the North Park neighbors were on edge, and therefore Kins parked where they could watch the street but not be conspicuous.

At 3:27 p.m., Tracy said, "If we don't see him in the next fifteen minutes let's go to the house."

Ten minutes later, Kins sat up. "There he is."

Evan Sprague walked the sidewalk toward the park entrance. He'd dressed warmly in a black knit hat and rust-colored Carhartt jacket, his hands shoved in the pockets. His breath preceded him in white bursts. The cold looked to have otherwise kept everyone else indoors. Evan approached the entrance to the park and stopped, as if he might walk down the trailhead.

"What's he doing?" Kins said.

"I don't know."

"The neighbor said he walked around the block, which explained why he didn't pass by her porch camera again."

"Maybe she's wrong," Tracy said.

"Or maybe he's contemplating—"

After a moment, Evan continued past the trail-head.

"Odd," Kins said. "Let's go."

He and Tracy pushed out of the car, crossed the

street, and came up behind Evan before Evan got to the end of the block. He turned as they neared.

"Evan," Kins said. "How're you doing?"

Evan stopped and gave them a blank stare, as if he didn't recognize or remember them, which was highly possible if Franklin had been truthful about Evan's memory.

"We're the police detectives who came to your house the other day and spoke to you," Kins said.

Tracy could have kicked him. It was the perfect opportunity to determine whether Evan's memory was as bad as Franklin claimed. "How are you feeling?" Tracy asked.

Evan didn't respond.

"Is your brother Carrol sick?"

"Carrol?"

"Is he home sick?" Tracy asked.

"Carrol works."

"Is he working today?"

"I don't remember."

"We were just on our way into the park," Kins said. "You want to walk in the park?"

Evan didn't respond. Again, he looked confused.

"Do you walk at this time every day?" Tracy tried.

"I got to go home." Evan turned and quickened his pace.

"We'll walk with you," Tracy said. She and Kins hurried to keep up.

Evan did not look comfortable, but he didn't protest and he didn't run. Kins walked beside him, Tracy behind them.

"We know you walked at this time on Wednesday, Evan."

"I don't remember," Evan said.

"Your neighbors have a video camera. It filmed you walking past their house."

"Bibby?"

"No. The Maxwells. You walked past their house, just like you did today. You walked down this street, past the entrance to the park. That was the day that a young woman, Stephanie Cole, ran in the park." Kins had pulled up a picture of Cole on his phone and showed it to Evan. "This is her, Evan."

Evan gave it a cursory glance but didn't respond. He looked worried.

Kins pulled up a second picture. "And this was her car. Look a little closer, Evan. It's very important we find that girl before she gets hurt."

Evan glanced quickly at the photo. "I didn't see any cars. I just walked."

Kins glanced at Tracy and she read his meaning. Evan remembered walking that day.

"What about the young woman, Evan? Did you see her?" Tracy asked.

"I didn't see her."

"We know she ran in the park that day, Evan."

Again, Evan didn't answer.

"Did you see the girl, Evan?"

"I was sick," he said suddenly. "I had the flu."

"Not Wednesday, Evan," Kins said. "You walked on Wednesday, and you mowed the lawns on Thursday. You weren't sick."

"Was she lost, Evan? Did she stop to ask for directions?" Tracy tried.

Evan brought both hands to his head. "I . . . I . . . I don't remember."

"Evan, we have to find that girl. We know you wouldn't want to see her get hurt. It's important that we find her."

"I have to go home."

Tracy changed gears. "Was Carrol at home sick yesterday?"

"Carrol works at the Home Depot."

"Did he get sick?" Kins tried. "Was he home yesterday—Sunday?"

"Carrol works at the Home Depot. Franklin works at a retirement home. I don't work."

"Was Carrol home sick yesterday and today, Evan?" Tracy asked again.

"I had to see the doctor," he said, seemingly more and more confused. "I had to go to the doctor."

"Evan?" He stopped and looked at Tracy. "It's okay, Evan." He appeared guarded. "Can I bum a cigarette?" Tracy asked.

Evan instinctively touched the breast pocket of his jacket, then he shook his head. "I have to go home. I'm not supposed to talk to you. I have to go. I have to go home." He resumed walking, nearly jogging. He turned right at the end of the block.

"He smokes," Tracy said, watching Evan disappear around the corner.

"But you're not going to convince a prosecutor or a judge to give us a warrant just because he patted his jacket."

"Not by itself. But we also know Carrol lied about his work schedule."

"Not about Wednesday."

"We know someone big enough to carry a 140-pound woman, knocked out, was lying in wait in the ravine, and the Sprague house backs to the same ravine."

"Franklin and Carrol both worked Wednesday, which is the day in question, and three other houses back up to that same ravine."

They started back to their car. "Let's try anyway," Tracy said. "Let's see if we can get Cerrabone on board."

They caught up with Rick Cerrabone in his office, preparing for trial. A senior prosecuting attorney in the Most Dangerous Offender Project, Cerrabone was always preparing for a trial, and his office inside the King County Courthouse usually looked as if a bomb had detonated. Cerrabone was old-school. He'd reluctantly accepted the use of laptop computers and other gadgetry, but he still maintained numerous black binders, some piled atop each other on his desk, others lining his office walls beside boxes containing exhibits, transcripts, photographs, and other material.

Cerrabone invited Tracy and Kins into his office out of professional courtesy—over the years they had worked many cases together—but he told them he didn't have a lot of time and might get called to the courtroom at any moment for a plea deal.

He gestured to the two chairs across from his desk. Tracy and Kins cleared stacks of paper and sat. Legal books lined floor-to-ceiling bookshelves, though the books were now just decoration. Every case had long ago been put online. The shelves included framed photographs of Cerrabone with his wife, and pictures of his three children—two grown boys and a daughter in a graduation cap and gown.

"Is that from college?" Tracy asked, dis-believing.

Cerrabone turned to look at the picture. "Medical school. Johns Hopkins."

"Hillary Cerrabone graduated medical school? She was just a little girl."

"And I was once young and had hair," Cerrabone said. "Don't remind me."

Cerrabone had never looked young. He had a

hangdog appearance, with perpetual dark bags under his eyes, a five-o'clock shadow, and skin that begged for sunshine. When Tracy first met him, she thought he looked like Joe Torre, the former Yankees manager. In court, Cerrabone reminded her of the stumbling, bumbling television police detective Columbo. It was an act that juries bought. After trials, jurors often expressed that they "felt sorry for Cerrabone" because he looked like he worked so hard.

"No wonder you're still working," Kins said.

"Not for that one," Cerrabone said. "We didn't pay a dime. She got scholarships for both her undergraduate and graduate studies. What wasn't covered by the scholarship, she took out in student loans."

"Can she talk to my boys? I have three in college and the tuition is killing me. One comes off the payroll this June, however. If he opts for graduate school, he's on his own."

"What can I do for you?" Cerrabone had removed his tie and had rolled the sleeves of his white shirt halfway up his forearms.

Kins gave Cerrabone the rundown on Stephanie Cole. The prosecutor had heard about the case, but not the details of their investigation.

"You think one of these three brothers had something to do with this girl going missing?" he said, cutting to the chase.

"We know the older brother lied to us about

Carrol working, and lied to us about Evan, the youngest, being sick."

"What evidence do you have that he lied?"

"We confirmed Carrol called in sick yesterday and today to his employer, and when asked, he didn't know Evan had been sick."

"And you think Carrol had something to do with getting rid of this girl because he didn't go to work?" Cerrabone sounded skeptical.

"We think that's a distinct possibility," Tracy said.

"But he worked Wednesday and Thursday?"

"Yes," Tracy said.

"And Evan smokes because he patted the pocket of his jacket?"

"Yes," Tracy said.

"How many cigarette butts did CSI find in the creek bed of that park?"

"Three or four." Tracy quickly added, "But only one behind the tree stump where Kaylee believes the person was lying in wait for Cole, and the Sprague backyard backs up to a trail leading down to the stump. If we can get a search warrant to find the cigarette brand that Evan . . ."

"You're not going to get a search warrant based on what you've told me," Cerrabone said matter-of-factly. "You confirmed Evan went to the emergency room—"

"He went after the fact—"

Cerrabone shrugged. "Doesn't matter. And

as for Franklin and Carrol lying about work, it could have been for any number of reasons. The key is they both worked Wednesday when this girl disappeared."

"The person behind the stump carried her up the hill, Rick. He didn't leave her in the ravine. Someone also moved her car. Probably the same person—or someone with an interest in this, like a brother. Both are indicative of a person or persons who didn't want us searching in that area. And that points to someone who lives there."

"Or someone who was in the ravine, saw her coming, hid, assaulted her, then used her car to transport her body someplace else so CSI wouldn't find any evidence." He held out his hands, palms up. "Or that person used her car to dump her body because it was convenient and meant not contaminating his own car, if he had one. Then he dumped the car."

"How many perpetrators do we come across who are that smart?" Tracy asked.

"Few," Cerrabone said. "Usually only the psychopaths."

"Which is around four percent of the population."

"And yet we've managed to have our fair share. You said there were also two prostitutes who went missing not far from North Park, didn't you?"

Tracy regretted mentioning the other two cases.

"This was a crime of opportunity, Rick. The person who did this was waiting for Cole at the end of the trail."

"You're speculating. You don't know that."

"Kaylee says that's what happened," Tracy said.

"You don't have any evidence it was . . ." Cerrabone looked at notes he'd scribbled. "Evan, or one of his brothers, which is what you'll need to get a search warrant for *their* house."

"We know Evan walked past the park that day."

"It's not enough."

"This woman may still be alive, Rick," Tracy said.

He shook his head and pointed to the picture of his daughter in her cap and gown. "You don't think I know what's at stake? Don't do that to me. You asked me for my opinion on what a judge was likely to do. I'm giving you an honest answer."

"No. Just—"

"You came to me for advice. I'm telling you it's unlikely a judge is going to issue a search warrant based on what you've told me. If you disagree, give it a shot."

Tracy and Kins left the courthouse and walked back to Police Headquarters in blustery and cold weather. They knew their chance of obtaining a search warrant without Cerrabone advocating for them was greatly reduced. In the A Team's bull pen they found Faz and Del seated at their desks. Maria Fernandez's desk remained unoccupied.

"If it isn't Starsky and Hutch, back from the dead," Faz said, rotating to face them.

"Let's hope not," Tracy said. "But it looks likely."

"I thought you were working cold cases," Del said.

"You and Nolasco," Tracy said.

"Somebody's cranky," Del said.

Kins said, "Go easy. We can't get Cerrabone to help us with a search warrant."

"Do it yourself," Del said, as if it were no big deal. "Save the time and the aggravation. Most of those guys over there don't got the balls, although Cerrabone usually does. Is this the missing girl up north?"

"We have witnesses lying," Kins said. "Three brothers who live together in a house close to where the girl went missing. Tracy thinks maybe they're protecting each other."

"Well, good luck," Faz said. "We're up to our eyeballs with that shooting in Pioneer Square. Try getting a deranged vagrant to tell you anything worth a shit."

"The world has turned upside down," Del said. "And we're all standing on our heads."

"Go on home," Kins said to Tracy. "I'll prepare the search warrant, take it to the judge, and let you know how kind he is when he rejects it."

"No. I'll stay and help," she said.

"Go," Kins said. "If I go home, I'll be eating leftovers alone. Shannah has book club tonight, which should be called 'wine club.' Half the time she doesn't even read the book."

"Sounds lonely," Tracy said.

Kins shrugged. "It's different when the kids move out."

"Tell me about it," Faz said. "When Antonio moved out, me and Vera looked at each other like two strangers."

"We have a set date every Tuesday," Kins said to Tracy. "In the spring and summer, we golf. This time of year, we have dinner and watch either a movie or a show. We trade off picking the movie and complaining. Go home. Go see Dan and your little girl."

"She took her first steps the other day," Tracy said. "Ahead of schedule."

"She's smart, that one," Faz said.

"Best to keep her away from you then," Del said.

As Tracy turned to leave, Nolasco and Maria Fernandez stepped into the cubicle. He wore his jacket and had his car keys on his index finger. He looked to Tracy, then announced, "Maria's case just finished."

"What happened?" Faz said. "You get a conviction?"

"He pled," Fernandez said. "First degree. Life in prison."

"That's good," Del said.

"You still working that missing girl investigation?" Nolasco asked Kins, now ignoring Tracy.

"Tracy and I were just about to put together a search warrant."

"Maria's available. Bring her up to speed."

"Tracy is already up to speed," Kins said.

"Tracy has her hands full working cold cases," Nolasco said.

"Tracy is standing right here," Tracy said. They all looked at her. "You have something to say, say it to me, Captain."

Nolasco smirked. "Maria's working the A Team now. I want Kins to bring her up to speed on the Cole investigation. Do we have a problem?"

Tracy shook her head. This was her case now. She didn't want to give it up, but she also wasn't going to fight with Nolasco in front of other detectives. "Not with Maria. No."

"Like I told you. Nunzio didn't do you any favors. You got big shoes to fill. I'd start filling them."

"I'd like to talk to you, in private."

Nolasco shook his head. "No can do now. I'm on my way out." He looked around the bull pen, turned, and left.

Fernandez grimaced. "I'm sorry, Tracy. I didn't

know you were working with Kins on this one. I told Nolasco about the plea deal and he told me to talk to Kins and get up to speed."

"Don't worry about it," Tracy said, seething that Nolasco didn't have the balls to talk to her in private. "I was going home anyway."

CHAPTER 26

Evan looked from the television to the sound of the garage door rattling open. Franklin was home. Evan had felt sick to his stomach for three hours, ever since those detectives came up behind him on the sidewalk. He felt like he was going to throw up.

Franklin had told him not to answer the front door. He'd said if the detectives came back, Evan was to hide, then call Franklin's cell phone. He said the detectives couldn't talk to him no more. Evan hadn't disobeyed him. He hadn't opened the door. The detectives hadn't even knocked. They'd come up to him on the street. They'd surprised him. He knew he shouldn't talk to them, but they kept asking him questions, confusing him.

Franklin would think Evan had said too much. He wouldn't give Evan a chance to explain what happened. He'd just start yelling. Then he'd beat him, like he'd always done. The way their daddy beat him.

"Keep your mouth shut." That's what Franklin had told him. "Keep your mouth shut. You're going to ruin it for all of us."

Evan didn't want the belt. Not again. His arms and legs still hurt, bruised purple and yellow. Franklin had made him wear sweats to the doctor, but the doctor had lifted Evan's sweatshirt to check his breathing. He made a face when he saw the bruising. He asked Evan what happened.

"He lost his footing and fell down the ravine behind the house," Franklin said. "It was a nasty fall over rocks."

The doctor asked Evan if that was what had happened. Evan said what Franklin said, so he wouldn't get beat again.

He didn't want to get beat again.

Car keys dropped on the counter. Franklin had driven back to Cle Elum and picked up Carrol, who stepped into the room just after him.

"Who cleaned up in here?" Franklin eyed the couches and the coffee table. Evan had cleared them of all the stuff. He'd even vacuumed so Franklin would be in a good mood.

"I did," Evan said. He looked again to the television.

"Yeah? Did hell freeze over?"

"What?" Evan gave Franklin a quick glance.

Franklin looked about the room. "Why'd you clean up?"

"You told me to."

"I tell you that every day. It don't mean you do it." Evan felt Franklin eyeing him and tried not to look at him. "How long you been watching TV?"

"I don't know."

"You clean the kitchen like I told you?"

"Yep."

Franklin walked from the room into the kitchen. Evan heard the refrigerator open and close. Franklin returned with a beer. Evan could tell without looking that Franklin was staring at him while drinking his beer. "It isn't exactly spotless, but it's clean."

Evan focused on the television. He thought he might throw up.

"What's wrong with you?"

Evan shook his head. "Nothing."

"Don't tell me 'nothing.' I can tell when something's bothering you. You cleaned the front room *and* the kitchen . . ." Franklin looked about the room. "You better not be lying to me." He sat in his recliner, which had been their daddy's chair. "What are you watching?"

"*The Big Bang Theory.*"

"I told you those were reruns. Half the jokes fly right over your head anyway."

"I like Penny," Evan said.

"Yeah, she's some piece of ass." Franklin sipped his beer. "Anyone come to the house today?"

"No," Evan said quickly. He kept his eyes glued to the television. Sweat trickled from his armpits down his sides. His stomach felt tied in knots, like he was about to throw up.

"What about those detectives?"

Evan shook his head. "They didn't come to the door."

He waited, but Franklin didn't ask him no more questions. He let out a held breath and started to relax. They watched television in silence for a minute. Then Franklin said, "You go on a walk today?"

"Uh-huh," Evan said.

"Boy! Look me in the eye when I'm speaking to you."

Evan looked at his older brother.

"Did you go for a walk?"

"I went for a walk," Evan said, trying not to gag on his words.

"You stop to talk with anyone?"

He felt his Adam's apple stick in his throat. "No."

"What about Bibby? You talk to Bibby on your walk?"

"I didn't see Bibby," Evan said.

Franklin sipped the beer. "Maybe that piece of shit finally died. Him and that damn dog."

Evan smiled. "I like Jackpot. I like Mrs. Bibby."

"You like it when she makes you them brownies. Don't be talking to either of them. You hear me? They're busybodies. I don't want them up in our business."

"I didn't talk to Bibby."

Franklin stared at him. "You said that already."

"I didn't remember," Evan said.

Franklin motioned with his beer toward the television. "That's because you're thinking with your pecker. You been thinking about that girl, haven't you?" Franklin smiled.

"Sometimes."

"I'll bet you have," Franklin said. "I'm off end of this week. Thought we better get up to the cabin and check on the girls. We'll take a drive, me and you."

Evan smiled. "What about Carrol?"

"Screw Carrol. He had time to himself up there. He can stay here and watch the house. Maybe I'll take your gal for a spin myself, break her in for you."

Evan felt panicked. The girl was his to play with. "You said you wouldn't."

"Maybe I changed my mind."

"You got your own girl."

Franklin laughed and finished his beer, then held the bottle out to Evan. "Get up and throw this out."

Evan got up from the couch. As he passed the recliner he reached for the empty bottle. Franklin grabbed his wrist. "Did Carrol tell you he touched my girl?"

"I didn't talk to Carrol."

"You ain't covering for him?"

"He didn't tell me nothing."

Franklin released Evan's wrist. "You're lying

about something," he said. "I can tell. And I will find out."

Evan had to go to the bathroom, before he pissed his pants. "I got to pee."

"Well, go then. And make yourself useful and bring me another beer when you come back."

Stephanie walked along the wall as far as the chain fastened to the post allowed her.

"Now what are you doing?" Donna asked. "More exercise?"

"I'm looking for a piece of board."

"You planning on starting a fire? Going to rub two sticks together, Little Miss Girl Scout?"

"I'm looking for something I can make into a weapon," she said. She held up the stone she'd dug up in the ground. "I might be able to sharpen an end with this."

"And then what?"

"I'll wait until he takes off my chains. Then I'll stab him and grab the key and unfasten your chains."

"Just like that? You ever stabbed a man?"

"No. Have you?"

Donna nodded. "Stabbed a john in the thigh once when he tried to get out without paying."

"What happened?"

"He paid. My point is, Little Miss Girl Scout, it isn't enough to have a knife. You have to be willing to use it without hesitation. You hesitate, he's going to grab the knife and use it on you, and maybe the two of us."

Stephanie hadn't thought of that. "You said they're going to kill us and leave our bodies up here for the animals."

"That's why we're here. You changed the game for them. You heard Franklin. Evan wasn't supposed to grab you. He called you a cheerleader."

"So?"

"So. Angel and I ain't no cheerleaders, in case you hadn't noticed. You know how many of us go missing, get beat up? You know what the police do?"

"No."

"Nothing. Absolutely nothing. But the police are going to look for a cheerleader. You got a mommy and a daddy likely pushing the police to find you. That's why we're here. That's why they're going to kill us. Because of you."

Stephanie looked to Angel, who simply nodded her head. Then she said, "Then I guess I can't hesitate. Can I? When I get the chance."

"You're going to get us all killed," Donna said.

"You said they're going to kill us anyway. What's the difference?"

Angel laughed. "Little Miss Sunshine has a point, doesn't she?"

CHAPTER 27

Tuesday morning, Tracy still seethed at the dressing-down she'd received from Johnny Nolasco in front of what had been her team, and at his cowardice. Maria Fernandez and Kins each called her cell phone after she left the office, but she'd let both calls go to voice mail. Neither was to blame for what had happened, but Tracy didn't want to say something in anger she'd later regret.

She'd spent a quiet night at home, and when Dan asked if everything was okay, she'd told him she was enjoying the family time.

Tracy made calls to the cell phone numbers for Bobby Chin's parents and his sister that she'd obtained from the preschool authorization form. None of the numbers remained in service. She turned instead to Chin's fraternity brothers in Phi Delta Phi. She wanted to determine if Chin had a history of violence against women.

One of the brothers, Peter Gillespie, worked as a director and coordinating producer for the Root Sports television station located in a building just off the I-90 freeway in Eastgate. Gillespie sounded surprised, then perplexed by Tracy's call, but he agreed to meet with her that morning. Before leaving home, she looked through

Gillespie's Facebook page and his LinkedIn professional page. Gillespie was popular, with more than fifteen hundred Facebook friends. His Facebook pictures dated back to his college years, including pictures of Gillespie with his fraternity brother Bobby Chin. They looked to have been close in college, and she expected to find postgraduation photos of the two of them but found very few. Gillespie posted pictures of UW football game tailgate parties, boating on Lake Washington, and of his five-year reunion. He also posted wedding photos and pictures with his wife and two kids. Tracy went through the pictures quickly. She did not see any others with Bobby Chin.

Tracy parked and made her way inside the building. She checked in at a reception counter and, minutes later, introduced herself to a heavyset man in slacks and an open-collared work shirt. Gillespie looked to have put on thirty pounds since college. He led her into a conference room on the first floor.

"I only have about twenty minutes," he said. "But I'm also happy to talk over the phone if you have additional questions. So, this is about Bobby?"

Tracy explained her connection to the cold case, and Gillespie asked the question everyone had asked.

"Has there been a new development?"

"I'm taking a fresh look at it. How well did you know Bobby Chin?"

"We were in the same fraternity in college, the same pledge class, so we were pretty close. We hung out a lot back then."

"Not so much anymore?"

"It's complicated."

"Did you have a falling-out?"

"No. We're still friends," Gillespie said. He looked to be struggling to define their relationship. "We just sort of drifted apart for a while. Bobby took a job with SPD straight out of college, which surprised those of us who knew him. He wasn't around much."

"What surprised you?" Tracy asked, expecting Gillespie to say that Chin had been wild in college.

"Never had any indication that's what he wanted to do. He studied computer science—what they call STEM: science, technology, engineering, and math. He was really smart. Good with computers. Always figured he'd pursue a tech job."

"You were surprised then because he chose SPD."

"Absolutely. I asked him about it after the fact and he said he wanted to get into forensics, and he thought being an officer and starting with a working knowledge would help him. Pissed his parents off something royal though."

"How do you know that?"

"Bobby told me. His parents are traditional Chinese. Bobby and his sister were the first generation born here. His parents wanted him to do something with computers and technology. A police officer was the last thing they wanted, at least according to Bobby."

"Do you know his parents or his sister?"

"I met the parents briefly at graduation. I met the sister a couple of times; she went to school at the U. I can't remember her name."

"Gloria."

"Right. She was a few years behind us. She and Bobby seemed close. I don't really know."

"You said you grew apart? When did that happen?"

"About the time Bobby started seeing Jewel."

"You know his ex-wife then."

Gillespie shook his head. "No. Not really. Honestly, I don't know anyone who really knew her."

"You didn't socialize?"

"We tried. I should say, I tried. She came to a couple of tailgates with Bobby, but you could tell it wasn't her thing. Bobby came for a while without her, but then he stopped coming too. A couple of us reached out to him, but I think with working full-time and with Jewel . . . After a while you give up trying, you know?"

"When was the last time you saw him?"

"Now? Now we see each other once or twice a month. He's working for a company here in Bellevue."

"When did your relationship start again?"

"Soon after he left Jewel. I saw him out to dinner in downtown Bellevue. He's remarried and has a little boy."

"Did you ask what happened? Why you didn't see him for so long?"

"I knew why."

"And what was that?"

"Jewel didn't like Bobby's college friends; she thought we were immature."

"Bobby tell you that?"

"Didn't have to. It was made clear by Jewel."

"Did Bobby talk about Jewel?"

"He said he was glad he got out of the relationship, and that his one regret was he wished he had put it together earlier, that maybe he could have saved his daughter."

"Put what together?"

"Jewel's mental illness."

"Who told you Jewel was mentally ill?"

"Bobby."

"Have you and Bobby spoken about his daughter's disappearance?"

"Not a lot," Gillespie said. "It isn't really something Bobby likes to talk about. He did say he thought Jewel and the boyfriend took Elle, but that they'll never prove it. You heard the boyfriend shot himself?" Gillespie asked.

"I did," Tracy said.

"Bobby thinks Jewel had something to do with that also."

"Did he say why?"

"He thinks Jewel was just using the boyfriend to make Bobby jealous, and after the divorce was finalized, and Elle went missing, she wanted to dump him for someone who made money, but the boyfriend knew what happened to the kid. So she was stuck."

"And Bobby thinks Jewel had him killed so he wouldn't expose her?"

Gillespie shrugged. "He didn't get into details. Just said he thinks she likely had something to do with it."

"He never gave you any evidence though?"

"Nah, shit, I don't know. Just Bobby venting, I guess."

"Did you ever know Bobby to become violent?"

Gillespie gave the question some thought, then shook his head. "No. Not really. We could all get a little out of hand when we were drinking, fraternity stuff, but never violent."

"Did he have relationships in college?"

"Bobby? Hell, yeah. He's a good-looking guy. He had a lot of girlfriends."

"Any issues of any violence with them?"

"No. Nothing I'm aware of."

"Do you know how he met Jewel?"

"I think he told me they met in a bar, but don't quote me on that. They got married six months later."

Gillespie stopped, though he looked like he wanted to continue. "Something more?" Tracy asked.

He shrugged and made a face. "I heard through the rumor mill that Jewel got pregnant; that's why Bobby got married so quickly. I don't know. I've never asked him about it. Not my business. But Bobby's family had money, and the rumor was Jewel was looking for a big payday. No insult intended, but SPD isn't exactly striking it rich."

"Far from it," Tracy said with a smile.

"Bobby doesn't talk about it and I don't ask. I'm just glad I got my friend back. You know?"

Tracy knew, but she wondered if Bobby Chin had started to resent Jewel Chin. If he had started to feel like maybe he'd been played, with her getting pregnant, and he got tired of Jewel bitching and complaining about his salary, his work schedule, his friends. Maybe he'd met the woman who is now his wife and wanted out of the relationship. She wondered if it all just got to be too much for Bobby Chin and he snapped, his daughter collateral damage.

Then again, maybe Jewel Chin did have a psychiatric disorder.

There was one way to find out.

CHAPTER 28

Tracy reached Bobby Chin at his employer in Bellevue and made plans to speak to him as she left Gillespie's office. She figured Gillespie would be on the phone to Chin the minute she departed, if he hadn't been already, which maybe was the reason Chin had been so amenable to meeting her on short notice. Curiosity was usually a great motivator. A former cop, Chin would think something might have developed in his daughter's case, and he'd be curious why Tracy was asking his friends questions about him.

Chin worked as chief of security at a Chinese-owned computer company. He'd left Seattle PD roughly six months after his daughter's disappearance. Tracy speculated, based on her conversation with Officer Bill Miller, and from her own personal experience, that Chin departed because of the focus of the investigation with him as a suspect, which had to be embarrassing for a police officer.

Tracy pulled into a garage beneath a blue-glass, high-rise building—the Bellevue city center. In the lobby she spoke with a security guard, then watched fresh-out-of-college workers with lanyards dangling around their necks pass through security turnstiles.

Bobby Chin greeted her dressed in a tailored business suit and tie. His clothing surprised her, and not just that he wore a suit in the casual-dress Pacific Northwest. The suit material looked to be of high quality, meaning expensive. She had expected Chin to be wearing a drab security guard's uniform, like the outfit worn by the man seated behind the lobby counter. After introductions, Chin handed her a pass on a lanyard for a company called Xia Tech, and Tracy followed him through a turnstile and into a glass elevator. As the elevator ascended, she had a stunning, west-facing view across Lake Washington's glass-calm, gray waters to the spires of downtown Seattle. The snow-capped Olympic Mountains served as a backdrop.

"What kind of company is Xia Tech?" Tracy asked on their ascent.

"It's a Chinese-owned tech company. We do business primarily in Internet translations." Chin sounded as if he had answered the question before. "Four years ago, Xia Tech opened this branch and hired engineers to focus on artificial intelligence and cloud-based applications."

Tracy was sure being near Microsoft and Amazon played a large part in the company's location choice.

She stepped from the elevator car onto the

fortieth floor and followed Chin along sparkling white hallways to an office door bearing his name. "Not a bad gig," Tracy said, entering an office with the same glorious views.

Chin smiled. "You look surprised."

A good-looking man, Chin wore his hair short, and it had started to gray at the temples. He had a strong jawline to support a million-dollar smile. The suit fit him; some men looked born to wear a suit. Chin was one of them.

"I guess when you said security, I was expecting you were a security guard." Tracy settled into a seat across from Chin, who sat behind a desk with the windows and the million-dollar view at his back.

"In a sense I am," Chin said. "I'm in charge of protecting the company's proprietary interests. I oversee a team of engineers who try to anticipate where we're vulnerable to hackers and head them off before they get there. The ideas the company generates are worth a lot of money."

"How did you go from Seattle PD to Internet and cloud security?" Tracy suspected she knew, but she wanted to hear it from Chin.

"I studied computer engineering at UW— my parents' choice—but there was something that always appealed to me about police work. My goal had been to eventually grow into forensic crimes at Park 90/5, but I never got that far."

Chin's desk phone rang. "Sorry. Let me get rid of this."

Tracy could tell Chin spoke to his spouse on the desk phone. She used the interruption to look around his office. A framed wedding photograph of Chin and a Caucasian woman sat prominently displayed on a shelf to his left. In another, a selfie taken at a hospital, the same woman held a newborn baby in her arms after giving birth, Chin close by her bedside. In a third photograph, one Tracy had in the cold case file, a Chinese girl stood wearing a colorful butterfly costume and a beaming smile. She held the wing tips so the colors could be seen. Elle Chin.

Tracy felt a wave of melancholy wash over her.

"Yeah, I will," Chin said. "I'm just starting a meeting. Love you too."

Chin hung up the receiver and pressed a few buttons to hold future calls. "Sorry about that."

"No problem. I make similar calls to my husband and the nanny," Tracy said to broach the subject.

"How many children do you have?" Chin asked.

"A daughter. Ten months. How old is your . . . son?"

"He's two now," Chin said. "I need to update the photos." He lost the smile. "Some of them anyway." Chin reached and picked up the framed photograph of Elle Chin. "This is Elle. I took this the night she disappeared."

"I'm sorry," Tracy said.

"I am too," Chin said, and he looked and sounded emotional. Though it had been five years since his daughter's disappearance, Tracy knew that day never left the forefront of a parent's being. She also knew that having a detective appear in your office to talk about it made it all the more real and all the more painful, especially when that disappearance came from horrific circumstances.

Chin sat back. "Pete Gillespie called and said you spoke to him. He said you asked a lot of questions about me."

"Wouldn't you?" Tracy asked.

Chin nodded. "I suppose I would."

"I've taken over the Cold Case Unit from Detective Nunzio."

"I figured as much. Did he retire?"

"He did."

"Good for him."

"I'd like to take another look at your daughter's case."

"Great. Is there some new information to warrant it, or do you just believe the husband of the crazy wife must be guilty?"

"Are you?"

He smiled, though not with humor. "The husband of the crazy wife? Yes. The husband who killed his daughter? Absolutely not." He sighed. "If there've been no new developments, why are you here, Detective?" Chin's tone clearly indicated displeasure. Tracy did what she always did; she used it.

"Does it upset you to talk about it?"

Chin gave a sarcastic chuckle. "Of course it upsets me. That day . . . those days, were the worst days of my life. I spent countless hours over countless weeks searching for Elle. I've never accepted she was gone. That's why I keep her picture here. I see her every day as I remember her. But . . ." He caught himself, looked away, and sucked in a breath. "I had to move on, Detective. We don't really have much of a choice, do we?" He glanced at the photographs on the shelves.

No, we don't, Tracy thought, but didn't say. "You've remarried."

Chin nodded. "And we have a little boy. And I miss my daughter every day. What else can I help you with? Do you want to ask what kind of an idiot would allow his five-year-old to play hide-and-seek in a corn maze? I've been asked and answered those questions a hundred times."

Since Chin had raised the painful issue, better to just rip off the Band-Aid in one swipe. "So what's the answer? Why did you?"

"Because I wasn't thinking clearly. I hadn't been thinking clearly for some time. Jewel screwed with my head. I know it's hard for everyone to understand. It's hard for me to explain, but it's true. I wasn't thinking like a parent. I was thinking like a pissed-off husband trying to curry favor with his five-year-old daughter whom he got to see Wednesday evenings and every other weekend." He rested his forearms on his desk pad. "My time with Elle was limited because of certain circumstances."

"The domestic violence charge?"

"I'm not proud of it, Detective. It happened. It's not exactly something to strive for, having your work colleagues come out to the house and ask you to leave, the last time in handcuffs. It's not like me. Wasn't like me."

"Why did you do it?" Tracy asked, knowing men often excused their behavior by blaming others.

"Like I said, I wasn't thinking right. Jewel baited me and I took the bait. But it was on me and I own it. It was wrong, and I regretted it the minute I slapped her. I knew she would use it to hurt me."

"Not sorry because you hit her?"

Chin sighed. "Of course I regretted hitting her." He sat back. "My ex-wife was sick, Detective, and I paid the price."

"Sick how?"

"It's in the reports, Detective."

"I haven't read the entire file. I just started a couple days ago," Tracy said, feigning ignorance.

She had read the file but didn't recall a report that Jewel was mentally ill.

Chin smiled. "I doubt that. You've been in homicide for more than a decade and have the highest success percentage of any detective. You're also twice decorated. The Medal of Valor. Impressive."

"You researched me."

"As you researched me," Chin said. "I still have friends in the North Precinct."

"Bill Miller?"

"No. Though I know who he is. You were pretty famous for catching the Cowboy. So, don't tell me you didn't read the file. I'm sure you read every word of it. Maybe talked to others besides Pete. Maybe my ex. You're trying to see what kind of guy I am. Whether I could get angry enough to kill my own daughter."

"Tell me about that night," Tracy said.

Chin took a moment, perhaps deciding where to start. He blew out a breath. "As I said, my time with Elle was extremely limited, and my wife did everything she could to undermine what time I did have with Elle. So, when I got Elle, I tended to spoil her. I just wanted her to be happy, Detective. I felt tremendous guilt leaving her in that house, with Jewel and the boyfriend. I loved that little girl and she loved me." Chin wiped a tear from his eye. "Elle wanted to play hide-and-seek. I initially said no, but she started to cry."

His eyes welled with tears. "She said her mommy and Graham—the boyfriend—let her play. Then she sat down in the dirt. I didn't want her to cry. I just wanted her to be happy. So, I let her play. I figured she wouldn't get far." He shook his head. "Then the lights went out. It was pitch-black." Chin blew out another breath.

Tracy gave him a second, then switched subjects. "Tell me about your wife's illness."

Chin exhaled and sat back. "There was never a diagnosis, okay? Never a court determination. We didn't get that far. Borderline personality disorder is the term that came up most often in my own counseling sessions following my daughter's disappearance to describe my wife's behavior and how I might deal with it."

"What behavior in particular?"

"My ex separated me from my friends and tried to separate me from my family. She isolated me. I didn't know it at the time, but looking back, that's exactly what she did. She didn't like my college friends because they were immature, and she didn't like my high school friends because she thought they were spoiled and entitled. She didn't like my parents because they were too judgmental. Then she started to use Elle to get what she wanted. She used everybody to get what she wanted. Me. Elle. Her new boyfriend. She used us until we were no longer of any use, or in my case, when I finally figured out how unhealthy our relationship was, and I left her. That's when she attacked."

"Attacked how?"

"She had the boyfriend when we separated. He was her personal trainer. I don't think she gave a shit about him, to be honest, but he was well-built and good-looking, perfect for her to try to make me jealous, to get under my skin."

"Did it?"

"No." He shook his head with emphasis. "As I said, I knew what she was doing, and I figured that maybe if she had someone else to torment, she'd leave me alone. I was just looking forward to the day when I'd no longer have to deal with her."

"But that day would never come, so long as you each had Elle."

"I know. And at one point I thought the only way out was if I checked out. That's how messed up she had me. I actually contemplated it."

"What stopped you?"

"I realized that would mean leaving Elle to Jewel, and that would mean condemning Elle to a life in hell. I couldn't do that to my daughter."

Tracy wondered, though, if that thought could have been the impetus for killing Elle. Especially if Chin wasn't right in the head, as he said. "Let me ask you something. It seems counterintuitive, doesn't it, that Jewel would use the boyfriend just to take Elle? If she's that calculating, she'd have to know she and the boyfriend would be forever stuck together."

"Unless she drove him to kill himself . . ." Chin shrugged. "Or manipulated someone to do it for her. I can only imagine the mind games she played on him, because she played them on me. They said it was depression from steroid use, but I know differently. I think it was depression from Jewel."

"There was a witness to Elle's disappearance—"

"Jimmy Ingram," Chin said.

"He said he told you the lights went out at ten, but you were insistent on going through the maze. Why?"

"As I said, I was just trying to give my daughter a good time, to make her happy. I was late getting to the house because I got tied up doing reports at work. Jewel refused to feed Elle the nights I picked her up." He shook his head. "What kind of a woman lets her child go hungry just to make a point against her husband?" When Tracy didn't answer, Chin continued, telling her about their arrival at the corn maze, Elle's need to use the bathroom, and her hunger. "By the time we ate, the maze was about to close. I told the guy I just needed a few minutes."

"I was curious. He said it didn't look like the little girl he saw was resisting the woman, that she didn't appear to be struggling or screaming or otherwise trying to get away."

"I know. I've wondered about that as well."

"You told the detectives you thought it was Jewel and the boyfriend."

"I know."

"Do you still believe that?"

"I don't know. What I believe doesn't really matter."

Tracy changed subjects. "Jewel claimed she left you, that you were obsessed with her."

"Yes, she did." Chin smiled and met Tracy's gaze. "But that isn't how it happened. I walked out on her, and she raced to get an attorney and to file for divorce to make it look like her idea. I didn't really care, but I couldn't have even started to fathom the storm she was brewing. Jewel hated me for walking out on her, Detective. She hated me because I didn't have the career she thought I was going to have, because my parents cut off all financial support when I joined the PD and married Jewel. My ex used Elle to try to hurt me. She used the domestic violence charge to hurt my position in the parenting plan and in the divorce. She was very calculating."

"You think she planned this from the start?"

"That part of it. I know she did. Remember, Detective, I worked. Jewel didn't. She had all day to think about this shit, about how she could hurt me, disgrace me, maybe get me to kill myself like the boyfriend, so she could get it all. I almost did too. In the end, I had to walk away, and all

I can tell you is that walking out that door was the hardest thing I ever did, because I knew I was leaving Elle behind in her dysfunctional care."

"Why do it, then, Bobby? If you were so certain of this, why leave your daughter with someone that sick?"

Chin shook his head, fighting emotions. "I always thought I'd get Elle. I thought a judge, the guardian ad litem, someone would see what I saw, what I'd come to know." He shrugged. "They didn't. I underestimated Jewel. And I paid dearly for it."

Tracy decided to ask the question intimated in the reports. "With Elle missing, you no longer have to deal with Jewel."

Chin closed his eyes and shook his head. "I married Jewel because of Elle, Detective. I took responsibility for my child. My parents. My sister. My friends. They were all dead set against me marrying Jewel. They saw what I didn't want to see. But Elle was my responsibility."

Chin sounded sincere, and it was a strong argument. "I tried to reach your parents and your sister, but the numbers I have no longer are in service."

"My parents and sister can't tell you anything, Detective."

"Where are they?"

"China. My sister met a student at the U—a Chinese national. They live outside Chengdu.

My parents went back home with them. And I've put them through enough as it is. I'd ask you to leave them alone." Chin stood. "Unless there is anything else, any new leads, I need to get back to work."

It sounded more like "I need to get on with my life."

Tracy arrived at Police Headquarters early afternoon, grabbed a cup of coffee, and sat at her desk in her office. She wanted to confront Nolasco, but she kept thinking of the Bobby Chin interview. Chin made a lot of sense when he said he took responsibility for his daughter, but at the same time, he didn't help himself. If his ex-wife had screwed with his mind so much that Chin was unstable, that he had contemplated killing himself, then wasn't it possible he saw the only other way out of the situation as well?

Under normal circumstances, Tracy would have said no, but Chin had said these weren't normal circumstances. They were far from normal, at least as he described them. Something was amiss, but Tracy was starting to doubt she would ever figure out what had happened.

Her computer pinged. An email from Kins. His attempt to get a search warrant had been denied. The judge had ruled as Cerrabone had predicted—insufficient evidence to warrant a search of the Sprague brothers' home.

The email frustrated her, but the court often frustrated her, seemingly more concerned with perpetrator rights than with the victims. She was convinced the brothers were behind Cole's disappearance. There were just too many coincidences, too many half-truths and outright lies. But as much as she wanted to work on the case, she knew she couldn't.

Nolasco had been direct about that.

She looked to the two cold case binders on her desk, one for Angel Jackson, the other for Donna Jones—the two prostitutes who had disappeared on Aurora Avenue North. Was that just another coincidence, that their disappearance was in roughly the same area as Stephanie Cole's, and under similar circumstances, with no body found?

When she broached the subject of the two prostitutes with Kins, he had suggested they work Cole's case, and if that led to the two prostitutes, they could work those cases as well. Tracy smiled.

Wasn't the reverse equally true?

If she worked the two prostitute cases and it happened to lead to Stephanie Cole, well, Nolasco couldn't very well discipline her for it, could he?

She pulled out her keyboard and started typing. Using King County land records, Tracy determined Ed and Carol Lynn Sprague purchased the house in North Park in 1957. She looked for whether Ed Sprague owned any other property, someplace out of the area, remote, where the sons could have taken a kidnap victim, either with the intent to keep her alive, or to bury the body. She did not find other property in Ed Sprague's name.

According to an obituary in the *Seattle Post-Intelligencer*, Ed had died of cancer ten years ago. He had worked as a machinist at Boeing. That fact got Tracy's attention. Brian Bibby had also worked as a machinist for Boeing. Given their similar ages, the two employments likely overlapped. That didn't necessarily mean they knew one another. Boeing employed thousands of machinists, but it was something to at least explore. She made a note to ask Bibby.

At the time of his death, Ed was survived by his wife, Carol Lynn, and his three sons, Franklin, Carrol, and Evan. The obituary also noted another child, Lindsay.

Tracy paused. It felt like the moment in an investigation when there was an unexpected breakthrough, a piece of critical evidence. No one had mentioned a daughter.

She read the ages of the children at the time of Ed Sprague's death. Lindsay was ten years younger than Evan. Simple math indicated Carol Lynn, the mother, would have been in her midforties when Lindsay was born. It wasn't impossible she'd had a child. Tracy knew that well. But ten years between children seemed a long time to wait. An unexpected pregnancy? Perhaps. Had they adopted Lindsay to give Carol Lynn the girl she'd always wanted? Again, if so, why wait so long to make that decision?

Tracy wondered where Lindsay was now.

She called the Washington State Department of Children, Youth and Families in Olympia. She wouldn't be able to get sensitive information, such as birth parents, assuming Lindsay had been adopted, but she could get basic information. Fifteen minutes later, after two different conversations, she hung up the phone with information that confirmed her suspicions. Carol Lynn had not become pregnant, nor had the Spragues adopted Lindsay. She came to the Spragues through foster care, living with them from ages twelve to eighteen, at which time she became an adult and left the DCYF system. Tracy obtained her birth name: Lindsay Josephine Sheppard.

She thought of the school just down the block from the Sprague house, and Brian Bibby's statement that it had been the shortest commute a teacher ever had to make to get to work. The same applied to neighborhood children. She made a note to determine if the Sprague children had attended the North Park elementary school and, if they had, whether the school had further information on any of them, particularly Lindsay.

Tracy switched gears. She checked whether any of the three Sprague brothers had a criminal history. Again, she got a hit. Franklin Sprague had been arrested twice for soliciting a prostitute. "Bingo," she said out loud. A possible connection to Angel Jackson and Donna Jones? She read further. Franklin had been picked up twice, both times not far from where the two prostitutes had subsequently gone missing on Aurora Avenue. Two more coincidences.

Her reading picked up speed. His first arrest, Franklin Sprague had solicited an undercover Seattle police officer working a sting operation. His second arrest, detectives working the strip observed him soliciting a known prostitute from his van. Tracy pulled up the criminal files. His first offense, Franklin had been charged with a misdemeanor, fined $1,000, and given a ninety-day suspended sentence, subject to his completing 250 hours of community service. Six months later, following his second arrest, Franklin served 120 days in the county jail.

Tracy clicked on the police report for Carrol Sprague and again got a hit. "Bingo," she said again. Coincidence number three. Carrol had also been pinched for solicitation, also on Aurora Avenue, and not far from where the two prostitutes subsequently went missing.

She ran a report on Evan Sprague but did not get a hit.

Tracy's police cell phone rang. Caller ID indicated Mike Melton at the Washington State Patrol Crime Lab.

"Had trouble tracking you down," Melton said. "I've called your desk number so often it's become a habit."

"What do you have for me? I could use a little Oz magic."

"A few of the cigarette butts were in too poor of a condition from the elements to pull DNA, but we did get DNA from three of them."

"Which ones?" Tracy asked.

"We pulled DNA from the butt behind the log at the end of the trail, and two located near the start of the trail."

Tracy clenched her fist. "Same DNA or different?" Tracy asked.

"Different. And, unfortunately, we ran all three through the FBI's criminal database and we did not get a hit."

"Did not?"

"Did not. Sorry."

The criminal database only recorded DNA profiles for persons convicted of a felony. Washington State did not require the defendant to give a sample when convicted of a misdemeanor. That likely ruled out Franklin and Carrol Sprague's DNA being in the database, their solicitation convictions being only misdemeanors.

Tracy had another thought. "If I could get you a DNA sample, you could compare it to the DNA from the cigarette butts and determine if it matched, couldn't you?"

"You know we can."

"And you could determine if the sample came from a relative?"

Seattle had recently been in the news for the trial of a man arrested after DNA found at a homicide was run through criminal databases and determined to be related to a convicted felon—a brother—whose DNA was stored in one of the databases. A similar case in California had also created significant controversy when a man was identified as the Golden State Killer—a former policeman who had raped and murdered multiple women—through the DNA provided by a distant relative to an ancestry database.

"Familial DNA? Yeah. You know we can do that too."

"Thanks, Mike. I'll be in touch." Before she hung up, another thought came to her. "Mike?"

"Still here."

"If anyone asks, tell them I asked you to run the DNA in two cold cases I'm working, Angel Jackson and Donna Jones." She provided Melton with the case numbers.

"Let me write this down." After doing so, Melton said, "Got it."

"Thanks, Mike."

"How's that little girl?"

"Growing quickly."

"You have no idea how fast the years go."

Tracy disconnected and called Kins; she arranged to meet him at a Starbucks down the street. She didn't want to talk over the phone or meet with him in the A Team's bull pen.

When Kins arrived, Tracy told him the crime lab results, what her own research had revealed about Franklin and Carrol's criminal records, and about the foster child, Lindsay Sheppard.

Kins's brow furrowed. "Even if you find her, her DNA won't help if she isn't a blood relative."

"I know that. I have another idea."

"You want to share?"

"No."

"I didn't think so. Just keep me in the loop." Kins sounded deflated.

"What's wrong?"

"Nolasco is pushing us to direct our attention to other cases."

Tracy nodded. "I'll forward Mike's results and keep you in the loop."

She looked at the clock on her phone. Three

thirty. Franklin told them Carrol went to a bar after work. Tracy wasn't sure if that had also been a lie, but there was only one way to find out.

And Carrol had not yet seen her.

CHAPTER 29

Tracy drove her pool car into the Home Depot parking lot and proceeded slowly up and down the aisles of parked cars, checking makes and models and license plates. Before leaving the office, she'd called the Department of Licensing and obtained a copy of Carrol Sprague's driver's license, with his photograph. He'd recently paid the license tab fee on a green 2017 Kia Rio. She found the car parked on the east side of the building near an exit for garden plants and supplies. She drove three aisles over, parked in a space where she could observe the car and the exit, and taped a blown-up copy of Sprague's driver's license photo to her dash.

Carrol Sprague was forty-seven years old, five feet eleven, and 230 pounds. He wore glasses and had thinning hair, just wisps atop his head. From his picture, he didn't physically resemble Evan or Franklin Sprague. His hair and skin coloring were lighter than his brothers'. He wasn't as tall, and was heavyset, but there was a similarity in their facial features.

Raindrops splattered the windshield and increased to a steady mist. Tracy intermittently turned on her Subaru's windshield wipers to clear the glass while she waited. The drops looked to have ice. Snow was in the forecast.

At 4:40, Tracy sat up. A man had exited the garden center and was walking toward the Kia Rio. Darkness, and the rain, made it difficult to see any features, and the man wore a green-and-black Gore-Tex jacket with the hood protecting his head. He used a key fob that illuminated the Kia's interior dome before he opened the door.

Carrol Sprague.

Sprague backed from his parking spot. Tracy started the engine, kept the headlights off, and pulled forward, giving herself plenty of room behind the Kia. Sprague wove his way through the parking lot to 244th Street Southwest, turned left, and drove to Aurora Avenue North, also known as the Pacific Highway. Tracy followed, maintaining a distance of several car lengths behind the Kia on the four-lane road. She had to be close enough to make the traffic lights and to turn, if Sprague suddenly turned.

Sprague drove for several miles, passing one-story fast food restaurants, motels, hotels, and travel lodges, as well as one-story businesses. Tracy thought again of Angel Jackson and Donna Jones, and how easy it would have been for Sprague to cruise the strip after work to snatch a prostitute without attracting any attention.

He made a right turn into a strip mall parking

lot. Businesses included a chiropractor's office, a video game arcade store, and a bar, the Pacific Pub. Tracy turned into the driveway and watched in the rearview mirror as Sprague parked the Kia and got out, again pulling the jacket hood over his head before entering the bar.

Creature of habit.

Tracy slipped on her raincoat, pulled her blouse from the waistline of her jeans to look a little less put together, then stepped from the car and hurried beneath the awning protecting the entrances to the businesses from the rain.

The pub's glass door and windows had been tinted black, so she couldn't see where Carrol Sprague sat. Tracy stepped inside to dim lighting from globes hanging over a bar, booths along the walls, and several tables with chairs. At a booth closest to the bar, Carrol Sprague removed his jacket and hung it on a hook before he lowered onto the bench seat.

Tracy sat in an empty booth where she could watch the back of Carrol Sprague's head. Above him, hanging from the ceiling, a television broadcast a college football game. A waitress appeared at Sprague's table with a laminated menu, but it never left her hand. She and Sprague exchanged a few words. They looked as if they knew each other. This was likely the bar Franklin said his brother frequented after work.

After a couple minutes, the waitress moved

down the booths to Tracy, welcomed her, and handed her the menu.

"Can I get you something to drink?"

"Maybe. I'm supposed to meet someone here. Let me look over the menu while I'm waiting."

The waitress left the menu on the table and departed. She returned to Sprague's table with a longneck Bud Light, again stopping to talk with him. *Girlfriend?* Tracy wondered. The woman again approached Tracy's booth. "I think I'll have a Budweiser while I'm waiting," she said.

"A bottle or a draft?"

"A bottle's fine."

Tracy kept her eyes on Sprague, but to any of the other half a dozen people in the bar, she looked like she was watching the football game on the mounted television. The waitress returned with her bottle of beer. Twenty minutes later, she delivered a basket of food, what looked to be a hamburger and French fries, and a second beer to Sprague. She didn't take the first bottle.

She approached Tracy's booth. "Still waiting?" she asked.

"Still waiting," Tracy said.

"Can I get you another beer?"

"Not just yet."

"Just flag me down if you need anything."

"I'll do that."

Another ten minutes passed. The bells hanging on the glass door jingled. In Tracy's peripheral vision, a man entered the bar. As he made his way to Carrol Sprague's table, Tracy paid closer attention.

Franklin Sprague.

"Shit," she said under her breath.

Carrol Sprague looked up from his hamburger, his mouth filled with a large bite, and mumbled a greeting to his brother sliding into the booth across from him.

Franklin did not respond.

"What's up?" Carrol asked. He wiped his hands and mouth on a napkin and set it on the table. Franklin had called him just before Carrol got off work and said he'd meet him at the Pacific Pub, that he had something to talk to Carrol about. The call had made Carrol queasy. The only thing worse than Franklin being upset about something was Franklin telling you he needed to talk to you, but not telling you about what. He made it feel like an interrogation, like he was asking you questions he already knew the answers to and really wanted to determine if you were lying or trying to get away with something.

The waitress appeared at the table and handed Franklin a longneck Bud. "Thanks, Janice."

"Can I get you any food?"

"Not tonight. I ate at work."

She tore off the bill and slipped it beneath the basket, departing.

"She wouldn't be bad if she lost twenty to thirty pounds in her ass," Franklin said, watching her leave.

"More cushion for the pushing," Carrol said, trying to keep it light. He sipped his beer.

Franklin turned his attention back to the table. "You talk to Evan?"

"Evan?" Carrol shook his head. "When?"

"What do you mean, when? Anytime. Did you talk to Evan last night when we got home?"

Carrol didn't know what this was about. He'd talked to Evan last night when he got home. Nothing of substance though. "Not really." That seemed like the safest answer.

"How did he seem to you?"

Carrol shrugged. "Seemed fine. I mean, same as always. We didn't really talk all that much. Why?"

"Did you notice he'd cleaned the front room and the kitchen?"

Carrol sipped his beer. Then he said, "Didn't you tell him to do it?"

"Yeah, I told him, but I've told him about a million times before. When's the last time he actually remembered to do it? Shit, he can't remember to take the garbage out when he's holding the bag in his hand."

"That's true." Carrol sipped more beer. "What did he say when you asked him?"

"He said he did it 'cause I told him to."

"Well, there you go."

"There I go where?"

"There's your answer."

Franklin drank from his beer. "If that was my answer would I be here?"

Carrol didn't respond. He figured the question was rhetorical, but just in case, he kept quiet and ate a couple of the French fries.

"He was squirrely," Franklin said.

"He's always squirrely around you, Franklin. He's afraid of you."

"Maybe. He seemed like he was hiding something he didn't want me to find out."

"What?"

"If I knew that, he wouldn't be hiding it, would he?"

"Did you ask him?"

"Course I asked him. He danced around it, avoided eye contact. I thought maybe he said something to you."

Carrol shook his head. They sat in silence for a moment, each sipping from their beers. "What do you think it is?" Carrol asked.

"I don't know. But I want you to talk to him when you get home, see if you can pry it out of him. Sober. Not drunk."

"Okay. Yeah. Sure."

"This whole thing is going sideways," Franklin said.

"What whole thing?"

Franklin lowered his voice. "What do you mean, what whole thing? What the hell do you think I'm talking about? The girls. Ever since he grabbed that young runner . . . The police have been all around the park, asking everybody questions, whether they have video. I spoke to the Maxwells, and they said the police asked for their surveillance footage for Wednesday, and guess who was on it?"

"Bibby."

Franklin shook his head and rolled his eyes. "Evan. He went for a walk past the house last Wednesday just before that girl went into the park."

Carrol set down the French fries. He'd lost his appetite. "Oh shit."

"Yeah. Oh shit."

Carrol took another sip of his beer. He wished he had a shot of whiskey, but Franklin might crack him over the head with his bottle if Carrol ordered it. "You . . . you . . . you think the police got something else?"

"Yeah, they got something else. Bibby saw that girl in the park. That's why they were down there looking for evidence in the first place. Now they got Evan out walking at the same time she went missing. They're just putting the pieces of the puzzle together."

"Did . . . did . . . did you throw out Evan's shoes and clothes?"

Franklin nodded. "What about prints? Could they have found your prints on the car?"

Carrol felt heat radiating through his body. "I . . . I don't think so. I . . . I . . . I wore the gloves the whole time, and the hat, just like you said. An . . . an . . . and I wiped down the car with the wipes you gave me. Inside and out. I did just what you told me to do."

Franklin finished his beer and set the bottle on the table. "I'm thinking we need to pull the plug before this gets out of hand."

"Pull the plug?" Carrol said.

"Get rid of the women."

"Let them go?"

Franklin spoke like he hadn't heard a word Carrol had said. "Evan and I are going to take a trip up to the cabin tomorrow."

"What about me?"

"You'll stay here."

"Why?"

" 'Cause you can't keep calling into work sick, that's why. It starts to look suspicious. And we don't need any more suspicion."

"What are you going to do up there?"

"I don't know." He turned and looked to the door, then reengaged Carrol. "Anybody comes around, like those detectives, you tell them I took Evan over to Eastern Washington. Tell them we're going to visit Uncle Henry, do a little bird hunting, check up on him. I'll get ahold of Henry and let him know, just in case anyone is interested enough to find out. He's got the dementia, so he won't remember much anyway."

"Okay." Carrol took another swig of beer and looked longingly to the bar, then to his brother. "What are you going to do up there, Franklin?"

"I told you. I don't know."

Carrol felt short of breath. The bar had become uncomfortably warm. "We ain't killers, Franklin."

Franklin shook his head. "How the hell did you think this was going to end, you dumbshit?" He raised his eyebrows in question. "Did you think we were just going to release those two women and they'd go on their merry way, not say a word to no one about nothing?"

"I . . . I . . . I . . . That's what you told me."

"I . . . I . . . I . . . ," Franklin said, mocking him. "You didn't think that far, did you? I told you that just so you'd shut the hell up."

"I . . . I . . . I just figured we'd ho . . . ho . . . hold on to them forever. That eventually they'd like us and could be like our wives," Carrol said, the words tumbling from his mouth.

Franklin shook his head. "What the hell happened to the family gene pool after me?"

"We ain't killers, Franklin."

Franklin shook his head. "You don't know the half of what we are."

• • •

Tracy swore under her breath, slumped low in the booth, and tilted her head to the side to cover her face. Carrol Sprague didn't know what she looked like, but Franklin certainly did. It didn't help that she was one of only three women in the bar, and the pub looked like the kind of place where a woman attracted attention just walking in the door. She thought about getting up and leaving, but Franklin sat across the table from Carrol, facing Tracy. He would certainly see her. Beyond that, Tracy had an opportunity here she might not get again.

Not soon enough.

She decided to wait.

The waitress approached the Spragues' table with a menu and a beer. Franklin waved off the menu but accepted the longneck Budweiser bottle.

Another fifteen minutes passed with the brothers in quiet conversation. Whatever they were discussing, Carrol looked like he had lost his appetite. Finally, they stood and grabbed their jackets. Tracy lowered her head and turned toward the wall, as if searching her purse on the bench seat beside her. She heard the two men shuffle past her table. They didn't stop. A moment later she heard the bells on the door. She looked up as the Spragues left. The waitress approached to clear their table.

"Miss," Tracy said. The waitress turned, set down the bottles she'd been collecting, and came to Tracy's booth. "I don't think I'm going to wait any longer. Could I get the check?"

"Sure," the waitress said. She looked at her pad and ripped off Tracy's bill, handing it to her.

Tracy handed her a twenty.

"I'll get you change."

"The bathroom?" Tracy asked, though she had determined the location earlier. The woman pointed past the Spragues' booth to a narrow hallway with an arrow above the word "Restrooms." "It could have jumped up and bit me," Tracy said.

When the woman returned to the bar to get change, Tracy stood with her purse and walked toward the sign. At what had been the Spragues' booth, she stopped as if to watch the football game. She set down her beer bottle on the table and picked up two bottles, one from each side of the table. She slipped them and the crumpled napkins from Carrol Sprague's food basket into her bag before she walked down the hall to the bathroom.

Carrol followed his brother outside, then realized he hadn't paid the bill. "Shit," Carrol said. "I forgot to pay."

Franklin shook his head. "You're a dumbshit. Go back in and pay it; I'll meet you at home."

Carrol pulled open the glass door and stepped back inside the bar, lowering his hood and shaking beads of water from his shoulders. Franklin had him so worked up he hadn't even remembered the bill. He hurried to the booth but didn't see the check. About to turn toward the bar and look for Janice, he noticed only two beer bottles on the table. A Bud Light and a Budweiser. The Budweiser remained half-full. It certainly wasn't like Franklin to leave a beer unfinished neither. Then again, Franklin's mind had been occupied. More for him, Carrol guessed.

He picked up the bottle to drain the remainder but noticed a funny taste. He set the bottle down, trying to figure out the taste. A woman walked down the hall from the bathroom and hesitated when she saw him at the table. She smiled, real friendly like, then stepped past him to the door. He'd never seen her in the bar before, and she was someone he would have remembered. As Franklin would have said, "She was a fine piece of ass." Tall, blonde, and good-looking.

"Miss," Janice called out, but the woman kept walking. Janice stepped out from behind the bar with money in hand.

"Something wrong?" Carrol asked.

"She forgot her change."

"Maybe she meant it as a tip."

"It's change from a twenty; she only had one beer."

Carrol smiled. "More for you, I guess. I forgot to pay my bill," he said.

"I know," she said. "I figured that woman distracted you, and I'd get it from you next time you came in."

"Never seen her in here before," Carrol said.

"She was waiting for someone. I think she got stood up."

Carrol made a face. "Really? Who would stand *her* up?"

"Don't know," Janice said. "She just ordered the one beer and said she was waiting for someone."

"Just the one beer?" Carrol looked back to the table where he'd been sitting. Then he answered his own question. *Who would stand her up?*

"No one," he said.

"What's that?" Janice said.

He looked to Janice. "Did you clear anything off my table?"

"Not yet. Why?"

Carrol suddenly felt warm.

"Carrol? You all right?"

"Yeah," he said, identifying the taste. Lipstick. "I . . . I . . . I'm fine."

When he arrived home, Carrol found Franklin in the living room peppering Evan with questions. Evan looked pale and scared.

"I know something is up, Evan. You've been squirrely since last night."

"No one came to the door, Franklin."

"Franklin?" Carrol said.

"Can't you see I'm busy?" Franklin said.

"It's important."

"So is this."

"Wh . . . wh . . . what did that female detective look like?" Carrol asked, knowing the question would get Franklin's attention.

"Why?" Franklin turned to him.

"Bl . . . bl . . . blonde hair? Almost as tall as me. Good-looking."

"Where'd you see her?"

Carrol felt sick to his stomach. He slumped into a chair. "In . . . in . . . in . . ." He couldn't get the words out.

"What?" Franklin said.

"In the . . . the . . . the bar tonight—"

"She wouldn't have been in the bar."

Carrol's stuttering worsened as what had happened dawned on him. He had trouble getting the story out.

Franklin sat. "Just slow down and tell me what happened."

In between his stuttering, Carrol told Franklin what had happened when he went back inside the bar. "It was lipstick," he said.

"How would you know what lipstick tastes like?"

"I know," he said.

"You're sure?"

"I'm sure."

Franklin ran a hand over his face, turned away for a moment, and paced the room. When he turned back, he was smiling, which really scared the shit out of Carrol. He snuck a glance at Evan, who looked equally terrified, then looked again to Franklin. "You okay?"

"She took the bottles for the DNA," Franklin said.

"Oh shit," Carrol said.

"No. That's the good news." Franklin laughed. "She'll run the DNA on the bottles, but it won't match any DNA they might have found in the park. It will clear us."

"What about the car? What if they found something in the car?"

"You wore the gloves and the hat?"

"Yeah, but I mean what if a hair dropped in the car, or like skin follicles or something."

"Shit, you don't have no hair to drop. And you wiped everything down?"

"Best I could."

"Then you don't have nothing to worry about. Least not yet."

Carrol still felt queasy. "What about Evan? If she found DNA at the site maybe it could belong to Evan."

"What DNA?" Franklin asked. He turned to

Evan. "Were you drinking anything before you nabbed that girl?"

Evan shook his head.

"Did she pull out your hair or tear the clothes you were wearing?"

Again, Evan shook his head.

Franklin smiled and spoke to Carrol. "She ain't thinking about Evan. He's got the best alibi of any of us. He's an idiot. She's thinking about you and me. We both worked Wednesday. Our employers will confirm it, if they haven't already. If that isn't enough for her, the DNA will be."

"We're in the clear?" Carrol asked.

"Looks that way," Franklin said. He turned to Evan. "Looks like you're going to get to try out that young girl after all."

CHAPTER 30

Early the following morning, Tracy dropped off the beer bottles and the napkins at the Washington State Patrol Crime Lab on Airport Way. Mike Melton greeted her warmly. They'd worked many cases together and helped raise money for Victim Support Services, a Washington nonprofit that assisted victims of crime and their families. Melton played guitar and sang in a band called The Fourensics at the nonprofit's annual fund-raiser, and Tracy had created a golf tournament that raised funds to honor a fallen detective, Scott Tompkins. The money also benefited the charity.

Tracy shared pictures of Daniella with Melton, which brought a smile to his bearded face. The big man melted, as he no doubt did with his own daughters and grandchildren.

"I don't envy you, and I really don't envy your husband," Melton said. "Raising daughters is hard on a father. You're always worrying about them, hoping they're safe, hoping some boy doesn't break their heart. There will be many sleepless nights for the two of you."

"There already have been. But you seem to have survived," Tracy said.

"This job doesn't make it any easier," he said,

"as you know all too well. But it does make you guarded, which is good, I think." He looked at the bottles and the napkins. "Am I to assume you believe that the DNA on those bottles and napkins relates in some way to the DNA we pulled off the cigarettes in the disappearance of that young girl?"

"You are."

"And you need it ASAP?"

"I never could get anything past you," Tracy said. "Do me a favor though—"

"I know. Run it under the two names and case numbers you gave me yesterday?"

She smiled. Telling Melton how to do his job was like telling Bill Gates about personal computers.

"I'll press the guys in the lab, again, and tell them you promised them all Rolexes for Christmas."

Tracy laughed. "They might have to settle for Casios."

On her way out, Tracy called Kins. She would have called him the night before, but Tuesday was Kins and Shannah's date night, and she decided not to interrupt. She told Kins what she had done and what she had obtained from the bar.

"He didn't have a clue who I was," she said, referring to Carrol Sprague. "Mike's asking the lab to expedite the DNA analysis and compare it to the DNA on the cigarette butts CSI found in the ravine."

"Familial DNA," Kins said.

"If we're right, it would place Evan in the park, likely behind the tree stump. That should be more than enough evidence to get a search warrant. I'll call you when I hear from Mike. Oh, and the lab is running the DNA under the investigations for Angel Jackson and Donna Jones."

"Who?"

"The two prostitutes who went missing on Aurora Avenue."

Kins didn't answer immediately, an indication he understood the reason for her using the cold cases to get DNA evidence for the Stephanie Cole matter. Then he said, "Are you on your way in?"

"I got another lead I'm pursuing."

"Also in the two cold cases?" Kins asked, his tone intimating he suspected the lead also related to the Stephanie Cole matter.

"I'll keep you in the loop."

Tracy drove to the North Park neighborhood. With school in session, cars filled the parking spaces along the street. Children ran around the school playground making noise. She parked around the corner and walked to Brian Bibby's home. She didn't want any of the Spragues to see her car or see her talking with Bibby again.

Bibby answered on the third knock. Tracy felt warm air blasting from the fireplace insert. Classical music played on a stereo. "Detective? I didn't expect to see you back so soon," Bibby said. "Where's your partner?"

"Pursuing a different lead in another case. I actually came to speak to your wife for a minute. Is she home?"

"Lorraine? Sure, she's home. Come on in."

Tracy stepped inside and Bibby closed the door behind her. "You find out anything more on that missing girl?"

"Still working the investigation. I did have a question for you also."

"Shoot."

"Do you smoke?"

Bibby looked to the hall as if about to be busted by a parent. He kept his voice low. "One cigarette a day when Jackpot and I go on our walk. Don't tell Lorraine, though I suspect she knows, but I don't want to rub her nose in it. It's my one nasty habit."

"What brand?"

"Marlboro. Why?"

"We found some butts in the ravine, and I may need to eliminate yours." Tracy reached into her purse for a DNA swab kit.

"That's easy. I don't throw my butts in the ravine. People have worked too hard to clean it up. I smoke my cigarette on the way up the trail and put it in that trash can outside. Lorraine?" Bibby called, starting down the hall as he shouted.

"Hang on a second," Tracy said. "I'm also wondering if you happened to know Ed Sprague?"

"The father? Sure. I knew Ed. Not well, but in passing. Neighbors. He's dead though."

"I understand. I also understand that he worked as a machinist at Boeing."

"That's true," Bibby said. "Do you mind if we sit? I overdid it a bit yesterday and my back is sore."

Lorraine Bibby came down the hall. "What is it?" she said to Bibby. She hesitated when she noticed Tracy.

"The detective here wants to ask you some questions," Bibby said.

"Me?" Lorraine sounded surprised.

Bibby took his place in his chair. Tracy sat on the couch, closest to the fireplace. Lorraine sat on the other end.

"I was asking if your husband and Ed Sprague knew one another from work."

"We didn't," Bibby said. "There are a lot of machinists at Boeing, Detective. I believe it's somewhere between fifteen and twenty thousand, but don't quote me on that number."

"I knew there were a lot," Tracy said. "I

assume then that you didn't commute together or anything."

"Also, a lot of different work schedules," Bibby said, shaking his head. "No. We didn't commute. I knew Ed, and ran into him a couple times at work, but we weren't close."

"What type of a man was he?" Tracy asked. "What you knew of him."

"Quiet," Bibby said, looking to his wife. "Ed kept to himself. Didn't share a lot. Not every neighbor wants to be close. Lorraine may have a different opinion, however." Bibby's tone wasn't condescending, but it had a bite to it.

Lorraine frowned at her husband before engaging Tracy. "I don't want to speak poorly of the dead," she said. "And Carol Lynn was a lovely lady. Meek, but lovely."

"Something about Ed Sprague rub you the wrong way?" Tracy asked.

Lorraine looked like she was grinding glass with her teeth and shooting spears at her husband from her eyes. "This was more than thirty years ago. Things were different then," she said, dismissive. Tracy waited while Lorraine ground up more glass.

"What was different?" Tracy asked, coaxing her.

"The boys would come to school with bruises and scrapes," Bibby said.

Tracy looked to Lorraine. "You think Ed Sprague beat them?"

"I don't know," Lorraine said, not happy with her husband. "And it doesn't really matter anymore."

"Did you ask the boys? I mean when they were in school, did you ask them?"

"Various teachers asked them on various occasions. The boys all said the same thing every time. They had been wrestling or playing football in the yard. There was always some . . . We'd even separate the boys, but they all said the same thing."

"Boys roughhouse," Bibby said. "It's part of being a boy. I had brothers, and we'd beat the hell out of each other growing up."

"So, you don't think Ed Sprague beat them?"

Bibby frowned. "Discipline was different back then. I can tell you my father hit me and my brothers, more than once. We usually deserved it, and we thought twice about doing whatever we did to get hit. But Lorraine's right. Times are different now."

"Did anyone ever report the incidents?" Tracy asked Lorraine.

"Not that I know of," Lorraine said. "The law allows a parent to physically discipline their children, but . . . Well, this seemed excessive."

Tracy changed gears. "What were the boys like in school?"

"Much like they are now. None were very good students. Franklin was the oldest and the biggest. He was a natural leader but also a bit of a bully. We had a few problems along the way. A few fights. Carrol had a stuttering problem and was overweight. If he got picked on, Franklin stepped in. Carrol mostly deferred to Franklin."

"Did Evan go to the school as well?"

"He did, but well after his brothers, and he was in a special education program. He was a sweet boy, kind, but he also deferred to Franklin, and it seemed like Franklin was always around to protect him."

"Were they afraid of Franklin?" Tracy asked.

"Some teachers got that impression."

"Did you?"

"Not really—I mean, they wouldn't all still live together if that was the case, would they? My impression is that Franklin takes care of them, particularly Evan."

"And none of them ever married?"

"Never did. Always lived in that house, as far as I know anyway."

"Did you know the girl who came to live with them from foster care?"

"Lindsay?" Lorraine sounded surprised. "She was there only a few years. Four or five, I believe." She looked to Bibby.

"I didn't really pay too close attention," he said. "Hardly remember her."

"She was much younger than Franklin and Carrol," Lorraine said. "Younger even than Evan. I often wondered if that was why they brought her in. So Evan would have someone closer in age around the house."

"Did you ever ask the Spragues why they decided to take her in?"

"I didn't. I guess I always just assumed Carol Lynn wanted a daughter but ended up with three boys and, well, after Evan was born, she likely decided against having any more children."

"What was Lindsay like?"

"I didn't see her like I saw the boys. I think she came in the seventh grade. She was quiet. Moody. Sullen. We had a few incidents of her acting out as well."

"Did she have the bruises?"

"Not that I recall."

"Anybody ever determine what she was sullen about?"

Lorraine shook her head. "Those kids coming out of foster care . . . They can have a lot of problems. I always admired Ed and Carol Lynn for doing what they did, or at least trying."

"Any idea if Lindsay ever married?"

"I don't know," Lorraine said. "What I recall was that as soon as Lindsay turned eighteen, she took off. I don't think she even graduated high school. We never saw her again."

"Never?" Tracy asked.

"Not once," Lorraine said. Bibby nodded in agreement.

"Did you ever ask Carol Lynn about her?"

"Once," Lorraine said. "Just in passing. You know, *whatever happened to Lindsay?*"

"What did she say?"

"I believe she said she moved out of state, didn't she?" Lorraine asked her husband.

"That was my understanding," Bibby said.

"Carol Lynn seemed sad about it, but she didn't say much. She did say once that Lindsay came to them with a lot of problems that manifested in her teen years."

"Those are the difficult years," Bibby interjected.

Tracy asked a few more questions, then thanked the Bibbys and left the house.

She drove to Police Headquarters and sequestered herself in her office, going through the foster care file from Olympia. Lindsay's foster care records ended with her placement in the Sprague home. There were a few reports documenting follow-up visits, but the contents of those were unremarkable.

After going through the foster care file, Tracy ran the names Lindsay Sheppard and Lindsay Sprague through state and federal databases for a driver's license, a social security card, tax records, and marriage records. She combed through numerous potential hits, but ultimately decided, based on the date of birth or the geographic location, that none were the Lindsay Sheppard she sought. She searched death records, again without success.

She also ran both names through four federal law enforcement databases: the National Crime Information Center (NCIC), the Combined DNA Index System (CODIS), the Integrated Automated Fingerprint Identification System (IAFIS), and the Violent Crime Apprehension Program (ViCAP). And she ran the names through Washington State's Missing Persons database. She did not get a hit on any database. With each search she began to feel less and less at ease.

Tracy knew from experience that, at least at one time, many cities and counties buried unidentified remains without attempting to collect DNA samples for later analysis. She also knew that even if they collected a sample, they didn't always enter the information into the federal or state databases. In addition, when Tracy had searched for her sister, she had learned there were upwards of 40,000 sets of human remains held in evidence rooms of medical examiners throughout the country that could not be identified through conventional means. One of those means was for family members to provide DNA for comparison to the DNA kept of missing or deceased persons. A lot of variables, but none applied to Lindsay Sheppard since she wasn't a Sprague blood relative.

Tracy searched through court cases using electronic systems such as Public Access to Court Electronic Records (PACER), as well as Westlaw and LexisNexis. She did not get a hit in the civil, criminal, or bankruptcy databases.

Lindsay Sheppard had turned eighteen and simply disappeared from the planet.

Just like Sarah.

Just like Stephanie Cole.

Tracy felt a wave of tension, enough that it caused her to stand from her desk and stretch. It didn't help. Her heart suddenly felt as though it was beating a hundred miles a minute. She was short of breath, sweating. She recognized the symptoms.

Fight or flight.

She took several deep breaths but felt dizzy and light-headed, causing her to sit. She lowered her head to her knees, fearful she might pass out.

After several minutes, her breathing returned to normal, but she felt weak. She wondered if she was diabetic or anemic. She'd heard of women giving birth and becoming one or the other. She also wondered if her search for Lindsay had triggered the subconscious memory of those horrible days after Sarah went missing, as Dan had feared possible, and Lisa Walsh suggested.

She needed to get her mind off Lindsay

326

Sheppard. She pulled out Elle Chin's file and quickly flipped through the pages. Then she made a few phone calls and, eventually, tracked down Jewel Chin.

She grabbed her purse and headed out the door.

CHAPTER 31

Tracy called the Seattle real estate company where Jewel Chin worked and obtained her cell phone number. Chin didn't sound thrilled to get Tracy's phone call. She indicated she was too busy staging a house for a showing that weekend and had a personal training session that evening. Tracy wondered if the personal trainer was a new boyfriend.

Tracy told Chin she'd make it convenient and come to the home on Queen Anne that Chin was staging.

"Do I need a lawyer?" Chin asked.

"I just want to ask questions about that night. I'm taking another look at the file."

"Why?"

Tracy had grown tired of answering that question. "I'm pursuing a new angle," she said.

"Does the new angle involve her father?"

Tracy sensed her answer would dictate whether Chin agreed to speak with her. "It does," she said.

Chin reluctantly agreed to meet.

Tracy parked across the street from a brick Tudor home with a moving van parked at the curb. Workers carried folded, padded blankets from the house, presumably used during transport to protect the staging furniture. Tracy estimated the home to be 3,000 square feet on a quarter-of-an-acre lot. It would likely be put on the market for a couple million dollars, give or take a few hundred thousand.

She climbed the front steps and knocked on an open door as she stepped across the threshold onto freshly redone hardwood floors. The interior felt cold and smelled like paint, which was likely the reason someone had opened the doors and the windows. Based on the strength of the smell, they'd need the rest of the week to air out the house. The front room was white on white. White walls and two white couches positioned perpendicular to a fireplace with an elaborate silk flower arrangement on the mantel. The flower colors complemented the tones in an abstract painting hanging over the marble mantel. Recessed, low-wattage LED bulbs gave the room a soft, warm glow.

Tracy couldn't imagine white couches and silk flowers in her home, not with the amazing shedding dogs and her cat, Roger, running around like bulls in a china shop.

"I'm sorry, the house isn't showing until tomorrow," Jewel Chin said as she walked into the living room.

She looked as put together as the staged front room in tight white jeans, red three-inch heels, and a navy-blue blouse cut low enough to reveal several gold chains. What looked to be an expensive watch and jewelry adorned her wrist and her fingers. Tracy wondered if Chin was staging the house or herself. The file indicated Chin remained single. Now, in her early thirties, crow's-feet already projected from the corners of her eyes, despite heavy makeup. "Worry lines," her mother had called them, and she said you could count them like aging rings on a toppled tree trunk.

"What's the listing price?" Tracy asked.

"One point two five, but it's likely to go above that price."

"Too rich for my blood."

"It's one of Seattle's finest neighborhoods with access to excellent schools."

"My little girl is only ten months. We have time."

"The Interbay Golf Center is close by. Do you golf?"

"Poorly."

"It also has easy access to downtown Seattle shops and restaurants," Chin said, as if repeating the sales flier. "What do you do?"

Chin's question surprised Tracy. She thought Chin knew who she was and was just making small talk. They had picked the time on the phone. "I'm a Seattle police detective," Tracy said.

Chin stopped smiling. "You're the police officer?"

"I'm the detective," Tracy said.

"I guess I just expected someone a little more . . . I don't know, frumpy."

"I'll take that as a compliment."

"Take it at the dining room table. As I told you over the phone, I don't have much time." Chin didn't sound or act the least bit intimidated to be speaking with a detective. "You said something happened in the case? Are you here to tell me they found Elle's body and evidence Bobby killed her?" Chin said the words without expressing any emotion, as if she were discussing the house and trying to determine where to put the sofa. True to Miller's recollection, she also seemed more concerned with blaming her ex-husband. She clearly had not moved on.

"No," Tracy said. "They didn't."

"Then why are you here?"

Pleasant. Jewel motioned to the modern dining room table, and they sat across from one another. Tracy again explained that she had taken over the Cold Case Unit and was following up on several cases, including Elle's.

"You said on the phone you're taking another look at my ex?" Jewel asked. "What is the new evidence?"

Tracy nodded. "I can't go into details yet, though I have spoken to him."

That response at least got Chin to pause for a moment. Then the paranoia started. "Did he tell you that I kidnapped Elle and buried her body somewhere? Or that I sold her on the black market? Maybe he told you I'm crazy? Borderline personality disorder? Narcissistic? The guilty always blame the innocent."

Tracy didn't doubt that little pearl of wisdom; unfortunately, it applied equally to each spouse in this case. Still, she could see that Jewel Chin was getting ramped up. Tracy would lose her if she didn't find some common ground. From everything she'd been told, Jewel was a predator who played on others' weaknesses. Tracy needed to let Jewel see one of hers. This time, it wasn't difficult.

"I have a newborn daughter at home. I know I'd be distraught if anything happened to her. A mother and a daughter have a special bond that fathers don't understand, can't understand. But I'm sure you know."

Jewel Chin looked distrusting, or at least suspicious; Tracy had interviewed enough people to make an educated assessment that Jewel believed everyone was out to get her, even her elderly former next-door neighbor, Evelyn Robertson. She doubted Jewel Chin ever let her guard down.

"Then you know exactly how I feel," Chin agreed.

"I do," Tracy said. "Absolutely. What I'd like to hear is your story, though I know it must be difficult for you to go back to those days."

"It is," Jewel said. She almost looked ready to cry. Almost. There wasn't a tear in her eyes.

"If you can, will you tell me about the night your daughter went missing? Your perspective."

Chin turned at an angle so she could cross her legs. "I wish I could. I wish I had fought more to keep Bobby away from her. I regret it now but . . . No, I can't. Not really. She was with Bobby."

Tracy asked Jewel many questions she already knew the answers to, so Jewel Chin would keep talking and get in the habit of answering.

"The fact that he was a police officer is the reason you people didn't investigate him the way you should have," Chin said.

"What do you mean by that?"

"I mean, it should have been obvious Bobby took Elle. Elle was with him and then suddenly she was gone. And his excuse was that he played hide-and-seek with her?" She made a face like the whole story was preposterous. "Elle was five. What kind of a father plays hide-and-seek with a five-year-old in a corn maze? Please."

Tracy nodded as if she and Chin were two aggrieved sisters.

"He wasn't even charged with reckless endangerment, though I pressed the prosecutor for months to charge him with *something*."

So far, Jewel sounded exactly as Bill Miller had described in his report and Bobby Chin had stated in his interview.

"Where were you that evening?"

Jewel rolled her eyes. "Really? Again? Is this the reason why you're here? I told the other detectives where I was. Ask them. Otherwise, you can speak to my lawyer."

"I didn't mean to upset you," Tracy said. "I'm just trying to catch up so I can move forward. The other detectives have retired, which is why it's a cold case. I understood you were at home."

Jewel straightened. "I'm sorry, but you've only been a mother for ten months. I was a mother for five years."

Uncertain what Chin meant, Tracy ignored the comment and again sought common ground. "I'm divorced also."

"Then you know what it's like to go through it. It isn't pleasant. I had to call the police three times because Bobby was beating me. The third time I'd had enough and agreed to file charges against him for domestic violence."

She sounded like the divorce remained ongoing. "Why did he hit you?"

"Because I told him I was done with him and wanted him out of the house. He couldn't take rejection. No woman rejected Bobby Chin. He had a lot of college girlfriends who I guess wor-shipped him. Well, I wasn't some college girlfriend, and I wasn't going to stand for his shit."

Tracy moved back to her questions about the night Elle went missing, asking Jewel what she did that night, and whom she was with, looking for any inconsistencies.

"But don't bother looking for him," Jewel said, referring to Graham Jacobsen. "The idiot shot himself."

Jewel didn't exactly sound broken up about it. "I'm so sorry to hear that," Tracy said.

"On top of everything I went through, I then had to go through that," Jewel said, shaking her head. "I had to move. There was no way I was living in that place after that. I don't care how many coats of paint they used."

"I thought the house was sold in the settlement of the assets," Tracy said.

"I would have at least considered buying it before that happened."

Tracy knew from a court order in the file that Jewel would have had to buy Bobby out as a condition to staying in the home. There wasn't much equity in the home, and Jewel couldn't afford to stay in it.

"Anyway, he told the detective we were together that night, except for the few minutes when he left to pick up takeout. So you can pretty much forget that witness's statement."

"Which one?" Tracy asked, though she suspected she knew.

"The one in which the kid said he saw Elle with an Asian woman and a man."

Jimmy Ingram had never used the word "Asian."

"I stayed at home. I can even tell you exactly what I watched that night. I made a list."

"When did you do that?"

"Sometime after I learned about the witness statement. My attorney suggested I do it, in case I was ever subjected to cross-examination. For all I know, Bobby paid the guy to say he saw me and Graham."

"Did the detectives ask for the list of the shows you watched?" Tracy had not found one in the file.

"No. But I wasn't about to let Bobby railroad me."

Unbelievable.

She asked Chin how she heard that Elle was missing, and her statement coincided with what Miller had put in his report. "I told him that Bobby had something to do with it, but he just stood there, staring."

"What did you want him to do?"

"His job. Arrest the person who was with my daughter when she went missing. I would have thought he'd call SWAT or something. Somebody. Maybe if he had, they would have found Elle."

"Do you think your ex was capable of harming your daughter?"

Jewel smirked. "Capable? He beat me, and the court let him off with a slap on the wrist and made him go to anger-management classes. He shouldn't have even been allowed to spend time alone with Elle. I had my attorney make that argument, but I lost. It was a male judge. A former prosecutor. Pretty sure a female judge would have had a better understanding."

"A better understanding?" Tracy asked.

"It's obvious, isn't it? Someone who can lose their temper that quickly and inflict hurt that quickly? Bobby's not a small man. He could have struck Elle and snapped her neck."

"Did you ever see your ex-husband strike your daughter?" Tracy asked.

"No. But he never struck me either . . . until he did. So clearly he was 'capable.'" She made air quotes with her fingers.

What struck Tracy was the way Jewel Chin painted herself as both a heroine and a martyr. Everything was couched in terms of what she did or how it had impacted her. She wanted to convince Tracy she was running the show—that she was a competent, capable woman whom the court system had seriously aggrieved—but still play the poor, defenseless mother abused by her husband. Tracy made a mental note to determine if Graham Jacobsen had an insurance policy and, if so, to determine who was his primary beneficiary. At this point, she didn't put anything past the woman.

"Do you have any siblings?" Tracy asked.

Another eye roll. "I have a brother who lives in Boston. He's got three kids of his own . . . The detectives checked him out too, and he didn't take Elle. He was in Boston that night. Besides his wife is Caucasian, not Asian."

There it was again.

"Who told you the witness saw an Asian woman?"

"I don't know. One of the detectives, I suppose. You should talk to Bobby. His mother and his sister are both Asian. Gloria. Mousy thing. Hardly speaks. Bobby used her to pick up Elle from school on days he had her so I wouldn't know about it. But I knew. I asked the school. And I kept a record of it."

"You think Gloria took Elle?"

Jewel shrugged. "I don't know what to think anymore. Doubtful." She stood abruptly. "If we're done, Detective, I have to get to my workout."

"Of course." Tracy stood and walked to the door. "The house looks beautiful. I wish I could buy it."

"Come up with the money. I could act as your agent and give you a deal."

I'll bet you could, Tracy thought. She bet Jewel Chin was adept at working every angle.

CHAPTER 32

Tracy entered Lisa Walsh's office at just before five o'clock on her drive back to Redmond following her interview with Jewel Chin. Walsh accommodated Tracy, who wanted to ask her counselor about the spell she had suffered at her desk and question whether she had anything to be concerned about.

She initially was concerned she'd had a mild heart attack or stroke. She worried she could be anemic. But other than being fatigued, she didn't feel any adverse physical effects. She had no numbness in her chest or her left arm. Her breathing had returned to normal. She didn't have a primary care physician to consult, and she didn't think her symptoms appropriate for her ob-gyn. As much as she hated to admit it, she believed her symptoms were more likely mental than physical.

She wondered if maybe she was on the same wall as the climber who Walsh had mentioned, and whether she had just taken a fall.

She thanked Walsh for seeing her on short notice.

Walsh smiled. "I'm happy I could accommodate you. Tell me what's going on."

Tracy took her seat on the couch. "I don't really know," she said. "I was working long hours and keeping busy on the cases I talked to you about. I learned that the brothers I was investigating had a foster sister, and I was pursuing that lead." Tracy gave Walsh the details of her conversation with Lorraine Bibby and her subsequent return to the office and search for Lindsay Sheppard, culminating in her attack.

"I'm smart enough to see the similarity in that girl going missing at eighteen and my sister going missing at the same age, but I've had similar cases and never suffered those physical symptoms. I feel fine now, fatigued after a long day, but fine."

"Tell me more about the symptoms," Walsh said.

Tracy did. "Should I go to the emergency room?"

"It sounds to me like you were having a panic attack, Tracy."

"A panic attack?" Tracy was not familiar with the term. "What's a panic attack?"

"It's a sudden episode of intense fear that triggers physical reactions."

"I was in my office; there was nothing to fear."

"Exactly."

"You mean I imagined something to fear?"

"No. What you experienced was real. The physical symptoms were real. When panic attacks occur, you might think you're losing control, having a heart attack, even dying."

"That's exactly what I thought."

"Many people have just one or two panic attacks in their lifetimes, and the problem goes away, usually when a stressful situation ends."

"Stress triggers it?"

"It can."

Walsh made sense, but . . . "So what can I do?" Tracy asked. "This is what a detective does."

"You can learn to manage it. There's also medication."

"I don't like medication."

"Nothing addictive and not forever. Just to get you through this time. If you need it."

"What I don't understand is why is it happening now? Why at this point in my life? I didn't experience these attacks when Sarah went missing, and that was the most stressful period in my life."

Walsh nodded. "But from what you told me, your focus back when your sister went missing was holding your family together, being strong for your mother and your father. Later, your focus changed to trying to find your sister."

"That's true," Tracy said.

"And you told me that finding your sister consumed you for many years. I think you used the word 'obsessed,' didn't you?"

"It did become an obsession."

"But that's over now. You found out what happened to your sister."

"I knew she was dead," Tracy said. "I always knew Sarah was dead. There's that faint hope you're wrong, those very few cases where the woman escapes and makes it home, but I knew how rarely that happens."

Tracy thought of Lindsay Sheppard, knowing the odds were more likely she, too, was dead. Sheppard had been high risk, coming from the foster care system with family drug problems. The odds had been stacked against her long before she entered the Sprague household. Stephanie Cole was also likely dead.

She was chasing ghosts. She was, again, surrounded by the dead.

"What's different now, Tracy?"

"What's different?" Tracy said. "You mean Dan and Daniella?"

"You met a good man and you fell in love. You got married. Had a daughter. Became a mom."

"You're saying I have something to lose."

"Do you fear something happening to Dan, or to your daughter?"

Tracy gave the question some thought. "I do. But that's natural, isn't it?"

"What would be the worst thing that could happen to you now?"

"Losing my daughter," Tracy said without hesitation.

Walsh nodded.

"Is that why I had the panic attack now?"

"Why did you pick this cold case to pursue?"

She thought of her conversation with Art Nunzio in his office. "Because somebody needs to speak for that little girl. Somebody needs to be her voice."

"Because somebody needs to give a shit," Walsh said. "I think that's how you put it."

Tracy smiled, thinking of Nunzio. "I do. I can't help that."

"And you can't help worrying about those you love," Walsh said. "So, what's wrong with caring?"

"Nothing."

"Nothing." Walsh smiled. "It's a mother's instinct to worry about her daughter; for a wife to worry about a husband. Unfortunately, because of what you do, you see horrible things happen to young girls and young women. You've got to learn to separate the two—your profession and your life."

"I thought I did."

"You told me you became a detective to find your sister, that you made it your profession and therefore that one was integral to the other. What you experience in your profession does not mean it is going to happen to you or those that you love. Statistically speaking, it is far less likely. Lightning rarely ever strikes twice in the same place. Almost never," Walsh said with a smile. "So rather than asking 'Can I do this job?'

you should ask 'Do I want to continue doing this job?' "

Tracy beat Dan home. She planned to cook him a nice dinner and to try to relax. She'd called Therese on the way and had her remove chicken breasts from the freezer and defrost them in the microwave, then start rice in the cooker. She'd make Dan chicken marsala, one of his favorite meals.

When she arrived at home, she found everything as she had asked, except Daniella, who was fussy and didn't want to be put down or ignored. Therese offered to stay, but she'd already worked late three days and she had her painting class. Tracy sent her off.

When Dan got home, Tracy had the parsley, mushrooms, and garlic on the kitchen counter and the chicken breasts in the pan, but she hadn't been able to get any further. She was pacing, walking Daniella.

"She's fussy," Tracy said. "Maybe she has a tooth coming in."

"You want me to take her?"

"And she's hungry."

"I can give her a bottle. What's cooking?"

"Nothing at the moment; it was going to be chicken marsala, but I haven't gotten that far. I was hoping to surprise you." She sighed. "Surprise."

Dan smiled. "You've activated my taste buds and it sounds too good to not follow through. I'll handle it from here."

Tracy's smile waned as Dan went into the kitchen and started to cut and dice. "Things are different, aren't they?" she asked.

"Sure they are," Dan said, chopping parsley.

"Better?"

He stopped the knife in midstroke and looked at her. "What's the matter? What's bothering you?"

She told Dan about the panic attack in her office and her visit with Lisa Walsh.

"Everything okay now? Is there anything I can do?" Dan asked.

"I'm fine," she said. "Really. Lisa just made me realize that Daniella has already changed our lives."

Dan nodded and smiled, but it looked uncertain. "But . . ."

"No buts . . . just . . . different," Tracy said. "A family."

He looked at the chicken. "Look, if we're being honest, I missed lunch and ate a sandwich at my desk about half an hour ago, so I was going to suggest we have something light and read by the fire."

Tracy laughed. "Why didn't you just say that?"

"Because I could tell you went to a lot of trouble and that this meal was important to you. So, I was going to keep my mouth shut, at least when I wasn't forcing chicken marsala down my throat. Are you hungry?"

"Not particularly."

"Why don't we save the chicken marsala for tomorrow? Unless you'd like to watch me split my pants."

The back door opened and Therese walked in. She dropped her keys on the counter with a clang.

"What are you doing back?" Tracy asked. "I thought you have painting class."

"I did," she said. "Until it started snowing."

Tracy and Dan moved to look out the windows. Snowflakes floated gently to the ground.

"It's not real heavy, but the teacher sent a text saying it's supposed to get worse." Therese looked at the food on the counter. "I can see you were planning an evening alone. I'll just grab something and go on back to my room so as not to intrude on your alone time."

"There isn't going to be a lot of alone time," Tracy said. "Not for the next eighteen years."

"Tell me about it. You have just the one. My parents had the seven of us. I shared a room with two sisters my entire life."

"Not sure how your mom did it?" Tracy asked.

"She didn't do it alone. I can tell you that."

"What do you mean?" Tracy asked.

"We looked out for one another, my siblings and me. The oldest helped to raise the youngest." Therese looked to be contemplating something.

"It was just natural, really, especially among me and my sisters. My brothers were lazy lots, but . . . Have you thought about a sister for Daniella?"

Tracy laughed. "I'm getting a little old to be thinking about having another baby," she said.

"You could adopt. Daniella's a social one. I can tell already. She and a sister would be two peas in a pod. The way I am with my sisters, some of them anyway. We know everything about each other. We still talk all the time."

Tracy and Sarah had been the same way. They knew things about each other that they'd never told their parents. Tracy missed that. She missed that intimacy.

And that's when the light bulb flashed.

"Tracy?" Dan said. "You okay?"

"Yeah," she said. She'd never checked to see if Lindsay Sheppard had a sibling, a blood relative, maybe even a sister.

CHAPTER 33

The following morning Tracy arrived early to her office and immediately checked Lindsay Sheppard's foster care file, then made a call to Olympia. After half an hour of probing, she learned that Lindsay Josephine Sheppard did indeed have two older siblings: a brother, Thomas Harden Sheppard, deceased, and a sister, Aileen Laura Sheppard. All three children had been removed from their parents' home after multiple incidents of domestic violence and drug-related charges leading to convictions. Lindsay, the youngest, had the best chance of being placed in foster care. The brother, Thomas, had been sixteen. Aileen had been fifteen.

Running the names through the same federal and state databases as before, Tracy learned that Thomas Sheppard had served time for multiple drug convictions, most notably meth, and eventually became the victim of a drug-related homicide. Aileen had also done jail time for possession of a controlled substance. A condition of her parole had been that she successfully complete a drug rehabilitation program. State records indicated Aileen had married and, according to her parole officer, her last known address was in Union Gap, just outside Yakima in Eastern Washington.

After tracking down the home number, Tracy placed a call, feigning to be a solicitor, and confirmed Aileen was home. Tracy jumped in the car. Some subjects, like the whereabouts of a sibling, particularly if that sibling turned out to be deceased, were best handled in person. The snowfall had subsided overnight. Little had stuck on the ground in Redmond, but much more had accumulated over the Snoqualmie Pass and in the towns in Eastern Washington. The sky that morning hung heavy, a dark gray shroud giving every indication of more snow to come. According to Tracy's weather app, that would happen by midafternoon.

Just under two and a half hours after leaving Seattle, Tracy pulled up to what looked to be a modular home with a small yard and a brown picket fence. The home looked to be well maintained. The shrubs in the snow-covered yard were neatly trimmed. A car sat in the driveway and, judging by the snow on the hood and the roof, and the uncompacted snow in the driveway, the car had not been moved since the snowfall.

Tracy stepped from her pool car, her boots leaving a distinct impression in the fresh snow. She'd dressed in jeans, a flannel shirt, and her black down jacket, but she could still feel the cold.

She knocked on the door and hoped for the best.

A woman pulled open the door. Aileen Rodriguez—her married name—according to her driver's license. Thirty-three years old. Barefoot, Aileen wore black stretch pants and a long-sleeve white shirt. She was stout, though not heavy.

"Aileen Rodriguez?" Tracy asked.

"Yes."

Tracy held up her badge and her identification and introduced herself. "I wonder if we could talk for a moment."

"You came all the way from Seattle?"

"I did."

"Why didn't you call?"

"The subject matter is best discussed in person."

Aileen squinted, intrigued. "And what subject matter is that?"

"Your sister. Lindsay Sheppard."

"Can't help you." She moved to close the door.

"I did come all the way from Seattle," Tracy said quickly. "And I won't take much of your time."

Aileen seemed curious and to be debating Tracy's response. She stepped aside. "You can come in, but it won't change my answer. I haven't seen my sister in years."

Tracy stepped onto a floor mat and cleaned her boots. "Would you like me to remove my shoes?"

"No need."

Inside, Tracy said, "Can I bother you for a glass of water? It was a long drive."

"Take a seat." Aileen nodded to a couch beneath the window, then departed, presumably into the kitchen. Tracy wasn't thirsty, but the time alone gave her a chance to look around the interior of the house. The furnishings were also well cared for, if a bit dated. On shelving she found family photographs, most in five-by-eight picture frames. Aileen had married a Hispanic man, and it looked as though they had two teenage children. Tucked behind one of those family photographs, only partially visible, was what Tracy had hoped to find.

Aileen returned with two glasses of water, handing one to Tracy. Tracy sipped it and sat on the couch. Aileen sat in a leather chair, adjusting the pillow at her back and pulling a bare foot underneath her. She set her glass on the coffee table between them.

"As I said, I'm trying to locate Lindsay," Tracy said.

"It's a little late for that," Aileen said.

"Why is that?" Tracy asked.

"Because she's been gone for about ten years, something like that."

"Is she still alive?"

"I don't really know."

"When did you last see her?"

"I don't really know; I suppose when foster care separated us."

The picture in the five-by-eight frame indicated otherwise, but Tracy didn't call Aileen on it. Not yet. It would only upset her. "So you don't know where she might be living?"

Aileen shook her head. "Nobody does."

"You're her older sister?"

"Yeah, so?" Her tone was defiant.

"And you said you were split up in foster care?"

She nodded. "Back then they didn't keep the siblings together. Tom, our brother, was sixteen and an addict. He didn't have a chance. Spent much of his time in juvie and had several prison sentences. He was shot in a drug deal. I was fifteen, so my chances of being placed were also not good. Lindsay was twelve. Why are you looking for her?"

"A girl went missing near the Sprague home—"

"How old?" she interjected. Tracy noted Aileen did not ask her who the Spragues were.

"Nineteen."

Aileen looked like she was biting her lip.

"Did you know the Spragues?"

"No. Who are they?"

The question was not convincing, but Tracy played along. "The parents are dead but the three brothers live together in the parents' home."

"You think one of them took this girl?"

"Why do you say that?"

"Seems the obvious reason you'd be here."

"That's what I'm trying to find out. One of the Spragues' neighbors said when your sister turned eighteen and became an adult, she moved away, and that no one, not even the Spragues, ever saw or heard from her again."

"Me neither," Aileen said.

Tracy noted Aileen wasn't showing a lot of emotion. "I'm hoping to find her. I'm hoping she's still alive and may have information helpful to finding the missing young woman."

"And you thought I might know."

Tracy reached into her purse and removed a photograph she kept in her wallet. "This is my sister. She went missing when she was eighteen. I was twenty-two. I searched for her for twenty years, until they found her body. But I've always kept this photograph."

Aileen lowered her head. Tracy saw her chest rise and fall. "I'm sorry, Detective. I wish I could help, but I haven't seen or heard from my sister in years."

Tracy decided to push her. "You've never looked for her?"

Aileen gave a sarcastic laugh. "I had my own problems, Detective."

"Drugs?"

"Yes. As a matter of fact, I'm an addict," she said. "I was offered rehab instead of jail."

"In Yakima?"

353

"That's right. That's where I met my husband. He's also a recovering addict. We've both been sober eleven years, four months, and twelve days. We're raising two kids in a sober house. When they graduate, they'll be the first in the family to go to college."

"Congratulations. That's something to be proud of."

"You have no idea."

"I do, actually," Tracy said. "After my sister disappeared, my father took his own life out of despair. My mother never recovered. A psychopath killed my sister. I searched for years to find the person who destroyed my family and I didn't marry until my forties. We now have a daughter, ten months. So I know family tragedies are hard to put behind you. I just figured maybe you had searched for your sister and got lucky, or had information I could use."

Aileen didn't respond. Not right away. She looked somber. Then she said, "I wish I could help."

"So do I. I'm worried about that missing girl. I was hoping maybe something your sister recalled could help."

"How long has she been missing?"

"Too long. The chances of her being alive, I'm afraid, are getting less likely every passing hour." Tracy pulled a business card from her jacket pocket. Aileen Rodriguez didn't reach for it.

Tracy placed the card on the coffee table, facing her.

"Thanks for your time."

Kinsington Rowe slid from his jacket and hung it in the locker beside his cubicle.

"Kins," Maria Fernandez said, getting up from her desk.

"Hmm?"

"Listen, before Del and Faz get in I just wanted to say I'm sorry about Nolasco pulling Tracy from this case. I know the two of you worked together for a long time, and I certainly don't mean to replace her."

Kins smiled. "Not your fault. The thing between Tracy and Nolasco goes all the way back to the Academy."

"Did she really kick him in the nuts and break his nose?"

The story had gone around the office and, even all these years later, officers, particularly female officers, knew of the incident. "She really did. Then she beat his score on the shooting range, and not by a little. Her score still stands."

Fernandez nodded. "A lot of us try to emulate her."

"Not easy. She's a pistol."

"And one badass bitch when she needs to be," Fernandez said.

"You're telling me?" Kins's desk phone rang.

"So we're good?" Fernandez said.

"We're good." Kins picked up the phone. "Detective Rowe."

"Kins, it's Mike Melton. Tracy told me to give you a call when we got the DNA back on the beer bottles and the napkins."

"Shit, Mike, that was fast. Who did you bribe or hold hostage to get that done this quickly?"

"You know better than anyone that when Tracy Crosswhite says jump, we here at the crime lab all shout, 'How high?'"

Kins laughed. "What do you got?"

"Two different DNAs, but they're related. Brothers."

"You're talking about on the beer bottles?"

"Yes."

Kins knew that was good. It was undisputable evidence that Melton's DNA analysis was correct since they knew one bottle had been Carrol's and the other Franklin's. "And you compared it to the DNA obtained from the cigarette butts?"

"We did. The DNA on the two bottles and the napkins doesn't match the DNA on any of the cigarette butts, but there is a familial relationship."

"Which cigarette butt?"

"The one found behind the tree stump."

Kins felt his adrenaline kicking in. "And what's the relationship?"

"Siblings. Brothers."

Kins made a fist. "Thanks, Mike. When can you send over the results?"

"I can send over a preliminary report within the hour."

"I just need enough to get a search warrant."

"I'm on it," Melton said.

Kins hung up, gave Fernandez a fist bump, and summarized the conversation. "I'll get started on the search warrant for the Sprague home. You get ahold of CSI and have them prepared to go in. Get the canines also. That's a big piece of property. I want to check the backyards."

CHAPTER 34

Tracy circled the block and parked so she could see the Rodriguez corner lot as well as the freeway entrance. Then she waited. Less than ten minutes after Tracy had left the house, the front door opened and Aileen emerged hurriedly, dressed in winter gear—boots unlaced, over her stretch pants, and a down jacket, unzipped. She walked carefully, so as not to slip, though with urgency toward the car in the driveway. She backed into the street, then turned right at the intersection.

Tracy waited a beat before she followed. Rodriguez entered the on-ramp to Interstate 82, which paralleled the Yakima River, heading northeast. Tracy stayed three cars behind. Several miles down the road, Rodriguez took the exit. The ramp looped and deposited her onto East Yakima Avenue, a major thoroughfare lined with restaurants, hotels, and fast-food eateries.

Rodriguez pulled into a discount tire store. Tracy pulled into a hotel parking lot across the street and watched Rodriguez enter the shop's glass door.

Tracy checked her watch.

Roughly five minutes after Rodriguez entered the store, she exited, this time with a blonde woman who looked like the one in the photograph in Rodriguez's living room. Like Aileen, the second woman was stout, but not fat. They had similar facial features. The two women spoke outside the store for a minute, then embraced before Rodriguez got back inside her car and drove off.

The blonde retreated inside the store.

Tracy set her seat back and got comfortable, expecting a long wait.

Franklin Sprague shouted up the stairs. "Evan. Get a move on or I'm leaving your ass here. Evan?"

"I'm coming." Evan shuffled down the steps carrying a handful of board games.

"What the hell are you bringing?" He checked Evan's shoes. "And you can't wear tennis shoes. It snowed last night. Which means it snowed at the cabin."

"I can't find my boots. They're not in my closet."

"Borrow a pair of Carrol's. He won't need them. And you can bring three games. That's it. No more."

Evan went back up the stairs.

Franklin walked into the kitchen, where Carrol sat pouting over a bowl of Frosted Flakes. "You got it down, what to do if the police come by?"

"Why would they come by? I thought you said the DNA would exonerate us."

"Look at you, using fancy, four-syllable words. 'Exonerate.' What, you been studying the dictionary?"

"I . . . I . . . I . . ."

"You . . . you . . . you . . . are a dumbshit. And memorizing big words ain't going to change that. Just answer my question. You prepared?"

"Yeah."

"Run it by me."

Carrol stuttered but not too badly. "If . . . if . . . if they come by, I tell them that you and Evan aren't home. I t . . . t . . . tell them you drove to Eastern Washington to hunt, and that I don't know where your camp is or w . . . w . . . when you're coming back."

"And if they have a warrant to search the house?"

"Why would they have a warrant?"

"I'm preparing for every contingency." Franklin counted on his fingers. "There's a four-syllable word for you to memorize that means something. What do you do?"

"I let them search the house like it's n . . . n . . . no big deal."

"And if they ask why you missed work Sunday and Monday?"

Carrol continued stuttering. "I tell them that I called in sick, but that I really w . . . w . . . went down to Vancouver to hunt elk. I went by myself and don't recall seeing anyone. I hunted until dusk, came home, and w . . . w . . . went back down Monday."

"And what else?"

Carrol looked confused.

"What do you say if they say I told them you were sick?" Franklin asked to prompt him.

"Oh yeah."

"Oh yeah," Franklin mimicked. "You forgot the most important thing."

"I t . . . t . . . tell them that I didn't tell you I was going hunting. I told you I was sick and not feeling well."

"Why?"

"Because you'd get angry. Because you're the one always doing all the work around here and buying all the groceries."

"And if they ask you to call me on my cell phone?"

"I t . . . t . . . tell them the hunting camp is out of cell range but give them your number and tell them they're w . . . w . . . welcome to try."

"You sure you can remember all of that?"

"I can remember."

"You screw this up and we're both going to prison."

"What are you going to do with the girls?"

"I haven't made up my mind yet. I'm gonna

play it by ear—wait and see if those detectives come and search the house."

"And if they do?" Carrol asked.

"Well then, I don't have much choice now, do I, brother? Would simplify my life if I just killed you and Evan with them and buried all your asses up there."

Stephanie and Angel Jackson finished a thirty-minute workout followed by thirty minutes of yoga and a twenty-minute meditation. The work-outs were getting harder because Stephanie was becoming weaker from a lack of food and water. What the men had left them wasn't much and mostly junk food. Angel and Donna said back in the basement they had been relatively well-fed. Donna said Carrol once told her that he and Franklin liked their women with a little meat on the bones. They didn't like skinny women.

"It's another indication they're going to kill us," Donna said. "They don't care anymore."

Stephanie reached under the hay the men had left and pulled out the six-inch piece of wood she'd managed to break off from one of the boards of the barn. She pushed hay up against it so it wouldn't be noticeable. She picked up her rock and started to run the sides of the piece of wood along the stone.

"You're dreaming, girl," Donna said. "You

couldn't stab nothing with that. You can't get it sharp enough."

Stephanie suspected she was right. The piece of wood didn't seem to be getting any sharper, which was why in between running the stone over the wood, she used the stone to pound a link of the chain against another rock, hoping to weaken it and maybe pull it apart. That, too, was slow going. Maybe too slow. The men had left them, but for how long? And even if she could break a link in the chain, where would she go? She shook off tears. One thing at a time. One step at a time. So she didn't become overwhelmed and feel her situation was hopeless.

"Leave her to it," Angel said.

"It's a waste of time," Donna said.

"For you. Not for her. Leave her be."

Stephanie ran the stone over the edges of the piece of wood. She needed to get the shackles off first. If the man came for her and released her shackles, then she'd use the wood.

Just after noon, the woman who had hugged Aileen Rodriguez stepped out the glass door and made her way to a dated Subaru parked along the side of the concrete masonry building. The Subaru backed from its spot, then turned right on East Yakima Avenue. Tracy followed. East Yakima Avenue was four lanes wide, with a center lane for cars to turn left or right into the businesses. Tracy remained several car lengths back and in the far right lane, figuring that if the woman turned left, she could easily follow, but if she suddenly turned right, she might not have enough time.

The woman turned left into a Subway sandwich store parking lot. Tracy drove past, keeping an eye on her rearview and side mirrors, making sure the woman didn't double back. She didn't. She parked and went inside. Tracy made a U-turn and parked so she could see inside the plate-glass windows.

She did not immediately go inside; she wanted to be sure the woman wasn't picking up an order to go. The woman stepped to the counter, then moved down the line as she instructed a young man what type of vegetables and condiments she wanted. She paid, then carried her bag and her drink to a table at the far end of the store. She sat alone, with her back to the entrance.

Tracy waited to see if anyone met the woman. When no one did, Tracy stepped from the car into a biting wind. She entered and stopped just short of the woman's right shoulder. About to speak, she saw her business card on the table.

"Hello, Detective," the woman said.

Tracy moved around the small, narrow table to the chair on the opposite side. "May I sit?"

Lindsay Sheppard nodded to the chair.

Tracy sat. Up close, Sheppard and her sister did indeed look alike, though Aileen had more wrinkles. "You knew I was waiting for you?"

"Aileen saw your car outside her home. I saw you in the parking lot across the street. We've had a lot of years to get pretty good at watching people."

Tracy filed that comment away. "Why didn't you just call my number on the card?"

"My husband owns the tire store. It's his family's business. I didn't want you to come into the store and use that name."

"He doesn't know about your past."

"No. And I'd prefer to keep it that way. I figured you'd follow me wherever I went." She set her sandwich, which she didn't open, on the table beside her. "How did you know I was still alive? I did everything possible to erase anything related to Lindsay Sheppard."

"You couldn't erase your sister."

Lindsay looked confused. "Aileen said she told you that she hadn't seen me in decades."

"She did," Tracy said. "But I saw a picture in her home, a five by eight."

"Yeah," Lindsay said. "I know the one."

"I took a chance it was you, and that if you were still alive, she'd know where to find you."

Sheppard's shoulders slumped. "Why?"

"She's your older sister."

Lindsay's eyes narrowed. "She said you had a

sister. She said you showed her a picture and said your sister had been murdered."

"She was," Tracy said. "And that was the one time I failed to look out for her. I've lived with that regret my entire adult life. Always will."

Lindsay sipped her soft drink through the straw, then set the cup down. "Aileen said you're looking for a girl, that you thought the Sprague brothers had something to do with her disappearance."

"I'm hoping to find her still alive."

"Tell me what happened."

Tracy told Lindsay Sheppard what she knew. "Based on what my partner called to tell me earlier, I think Evan grabbed her. I think Carrol got rid of her car and drove it to Ravenna Park to misdirect our investigation. Maybe also her body. I'm hoping that isn't the case."

"You said that you think Evan grabbed this girl?" There was something in the young woman's tone and facial expression that indicated she was having a hard time believing that to be true.

"We've confirmed that both Franklin and Carrol were at work," Tracy said again. "And the DNA on the cigarette butt is conclusive, as is the video showing that Evan went for a walk about the time the young woman disappeared."

"Franklin would be the one to run things in that house after Ed died. He's the oldest, the biggest, and he's mean, like his father." Sheppard took a breath. "Carrol was always fat and lacked self-confidence. He had a stuttering problem, especially if he got nervous. Franklin protected him, but he also beat on him physically and verbally. He beat on Evan too. He used to call him an 'idiot' and a 'retard.' But Evan . . ." She shook her head. "He was a sweetheart when I lived there, Detective. He wouldn't hurt anyone. He was my lifeline. We played cards and board games together. It was the only thing that kept me from losing my mind."

"Could Evan have acted on Franklin's orders?"

"I suppose. He's afraid of Franklin . . . and he is slow. I mean he went to special ed. It was something about a lack of oxygen when he was born. But he isn't stupid," she rushed to add. "They just always treated him that way. They never took the time to get to know him and, after a while, he sort of just believed it."

"What happened, Lindsay? Why did you go to so much effort not to be found?"

"I don't know that name anymore, Detective. It's been years since I heard it. I'd prefer you not use it."

"What name do you use?"

"Jessica. Jessica Whitley. Whitley is my married name."

"Tell me what happened, Jessica."

"I don't like to talk about it. I put the past behind me. I didn't really have a choice. I'll tell you though, for that girl. If you think she could still be alive."

Tracy nodded. "I do."

"Why do you think they took me in?" The question sounded like a challenge.

"I thought maybe the mother, Carol Lynn, wanted a daughter after the three boys, but didn't want to try because of Evan's condition."

Lindsay smiled, but it had a sad quality to it. "Carol Lynn didn't have a say in anything in that house, or a desire to have a daughter. I think she knew what would happen if she had a daughter." Tears leaked from the corners of her eyes. She dabbed at them with balled-up napkins. "She knew what went on in that basement."

Tracy felt sick to her stomach, anticipating what was to come. "How bad was it?" Tracy asked.

"As bad as you can imagine," Lindsay said. "Times ten."

CHAPTER 35

Kins stood when Judge Ken Schwartz entered his courtroom in a dress shirt and tie, but no robe. Schwartz was midfifties, having ascended to the bench after serving in the prosecutor's office for some twenty-five years. He looked like each year had taken a toll. He was heavy, carrying most of his weight in his lower half, and bald, with wisps of hair that a comb could not tame. Kins had never sat in a trial with Schwartz, but Faz described the judge as pedantic about properly admitting evidence, and a real stickler for the minutiae. His direct and cross-examinations reflected his neurosis, often taking hours.

"The guy could bore butter," Faz once said. Whatever the hell that meant.

"Detective Rowe," Schwartz said. Kins, already standing, stepped forward. "You're seeking a warrant to a house belonging to three brothers. Is that correct?"

It was on the paperwork Kins submitted in black-and-white. "That's correct."

"I haven't had a lot of time to review it, so bear with me. This request is based primarily on DNA found on bottles obtained in a bar indicating a familial relationship between the bar patrons and the person who left their DNA on a cigarette butt in a park where a young girl went missing."

"Primarily, yes."

"How did you obtain the beer bottles?"

Kins told him.

Schwartz blew out a heavy breath, as if pondering the legality of what Tracy had done. Then he asked, "What evidence is there of a crime committed in that park?"

Kins wanted to scream. He pointed to the paperwork and went through it. Concluding, he said, "CSI located the cigarette butts."

"I understand that, but the cadaver dogs did not locate a body."

"No, but the CSI detectives did locate blood, and a man-tracker will testify that a person lay in wait behind the log and carried the woman from the park."

"The man-tracker," Schwartz said with a smile.

"Sign-cutter," Kins said. "Whatever you prefer."

"I'd prefer hard evidence to speculation."

"It isn't . . ." Kins caught himself, not wanting to get into a debate with Schwartz about the scientific validity of Wright's analysis. "CSI detectives located an earbud, and an eyewitness who saw the woman in the park referenced her running with earbuds."

"And the assumption is this person who Detective Wright concluded hid behind the log came down into the ravine and hurt this woman, then carried the victim back up the hill to the house you want to search?"

Kins bit his tongue. "Yes, Your Honor."

"Can she be certain the person carried some-one?"

"The shoeprints indicate that was the case."

"Detective Wright mentioned a toe dig. Couldn't that toe dig be the result of a person climbing up a hillside, trying to gain footing, with or without carrying something?"

Kins tried not to get frustrated. "The broken plants and bruised brush and the blood indicate there was a struggle between the runner and someone much bigger than her. We believe the person behind the log surprised the runner and struck her, then pulled her into the brush. That person then carried the woman up the hill. The cigarette butt evidences the person was Evan Sprague, and the Sprague house backs up to the park. We believe one of the other two brothers moved the victim's car to draw attention away from the park."

"You interviewed him?"

"The older brother?"

"The brother you believe moved the car."

"Detective Crosswhite interviewed him by phone and we spoke to his store manager."

"What was his response?"

"Detective Crosswhite opted not to press him at

that time, believing it best to ask him in person, where she could gauge his physical reactions."

"And Evan . . . Is that the name of the brother you believe took the girl?"

"We spoke to him, but with the older brother present and, we think, influencing what Evan said. Evan is slow, Your Honor," Kins rushed to add. "His brother answered many questions for him. We also have videotape evidence of Evan walking past a home in the direction of the park just before we know the girl was in the park. He claimed he didn't remember walking that day, but again, that was with the older brother orchestrating the conversation."

"What would you be looking for inside the house?"

The girl's body! Kins wanted to say, but again he refrained. "Further evidence tying Evan to the crime scene, such as shoes and clothing Evan might have worn that could contain bloodstains. Possible items belonging to the young woman. As I said, CSI found one earbud. The other could be in the home."

"Why cadaver dogs?"

Because we like pets. Kins couldn't believe he was having this conversation. "Ultimately, we're looking for a body, Judge. Statistically speaking, the chances of this young woman still being alive are not strong." And growing more remote by the minute.

Schwartz grimaced and scratched his scalp, leaving those stubborn strands of hair ruffled. It was no wonder he was bald; the guy had worried away every hair in his head. "I'll grant the search warrant," he said suddenly and without elaboration. He quickly signed his name and handed the paperwork to Kins, as if worried he might change his mind.

"Thank you, Judge." Kins took the paperwork and turned to leave before Schwartz did change his mind.

"Detective?"

Shit. Kins shut his eyes, then turned. "Yes, Judge?"

"I hope you find the young woman alive."

"So do I," Kins said, though he left the courtroom not believing that either.

Franklin worried the van would not make it up the snow-covered dirt road. In the winter, the accumulated snow could pile as high as seven feet, and there wasn't any snowplow service—no one lived out here in the winter. Which was why Franklin couldn't leave the three women here any longer. He couldn't get here to feed them, and he couldn't leave them alone, chained to posts, to care for themselves. He either had to bring them back to Seattle—or get rid of them.

Though he'd covered his bases as best he could, Franklin knew the police would keep looking for the runner, and the detective going to the extreme to get their DNA was proof they were prime suspects. As much as he hated to give up a sure thing, Franklin knew it would be near impossible to bring the three women back home—not now. Maybe not ever.

And that really only left one alternative.

We ain't killers, Franklin, Carrol had said.

Not yet, they weren't. But they'd gone down the same path their daddy went down. Franklin figured it was in their genes. He figured the Spragues did what they did to survive. And they would survive this. Franklin would see to it. He'd see to it for all of them. He always had. And likely always would.

Franklin parked at the cabin and grabbed Evan's arm before he ran from the van. "I got to turn on the generator in the pump house, so we have electricity and water. Put the damn board games down, get that diesel can from the back of the van, and bring it with you to the pump house."

Evan did as Franklin instructed. The generator provided power to the house, which was necessary to get electricity for the heat and lights, and water from the pump. Franklin filled the generator with diesel fuel and started it. He flipped a switch in the garage and the lights went on.

"Let me check the water. Then you can go play."

He walked around the cabin to the pump house, turned the spigot his daddy had installed, and waited a beat, in case there was air in the line. No water came out, which could indicate any number of things. None of them good.

"Shit." He wasn't interested in standing in the cold trying to figure out how to fix the problem. Then again, they'd have no water if he didn't.

Franklin turned to Evan. The idiot looked like a cat on a hot tin roof. He figured he might as well let him play. He wouldn't be no good to him anyway, especially if his mind was elsewhere. He'd toy with him a bit though, because . . . well, he could. "We need to split firewood to keep the house warm until I get this fixed. I'm thinking two or three cords ought to about do it."

Evan looked like someone had slapped him. "You said I could play after you turned on the generator."

"Maybe I changed my mind."

Evan now looked as if he might cry.

Franklin laughed. "Get me my toolbox from the van. Then get the hell out of my sight before I change my mind."

Might as well let him have his fun. The young woman wasn't coming back with them anyway.

Stephanie and the other two women had heard the sound of a car engine straining, likely because of the snow. Someone had come, likely one or more of the men. She was out of time.

She grabbed the piece of wood and put it down the waistband of her running tights at the small of her back and covered the tip with her shirt. Was it sharp enough to do any damage? She didn't know, but she refused to give up hope.

She heard footsteps outside the door. Someone was coming. Angel and Donna each had their head down. Stephanie heard someone fumbling with a lock, then the sound of deadbolts disengaging. The door pulled back. Light filtered in the opening. She saw the silhouette of one of the men. A light came on, a small glow from a bulb fastened to one of the overhead rafters.

Evan.

She felt her heart start to race. This was it. This was what Donna had kept warning her about.

He walked to where she sat, a broad smile on his face. She shook her head and pushed back against the wall. "No. Please," she said. "Please don't."

Evan sat on the floor, legs crossed. He looked sad. "You don't want to play?"

She put a hand at her back, feeling the piece of wood, but first she had to get him to remove the shackles. Her mind was jumbled. Everything was happening too quickly. "No. Please. Just let me go," she pleaded. "I won't say anything. I swear. I won't. Just let me go."

"These are my favorite games," he said, setting out the boxes in front of her. "You can pick one. Or we can play cards. Lindsay taught me how to play. She taught me kings in the corner and go fish. And crazy eights."

Stephanie looked to the two other women, uncertain, but it seemed as though Evan really did want to play one of the games.

"I'd play," Angel said. "Whatever game takes the longest to play."

Tracy listened intently. She didn't interrupt, didn't ask questions or seek clarification. She let Jessica talk, and it became apparent Jessica had locked Lindsay in a box, much like Tracy had locked Sarah in a box, so Jessica could survive, move forward, and live a life, in one manner or another. Now she'd let Lindsay out to tell her story. She told Tracy as if she were reporting something that had happened to someone else, something she'd seen in a movie. She unburdened her soul in a way Tracy sensed she had never done before, not even to her sister. Tracy knew it was . . . easier . . . if she could use that word, telling someone Lindsay didn't know and who didn't know her. Someone who would not judge her. Someone who knew Lindsay had done what she had to do to survive. She spoke without tears or much expression, detailing the horrible things Ed Sprague had inflicted upon her.

And it had been horrific. Times ten.

Though Tracy fought to stay present, to keep her mind from slipping back to the moment when she had walked into the dank and abandoned room in the mine shaft, the place where Edmund House had kept her sister locked and chained for so many months. Up until that moment, when she saw the restraints and the paperback books and the grimy bed, she had no idea what horrors her sister had experienced.

And they had been horrors. Times ten.

And just as with her sister, there was nothing Tracy could do about what had happened to Lindsay Sheppard. She couldn't change the past. Lindsay had gone from a drug-addicted home into the depths of hell. She couldn't change that. But maybe she could make sure Stephanie Cole didn't suffer the same fate. If she wasn't already too late.

"In high school, Ed started to lock me in the basement for periods of time. Evan would sneak down with board games and a deck of cards. No one else ever knew. Carol Lynn bought them for him, but no one ever played with him, or taught him how to play. I taught him. At first, it was because I loved him for his simplicity and his sweetness in a house that had none. We'd play those games for hours, until his mother or father called him upstairs."

"The mother knew what happened in the basement," Tracy said.

Lindsay nodded. "She knew. Ed used to beat on her too. She was as afraid of him as I was. He threatened her, and he threatened me. He said if I told anyone, if I said anything, he'd make it bad for me, and he'd make it bad for Carol Lynn and for Evan. He said he'd kill me and bury me in the cellar, with the others."

"There were others?" Tracy said, feeling both sickened and angry.

"Ed said there were. He said they were women no one cared to look for, women who could just disappear and generate no interest, no concern. He said I'd be just like them. He'd tell anyone who came looking that I'd run away. He said no one would ever find my body; no one would give a shit to look for me. He said I'd just be gone."

She smiled for the first time. "And that's when I first got the idea of running. Getting away. Figured if I could, no one would come looking for me. That maybe Ed would just act like I had died."

"How did you get out of the restraints?"

Her smile faded. "I didn't want to use Evan. I didn't want to take advantage of him the way everyone else did. They made him clean the house, do chores for them and others in the neighborhood, then they took the money he earned.

But I also knew Evan was my only chance. He had a conscience and a soul the others didn't have." She took another sip from her straw. "It took months to convince Evan to take off the shackles around my legs. He was terrified of Ed, and Franklin too. Franklin had started to assert his dominance around the house. He was as big and as strong as Ed, more so. Ed stopped beating him because he had to."

"How did you convince Evan to remove the shackles?"

"I made up a game. I made up the whole thing in my head, and I convinced Evan it was real. I used what had happened to me; I said the game had a dark castle with a dungeon where an evil king kept a princess captive. I said this king had two fire-breathing dragons who guarded the castle, but also a son, a prince, who was kind and gentle, and felt compassion for the people who lived in the village, but especially for the princess, Jessica. I said the prince wanted to help the princess because he loved her, but he feared the king and he feared his two dragons."

"It's brilliant," Tracy said. She had a sense Lindsay was bright and resourceful, that under other circumstances she could have done almost anything she wanted with her life.

"Evan used to get so excited when I'd tell him." A smile leaked onto Lindsay's lips. "I told him he could never mention the game to anyone, not to Carol Lynn and especially not to his daddy or his brothers. I told him they would think it was a dumb thing to spend money on, and they would never let Evan buy the game. I told Evan I'd stop telling him about the game if he told them. As the weeks went on, I could see his desire to play the game growing stronger and his fear receding. When he asked how we could get the game, I said that I knew where to get it, but that we needed money. I told him that if he hid some of the money he earned for doing his chores around the neighborhood, maybe we could save enough to buy the game. Each week he'd tell me how much money he had hidden. After several months, he had sixty dollars. I told him it was enough to buy the game, but that we had another problem. No one in his family would ever drive him to buy it. I made it seem like an insurmountable problem, but I told him I'd try to come up with a plan to get the game. Each day he would ask me if I'd thought of something, and I kept telling him I hadn't, which only made him more agitated and desperate. Finally, I told Evan I'd thought of a plan. I told him I could sneak out and buy the game while his father and brothers were at work. I told him I'd sneak it into the basement and hide it, and no one would ever know we had it except him and me."

"And Evan removed the shackles," Tracy said.

"And left the pantry door unbolted."

"The pantry door?"

"It's a false wall. Ed had the boys dig out the basement and reinforce the walls and ceiling. That's where I was kept. That's where Ed said the other women were buried."

"What about the mother? Did she work?"

Lindsay shook her head. "She was a lot like Evan, I think. Maybe a little slow. I didn't love her though. I hated her for not stopping what was happening. When I walked up the stairs and came through the door, Carol Lynn stood at the stove making coffee. When she saw me, she dropped the pot. She just stood there, staring at me, like I was a ghost, or like she knew this day would eventually come. I think she thought I was going to harm her, but I just wanted to get away before Ed killed me."

"What did she do?"

"Picked up the pot and put it back on the stove." Lindsay shrugged. "I slipped out the back door, ran to a main thoroughfare, and took the first bus that came. I was eighteen, an adult. I called Olympia and said I wanted to find my brother and my sister. Eventually, I learned my brother had been killed, but they gave me the name of the family that had taken in my sister. I tracked them down, but they told me they hadn't heard from Aileen in years. They said she'd had a drug addiction, and they had dropped her at a recovery clinic in Eastern Washington. They said she'd taken up with a young man. It took time, but when you're desperate you don't have a choice. I had to find Aileen. I made my way to the clinic in Yakima, and I learned that Aileen had married a man at the same clinic. They gave me his name.

"When I found her, we decided to play Ed's game and let Lindsay Sheppard die. I was still afraid of him, that he'd come for me, but with each day that passed, I feared him less and less. Years later I was curious, and I looked up his name online. I found an obituary. That was the first day in years that I took a deep breath.

"I felt bad for Evan. I hoped that maybe Carol Lynn didn't say anything, but I figured Evan got beat good when Ed got home that night. Maybe her too."

"I'm sorry," Tracy said. "I know that doesn't mean much coming now. It didn't when people said it to me after my sister disappeared."

Lindsay nodded. "I stopped blaming everyone else, including myself, a long time ago, Detective. Ed was a psychopath, plain and simple."

Remarkable, Tracy thought, *that this young woman could go through hell and not blame anyone.* "I'm holding out hope we might still find Stephanie Cole alive also," she said.

"The apple doesn't fall far from the tree, Detective. Franklin and Carrol could very well have kept her alive for the same reason Ed kept me." She shook her head and closed her eyes. "But maybe not."

"What do you mean?"

"There are graves in the basement, and at the cabin in the mountains."

The last comment caught Tracy by surprise. She'd done a property search for Ed Sprague and not found any other property. "What cabin?"

"They had a cabin near Cle Elum. In the canyon."

"I looked up land records for Ed Sprague—"

"It isn't in his name. It was the wife's, Carol Lynn. Her family."

It could have been where Carrol had gone the two days that he called in sick to work. It could be where he brought Stephanie Cole. A remote location. For the first time in days, Tracy had hope Stephanie Cole remained alive. "Do you know where the cabin is?"

"I can draw you a map." She paused. Then she said, "My one regret is that I never said a word. I was afraid it would lead Ed back to me . . . Maybe I could have saved one of the others. I live with that thought every day."

During her career, Tracy had dealt with her fair share of young women held captive. Most didn't survive. Many eventually acquiesced to their captors' needs and wants, some even sympathized with them. "Stockholm syndrome," they called it. That Lindsay Sheppard, just fourteen when the abuse began, just eighteen when she ran, had never succumbed, after all she'd been through, after all the years, was truly a testament to the woman's inner strength.

"What gave you the courage to do what you did, Jessica?"

"To run?" Lindsay closed her eyes and lowered her head. She began to cry. Tracy handed her another napkin to blot the tears. After a minute, Lindsay said, "I wasn't going to let what happened to me happen to my child. I did it for her. I escaped for her, and I hid for her."

And the reality hit Tracy like a freight train, where Lindsay's strength had come from. "You were pregnant."

"I have a daughter . . . and a son now. We live here in Yakima. My daughter has a good life. So do I. She doesn't know any of this. And I'll never tell her. Never. She wasn't conceived in love, but I've done my best to raise her in love."

"That's why you ran—why you needed to find your sister."

"I knew I would be better off with people thinking I was dead than living another day in that house. I wasn't going to let them do to my daughter what they did to me."

They. Tracy sensed something in the word, in Lindsay's intonation. "Is Ed the father?" she

385

asked, though she thought perhaps it could be Franklin or Carrol.

"It could only have been one of two people," she said. "And Bibby always wore a condom. Always."

CHAPTER 36

Kins peered into the cluttered living room where Carrol Sprague sat, looking forlorn. He had his hands cuffed behind his back, his knees vibrating like a man on speed. Kins took Carrol into custody and sent Faz and Del to the retirement home to take Franklin into custody and bring him downtown. He wanted to keep Franklin separated from the other two brothers, but Faz and Del had learned that Franklin was not at work—it being his regular day off—and Evan wasn't at the house.

Through a lot of stuttering, Carrol told Kins that Franklin and Evan had gone hunting somewhere in Eastern Washington and were not reachable. Calls to Franklin's cell phone went straight to voice mail.

"You've hunted before?" Kins asked.

Carrol nodded. "Our f . . . f . . . father taught us to hunt."

"Where?"

"All over."

"But you don't recall where exactly they went hunting?"

Carrol shook his head.

"Where are those weapons, Carrol? Are they here in the house?"

"No," Carrol said, shaking his head. "We . . . we . . . we . . ."

"We what?" Kins said. "Where are the weapons?"

Carrol shook his head. "I . . . I . . . I . . . don't know."

Carrol was lying. Unlike Franklin, Carrol had no poker face, and his stuttering increased exponentially with the rapid beat of his knees, so severely that Kins almost felt sorry for him.

Almost.

At present, Carrol was not saying a thing.

Dale Pinkney, CSI's detective sergeant, and his team, found the house filled with newspaper and magazine stacks going back decades, making it difficult to get down the hallways. He said they could be searching the house for days.

Kins found a locked door on the second level and asked Carrol for the key. The brother said the room had belonged to his parents, and only Franklin had the key. Kins had the lock removed, uncertain what he might find inside, hoping to find Stephanie Cole.

The bedroom was surprisingly well kept, neat, if not clean. A half-inch-thick coat of dust had settled on the bed frame, dresser, and ornate mirror frame. The closet remained packed with clothes, also covered in dust. Men's and women's shoes lined the floor. It was like some macabre shrine.

He did not find Stephanie Cole, or any evidence she'd been kept there.

Kins returned downstairs and sat in a cushioned chair across from Carrol. He placed his phone on the table between them and pressed "Record." He'd already read Carrol his Miranda rights. "You don't know where your brothers are, Carrol?" Kins asked again.

Carrol shook his head, then lowered his gaze. His knees pounded like engine pistons. Through his stuttering, he eventually repeated what he'd already said. "They went hunting in Eastern Washington."

"Why didn't you go?"

"I . . . I . . . I had to work. I . . . I . . . I . . . had too many sick days."

"Is that because you called in sick Sunday and Monday?" Kins asked.

Carrol didn't answer.

"Franklin said you were working. Your boss says you called in sick. Why is that?"

Carrol didn't answer.

"We're going to find your brothers, Carrol. You might as well tell us where they are."

"I . . . I . . . I don't know," he said, working hard to get the words out.

"Tell me what you know about Stephanie Cole."

The knees continued to fire. "I don't know anything."

"Carrol, I'm trying to help you. We have DNA from the Budweiser bottles you and your brother drank at the bar on Aurora."

"Then you know we didn't do it."

"Didn't do what?" Kins asked.

"Nothing," Carrol said under his breath.

"Take that girl from the park? We know you didn't take that girl from the park."

"We were at work."

"We checked that also. But we compared the DNA on the Budweiser bottles to the DNA on a cigarette butt we found behind a log in the ravine. And guess what we learned?"

Carrol shook his head. "We didn't do it."

"The two people who drank from the bottles are related to each other, and to the person who smoked that cigarette. They're siblings. Brothers."

Carrol looked so pale he was almost white.

"We know Evan waited behind the log for Stephanie Cole, and we know he took her. Did you or Franklin move the car to protect Evan?"

"I went fishing," Carrol said, rushing to get the words out. "I went f . . . f . . . f . . . fly fishing for steelhead on the North F . . . F . . . F . . . Fork of the Stillaguamish."

"Who'd you go with?" Kins asked.

He shook his head, almost gagging to get the words out. "No one. I went alone. I didn't see no one."

"Why did your brother tell us you were sick?"

Sprague looked like a man drowning. Kins waited. He had time. CSI would be all day, likely more than one. " 'Cause I didn't tell him. I . . . I . . . I told him I was sick."

"Why?"

"Because F . . . F . . . F . . . Franklin gets angry. He . . . he . . . he'd say he's the one always doing the work around here . . . a . . . a . . . and buying all the groceries."

"Are you afraid of Franklin?"

"No."

"But you didn't tell him?"

Carrol lowered his head like a schoolboy caught in a lie. He looked like he was tied in knots. "I . . . I . . . I . . . don't know."

"Here's what I'm going to prove, Carrol. I'm going to prove that after Evan took Stephanie Cole, he brought her here, to this home. We'll find DNA for sure. You, or Franklin, moved her car and parked it at the Ravenna parking lot. We have an investigative team going over her car. They're going to find fingerprints and hair, and with the science we now have available to us, we're going to match that DNA to you or to Franklin. It's just a matter of time, Carrol. I know you think you're helping your brothers. Everyone wants to help his family. It's noble, Carrol. But there's a young girl missing, and it's my job to find her. She has a family also—one that is very worried about her." Kins paused to let that sink in.

"Tell me what happened, and I will do my best to help you, to get the prosecutor to make you a deal. But if you keep lying, then there's nothing I can do. You'll be on your own."

Carrol looked like he wanted to say something, but as he stuttered, he swallowed whatever those words had been. "I . . . I . . . I . . . was fishing."

"Detective?" Kaylee Wright stood in the hallway. "You got a second?"

Kins looked to Carrol. "I'm going to talk to the detective for a minute, Carrol. While I'm gone, I want you to think about what I said. I want you to think about allowing me to help you. When I come back, I'm going to expect an answer. And I'm not going to give you a third chance."

Kins met Wright on the front porch. The circus had come to town, and that had brought out the neighbors. They stood in winter clothing; the temperature had dropped into the thirties. Having had police officers and detectives knock on their doors, the neighbors knew the police were searching for a missing young woman. Watching the police descend upon a neighbor's house—detectives wearing gloves and booties, a CSI van parked in the street, and detectives with dogs—made it all too real.

"We haven't found the shoes," Wright said. "Not the ones worn in the park, but . . ." She had a wry smile on her face. "The size of other shoes in Evan's room match the size of the impression of the shoe I found behind the log and in the ravine, and the wear indicates he distinctly pronates."

Kins nodded. It was something, but he could hear a skilled defense attorney asking him what percentage of the population pronates when they walk. "I'd rather have the shoe."

"We'll keep looking."

Pinkney joined them on the porch. "We found cigarettes," Pinkney said. "A lot of them. All over the house. Including the bedrooms."

"Do any match the brand we found behind the stump?"

"No doubt. Marlboro."

Kins looked to Kaylee. The DNA from the cigarette butt would place Evan at the site where Cole disappeared. His shoes, with a distinct wear pattern, would make it highly probable he'd been hiding, lying in wait.

"What else?"

Pinkney made a face like he smelled something awful. "A whole cache of pornography going back decades. Prurient shit. It runs the gambit from soft porn to some really nasty . . . bondage, sadism. There are unlabeled videos, boxes of them. I have a feeling they contain some nightmares. There are also multiple computers. We're going to need to have the drives analyzed. It could take weeks."

"Then let's get started. I can modify the search warrant as we go."

Kins's cell phone rang. Caller ID indicated Tracy. He stepped away to take the call. "Tracy? We're at the house now. Carrol is here, but Franklin and Evan aren't, and Franklin isn't at work. It's his day off."

"Kins—"

"Carrol says Franklin took Evan hunting in Eastern Washington but claims he doesn't know where."

"Kins." Tracy raised her voice and said his name in a tone he recognized. It meant she had something to say and needed to say it quickly.

"Go ahead."

"Did you bring the dogs?"

"They're outside, going over the yard."

"Bring them inside. Take them into the base-ment."

"There is no—"

"Go into the kitchen."

"Where are you? Sounds like you're driving."

"I'm on I-90, just outside Cle Elum."

"Why?"

"I found the sister."

"Where?"

"I'll tell you more later. There's a second

property, a cabin near Cle Elum. I'm going there now. But right now, I need you to go into the kitchen and check out something Lindsay told me."

"Hang on." Kins walked inside, the phone pressed to his ear. The rooms and hallways were teeming with CSI detectives. White bags contained confiscated evidence. He stepped around the bags, his blue booties making a swishing sound on the worn hardwood floor. He stepped into the kitchen. "Okay. I'm in the kitchen."

"Go to the pantry to the right of the back door."

Kins did so. "What am I looking for?"

"A hidden door at the back of the pantry. You should find a deadbolt in the upper right corner and another at the bottom."

Kins turned on his phone light since there was minimal ambient light and put Tracy on speaker. "Yeah. I see them," he said. His stomach flipped in anticipation of what was to come next.

"Unbolt them and pull the door open. There should be a string for a light. You'll find stairs."

"Where do the stairs go?"

"It's a house of horrors, Kins. I'm not sure what you're going to find. Send in the cadaver dogs."

Kins snapped the bolts and pulled the door open. The bottom scraped the cheap brick linoleum, leaving a white streak. He had to move cans of food and bags of rice to pull the door open the last few feet. He reached inside and felt the string hit the back of his hand, gripped it, and pulled. A bulb screwed into a socket attached to a floor joist illuminated a wooden staircase.

"You think Cole is down here?" Kins asked, feeling nerves tingling all over his body.

"I don't know. That's what I need you to tell me."

Kins held up his phone for more light as he carefully stepped down, making certain of his footing. Another bare bulb hung from a joist in the center of the room. He pulled the string. The light emitted a dull glow. The room looked to be eight feet square and perhaps six feet below ground. The walls were railroad ties. Wooden posts braced the floor joists and continued below ground. Attached to the posts were chains and shackles. In the corner was a table. Over it, tools. In the other corner, a mattress.

Kins swore. "Holy shit."

"Is she there? Kins?"

"Huh?"

"Is Cole there?"

"Not above ground," he said. He covered his nose and mouth with the collar of his shirt. "It smells like death down here."

"Does the floor look freshly dug up?"

Kins shone the phone's beam of light around the room. "Nothing I can see."

"I think Franklin and Evan are at the cabin, Kins, hopefully with Stephanie Cole still alive. I need you to find Brian Bibby."

"Bibby? Why?"

"Go down the street. Knock on Bibby's door and tell me if he's home. If he is, arrest him. He's had a hand in all this."

CHAPTER 37

The drive from Yakima to Cle Elum took an hour. It had started snowing as soon as Tracy jumped on the I-90, west out of Ellensburg. The snowfall intensified as she neared the town, at times swirling. She'd got what information she could on the cabin from Lindsay. She'd contemplated, but only briefly, bringing Lindsay with her, but she couldn't do that to the young woman, not after all she had been through, all she had somehow managed to survive. Tracy knew what it was like to go back to a place of your worst nightmares.

Tracy called the Cle Elum police department and spoke to Chief of Police Pete Peterson. Peterson knew the cabin in Curry Canyon but said he had not seen the gate across the access road open in years. He thought the property might have been abandoned, and more than once he'd contemplated looking up the owner at the registrar's office.

"The roads aren't cleared in the winter. Not enough money in the budget, and no one goes there this time of year to justify it," Peterson had said.

"Can you get there?" Tracy asked.

"It's dumping buckets," Peterson said. "But we got a four-wheel drive with a plow. We can get you there."

Tracy and Dan had visited Cle Elum on weekends, though usually in the summer. It was roughly a square mile with fewer than 1,000 homes. A 120-year-old former mining town, Cle Elum was quiet and peaceful in the summer, more so in winter when there were fewer tourists. A developer had built the Suncadia Resort, a mountain retreat with golf courses and fly fishing just outside of town that brought in tourists.

Tracy followed her GPS's directions to the police station on West Second Street—a one-story, clapboard building surrounded by pine trees, their branches burdened with snow. It reminded Tracy of the police station in Cedar Grove.

As she pulled into a parking space, her cell phone rang. Kins.

"Bibby isn't home," he said. "He told his wife he was going down to the Edmonds Marina with Jackpot to work on the boat and wouldn't be home until late. She gave me the slip number. I called the Edmonds Police Department and an officer made a run out there. Bibby's car isn't in the parking lot, and he isn't at the boat. What the hell is going on?"

Tracy quickly explained what Lindsay Sheppard had told her, but she didn't have time to be detailed. "I called Boeing on my drive. Bibby did retire with a back injury like he tells every-one, but he was also months from aging out."

"And he and Ed Sprague were . . . what, friends?"

"I don't know what you call people like that."

"The house . . . There's shit everywhere, Tracy. Pornography. We took the cadaver dogs into the room under the house and they went crazy. I've called in Kelly Rosa," he said. Rosa was King County's forensic anthropologist. "This is not going to be good."

"I think I know where Bibby's gone, and if I don't get there quickly, there might be more graves to dig."

"Don't be cowboying this, Tracy, and don't think about going in alone. You got a little girl at home. According to Carrol, his brothers went hunting. That's unlikely, but he said they hunted with their father as kids and own shotguns and rifles. I asked about the weapons, and he started to tell me where they were but caught himself. Now I know why. They're probably at this other piece of property, which means it's likely Franklin has access to those rifles and shotguns and knows how to use them. Get some backup."

"Way ahead of you, partner. I got the local police with me." Tracy had no intention of being a cowboy.

She disconnected her cell, shoved it in her pants pocket, and checked her Glock. She put two additional magazines in her coat pocket and stepped from the car into a foot of snow that continued to fall in large flakes and cling to the roof.

Peterson met her in the building lobby in full uniform. A tall, thin man, he wore a handgun at his hip and carried a rifle. Peterson introduced a young officer as Mack Herr. He, too, wore a pistol and carried a rifle. Peterson had a full head of red hair laced with gray. Wrinkles indicated he had years under his belt. Herr, on the other hand, looked to be in his twenties. Tracy quickly and fully advised them of the situation. She assured Peterson they had exigent circumstances—that the young woman's life was in imminent danger, negating the need for a search warrant.

"Sounds good to me," Peterson said. "We can always get one later to do a full search of the property. Let's go."

Tracy did not offer that Stephanie Cole could already be dead, and Peterson didn't ask. He had the look of a man ready for a confrontation. Herr, on the other hand, looked nervous.

The three slid into the cab of a four-wheel-drive truck with a snow blade attached to the front bumper. Peterson drove east on West Second Street to North Stafford Avenue, cutting through several city blocks to Summit View Road. The streets in town had been cleared but not Summit View.

Peterson pointed to relatively fresh tire tracks quickly filling with snow. "Those would appear to confirm what you just told us." He kept up the truck's speed, whipping the steering wheel left and right around turns. Tracy, in the middle of the front seat, pitched and bounced with each bump in the road, unsuccessfully bracing herself with a hand on the dash. She'd driven on roads like this, in the snow, and she could tell this wasn't Peterson's first rodeo either. He followed the tracks around turns and drove up and down hills without lowering the blade. The thick snow tires plowed through the snow, and Peterson kept up the truck's speed.

The tracks led them to a three-bar, metal-tube gate across a snow-covered road not much wider than the truck. Herr slid from the passenger seat and pulled a lock cutter from the truck bed. At the gate he bent to cut the chain but looked hesitant. He pulled the chain from the fence, holding it up for them to see.

The lock had already been cut.

Tracy got a bad feeling. Franklin would have known the combination to a lock on a fence leading to property they'd owned for decades.

Franklin had his head down and his hands in a hole in the ground inside the pump house. After half an hour freezing his ass off, he'd found the problem to be the pump. His fingers had gone numb, despite his blowing warm air on them to maintain some dexterity. He just about had the problem temporarily fixed; he'd have to eventually go into town and get a new one. He heard Evan shuffle into the building behind him.

"You through already?" Franklin said, not looking back. "Boy, you're quick. Hand me the half-inch socket wrench." He reached back with his arm.

"Your father hated it when the pump went out. One winter we had pipes bursting all over the Goddamn place."

Franklin recognized the voice. He'd heard it more times than he had cared to over the course of his life.

Bibby.

He hated the man, hated him since he was a boy. Seemed Bibby had always been around, in the basement at the house and in the room at the back of the barn.

Franklin sat up and turned. "What are you doing here?"

Bibby stood in the door frame, the falling snow illuminating him. But he didn't look like no angel, far from it. He looked like the piece of shit he'd always been.

"Good to see you too, Franklin."

Bibby wore winter clothes—Carhartt pants, a heavy down jacket, boots, and a hat with earflaps. Jackpot stood at his side, his entire body wagging and jumping around like the ground was electrified. Bibby held a rifle, one that Franklin recognized.

"What are you doing with my dad's deer rifle?"

"You're a creature of habit, just like your dad. I knew I'd find you here, and I knew I could count on your dad not changing the lock on the gun closet."

"What the hell are you doing here, Bibby?" Franklin asked again. He no longer feared the man. Age had a way of evening out the odds.

"I'm looking for the girl, Franklin. I know you got her here because you're too smart to keep her at your home with the police going over it. You were always the smart one."

Franklin kept the pipe wrench in his hand, wiped it with a rag. The police were searching the home. "What girl are you talking about?"

Bibby laughed. "You know what I'm talking about."

Franklin didn't respond. He kept his face placid, not giving anything away. "The police are at the house?"

Bibby smiled. "And you know what they're going to find under the floor in the basement. They brought the dogs. Dogs can smell the dead."

It had been the reason Franklin never moved from the house. He had wanted to, many times, but he couldn't very well sell it to someone, not with his daddy's and Bibby's "hobbies" buried beneath the basement floor. What was he going to say, that he didn't know about it? That wasn't going to fly. They'd think he had something to do with it, he and his two brothers. His father had screwed them all. He'd screwed them good. Franklin figured he'd live there until he died. Then he'd no longer give a shit.

"Have you added to our hobby?" Bibby said.

"I ain't my daddy. And I sure as shit ain't you. We don't have no girl at the house."

"Not anymore you don't." Bibby smiled.

"I told you. I don't know what you're talking about. Now get the hell out of here."

"I think you do know what I'm talking about. And I'll shoot you right here and find her myself. Evan with her? I'll kill him too." Bibby leveled the rifle, the stock under his arm. "They might find you when the snow melts, but given that nobody has been up this way in years, I doubt it. You'll rot right here in the pump house, though I imagine the animals will take most of you."

"What business is it of yours, Bibby, *if* we had the girl?"

Bibby stared at him. "You're either a damn good poker player or you're truly ignorant, like your brothers. Which is it?"

Franklin didn't answer. He didn't know what Bibby was talking about and figured keeping quiet might not give away his ignorance. Besides,

Bibby had always had a big mouth. Franklin figured Bibby would tell him what the hell he was talking about, eventually.

Bibby smiled. "He didn't tell you, did he?"

"Who?"

"The idiot. That brother of yours."

"Don't call him that. You ain't family."

"Not yours, thank God. Evan."

"What didn't Evan tell me?"

Bibby laughed. "I'll be damned. He wanted her for himself, just like he wanted that sister of yours for himself."

Franklin still didn't understand what business the girl was to Bibby, unless he wanted her for *himself*. "I still don't know what you're talking about. So, if you don't mind." Franklin stepped forward, the wrench in hand.

Bibby fired a round into the dirt, just missing the front of Franklin's boot. Jackpot jumped and raced from the pump house. "I do mind."

Franklin stopped.

"The girl, Franklin. Where is she? Did you put her in the room at the back of the barn?"

Franklin stared at him and the realization slowly dawned—what business the girl was to Bibby. Shit. How did he miss it? His anger with what Evan had done, disobeying him, had blurred his vision and his common sense. Evan wouldn't hurt a fly, never had it in him. He never would have struck that girl.

"You were in the park that day," he said. "Taking Jackpot for a walk."

"And old Jackpot is a chick magnet. Everyone knows Jackpot and I walk that ravine same time every day. Figured once the word got out, somebody would say, 'Old Bibby walks that park every day' and the police would be on me like stink on shit. In this case I figured the best defense to be a good offense. I decided to call it in myself, say I saw her and that was it."

"You did more than see her. Didn't you?"

"Girl came running down the trail half-dressed and not to be ignored." Bibby licked his lips. "I'd never seen her before. And I make it a point to know everyone in my neighborhood. It was just too good an opportunity to pass up. Like old times again. Been some years, but the urges never go away, not even for an old fart like me."

"You hit her in the head with a rock or something. I should have known Evan never could have done that."

"She ran right past me, gave me a smile and a nod. She had no idea she was running into a dead end."

~

Bibby watched the young woman slow her pace, then stop. She stared at the metal guardrail across the trail and the red and yellow signs telling her to stop and not to trespass. She jogged in place and looked about, trying to determine

407

whether the trail continued to the right or the left. It didn't.

Time to let Jackpot work his magic. He released the dog and sent him down the path. Jackpot ran right up to her. She lowered and removed an earbud from her ear.

"Hey," she said, petting him. "Where'd you come from?"

Bibby stepped out and went down the trail calling for Jackpot. "Jackpot. Bad dog. Come over here. I'm real sorry, young lady. He got off the leash and never could resist a good-looking woman."

"That's okay," she said. She took a step back, away from him. "I grew up with dogs. You wouldn't know if the trail continues, would you?" she asked.

"Afraid not. Dead end."

"I was afraid of that." She gave him a worried smile. "Well, I better get a move on if I don't want to be running in the dark."

"No, you don't," Bibby said. "Let's think of something else you could do. Shall we?" He removed his hand from the pocket, the one holding the stone.

~

"Women never could resist Jackpot," Bibby said.

"Why didn't you just kill her when you had the chance?" Franklin said.

408

"I would have, except for that idiot brother of yours interfering."

"I warned you once not to call him that."

~

Bibby dragged the young woman from the trail into the bushes. He had always kept a fresh condom in his wallet. Didn't want to leave behind any DNA. Never had. Never would.

He looked down at the young woman, eager for another chance with something so young. She wasn't dead, not yet. But that wouldn't be a problem. And he had a perfect alibi, in case one of the neighbors brought up the fact that he walked Jackpot at this time every day. No one was going to believe a seventy-five-year-old man with a bad back raped and killed a fit, young woman out for a run. If the police came asking, and likely would, he'd tell them he'd seen her in the park, that they'd passed on the trail. That was it. Who was going to dispute it? Like Ed Sprague had always said: "The dead don't see. And they don't talk."

He had unbuckled his belt and the button on his pants when something rustled the bushes at the end of the trail. Odd, since there was no wind at the bottom of the ravine, and Jackpot was at his side. In the fading light he didn't see anyone. Jackpot, however, was better than night vision goggles. He had a nose infinitely more powerful than a human and ran up the hillside. Bibby saw cigarette smoke wafting above the bushes. He made out clothing, unnatural colors.

Bibby almost called out to him, then decided to leave him be.

～

"Evan was hiding on the hillside, or thought he was. Jackpot sniffed him out. You know what your brother said?"

Franklin shook his head. He could only imagine.

" 'Hey, Bibby.' " Bibby smiled. "Just like that. 'Hey, Bibby.' Then he said, 'What are you doing?' Either he hadn't seen a thing or had already forgotten. Back in the day I would have beat him and sent him home with a message to keep his mouth shut. But I'm not young anymore."

"No, you ain't," Franklin said.

"I figured I could be in a real bind if I didn't play it right. So I told him I'd found the girl there, unconscious, that it looked like she'd hit her head. He asked me what I was going to do. I said I was going to call the police but now I didn't think it was a good idea, that the police would consider him to be the primary suspect. By then I realized the idiot had left behind all kinds of evidence that would lead back to him and to you and Carrol. The Maxwells got that camera on the porch. I figured it would show Evan out walking around the same time the young girl headed to the park. And I knew they'd find his bootprints on the hillside. Didn't know he'd also left behind DNA."

"DNA?"

"The cigarette butt. I deduced that from the police questions. He left a butt behind the bushes. I told Evan, 'We can't call the police, not knowing who hurt her, maybe killed her.' I told him the police would think he did it, and they'd put his ass in jail."

Franklin clenched his jaw and balled his free hand into a fist.

"That scared him good. I thought he might cry. But I told him I'd help him. I told him that he needed to hide the girl, carry her back up to the house and put her in the basement. He was hesitant, until I said, 'I'll bet she'd play games with you for saving her, the way Lindsay did.'" Bibby laughed. "He actually smiled at that. Your brother was my perfect alibi. Hell, I doubted he'd even remember what had happened by the time he got her up to the house. Once he did, I knew I'd put the turd in your pocket. Even if Evan could remember, who were you going to call? You had your dad's problems to worry about buried in your basement."

"If you're so smart, Bibby, if the turd is now in my pocket, why'd you come up here?"

"Because the police kept coming by, asking me questions. My bootprints were in the ravine also, and Jackpot's paw prints. I came up with a story

411

for them. But then they came with questions for Lorraine."

"Lorraine? What'd they want with Lorraine?"

"They asked her about Lindsay."

"Lindsay?"

"That's right."

"Lindsay's dead."

"Presumed dead. We never did find out one way or the other. We don't know for certain. If they find her, well, then, I got problems as big as you."

"That's nonsense, Bibby. And Lindsay is dead. Hasn't been around in years."

"Maybe. Maybe not. I don't like loose ends. I learned that from your daddy."

Franklin looked at the gun, wondering if he could somehow get it. "Lindsay's dead and nobody's going to believe a word Evan says, Bibby, even if he could remember. Which he don't. And like you said, I can't say shit. So just walk on out of here and I'll take care of the rest. Why do you think I came up here?"

"You might be able to do that. But I figured Evan would tell Carrol, if he didn't already know, and Carrol never was a good liar, not with all that stuttering and spitting. And now he's at the house with a whole lot of police detectives. I don't like it."

"Evan didn't tell Carrol, and he didn't tell me. That should be clear by now. I'll take care of the girl, Bibby."

"So, she's still alive." Bibby looked out the door, to the barn.

"She's alive," Franklin said. "But I brought her up here to get rid of her. Let me do it. Like you said, my daddy left me with a whole bunch of turds. I can't very well run to the police."

"Something else your daddy liked to say."

"What was that?"

" 'The dead don't see. And they can't talk.' "

Bibby squeezed the trigger and the rifle fired.

CHAPTER 38

Herr pulled open the gate and Peterson drove through, then waited for him to get back into the cab on the other side. Tracy felt the cold air when Herr opened the cab door, and snowflakes fell onto the seat as Herr kicked his boots against the truck's side to knock off the snow.

The distinct crack of a rifle shot broke the snowy silence. Tracy turned to Peterson. He'd recognized the sound as well. "Let's go," he said.

Peterson drove forward before the door fully closed, nearly clipping it on a tree trunk. He drove as fast as the conditions allowed. The fresh tire tracks had compacted the snow, making it somewhat easier to get traction. The immediate problem was the wind-driven snow falling from the sky and from the tree branches, making for near whiteout conditions. Several minutes into the drive, a second rifle crack echoed.

Stephanie Cole sat shivering on the dirt floor, despite the blankets the men had left for her and Donna and Angel. Evan had offered her his jacket, but she had declined. She couldn't very well put it on with her hands chained to the pole, and when she asked him to remove the shackles, Evan said, "Franklin said I can't. I'll get a beating if I do."

He had taught her how to play the card game kings in the corner, and they had played twice already. He'd also brought board games—older games like Monopoly and something called Snakes and Ladders. Stephanie figured Evan had been the person who carried her from the ravine up to the basement in the house. That was why Franklin had been so upset, why he'd beaten Evan. She was having difficulty believing Evan had been the person who hit her or had presumably tried to rape her. He didn't seem the least bit interested in sex, and he gave no indication of an intent to harm her. He seemed only interested in playing games.

"Do you like board games?" she asked, looking at the stack behind him.

"We can play Monopoly after this," he said. He put a black six on a card trail. "Your turn."

Stephanie considered her options and put down a red five on the black six. She moved a black four from another string and put down an ace of spades on a third card trail.

"I hate aces," Evan said, rocking. "You can't do anything with them."

"Who taught you all these games?" Stephanie asked.

"Lindsay." He studied his cards, then picked

up one at a time from the pile in the center. As he did, he sang. "Pick 'em up. Da-da-da-da. Pick 'em up."

"Who's Lindsay?"

"My sister. We used to play all the time."

"She taught you?"

"Uh-huh."

"Where's your sister now?" Stephanie asked.

"Gone."

"Gone where?"

Evan played a card and shrugged. "Your turn."

As Stephanie considered her moves, she heard a sound in the distance like a car backfiring. She looked at Evan, who seemed not to have noticed the noise. Donna and Angel, though, stared off in the direction of the sound.

"It's your move," Evan said again.

She put down a red two, looking in the direction of the noise.

"You're not done," Evan said. "I liked to help Lindsay too."

As she studied the game, she heard another blast. So did the two women. No mistaking it now. Gunshots. Her hand trembled as she moved the black ace, and used the free space to put down a run of seven, eight, and nine in alternating colors. Then she put down a king in the corner. Her final card.

"You won," Evan said, looking up and smiling.

She felt sick to her stomach, but also a sense

of urgency. "Does your sister live near here?" She just wanted to keep him talking, find out as much as she could, maybe get him to trust her, to remove the shackles.

Evan gathered the cards. "I don't know," he said.

"Don't you ever get to see her?"

He shook his head and turned quickly for the stack of games.

"Evan—" she said.

"Let's play Monopoly."

"Evan—"

He looked to the other two women. "Do you want to play?"

"I do."

The voice came from the door behind them. A male voice. Stephanie looked up at a man in the doorway, his head covered in a cap with earflaps, a rifle in his hands. He looked vaguely familiar. What she remembered more distinctly, though, was the dog, a Jack Russell terrier wagging its tail and shaking its body.

"Hey, Bibby," Evan said. "Hey, Jackpot."

"Jackpot," Stephanie said under her breath and looked from the dog to the man. He smiled at her, the way he'd smiled at her on the trail. It gave her the creeps. In her memory she watched him raise the rock overhead.

Bibby motioned with his hand. "Go," he said to the dog.

Jackpot ran to Evan, who petted him. "What are you doing here?"

"Franklin invited me up to the cabin. Didn't he tell you?" Bibby asked.

Evan shook his head. He looked confused. "Franklin doesn't like you. He says you're a busybody."

"Did he? Well, I like Franklin. Who is your friend?" Bibby asked.

"That's Stephanie," Evan said. "She's my new sister."

"Is she? Where did she come from?"

Evan made a face. "I don't remember."

"You don't remember?" Bibby asked. He looked to Stephanie. "But you remember, don't you, young lady? I can see it in your eyes."

Stephanie didn't answer, but she put a hand to her back, feeling the piece of wood.

Evan said, "We're going to play Monopoly."

"That'll have to wait, Evan. Franklin asked me to come get you. He needs your help behind the house. He's splitting some wood."

Evan looked to the games. "He said I could play."

Bibby shook his head. "Guess he changed his mind. Said there were chores needed to be done. He said you could play after you helped him. Said to tell you that if you didn't come with me, he'd come get you, and he wouldn't be happy."

Evan let out a breath of air and stood. "Okay."

"Evan," Stephanie said, looking between the two men. "I don't think you should go."

"Now why would you involve yourself in something that has nothing to do with you?" Bibby said. "Come on, Evan."

"Evan," Stephanie said again. "I want to play Monopoly. Let's play now."

Evan shook his head. "I got to do what Franklin says."

"Evan," she called out, but he'd run out the door.

Bibby looked back at her and smiled. "I'll be back. Maybe we can play our own games."

CHAPTER 39

Peterson gunned the engine up the final slope in the road. Tracy felt the truck tires spinning, the back end fishtailing. The tires gripped and the truck lurched forward. Peterson stopped behind a Jeep Cherokee and a white van parked in a turnaround. Snowflakes fluttered to the ground, making it difficult to see. The three officers exited the cab. Peterson and Herr kept the rifles at their side. Tracy removed her Glock. They proceeded cautiously, watching the windows in the house, the barn door, the tree line.

They moved along the side of the house to a small shed.

"Pump house," Peterson said softly.

When they reached the doorway, a blood-red streak in the snow led away from the pump house, as if someone had been dragged. Tracy saw fear in Herr's eyes. She figured this was a baptism by fire. Tracy thought of the two shots they had heard, as she followed the trail of blood around a corner, the pistol extended. Halfway across the snow-covered ground, a body lay facedown, already partially covered with falling snow. The body had not been dragged. Tracy could tell from the divots in the snow where the man had dug in his elbows, knees, and the toes of his boots; the

420

man had crawled on his belly. They approached cautiously.

Tracy dropped to a knee and rolled him over. Franklin Sprague.

Bibby beat them here and was tying up loose ends, as she had feared.

Franklin's eyes were shut. His face ashen. She checked his neck for a pulse, didn't find one. All the while she had her head up, eyes scanning her perimeter, the tree line, and the distant barn. Peterson, too, kept his rifle raised, swinging it left and right.

Peterson spoke to Herr. "Go back to the truck. Call the station and ask for all available officers. Have them radio the sheriff in Kittitas County. Tell him to send officers."

Herr took off for the truck. Tracy looked to Peterson. "That's a rifle wound. We might be sitting ducks out here in the open."

"Thinking the same thing. Let's move."

Tracy stood and together they moved toward the barn, pointing at multiple sets of footprints in the snow, including dog prints. Jackpot. She looked to Peterson for an acknowledgment that he, too, had seen the tracks. He nodded.

She and Peterson moved quietly but deliberately. No time to waste now.

At the barn, they didn't have much cover. The walls were dilapidated wood. Peterson stood to the side and used the rifle muzzle to push on the barn door. It swung in. The interior was dark, lit only by the ambient light filtering through the wood slats and rough holes in the wood siding.

A huge barn owl screeched and launched from an upper rafter, swooping down at them. Startled, Tracy ducked just as the owl passed a foot from the top of her head, then continued out the barn door. Peterson let out a held breath.

"Evan?" A woman's voice. "Evan, come back."

They moved inside, to a horse stall at the back of the barn. A door had been opened. It looked to have been added sometime after the original barn was built. She pulled on a handle and slid the door farther back, then waited a beat. When the response wasn't a rifle shot, she and Peterson went in with guns aimed. Tracy moved to the left, Peterson to the right.

Handcuffed to three wooden poles in the center of a rectangular room were three women. They sat wrapped in horse blankets. Tracy recognized the one closest to the door. Stephanie Cole. She looked to the others and recalled the two cold case files, Donna Jones and Angel Jackson, though the two women were painfully thinner than their pictures in their files.

"He took Evan," Cole said. "He said Franklin wanted him."

"Who?" Tracy asked.

"Evan called him Bibby."

"Which way did they go?" Tracy asked.

Cole pointed to an open door on the other side of the room. "They went out that way, just a few minutes ago. The man has a rifle."

"Stay with them," Peterson said.

"No," Tracy said. "You stay. In case the man comes back."

"Take my rifle," Peterson said.

"Don't need it," she said. Tracy could put a bullet in a bottle opening at ten yards.

She hurried out the back, following the footprints. Two sets. They could not have gone far, not in this deep snow. She moved between the trees, hoping to reach them before she heard another rifle crack. A few minutes into her trek, she was sweating and out of breath but glad she'd stayed in shape during her time away. Her hands hurt from the cold. She stopped. Listened over the sound of her own breathing.

Voices. Faint.

She pushed away from the tree and followed the trail to a bend. The snowfall intensified, making it difficult to see. An eerie silence enveloped her. Around the bend she spotted two men in the falling snow. They stood twenty-five yards down a shin-deep path they'd forged. Bibby and Evan Sprague. Evan walked in the lead. Bibby was behind him, holding a rifle. She could hear the muffled sound of their voices, but with the wind and swirling snow, she could not decipher their conversation.

• • •

"Why would Franklin be out here?" Evan asked as he trudged through the snow. "This isn't where we keep the woodpile."

"I couldn't tell you," Bibby said. He had trouble catching his breath. He wanted to get the idiot as far away from the house as possible, where the coyotes would come and eat the body, maybe even gray wolves, which were said to have returned to the area. "But this is where he told me to bring you."

"There's no trail. He would have left a trail," Evan said.

Maybe he wasn't such an idiot after all, Bibby thought. "Sometimes it's like a light comes on in that thick skull of yours, Evan, and you aren't as dull a bulb as everyone thinks, are you?"

"I don't understand you, Bibby." Evan called out Franklin's name several times.

Bibby had run out of steam, but he figured they'd gone far enough. "Okay, Evan. I think this is the spot."

Evan turned. "I don't think—why are you aiming the rifle at me, Bibby? Daddy always told us to point the muzzle at the ground until we mean to shoot."

"There you go remembering again. Your memory comes and goes, doesn't it?"

"I guess."

"And that is the problem. You don't remember

what happened on the trail, with that girl, but one day it might just come back to you."

Evan scrunched his face. "I don't understand you, Bibby."

"That's not important now." Bibby leveled the rifle at Evan's chest.

Tracy slid behind a pine tree but kept her eyes on the two men. She'd moved closer, fifteen yards. She didn't trust her aim at this distance, not with the wind and the driving snow. Not with her body shivering and her hands cold and numb. She should have taken Peterson's rifle. Arrogance. She hoped her arrogance didn't get Evan and her killed.

She blew on her hands, alternately shifting the gun from her right to her left. Then she moved forward, behind the trees, approaching from the side so she had an angle to shoot, if she had to. She didn't want to be behind Bibby and miss, hit Evan.

Confusion was etched on Evan's face. Bibby had the muzzle pointed at him. Tracy moved again, to the next tree, slow going in the unpacked snow. Ten yards.

She leaned out from behind the tree trunk, her pistol aimed at Bibby. Evan spotted her and shifted his attention to her. Bibby turned his gaze from Evan to Tracy and quickly got off a round. She pulled behind the trunk and heard the bullet graze the tree, a chunk of bark splintering near her face. She yelled, "Evan. Run."

When she leaned out, Evan had stumbled to his right. Bibby had moved to his left, seeking cover behind a tree trunk. He pointed the rifle in the direction Evan had run. Tracy fired two shots, hitting the tree trunk and forcing Bibby to pull back the rifle barrel.

When she could no longer see Evan, who had disappeared into the tree line, she yelled, "It's over, Bibby. We know all about you and Ed Sprague. We know what you did. There are cadaver dogs in the space under the house. We'll bring them out here and find more bodies."

"I don't know what you're talking about," Bibby said.

"We know you killed Franklin, Bibby. And Cole remembers you from the trail," she said, to make Bibby's situation seem even more hopeless. "It was you who hit her. That's enough right there."

No answer.

"There are officers at the barn. They heard the gunshots. They'll be coming, Bibby. Your only chance is to put down the rifle."

No answer.

"Bibby, don't do this to your wife and your family. Just come."

A rifle crack broke the silence, but no bullet hit the tree or brushed past it. Tracy waited a beat, then leaned out. The rifle had dropped from

Bibby's hands. A moment later, his body toppled to the side and fell into the snow.

"Coward," Tracy said, stepping out from the scene. "Coward in life and a coward in death." She hoped he burned in the same hell he'd created for so many women here on earth.

CHAPTER 40

Minutes after the final crack of Bibby's barrel, Tracy heard the sound of boots crunching snow and someone breathing heavily. She looked up from taking pictures with her cell phone. Pete Peterson came up the trail Evan had made fleeing. He looked at Brian Bibby lying in the snow, then to Tracy.

"He shot himself," she said.

After a moment, Peterson said, "I'll tell the paramedics it's a body retrieval. Who is he?"

"A neighbor of the Spragues down in Seattle, but that isn't the whole picture, far from it," she said. "I assume Evan made it back to the barn?"

Peterson nodded. "The young man? He's kneeling over the body in the snow. I had Herr handcuff him and stay with him. I'm going to need copies of any photographs you've taken and to get a statement."

"What you're going to need to get is a CSI team with cadaver dogs out here when the snow melts to look for more bodies."

Peterson's eyes narrowed.

"There could be many," Tracy said. "In the interim, you may want to search for the names of any missing girls from around here, though I suspect they're more likely to be women from Seattle."

Peterson swore. "What the hell was this place?"

"My partner stumbled onto a house from hell in Seattle," she said. "The Spragues own this cabin as well. The father was a psychopath. Bibby here also. Two on the same block. One playing off the other, perhaps, feeding their sickness. They preyed on women. I assume they did much of it here." She blew on her hands. "Is Herr watching the girls?"

"We cut them loose with the bolt cutter. They're wrapped in thermal blankets and eating PowerBars. We'll get them to the KVH Hospital in Ellensburg for treatment. I imagine they're dehydrated, among other things."

"Dehydration will be the least of their problems," Tracy said. "Let's get back. You can lead the evidence team out here."

They walked back down the trail to the cabin. The three women stood inside the barn wrapped in the silver thermal blankets, looking uncertain and unsure what to do. Outside, Evan knelt in the snow, like a penitent over his brother's body, which was covered by a blue tarp. Evan had his head down, his hands cuffed behind his back. Tracy checked on the three women, but they said little. They looked to be in shock. She reassured them they had ambulances and medical personnel coming, and that she would stop by the hospital

429

later to ask them questions and take a statement.

"Can I call my parents and tell them I'm okay?" Stephanie Cole asked.

"Sure." Tracy handed the young woman her cell phone.

Cole accepted the phone with thanks but didn't dial right away. She looked to Evan. "Is he slow?" Cole asked.

Tracy nodded.

"Is he the one who carried me from the ravine and took me back to his house? His brother said he did. He beat him for doing it."

"I imagine," Tracy said.

"He never touched me though. He never did anything to me."

"We'll get all the details later," Tracy said.

"What will happen to him?" Cole asked. She sounded genuinely concerned.

"I don't know," Tracy said.

"He just wanted to play games. He said his sister taught him."

Tracy nodded. "Make your call. I'm sure your parents are beside themselves with worry."

"I never should have left," Cole said. "I just want to go home."

Tracy thought Cole was lucky to say those words and to mean them. For so many, home wasn't a place of comfort and love, far from it.

She walked to where Evan knelt. *He might be slow,* she thought, *but he wasn't stupid.* That's what Lindsay Sheppard had said. No one had ever taken the time to teach him.

She put a hand on his shoulder. Evan looked at her. Tears streaked his cheeks. "Are you all right, Evan?"

"Bibby shot him. Bibby killed him."

"I'm afraid so."

"Franklin hated Bibby. Bibby was mean."

"I know," she said. "Did you see Bibby on the trail that day you found Stephanie?" Tracy pointed so that Evan knew who she was talking about. Evan put his head down. "It's okay, Evan. You're not going to get in trouble if you tell me."

"I liked her. She reminded me of Lindsay."

"Did you hide behind the log?"

"I just wanted to see her and ask if she wanted to play games."

"Did you see what happened?"

"I don't remember."

"It's okay," Tracy said.

She wanted to tell him that Lindsay was still alive. She thought, in his moment of sorrow, he could use some good news. But it wasn't her place. It wasn't her place to assume Lindsay would want Evan to know she was still alive. She'd lived once in the house of horrors. She might not want a reminder of those days.

"You saved her life, Evan. You saved Stephanie's life, twice."

"Bibby was bad. Franklin said so."

"Let's get you a blanket before you freeze."

Evan stood with Tracy's help. "Franklin took care of me. Who will take care of me?"

Tracy didn't say anything more, not wanting to lie to the man. He'd been mistreated and lied to most of his life.

She looked to the barn, to where Stephanie Cole, Donna Jones, and Angel Jackson stood watching. They were alive, she told herself. They were all still alive. That was something to take pride in, but at the moment she couldn't take much joy in it. She knew there had been many before them who had not lived. Many they would find in the months to come.

CHAPTER 41

Late that night, Tracy met Kins in the Polar Bar on Third Avenue in downtown Seattle. Neither felt like going home. Tracy had called Dan and told him she'd be late. She gave him a brief accounting of what had happened but didn't share details.

"Are you all right?" was all he asked.

"I'm looking forward to coming home," she said. "But first I need to meet with Kins."

The A Team occasionally met after work for a drink at a bar, a place to socialize, catch up on each other's lives, and do just about anything but talk shop. A place to reset. The Arctic Club hotel harkened back to an early time in Seattle's history. The hotel and bar had been a social club for men returning from the Yukon gold rush flush with money and stories to tell. They sat on plush leather seats amid fine Alaskan marble, and grand crystal chandeliers and velvet drapes.

The Polar Bar had developed from that same theme, featuring a mahogany bar atop blue glass that looked like glacial ice.

Kins had chosen the bar. Tracy understood why. Kins needed to be someplace completely unlike the Sprague home. He needed to be in a place of luxury and opulence, even for just a few hours. When Tracy entered the room, he sat on a stool at the end of the bar with his back to the wood-paneled walls.

"Is this seat taken?" Tracy asked.

Kins smiled. He gripped a glass of what was most likely Johnnie Walker Black. "Crosswhite, are you hitting on me? I'm a married man."

Tracy chuckled and slid onto the barstool. This late, the place was quiet. When the bartender caught her eye, she said, "What he's having. A double." She turned to Kins. "Did you call home?"

"Told Shannah I'd be late. You?"

"Yeah."

"You're lucky," Kins said.

"Why's that?"

"You have a kid to go home to."

"You miss your boys," she said.

"Every day. Every night when I get home. I keep asking myself where the years went. Don't get me wrong, I love the time with Shannah, but those years with the boys . . ." He chuckled and shook his head. "As frustrated as I could get by all the things they did, those were the best years of my life." He paused, thinking. "It wasn't the sporting events or stuff like that I remember."

"What was it?"

"It was Christmas mornings, birthdays, special occasions—those quiet times when their eyes lit up and they believed that anything in the world was possible. Magical. Beautiful."

"You gave them those memories, Kins. You and Shannah. You were a good father to them. You still are." She thought of Nunzio. "You know why?"

Kins looked at her.

"Because you give a shit."

Kins chuckled.

In the darkness, the evil, and the horrors they often experienced, it was important to be reminded that there were still beautiful things in the world. There was still goodness. Still joy. Light.

Like Shannah and Kins's boys.

Like Dan and Daniella.

The bartender put her drink on a coaster. Kins motioned for another. The whiskey was smooth and warmed her body.

"Kelly make it out to the house?" Kelly Rosa, the forensic anthropologist, had been the one to exhume and identify Sarah's remains. She'd be the one to dig up the bodies buried in the basement, however many there were.

"We'll start again in the morning," Kins said. "I suspect we'll end up tearing the whole house down to find out how many bodies are there. It's a cemetery."

"I think the cabin might be also," she said, and she told him about what had happened, about Franklin and Bibby and about Evan. "She's alive, Kins. We found Cole alive, and the two other women, Angel Jackson and Donna Jones. Cole will go home to her family. That's something, Kins. Something to be proud of."

The bartender brought Kins's second drink. He lifted his glass. Tracy reciprocated, but neither made a toast. Nothing seemed appropriate. No words could put it all in perspective, no pearls of wisdom, no joke to make them smile.

CHAPTER 42

As the weeks passed, the body count grew. By the time Kelly Rosa had finished at the house, she'd identified seven bodies, female, buried in the basement. She estimated the oldest had been there for decades. It would take months to identify them, all young women, long forgotten but for the people who had loved them most. When spring came and the ground in the canyon thawed, Tracy was certain they would find still more bodies. But that would wait. Seven bodies. Three women still alive. One active case and, hopefully, nine cold cases solved. Nine tombstones she would be able to remove from Nunzio's shelves. She'd remove more in the spring. She was, unfortunately, sure of it.

She'd been back to the neighborhood and spoke to the neighbors. No one knew anything about what had transpired in the house. Even Lorraine Bibby looked sickened. She told Tracy that Bibby had always told her he was going hunting with Ed when he'd left the house. She'd never suspected there had been anything more to it. Either she was telling the truth—or telling herself what she wanted to believe.

Marcella Weber, Seattle's recently hired chief of police, quickly got out press releases of the solid police investigation in Tracy's first week on the job that was expected to solve multiple cases. She made Tracy available for media interviews. One morning she called Tracy into her office and advised that Tracy would receive the department's Medal of Valor, its highest honor, for a third time.

"I'm honored," Tracy said, though medals weren't really her thing. "But I won't accept it, unless Kins receives it also." She thought it would be the perfect remedy for Kins—who remained depressed—to have his sons see their father honored.

Weber agreed.

The medals were presented at a Seattle Police Department awards ceremony in the Washington State Criminal Justice Training Center's auditorium in Burien. Tracy had one other request of Weber, and again the chief of police agreed.

As Tracy and Kins stood onstage in their dress blue uniforms, the auditorium filled with their colleagues, family and friends, and news media. Weber stood at the podium, speaking to the assembled crowd.

"The Medal of Valor is awarded to any officer who distinguishes him- or herself by an act of bravery or heroism, at risk of his or her own personal safety, or in the face of great danger, above and beyond the call of duty. Today we honor Violent Crimes detectives Tracy

Crosswhite and Kinsington Rowe for acts of heroism and bravery that led to the solving of at least two cold cases, more pending forensics review, and one active file. Because of their heroism and unrelenting investigative work, families have been reunited, and others will finally obtain closure.

"Detective Crosswhite has requested that their medals be bestowed on them by their captain, Johnny Nolasco."

Nolasco rose from his seat in his blue ceremonial uniform and white gloves. He placed his captain's hat squarely on his head. Kins glanced over at Tracy and spoke out of the corner of his mouth. "Crosswhite," he whispered. "You are a vengeful bitch. If I die of laughter on this stage, I am taking you with me."

Tracy tried not to smile. She was saving it.

Nolasco approached a table draped in blue that contained two black wooden boxes. He opened the first and removed the medal, then walked stiffly to where Kins was doing his best, but failing, to stifle a smile.

"Officer Rowe," Nolasco said, "for valor beyond the call of duty, the Seattle Police Department awards you the Medal of Valor." He slipped the blue ribbon with gold trim around Kins's neck and shook his hand. "Congratulations."

"Thank you, Captain," Kins said.

Nolasco stepped back, bent his arm at the elbow, and gave Kins a stiff salute. Kins returned the gesture, which the two men held for several seconds while cameras clicked and whirred.

Nolasco stepped back to the table, opened the second box, and removed the medal. He pivoted and stepped stiffly until he stood in front of Tracy. He pivoted a second time and faced her. Though Nolasco did his best not to show any emotion, Tracy knew her request to Weber that he bestow her medal was killing him. Chief Weber, not cognizant of their dislike of one another, had told Tracy that Nolasco seemed surprised that she had specifically asked that he award her the medal.

Surprised. No doubt.

"Detective Crosswhite," Nolasco said. "For valor beyond the call of duty, the Seattle Police Department awards you the Medal of Valor." He stepped forward and slipped the ribbon around Tracy's neck, looking her in the eye. She smiled.

Nolasco did not. He stepped back and shook her hand. "Congratulations."

"Thank you, Captain," Tracy said, maintaining eye contact.

There was a momentary pause, as if Nolasco almost couldn't bring himself to salute her, but he snapped rigid and did so. Tracy held the salute while the cameras whirred and clicked. She and Nolasco locked eyes. She refused to look away.

After several seconds, Nolasco broke the salute.

At the reception following the ceremony Tracy stepped toward Dan, Daniella, and Therese. She would have taken her daughter, but Vera, Faz's wife and Daniella's godmother, held her, and Tracy could tell Vera wasn't about to let her go.

Dan kissed and congratulated her.

"You looked grand up there in your blue uniform," Therese said. "Something about a lady in a uniform. Am I right, Mr. O?"

Dan smiled. "You have no idea," he said.

Therese lowered her voice. "I don't want to say anything out of turn, but I think your captain held your salute a bit longer than with the other bloke."

Tracy smiled. "I think you're right." She looked at Dan, who knew what she had done. He shook his head, smiling. "All Crosswhite. What am I going to do with you?"

She smiled. "We'll think of something."

"Hey, Professor." Faz approached with a plate of food. He flipped her the middle finger.

"Vic," Vera said.

"What? That's an Italian salute. It's a show of respect."

Vera rolled her eyes. Tracy and the others laughed. Faz leaned in, lowering his voice. "I took about a thousand pictures so you can document the look on Nolasco's face. He looked like he was sucking on yellow jackets while someone was giving him a wedgie, and he was wearing a thong."

Tracy laughed. "TMI, Faz. TMI."

She walked through the crowd to Kins and his family, greeting Shannah and their three boys. They looked like him. After greetings, Kins took her elbow and they stepped aside. "Did you hear Kucek is retiring end of the year?" Kins asked.

"No."

"Fernandez has volunteered to take his spot on the B Team. Looks like I'm going to get my partner back."

Tracy smiled, but she wasn't sure she'd go back, not right away. Working cold cases gave her an autonomy she'd never had working active cases. As Nunzio had pitched it, she could make her hours, spend more time with her family, and there was certainly something to be said for that. She wasn't naïve. She knew, as Nunzio had warned, that you couldn't let your emotions get too high or too low, but she was certainly enjoying the high.

She'd go see Lisa Walsh again, probably more than once, for those moments when her cases brought her too low, and she'd remember what awaited her when she got home, Dan and Daniella. Like Stephanie Cole, she was lucky. She couldn't imagine a time when she wouldn't want to go home to her family.

CHAPTER 43

A week later, Tracy drove her Subaru east on Interstate 90. Evan sat in the passenger seat, a stack of board games in his lap.

Carrol Sprague, upon learning of Franklin's death, spilled his guts. He told Tracy and Kins in multiple interviews that taking the prostitutes and holding them captive had been Franklin's idea. Maybe so. But Carrol had been a willing participant, and Donna Jones provided Tracy a statement of the intimate details of Carrol's mistreatment of her during her months in captivity. At Carrol's preliminary arraignment, the Superior Court judge denied bail, not because she thought Carrol was a flight risk, but because of the heinous nature of his alleged crimes.

Rick Cerrabone told Tracy and Kins that Carrol's court-appointed defense attorney was inquiring about a plea deal, one that would keep Carrol locked up for decades, possibly for the remainder of his life. Tracy felt relief. A plea deal would not require Lindsay Sheppard to testify in court about what had happened in that home.

Lindsay and Tracy had met on several more occasions, usually with Aileen present to provide moral support. Each meeting, Lindsay provided further details about what she knew of the other women Ed Sprague buried in the basement of his home and around the cabin, which wasn't a lot. It was mostly perfunctory. With Ed Sprague dead and Brian Bibby's suicide, there was no one to prosecute. No one to convict. No one to bring to justice for the women's families. There was no evidence to prove Lorraine Bibby knew more than she claimed, and Tracy doubted she had known much anyway. She believed the old woman's only real crime was a failure to look too deeply into the tortured and horrific things she undoubtedly speculated her husband had participated in. She'd live in her own hell for the remainder of her life because of it.

But closure was important to the families, Tracy knew, and she'd bring it to those she could.

Tracy asked Lindsay during one of her interviews if telling her story was too difficult. With Ed Sprague and Brian Bibby both dead, there wasn't a real need. Lindsay gave the question a lot of thought before she said that talking about what had happened to her had been "cathartic" for both her and her sister. "I finally have the chance to tell my story to someone, instead of hiding it."

The two sisters were seeing a psychologist, to learn how to better deal with their anger and pain.

They'd also told their husbands. But Lindsay said she'd never tell her daughter, that she'd never burden her with that knowledge. She had not been conceived in love, but she'd been born and raised in love. That was enough.

During one of the interviews, Lindsay asked what would become of Evan, if he, too, would go to jail. Tracy told Lindsay that Cole told her and the prosecutor that Evan had never harmed her, never touched her or the other two girls, and how Evan had likely saved her life that evening in the ravine. They had no evidence of any other crime.

"Where will he go?" Lindsay asked.

"He'll be placed in a state institution," Tracy said.

Lindsay cringed.

"It's not like *One Flew Over the Cuckoo's Nest*," she said. "They're more regulated. Evan will be allowed to work and learn to do things he never had the chance to do before."

Lindsay smiled, though with tears in her eyes. "Can I visit him?"

"Of course," Tracy said. "Whenever you're ready."

An hour and a half into their drive, Tracy pulled up to the one-story modular home with the brown picket fence on the corner lot in Union Gap.

As Evan and Tracy stepped from the car, the front door to the house opened. Lindsay came down the walk. The rest of her family, her husband, daughter, son, sister, brother-in-law, and their children and grandparents, remained in the threshold, watching.

Evan studied her, but only for a moment. Then he smiled. "Hi, Lindsay," he said, as if he had just seen her moments ago, not years.

"Hi, Evan," she said.

"I brought board games," he said.

Lindsay nodded, tears streaming down her cheeks. "I can see that. Do you want to play?"

CHAPTER 44

Tracy kept a scheduled Monday morning visit with Lisa Walsh. It was a chance to check in, to reset, and to get prepared for what lay ahead that week. She'd come to enjoy the sessions, though the subject matter was, at times, difficult. She was working through it.

She'd decided not to retake her position on the A Team. Not yet. Before she'd turned it down, she'd spoken to Chief Marcella Weber and told her she wanted to work cold cases for a while, and she'd like a greater commitment on the department's part, another dedicated detective to help ease the load, and a directive to make the cases a priority when Tracy sought the crime lab's help.

Weber was receptive to each of her suggestions.

She asked for one more concession. "I want to keep working a few active cases, if the A Team needs my help. And if I burn out working cold cases, I want the chance to return to the A Team, if I can be accommodated without it impacting anyone else."

Weber, a tough African American woman who had come from Baltimore, nodded. "The detectives sure want you."

"I know," she said.

But now, so did the families of the other cold

case victims. After word spread that Tracy had solved two cold cases, with more being solved in Seattle and Curry Canyon, the phone in her office had been ringing off the hook. Family members of other victims pleaded with her to look at their file next. It had been heart-wrenching.

After her visit to Walsh, Tracy returned to Police Headquarters, grabbed a cup of herbal tea, and made her way to her office. It was a mess, binders all over the place. Whenever Kelly Rosa identified another victim, Tracy spoke to the family, then closed the file. It was an elaborate process, but she wanted a hand in it. She didn't want those families to simply receive a phone call. She delivered the news in person if she could. If the family was out of state, she made the telephone call herself, and she helped each make arrangements to have the body properly buried. Advocates from Victim Support Services also helped the families, and they ensured each was treated with dignity and respect.

Most families expressed relief amid their anger and their pain, happy to finally know what had happened to their child or their sister. Happy to no longer be in a state of limbo. They didn't ask for many details. They didn't want to know. As one mother said, "It's enough that we have the chance to bury her, and to know that she's now in a better place. Retribution doesn't bring closure. Peace of mind brings closure."

Tracy knew that too.

Tracy vowed to straighten her office that morning and started with the black binders. Those cases she had closed, she prepared for storage. Those she had not, she marked with a blue sticker and put back on the shelf. In the process, she found the Elle Chin binder open on her desk. It gave her pause.

She had no new leads, and she worried this might be one of those cases Nunzio said she'd just have to learn to live with. She couldn't save them all.

She sat in her desk chair and looked through her interview notes, some she had not yet had the time to type up. She found the notes of her conversation with Evelyn Robertson, the Chins' neighbor, and scanned what she had written. She had noted Robertson's final comment, and she could still recall the woman's face when she'd said it. Robertson had looked pensive, as if not finding Elle Chin might not have been a bad thing.

"So sad they never found that little girl, but . . ."

Tracy waited. "But . . ."

Robertson shook her head. "Nothing," she said. "It's just sad."

Officer Bill Miller had made his own sad commentary on the entire situation. *"I just hope, for the little girl's sake, that she's alive somewhere. Alive and safe and that neither of them has any further contact with her. That's the kid's only hope for a normal life, in my opinion."*

She thought of her interview of Jimmy Ingram and the brief glimpse he'd had of the little girl. She hadn't been crying or struggling. She'd been holding the woman's hand. Tracy sat back. Ingram had never said "Asian woman." But Jewel Chin had repeatedly used the word "Asian."

Bobby Chin said he'd found Elle's wings on the ground. He said Elle had been proud of those wings, so much so that he couldn't get her to put on a coat. Wouldn't she have been upset to leave them?

Ingram said the little girl he saw wore a coat, which led Tracy again to believe it had not been Elle unless . . . What if Ingram had been accurate? What if it had been Elle? What would that mean about the woman Elle had gone with?

"Someone Elle knew. Someone she would have trusted. Someone Elle loved," Tracy said aloud. But if that were the case, then the abductor would have had to have been someone who also understood Elle's situation and took Elle believing, as Robertson and Miller had believed, that Elle was better without either parent.

Tracy recalled her interview of Elle's preschool teacher, Lynn Bettencourt. She'd thought the same thing, and Bettencourt had spent every weekday with Elle.

"Detective?" Bettencourt had said.

Tracy stopped. Bettencourt looked troubled. "Something else?"

"Earlier, you asked for my judgment."

"Yes."

"I don't think either living situation was a healthy environment for that little girl . . . Let me put it this way. I see a lot of kids in difficult home situations, and usually one of the parents is more to blame—they're lashing out and blaming their spouse for what has happened. The other spouse becomes the child's protector, the person who swallows their own pain or pride and puts the child first."

"But not here."

She shook her head. "Unfortunately, not."

Tracy again thought of Jewel Chin, of the interview in the dining room of the staged house. Jewel Chin had certainly been a piece of work, but she didn't strike Tracy as sick or mean-spirited enough to harm her own daughter just to spite her husband. Neither had Bobby Chin. But Jewel kept repeating evidence that no one else said. She kept saying the woman who had taken Elle had been "Asian." Was it just a casual slip of the tongue or did Jewel know, or perhaps suspect she knew, who took Elle? If Jewel did know or suspect, why had she not told the detectives . . . not told Tracy?

It made Tracy think of Evan Sprague. No one, not even his mother, had acted in his best interests. He was better off without his family. He was better off with Lindsay, not a parent, more a sibling who had been willing to do the right thing and look out for Evan's best interests.

Tracy would never forget what Lindsay had said to her. What had compelled the young woman to run away.

"I knew I would be better off with people thinking I was dead than living another day in that house."

And that was when it all came together, not like a lightning bolt, but like an electrical pulse, just enough to make Tracy sit up and go back through the notes, back through what they had all said. Who was in a position to know the damage Elle was suffering, the little girl's pain? Who spent time with Elle during the divorce? Who would Elle have trusted, loved enough to leave her wings?

She pulled out the file she'd copied from Lynn Bettencourt, the one with the names of the people authorized to pick up Elle from school. Tracy sat back and wondered how she and Nunzio, and the detectives working the active case, had missed it. Had it just been too difficult to even imagine? Had it been unfathomable that a sibling would inflict such pain on another sibling?

What if that pain was to save an innocent child?

And maybe to save the sibling, who had been spiraling out of control, as well.

A sister. An Asian woman. Gloria Chin.

EPILOGUE

Chengdu, China

Tracy stepped from the Chengdu airport, tired after a long flight with a stopover in Beijing. It didn't help that she was put through an extensive customs search and barely made her connecting flight. She knew little of Chengdu, except that it was one of the most populous cities in China, with more than fourteen million residents. It was most famous, however, for its nonhuman inhabitants—the giant pandas kept at the Chengdu Research Base of Giant Panda Breeding, which attracted tens of millions of tourists each year.

Her guide for the day, a midthirties Chinese man, held a sign with her name on it amid the throng of people waiting behind baggage-claim barriers. Tracy had only brought a carry-on. She didn't plan on staying in the country long. She'd managed to obtain a visa after much sweat and only with some high-level help within the United States government. She had not come in an official SPD capacity, and she'd used personal funds to obtain the visa and to fly to China.

Tracy was grateful to learn that her driver had a strong command of English, though accented.

453

"How was your flight?" he asked.

"Long," she said.

"China is a very big country. Like your country."

"What is your name?" she asked.

"Bruce Wayne," he said.

"Bruce Wayne is your name? Like Bruce Wayne from the *Batman* movies?"

He smiled. "Yes. That is my *English* name. Bruce Wayne. I'm Batman." He mimicked the character's signature movie line.

Tracy laughed. "Okay, Bruce. Lead the way."

Bruce led her to a black Nissan in the garage and put her bag in the backseat. She kept her briefcase with her. "You wish to go to the hotel to sleep, or go to see the giant pandas?"

"I have an address." She pulled the sheet of paper from a file compiled for her by an investigator in Chengdu she had personally hired without SPD's knowledge and also using her own funds. She handed the paper to Bruce Wayne. "Can you take me here?"

"Yes, yes. We can use 'Find,'" he said putting in the address on his phone. "No problem. We find. You here for business or pleasure?"

"Pleasure," she said, smiling but not saying more. "How long is the drive to that address?"

"About forty-five minutes," he said. "But I am fast driver, like Batmobile."

Tracy checked her watch. "Don't worry about driving fast. I prefer to get there alive."

They talked about China and what she was seeing along the drive. All around the freeway stood high-rise apartment complexes, dozens of them. Each building looked identical to the next, lined up like dominoes. "I've never seen so many apartment buildings," Tracy said.

"The government is building them for the people," Bruce said. "It is part of the movement of people from rural areas into the city. The government helps the farmers losing their land." Tracy had read that China was moving away from small rural farms to large industrial farms.

"Do the farmers own the apartments?" she asked.

"The government owns the land but it provides a seventy-year lease."

"What happens after seventy years?"

"The government has not told us."

"That wouldn't fly in the United States."

"Fly?"

"The people wouldn't agree to do that. When we buy something, we own it for as long as we want, until we die or decide to sell it."

"You know what is problem in United States?" Bruce asked, though it sounded rhetorical.

Tracy was curious. "No. What is the problem, Bruce?"

"You have too many choices."

"Do we?"

"Here, the government tells us what to do and it is done."

Tracy nodded, but she didn't take the bait. For all she knew, there were cameras and microphones in the car. The private investigator had willingly helped her, but he did not want to be with her in China. She checked her watch, which she'd set to Chengdu time. "What time do children get out of school?" she asked.

"This depends on school. Age of student. I would say between three and three thirty."

Tracy looked at her watch. She'd have a few minutes to wait.

After forty minutes, Bruce Wayne exited the freeway, driving surface streets past apartment buildings and business parks. Most of the businesses were vacant, as were most of the apartment buildings. They continued until they came to two-story detached homes in a more rural neighborhood. There were lawns and trees. In fields behind the homes, smoke drifted from small burning piles of leaves, adding to the already smog-choked air.

"I know this area," Bruce said. "Much money here."

"These are homes?" she asked.

"Villas."

Bruce slowed further, turning left and right, listening to his GPS. He came upon a three-story stucco home with a red-tile roof and a circular driveway. "This is villa. Bruce Wayne never fails. This a friend of yours?"

"Yes," Tracy said, considering the house. It was, by American standards, rudimentary. The top floor looked to be open, without windows or doors. Articles of clothing hung on a line stretched from one side of the building to the other. "But they're not expecting me. My coming will be a surprise. Park down the street."

Bruce looked confused, or concerned, but Tracy offered no more information. "This is stakeout? *Hawaii Five-O?*"

"No stakeout, Bruce. Just waiting." She was paying him by the hour, and figured he'd do as she asked. They drove down the street to wait. The private investigator had confirmed that Gloria Liu, her married name, had a daughter, age ten.

After fifteen minutes, schoolchildren walked down the sidewalk toward them, all dressed in the same light-green uniform with red scarves and carrying the same gray backpack. The students peeled off from the herd to the surrounding homes. A girl, who looked to be the right age, walked down the circular drive to the home Tracy and Bruce sat watching.

Tracy started from the car.

"You want me to come? Be translator?" Wayne asked.

"It won't be necessary," Tracy said. "They speak English. Wait for me here."

"Stakeout," Bruce said, smiling.

Tracy turned down the driveway to the front door. She didn't see a peephole, likely a good thing. She knocked. Moments later the door pulled open. A Chinese woman, who looked the right age, stood dressed in a blue cashmere sweater, blue jeans, and flats. It only took the woman a moment to register Tracy's blonde hair, blue eyes, and her height. Her eyes widened.

"Gloria Chin?" Tracy said.

The woman shook her head, speaking Chinese. She started to close the door.

"Bobby Chin's sister." Tracy held up the photograph she'd pulled off the Internet, a picture of Bobby Chin and Gloria standing together on a beach. The resemblance between the siblings was uncanny.

The woman sighed. Her shoulders slumped. "Who are you?"

"My name is Tracy Crosswhite. I'm a detective from Seattle."

"Private detective?" Gloria blew out a breath. "Did she hire you?"

"Jewel Chin? No. Bobby didn't hire me either. I'm not here on official police business. I'm here on my own, though I am a detective with the Seattle Police Department."

"I don't understand."

458

"It's complicated," Tracy said. "But I'm not here to cause you or Elle any pain." She meant this. She came to Chengdu with one intention—to determine what was in Elle's best interest. Coming through the ranks at SPD, Tracy had worked for a year in the Domestic Violence Unit. She'd seen horrific cases tear families apart and cause damage to the children. She'd never dealt with an international child abduction case, but she knew of such instances and knew that certain of those cases were governed by the Hague convention on international child abduction.

"May I come in?"

Gloria Liu stepped back from the door so Tracy could enter. The house was neat and simply furnished. Framed photographs lined a black-marble table in the entryway. On it, Tracy saw photos of Gloria with her husband and her niece.

Gloria led Tracy into the kitchen. A young girl sat at the counter eating cookies and drinking milk. She looked at Tracy as if she had two heads, and stopped chewing in midbite.

"We don't see people with blonde hair very often," Gloria said, putting her arm around Elle Chin.

"You must be Elle," Tracy said, smiling to try to ease the girl's discomfort.

Elle nodded, still looking uncertain.

"It's nice to meet you." Tracy held out her hand.

Elle looked to her aunt, who nodded, then held out her hand. Tracy shook it. "Who are you?" Elle asked.

"I'm a friend." She knew the little girl was struggling to figure out the relationship and worried what it could possibly mean. "I know your father in Seattle."

Gloria spoke Chinese and Elle picked up her backpack and left the room, looking back warily.

"Does Bobby know?" Tracy asked.

"He didn't, but now he does. As you said, it is complicated." Gloria slumped onto a barstool at the kitchen counter. "You are wondering how a sister can do something so hurtful to her brother, to inflict so much pain."

Tracy had been, but with time to think it through, she suspected Elle had not been taken to inflict pain, but to alleviate it. "I assume you did it because you love him, and you love your niece."

"Where there is a purpose in pain, it is not cruel," Gloria said softly.

"A Chinese proverb?"

Gloria smiled. "The nature channel. A show I watched in the United States about lion cubs. The mother will let one of her cubs die, so the others can live and grow strong." She sighed. "My parents are traditional. They did not want Bobby to marry Jewel. They didn't like her. I didn't like her. Jewel got pregnant. We all thought she trapped my brother, that she saw my family's wealth as a prize." She sighed. "This must sound like a rationalization."

"No," Tracy said.

"Maybe that's just a sister looking out for her brother, but Bobby was not blameless in this. Bobby was pigheaded. He often rebelled against my parents' wishes and did what he wanted. My father wanted Bobby to go into computers, but when he graduated from college Bobby became a police officer. Is that how you know him?"

"Sort of," Tracy said.

"When Bobby and Jewel had Elle, my parents wanted to accept Jewel, for their son and their granddaughter's sake. They were thrilled to have a granddaughter. They doted on Elle. But Jewel was difficult. She became more difficult, more unstable each year. She isolated my brother from his friends, then from his family. She would keep Elle from my parents when she did not get what she wanted. She used her as a pawn. Bobby would sneak Elle over to their house to visit when he could." She shook her head.

"Bobby told us he was getting a divorce. He opened up about the person Jewel had become. He told us he worried about Elle. Worried about her living in such a toxic home. I already knew their house was not a home for a little girl."

"You picked her up from school."

"Many times when Bobby couldn't get there.

He didn't want to call Jewel, and he preferred not to call my parents. I loved picking up Elle and spending time with her."

"When did you formulate the plan to take her?"

"When Elle began to tell me things—about that house. About her mother. About Bobby. We knew Bobby had been violent with Jewel. That was not how he was raised. We feared what could happen to Jewel and to him if his anger escalated." She paused and went to a cabinet for a glass, then poured herself water. She lifted the glass to Tracy, who declined.

Back on the barstool, Gloria sipped her water before she continued. "Jewel had a boyfriend before the divorce. The boyfriend moved into the house." Gloria took another sip of water. "Elle began to tell me things—that he would put Elle on his lap and rock her as if on a horse. She would tell him to stop, but he would not." Gloria lowered her head.

"You believe he was abusing her."

Gloria nodded. "And I'm sure it sounds like justification to you, but . . . I believe what Elle told me." She sipped her water again, gathering herself. "The domestic violence charge brought much shame to my parents and our family. I worried about the impact all the fighting would have on Elle, about the boyfriend and what he was doing, what he would do, about the irreversible damage to Elle, and what Bobby would do if he found out. He would kill him. He would shoot him. I was sure of it. Removing Elle from the situation was the only way to save her and to save my brother." Gloria sipped her water. "When I picked up Elle from school she was often angry and volatile and would act out. I would calm her and ask why she was so mad." Gloria looked at Tracy.

"What did she say?"

"She didn't want to go home," Gloria said.

Tracy thought of Lindsay Sheppard. *I would be better off with people thinking I was dead than living another day in that house.* She thought of Stephanie Cole and her desire to go back home. How sad that a little girl, just five, would not want to go home.

"She asked if she could live with me and Uncle Bo," Gloria said. "She would beg me to let her stay when Bobby came to take her home. 'I want to live here, Auntie. Why can't I live here with you?' she would say. It broke my heart. It broke Bobby's heart."

"Do you have other children?" Tracy asked.

Gloria shook her head. "My husband and I tried, but I was unable to conceive. Elle was going to be the only grandchild. At least it appeared that way." She took a deep breath and exhaled. Tracy could see the weight of the years of torment. "My husband and I were leaving. He was returning to Chengdu for a job. He has family here. My parents decided to also come. We talked about going to Bobby and Jewel and offering to take Elle, but we knew Jewel would never agree. She wouldn't see the benefit to Elle. She would see it only as a win for Bobby."

"And if you asked to take Elle, you'd be prime suspects when she disappeared."

"Yes. Bo and I decided we could not tell either parent. You have to believe me when I tell you this. We decided we had to wait to tell Bobby because we didn't want him to be arrested, for the police to think he was involved. He was not." Her eyes widened in fear.

"I believe you," Tracy said.

"I knew what it would do to him, but I also knew that it was the right thing to do. He needed to suffer the pain of losing Elle to understand what was in *her* best interests, to do the right thing. This was not about punishing Jewel. It was about saving Elle."

Tracy thought of her interview with Bobby Chin in his office, of the tears he shed and the hesitation in his voice. It had not been an act. It had been the pain and the guilt of a father who knew he had been, in part, responsible for losing his daughter, that he had not earned the right to raise his child.

Gloria grabbed a tissue from a box on the counter and blotted her eyes. "It hurt me deeply to know how much I hurt my brother, but I couldn't let Elle live in that house, not with Jewel, and not with that boyfriend. I knew the longer Elle stayed there, the more damage she would sustain. I did what I did out of love. I love Bobby and I love Elle. I did it to protect both of them."

"I don't doubt you," Tracy said. "When did you finally tell Bobby?"

"We asked him to come to Chengdu for my father's sixtieth birthday. We sat Bobby down and explained that Elle was here, with all of us."

"How did he react?"

"The pain of parting is nothing compared to the joy of meeting again."

"That doesn't sound like the nature channel."

"Charles Dickens. I studied English literature at the U." She smiled. "Bobby cried. He fell to the floor and he cried like a baby. He cried because he realized he had failed his daughter. He had failed as a father. He was racked with guilt, but he was also happy Elle was alive, and that she was safe. He didn't ask for an explanation. He knew why we did what we did, and he knew he could never take Elle home again, never could act like she was still alive, because Jewel would take Elle, just to spite him. Bo helped Bobby to get a good job with a Chinese company that opened an office in Seattle. It is an excuse for Bobby to travel here to see Elle."

Tracy had never been in these circumstances, but she had done research before leaving Seattle.

First and foremost, she had no legal recourse she could enforce. China was not a party to the Hague child abduction convention, nor was there any indication that China intended to join the convention. There were no international or bilateral treaties in force between China and the United States dealing with parental child abduction, and it was highly unlikely a foreign court order would be recognized in China, especially an order related to foreign child custody. Chinese law required the existence of a treaty or de facto reciprocity to enforce a foreign judgment; neither existed between the United States and China. Beyond that, the convention specifically required that hearings be conducted expeditiously and concluded within six weeks. A Hague case instituted more than a year after the abduction of a child was subject to the exception that if the child had become settled in the new environment, it was highly unlikely the court would send the child back.

Beyond all of that, Tracy suspected that if Jewel found out about Elle and made some attempt to recover her, Elle could again disappear into a population of more than a billion people. And what good would it do, to pull the little girl from a safe environment, a loving environment, a place she could truly call home, and return her to a dysfunctional mother and a dysfunctional parenting plan? Tracy knew that to send Elle back would only cause her further damage. Even if the Hague convention were applicable, it emphasized the interests of the child to be paramount, and any order would not be enforced if there was a grave risk that her return would expose the child to physical or psychological harm or otherwise place the child in an intolerable position.

"What did you tell Elle?" Tracy asked.

"Initially we told her that her mother and father agreed that she would come and live with me, her uncle, and my parents until after the divorce. When I told her that she didn't have to go home, she cried. She was so happy."

"She'll have more questions when she gets older."

"Already. And at some point, Elle will have to decide for herself."

"Does Elle ever ask to see or talk to her mom?"

"Initially she did. But mostly she asked to see her daddy. She rarely asks about Jewel, and she never says that she wants to go back."

Tracy wondered if Jewel Chin knew or perhaps suspected Gloria Chin had taken Elle—if that was the reason she mentioned, three times, that Elle's abductor had been an Asian woman. Did she know Gloria had taken Elle? Did she acquiesce because she knew it was in Elle's best interests, or because she never wanted to be a mom in the first place, and the burden to her lifestyle outweighed whatever pain she could inflict on her former husband, and it was enough to know that he didn't get to keep Elle either? Tracy hoped it was the former.

"What does Elle call you?" Tracy asked.

"Lola. She calls my husband Uncle Bo."

"And she's happy?"

"You see for yourself." She motioned for Tracy to look in the other room. Elle sat watching television. Back in the kitchen, Gloria asked in a soft voice, "Why did you come all this way?"

Tracy knew Gloria remained concerned that Tracy's motives were not altruistic, that she had come to take Elle. She explained to Gloria what she had learned about the Hague child abduction convention, though she suspected Gloria knew much already. Then she explained that was why she had come without official authority. "I recently started working cold cases, and this case caught my attention because it seemed so tragic on so many levels. I have a counselor." She paused. "I lost my sister when she was eighteen. I was supposed to watch her, but I failed. She never came home again."

"I'm sorry," Gloria said.

"My counselor thinks I have an obsession to save young women." Tracy shrugged, smiling. "I guess she's right. There could be worse obsessions. When I figured out what happened to Elle, where she was, I guess I just needed to know she was safe."

Gloria waited. Then she asked, "And what have you found?"

"I think Elle is going to help me understand that I can't save every young woman, and in some cases, that I don't need to. Her aunt and her uncle have already saved Elle."

Tears rolled down Gloria's cheeks. "Will you tell Jewel?"

"No. I think to do so, without Jewel having any recourse, would only be cruel to her and to Elle. And a part of me thinks Jewel already knows but isn't saying because to admit it would be to admit that Bobby won. This way, neither of them won." Tracy thought of her conversation with Jewel Chin, and of the investigative reports in the file that each said Jewel had moved from the house to a hotel and refused to cooperate in the investigation to find her daughter. Tracy had no doubt that if she told Jewel about Elle, Jewel would then be forced to use Elle to reopen old wounds. She'd once again blame Bobby, say that he had orchestrated the taking, and maybe make Elle the center of an international tug-of-war that could threaten to tear her apart, maybe this time irreparably. "Do you know the story of King Solomon?"

Gloria shook her head. "I do not."

"It's in the Bible. Two women claimed to be the mother of a child. To determine the true mother, Solomon suggests cutting the baby in half. One

469

woman agrees, but the true mother begs that he give the child, unharmed, to the other woman."

Gloria nodded her understanding.

"I think you and your husband are handling this situation correctly," Tracy said. "I think the person with the right to decide what is best for Elle is Elle, when that day comes. Until then, the file will remain open, and unsolved."

Gloria again dabbed her eyes with the tissue. "It's admirable," she said. "That you would come all this way just to find out that Elle is all right."

"My husband wasn't so diplomatic when I told him I needed to take a trip to Chengdu."

"Is he here with you?"

"He's at home, with our daughter."

Gloria smiled. "So, you know why I did what I did."

"I know."

"How old is your daughter?"

"About a year. I've only been here a day and I already miss her."

"Then I'd say your daughter is very lucky to have a mother who loves her so much. She will grow up to be a wonderful woman."

Tracy smiled. "And I would say that Elle is lucky to have an aunt and an uncle who love her so much, and that she, too, now has the chance to grow up to be a wonderful woman. I hope everything works out for the best, for all of you."

Tracy grabbed her purse and prepared to leave.

"Can you stay for dinner?" Gloria asked. "My husband will be home soon, and my parents. And I'm sure Elle would love to speak English with someone."

Tracy smiled. "I'd like that," she said. "Very much. Let me tell Bruce Wayne I'm going to be a couple more hours."

"Bruce Wayne? You mean like the Batman?"

Tracy smiled. "He seems to think so. And it really isn't my place to say he's not."

She left the table and walked outside, feeling as though a weight had been lifted from her shoulders. She couldn't save them all.

Maybe she didn't have to.

But there was nothing wrong with trying.

ACKNOWLEDGMENTS

I wrote much of this novel while sheltering in place amid the COVID-19 pandemic. Every morning I would go online and check the numbers of infected and dying here in my home state of Washington. The first few weeks were especially scary as my son was traveling in Southeast Asia, and the in-state outbreak occurred in a nursing home just a few miles from my house. Like many, I initially compared the pandemic to the flu. I was wrong. We got my son home through Australia, my daughter came home from school, the world shut down, and we hunkered down for the long months. I learned to do Zoom book clubs, Zoom workout classes, and to make other video appearances. With time to reflect, I realized I had been born of a generation that had never suffered through the difficult times many Americans experienced during the First and Second World Wars and the Depression, and I am too young to have fully understood and appreciated the impact of the Korean and Vietnam wars on the young in our society.

I spoke to an older friend one afternoon, checking in to make sure he was okay, and I told him I felt bad for the young, to have had their lives disrupted. I told him of my nieces and nephews who would not get to celebrate their college and high school graduations. I told my friend about my nephew who was valedictorian of his high school class and would not get to give his speech or go to his senior prom, or finish out the school year with the classmates he started high school with four years ago. I told him of my son, living at home, rather than with friends as he embarked on a new career.

My friend said to me, "This has been a couple of months. Think of the people who went to Vietnam for an entire year, or who lived in Europe during World War II and suffered for a decade."

He was right, of course. Perspective, however, often only comes with age.

I bring this up because many authors I spoke to during these difficult months have asked whether I will include COVID-19 in my novels. I have chosen not to. During the shelter-in-place months, I received numerous emails from readers thanking me for the chance to escape their homes and the difficulties and loneliness they were enduring. This, I believe, is the primary purpose of a novel, to entertain a reader in the comfort of his or her home. To spur his or her imagination, make him or her tense or cry tears of joy or sadness. The really good novels can make us all reflect on our own lives, and all we have experienced, the good times and the not-so-good times.

So you will not find a reference to COVID-19 in *In Her Tracks*. Whether I put it in future novels will depend on the subject matter. As with the pandemic, time will tell. In the interim, I hope you are all surviving, and that this pandemic has not been too painful for you or those you love. I hope that life will return to normal, and we can all see and be with one another again at writers' and readers' conferences and at bookstores.

As with all the novels in the Tracy Crosswhite series, I simply could not write this one without the help of Jennifer Southworth, Seattle Police Department, Violent Crimes Section. Jennifer has been invaluable helping me to formulate interesting ideas and with the daily police routine, as well as the specific tasks undertaken in the pursuit of a perpetrator of a crime.

My thanks also to Kathy Decker, former search-and-rescue coordinator of the King County Sheriff's Office and a well-known sign-cutter and man-tracker. Kathy has assisted me with multiple novels, and I'm fortunate to have access to her wealth of knowledge. She kindly took the time to review and help me with the tracking in this book.

To the extent there are any mistakes with respect to police procedure in this novel, those mistakes are mine and mine alone. In the interests of telling a story, and keeping it entertaining, I have condensed certain timelines, such as the time it takes to have DNA analyzed.

Thanks to Meg Ruley, Rebecca Scherer, and the team at the Jane Rotrosen Agency. They are literary agents extraordinaire. They have supported my work all over the world, and we've had fun together in New York, Seattle, Paris, and Oslo. I'm thinking an Italian book festival should be next on the list, once this pandemic has left the country of my heritage. Thanks for all your hard work negotiating all the contracts, providing me with advice on my career, guiding me through Hollywood, watching over my backlist, and being such kind human beings.

Thank you to Thomas & Mercer, Amazon Publishing. This is the twelfth book I've written for them, and they have made each one better with their edits and suggestions. They have sold and promoted me and my novels all over the world, and I have had the pleasure of meeting the Amazon Publishing teams from the UK, Ireland, France, Germany, Italy, and Spain. These are hardworking people who somehow make hard work a lot of fun. What they do best is promote and sell my novels, and for that I am so very grateful. During this time of sheltering in place and social distancing, they have come up with creative new ways to keep me in contact with readers through fun videos my family and I have enjoyed making.

Thanks to Sarah Shaw, author relations, who does such a terrific job celebrating my milestones. Thanks to Sean Baker, head of production; Laura Barrett, production manager; and Oisin O'Malley, art director. It's getting redundant, I know, but I love the covers and the titles of each of my novels. I am always amazed at the ways you take care of me. Thanks to Dennelle Catlett, Amazon Publishing PR, for all the work promoting me and my novels. Dennelle is always there, always available when I call or send an email with a need or a request. She actively promotes me, helps me to help charitable organizations, and makes my travel easy. Thanks to the marketing team, Lindsey Bragg, Kyla Pigoni, and Erin Calligan Mooney, for all their dedicated work and new ideas to help me build my author platform. I hope they never stop asking, because they make each new idea a great experience. Thanks to publisher Mikyla Bruder, associate publisher Hai-Yen Mura, and Jeff Belle, vice president of Amazon Publishing, for creating a team dedicated to their jobs and allowing me to be a part of it.

This past year, when sales of my Amazon novels surpassed five million, they threw a party for me, and I had the chance to tell them in person how much I appreciated all they have done for me. I am sincerely grateful, and even more amazed by the additional million readers we have now reached.

I am especially grateful to Thomas & Mercer's editorial director, Gracie Doyle. Gracie helps me find new ideas and new ways of telling stories. She pushes me to take stories to a depth I hadn't initially considered. We've had a lot of fun at author events, and I hope we will do so again in the near future.

Thank you to Charlotte Herscher, developmental editor. All of my books with Amazon Publishing have been edited by Charlotte—from police procedurals to legal thrillers, espionage thrillers, and literary novels, and she never ceases to amaze me with how quickly she picks up the story line and works to make it as good as it can possibly be. Thanks to Scott Calamar, copyeditor, whom I desperately need. Grammar has never been my strength, so there is usually a lot to do.

Thanks to Tami Taylor, who runs my website, creates my newsletters, and creates some of my foreign-language book covers. Thanks to Pam Binder and the Pacific Northwest Writers Association for their support.

Thanks to all of you tireless readers, for finding my novels and for your incredible support of my work all over the world. Hearing from readers is a blessing, and I enjoy each email.

Thanks to my mother and father for a wonderful childhood and for teaching me to reach for the stars, then to work my butt off to touch them. I couldn't think of two better role models.

Thank you to my wife, Cristina, for all her love and support, and thanks to my two children, Joe and Catherine, who have started to read my novels, which makes me so very proud.

I couldn't do this without all of you, nor would I want to.

ABOUT THE AUTHOR

Robert Dugoni is the critically acclaimed *New York Times*, *Wall Street Journal*, and Amazon bestselling author of the Tracy Crosswhite series, which has sold more than six million books worldwide; the David Sloane series; the Charles Jenkins series; the stand-alone novels *The 7th Canon*, *Damage Control*, and *The Extraordinary Life of Sam Hell*, for which he won an *AudioFile* Earphones Award for narration; and the nonfiction exposé *The Cyanide Canary*, a *Washington Post* best book of the year. He is the recipient of the Nancy Pearl Book Award for fiction and has twice won the Friends of Mystery Spotted Owl Award for best novel. He is a two-time finalist for the International Thriller Awards and a finalist for the Harper Lee Prize for Legal Fiction, the Silver Falchion Award for mystery, and the Mystery Writers of America Edgar Awards. His books are sold in more than twenty-five countries and have been translated into more than two dozen languages. Visit his website at www.robertdugonibooks.com.

Books are produced in the United States using U.S.-based materials

Books are printed using a revolutionary new process called THINKtech™ that lowers energy usage by 70% and increases overall quality

Books are durable and flexible because of Smyth-sewing

Paper is sourced using environmentally responsible foresting methods and the paper is acid-free

Center Point Large Print
600 Brooks Road / PO Box 1
Thorndike, ME 04986-0001 USA

(207) 568-3717

US & Canada:
1 800 929-9108
www.centerpointlargeprint.com